AN ANTHOLOGY OF CHINESE SHORT SHORT STORIES

Selected and Translated

by Harry J. Huang

First Edition 2005

ISBN 7-119-03881-8
©Foreign Languages Press, Beijing, China, 2005
Published by Foreign Languages Press
24 Baiwanzhuang Road, Beijing 100037, China
Website: http://www.flp.com.cn
E-mail Address: info@flp.com.cn
sales@flp.com.cn
Distributed by China International Book Trading Corporation
35 Chegongzhuang Xilu, Beijing 100044, China
P.O. Box 399, Beijing, China
Printed in the People's Republic of China

Contents

Supplement: Essays and Comments on the Chinese Short Short Story

Preface

The Chinese short short story, or mini-story, is no longer a dwarf. In China, it has become an equal member in the family of fiction. According to Liu Haitao, one of the contributors of this anthology, ancient Chinese short short story writing reached its peak in the Ming and Qing Dynasties (1368–1911). However, the Chinese short short story did not gain official recognition until the 1990s, as pointed out by Yang Xiaomin, another contributor and Editor-in-Chief of the Chinese monthly *Selected Chinese Short Short Stories.* Last year, more than 400 books of Chinese short short stories were published. More significantly, short short stories have been included in university and college textbooks. Nonetheless, the Chinese short short story is hardly known to the reader in the English-speaking world.

With the intention to introduce the Chinese short short story to the English reader, I have translated 121 such literary pieces, including ten ancient ones, which thus comprise this anthology. These stories were selected from a pool of more than 20,000. What should be pointed out is that the ten ancient stories are not intended to represent the different periods or writers of various dynasties, but merely as a glimpse at this form of narrative literature in ancient China.

Submissions and Selections

Every effort was made to produce a best possible anthology. My call for submission was published in the *New Star Chinese Weekly* and on its web site, and was spread by the delegation of the Chinese Writers' Association who visited Canada three years ago, the Short Short Story Writers' Society of China, and several provincial writers' associations in China. Writers also recommended peers. In addition, I selected authors directly from selections of award winning stories. Authors were citizens or permanent residents of the Chinese mainland, Taiwan, Hong Kong or Macao, at the time their stories were published.

The average length of the short short stories is about 1,500 Chinese characters, approximately translated into 900 English words. "Coming to Life," the shortest story, consists of 91 Chinese characters. A few pieces, such as "My Wife's Hands," exceed 2,000 Chinese characters.

I attempted to find stories that demonstrate some Chinese culture which readers at different levels may enjoy. I would feel honored if each story could impact the readers in some way: either thrill them, amuse them, enlighten them, make them smile, laugh or cry, weigh them with sadness, arouse curiosity, strike a chord in their heart, or impress them with unforgettable artistry.

The anthology is divided into sections by theme for easy reference. Also included are seven essays on the Chinese short short story and brief biographies of the authors.

It is my hope that another edition or anthology will be published to include best new Chinese short short stories. Writers and readers are invited to recommend stories in Chinese by e-mail to harry8899@yahoo.com.

Rules of Translation

The reader is my boss whose expectations have become my guideline. I conducted two surveys to find out what readers look for in a translation. Three translations of Cao Xueqing's poem "*Hao liao ge*" done by Yang Xianyi and Gladys Yang, David Hawkes, and myself (with our names removed) and two versions of Cui Hao's *Huang he lou* done by myself (with my name removed) were respectively given to 102 and 50 Canadian college students to grade. The students were then asked to explain why a certain grade was given and/or why they preferred one version over the other. The results indicate that 56% preferred one version to another for its clarity and understandability; 13% stressed the importance of content; 31% listed stylistics as a priority. They said that they liked a translation when it was "clear" and "easy to understand" with "good content" and "elegant style." I heeded their words and did whatever I could for the readers on behalf of the authors.

Knowing readers from diverse cultures with individual tastes look for different merits in a translation, I opt for readability. An English-speaking audience with high-school education remains my primary target. Thus, throughout the process of translation, additional notes would be added if any point was deemed difficult for the reader. Any repetitive words and sentences that should be combined or simplified would be treated with due attention.

Before the translation started, every contemporary story was reviewed and, where necessary, edited, in some cases substantially, by the Chinese author or the translator with the authorization of the writer. The translation was not done word for word or line for line. Taken as a whole, every story was recreated in English, sentence by sentence, paragraph by paragraph, with the aim to render every Chinese character. The English text may not fully match the original text if compared line by line. The ancient Chinese short short stories, which are often deemed untranslatable, were translated in a more unconventional manner, simply based upon my paraphrasing of the outdated text. In my view, only in this way can ancient Chinese literature be translated into readable English. I hold the opinion that a translation not only should be faithful to the original, but also as good in the target language as it is in the source language. For details of this criterion, see my essay "FRB Translation Criterion & COSB Model for Translation Quality Analysis & Evaluation: Illustrated with Poems Translated from Chinese" in *Chinese Translators' Journal*, Vol. 25, No. 4, 2004.

From start ("Invisible Label") to finish ("What Scares the General"), it took me twenty years to complete this anthology. With the generosity of the Chinese authors, I am adding to the literary flowerbed a fresh flower to beautify the reader's life. May this new flower never wither and fall!

Acknowledgments

First of all, I wish to express my sincere thanks to all the authors who responded to the call for submission to this anthology. I owe a debt of gratitude to all the living authors who have granted me the exclusive right to translate their stories into English as well as their understanding and support.

Special thanks go to Dr. Robert Price, professor of English; Dr. Lien Chao; Professors Lynn Holmes and Elizabeth Holmes; Dr. Stephanie Fysh; Patria C. Rivera; Professor Patricia Reeves; and Ms. Chen Haiyan, director of the Panda Books Department of Foreign Languages Press, for their invaluable editorial input; to Mr. Gao Weixi and Dr. Mark Moss, for their advice on various issues; and to Ms. Li Fang, Ms. Wang Rui, the other staff members, the Editor-in-Chief and the Director of Foreign Languages Press, for their consistent support.

Thanks also go to the Chinese Writers' Association, the Short Short Story Writers' Society of China, *New Star Chinese Weekly* in Toronto, and Seneca College.

The following individuals deserve my heartfelt thanks for contacting the many authors whose addresses were originally unknown to me: Mr. Jiang Zilong, vice-chairman of the Chinese Writers' Association; Mr. Ling Dingnian; Ms. Cai Qing; Mr. Sun Fangyou; Mr. Zha La Ga Hu, Mr. Ma Baoshan; Mr. Lin Ruqiu; Mr. He Baiyuan; Mr. Tao Ran; Ms. Huei-Wen Vivian Chung of National Sun Yat-sen University in Taiwan; and numerous other friends and readers.

I also wish to thank my wife for helping me understand the Cantonese slang and other difficult points, my elder daughter Wendy Huang, for reading every one of the stories and making extremely useful comments, and also my five-year-old daughter, Alice, and two-year-old son, Jeffrey, who have sacrificed much playtime with me for the sake of this book.

It is the unreserved help of all these individuals that has enabled me to crystallize for the English reader in book form the artistry of Chinese short short story writers.

Harry J. Huang
Toronto, Canada

My Views on the Chinese Short Short Story

What a short short story does, often in a more attractive and direct way, is what a lyric poem is designed to do: it gives a direct perception of an event, or a feeling, a situation, a character, an interaction. However, it is given without the historical or cultural context in which the perception is embedded. Or almost: there may be allusions or hints, and if the reader misses them, the point of the story is lost, or the story may be misread. That is why it is especially difficult to translate a short short story, or to deal with one from even a few decades in the past, or from a neighboring country (or community). Many or all of the historical or cultural conditions cannot be provided or explained — the author may not even be consciously aware of them. The annotations and footnotes needed would be endless, which would swamp the story itself.

Here, the tact and skill of the translator Harry Huang deserve our gratitude. He provides just enough illumination, without obliterating the storyteller's reticence, limiting and controlling the information the story gives: the rhetorical strategies employed. Why would we want to read the stories, if the teller did not control, withhold, position the elements in a skilful way?

Our interest, of course, may be just as much in the aspects not foregrounded by the storytellers: the histories and lives of the contemporary Chinese writers Mr. Huang has selected, and the characters they present. (How representative are they, and how can we tell?) We are curious, inquisitive, often reading with a meddling scrutiny, not always with the best of intentions. Often we lack the patience required to read the stories appropriately or do not expect to enjoy the stories anyway. But what we have in Mr. Huang's anthology is not a duty-read, not something we have an obligation to understand.

First, there are enough stories here to inform us of what is behind Chinese storytelling, the purpose if there is one: the expectation that each story will have a moral, a point, a positive value in our own lives or community. What may appear to us at times as old fashioned, a remnant of (or possibly an unconscious throwback to) the didactic monitory devices of older political regimes are really traces of a much older tradition. Literature that teaches, guides, instructs, improves (in our own schools, and not so long ago), that makes us more civilized, more sensitive to others, or just better informed about everything has been part of our tradition for thousands of years.

If such didacticism or moralizing is out of fashion in our modernist and postmodernist times, that does not mean readers have completely lost their taste for it, and the pendulum may swing back. Reading that challenges our moral and ethical values can open our minds and reinforce our prejudices. Stories (such as many in this selection) which may strike us as partisan, as special pleading, or express a self interest without nuance or balance or awareness of counter arguments can still be effective and stimulating, as prods to our complacency, and fixed ideas.

So much for moralizing: it is best to read short short stories the way we listen to anecdotes and jokes: moments of uncensored privilege when we find ourselves outside the "politically correct" framework of our everyday lives — almost in a dream-world where taboos can no longer apply: licensed irresponsibility.

In our carefully controlled and self-monitored transactions with others in a multicultural society, we wander in a fog, encountering other people as opaque, well-meaning, but enigmatic, seemingly unknowable. If fiction (serious fiction at least) is designed to give us imaginative access to other selves, and since to be human is necessarily to suffer and to face the unpleasant, what we gain from our reading is an extra concentrated dose of simulated life.

What do we want from life, from other people? We choose to escape from them, to go to another country and reinvent ourselves, which may be the point of Harry Huang's "Should I Stay or Go." We choose to seek revenge on those we have lived with, or at least tell the Truth about them; to memorialize the weird, inexplicable, often senseless things that do happen, or the very odd things people can think. We choose just to enjoy and marvel at the patterns, coincidences, juxtapositions of characters, what happens to them, and what it might mean; to celebrate the endurance, nobility, pathos of life at a minimal level: lost in a desert, condemned to death, offered as a sacrifice for the good of the community, committed to duty such as keeping the furnace stoked with coal. These things sustain us.

And what of the new, young Chinese writers? From the stories in Mr. Huang's anthology what I see are the survival of naïve romance, men chasing women, women choosing not to be dominated by men, families still more important than the community at large, the need for release through humor and wild behavior, economic uncertainty and recognition that some aspects of the recent past are just fading away. The problems facing rural communities as employment disappears are hinted at in some of the stories; the new explosion of urban life is cautiously celebrated without as much apprehension as one would expect. The short short story offers little scope for deeper examination of where society is heading, but what literature does? There is less science fiction, less fantasy writing here than one would expect (but certainly enough to my taste), and perhaps less exploratory, adventuresome imagination of psychological possibilities than there should be. Maybe that is what we will see if collections such as this appear in the future.

Lynn Holmes

Teasing in Life

Restaurant Business

By **Liu** Wanli

I had to stay home for some time after I graduated from university, for I could not find a job immediately.

To help me find a job, my father was busy all day long, sending big gifts and small gifts to connections. This made me feel rather guilty, so I thought I might as well look for a temporary job to somewhat ease the financial burden of my family. My father had read my mind and said, "I have an old army friend. He's now the chairman of the county's People's Congress. He has just opened a restaurant and still needs workers. I mentioned you when I was talking with him. He said if you like, you can start working for him tomorrow."

I had studied hotel management, and could still use my knowledge if I worked for a restaurant. So I gladly accepted his offer.

My boss was called Qian, but because he was my father's friend, I did not call him Mr. Qian. Instead, I called him Uncle Qian. Uncle Qian treated me very well. The first day I went to work, he appointed me general manager, asking me to keep accounts for his business.

"Our customers are God," he told me solemnly. "We must win their patronage with high-quality delicious food, generous in weight but at low rates."

I nodded in agreement.

I put whatever I had learned from my books into practice. Thanks to my proper management, I made him a net profit of several thousand yuan* the first month. But when I reported it to Uncle Qian, he looked

---

* Translator's note: One yuan of the Chinese currency, Renminbi, equals about 12 cents (US) at present.

somewhat displeased. "Our customers are God," he said. "We must give more to them. This way we can attract more and more returning diners. Don't forget the long-term interest."

I thought there was something in what he said. Accordingly, I worked on the quality of our food and reduced the prices until they became the lowest in the city. Not unexpectedly, our business was booming. Customers swarmed into our restaurant, and all our tables were booked up every day before we opened.

When the accounts were cleared by the end of the month, revenues and expenses were roughly balanced. I reported it to Uncle Qian, and he said in a serious tone, "Our customers are God. How many times have I said it? Next month, you are only allowed to lose money. No profits allowed!"

I was puzzled that the owner of a business did not want to make money, but since he had given the word, I just had to do it. The final calculation of the third month's revenues and expenses showed a loss of 10,000 yuan. I reported it to Uncle Qian, readying myself for reproaching. Unexpectedly, on hearing my report, he repeated the word "good" three times. "Good job well done!" he finally said, smiling. "We lose money first and will profit later. Just do the same next month." Then he thrust a cash bonus* into my hand.

The restaurant lost another 10,000 yuan in the fourth month. The same loss also occurred in the fifth month.

"This is no way to run the restaurant!" I said to Uncle Qian.

"Don't worry. You can't worry just about short-term interest," he said.

"I feel I can't bring my talents into full play here. In other words,

---

* *Translator's note:* Apart from the regular month's salary, nearly all salaried employees get additional income known as "bonus" from their employers. Bonuses differ greatly from place to place, depending on how well off the employers are. Generally speaking, the better off the employer is, the higher the bonuses the employees are likely to get.

this is not the right place for me to demonstrate my abilities. So I have decided to resign."

"Since you have decided to leave, I won't insist on keeping you," he smiled carelessly.

Not long after that, I went to the south to start my own career.

One year later, I returned home for the Chinese New Year. On this day, Uncle Qian came to visit us. This time he drove an expensive car. When I asked him about his restaurant, he said, "We won't talk about work or business today." Then he raised the wine glass and started to drink. My father also said, "Drink!"

While they drank, they talked about past events. Uncle Qian was in a good mood, so he drank more than he should. When he was drunk, he began to mutter and mumble.

"Do you know why I opened the restaurant? In fact, it's just a cover," he said. "I raked in plenty of cash when I was the bureau leader and the chairman of the People's Congress of the county. I never dared to use any of that money, for fear of arousing people's suspicion. So I opened a restaurant to create a facade. I only lose money, instead of making money. In this way, my business keeps booming, so others will think I am making lots of money. As a result, I can buy my villa and car—anything—free of fear."

Finally, I understood why the restaurant owner was just interested in losses instead of profits. I stood there as if in a trance, unable to speak for a long time.

He Lost Himself

By **Xing** Ke

Du Baotian's father was an outstanding Chinese chess player who beat all the locals. At the age of five, Du began to learn to play chess from his father. A gifted player, Du learned quickly. By the age of twelve or thirteen, he was beating his father mercilessly on the chess board. In those days, playing chess was fun and pleasure for him. All he saw were the chessmen, and all he cared about was the chessboard. Father and son would go all out, each trying to defeat the other. At a moment of joy, Little Du would clap his hands on his knees, or burst into happy laughter, or shout "hurray." What a jubilant player he was!

But after he started working, Du was never a happy player again, though he frequently played chess. When playing with people working under him, he always won, whether they were good players or bad ones. He was never really challenged, and his chess skills were never fully used. Furthermore, he also felt insulted, so it was just boring.

When he played with his own bosses, on the other hand, he always had to keep them in a winning situation and let them win in the end. Playing it this way was just like choking himself, but he knew he could not do it otherwise. The minister of the province loved playing Chinese chess, so he often held ministry-wide chess contests, and he was always the champion. Yet, each time, Du knew well that he could easily defeat the minister, but . . .

Du not only had to let the minister win, he had to be defeated by the deputy ministers. As a result, he was never among the top three winners. He felt wronged and tortured, but he could only endure it.

5

Now he would soon leave this world. "The ship has anchored at the harbor and the bus has reached the terminal." He needed nothing more; he didn't have to wrong himself like before. He wanted to play a real game with the minister to show his real talents on the chessboard, so as to enjoy the simple pleasure of the game. By doing so, he could also let the minister know that Du was the real champion. Yet whenever the minister asked him if he wanted anything before leaving this world, Du would open his mouth then close it immediately without uttering the last but most important wish in his life.

This wish had now turned into an unendurable pain in his heart. It worsened daily, adding agony to his ailment.

One day, when the minister came to visit him again, he asked Du once more if there was anything he could do for him. Plucking up all his last courage, Du told him his last wish.

"Fine. Fine. Let's play a game right now," smiled the minister on hearing him.

Placing the chessboard on the hospital bed, they started to play at once. With one charging and the other advancing, the two had a fierce, dogged fight. At a crucial point, when Du could have advanced his horse one step to defeat the minister, he became soft-hearted, hesitated and made a useless move. This break allowed the foe to counterattack, which eventually led to victory.

Du regretted his loss miserably, tears welling up in his eyes.

He left this world the next day.

Chinese Teacher Wanted

By Harry J. **Huang**

Yesterday was Youth Day. We had an exciting get-together in the town hall. We also invited Secretary Guo of the town's Party Committee to our party. To "improve the transparency of work," he even had a dialogue with us young people. Obviously, it was an enjoyable dialogue, because my colleagues laughed from the beginning till the end while he spoke. Some, I should say, sounded pretty impolite. They not only interrupted him all the time, they also made all sorts of contemptuous noises right in his presence. I have little education myself, so I did not understand much of what he said.

This morning, when I was on my way to work, I happened to see a large poster:

Chinese Teacher Wanted
Immediately

Secretary Guo of the town's Party Committee is in
desperate need of a teacher who can help him improve
his knowledge of the Chinese language and logic.
Requirements:
(1)   Three years of primary schooling or more
(2)   Ability to speak with a little logic
(3)   Two weeks of teaching experience
Salary: 15 yuan per hour

An Anthology of Chinese Short Short Stories   Translated by Harry J. Huang

Apply in person at Secretary Guo's office.*

It was great news for me. I had four years of schooling, I had once taught my little niece about five Chinese characters in twenty-one days, and I believed I did speak with a little logic. I phoned the operator for Secretary Guo's phone number when I got to my office, then called him. But when I asked if the position was still available, his secretary could not understand me at all.

I even had to read the whole poster to her.

"No. He doesn't need any teacher now!" she shouted unhappily after hearing me.

"But why did you put up that poster, then?"

She hung up. Perhaps she wanted to keep the position for her own relatives or friends.

I was in need of money because I planned to get married the next month. I calculated for myself: if I taught Secretary Guo two hours a day, six days a week, I could make 180 yuan per week. In six weeks I would make over 1,000 yuan easily. Why not try again, then?

I went to read the poster for a second time, then tore it from the wall and brought it with me to the Party secretary's** office.

"Look, here is your poster." I showed it to the secretary in Guo's office. "I just phoned to ask about the position."

"It's filled now!" She then snatched the poster from my hand, tore it into pieces and threw it right into the garbage can.

"I simply don't understand what you are doing."

"Then you'd better find a teacher for yourself first."

"I'm all right. I have four years of education. My Chinese is pretty good. I can speak with a little logic, and I have taught for about twenty days. I'm even better than Secretary Guo—why should I find a teacher for myself?"

8

She then went away, leaving me in the office all by myself. Just as impolite as any other secretaries you see elsewhere. Weren't they stupid? They said Secretary Guo needed a teacher desperately, but when I went to apply for the position, they turned me down!

* *Translator's note:* The monthly income of a university graduate was about eighty yuan at the time, likely late 1980s, when the story took place.

** *Translator's note:* The Party secretary is the director of a Party branch or committee, the most powerful person of a province, county, factory, school or department store, for example. He makes the decisions and approves or disapproves anything of whatever unit is under his control. Chinese Party secretaries may be ranked as follows:

- General secretary of the Central Committee of the Communist Party of China
- Secretary of a provincial committee of the Communist Party of China
- Secretary of a county committee of the Communist Party of China
- Secretary of a town committee of the Communist Party of China
- Secretary of a district general branch of the Communist Party of China
- Secretary of a village branch of the Communist Party of China
- Head of a group consisting of three or fewer than three members of the Communist Party of China

Different organs and institutions other than those mentioned above are generally classified as provincial-level units, county-level units, and so on, and Party secretaries of such units are granted the power and receive benefits accordingly.

Ten Pig Heads

By **Ma** Fengchao

The locals had the habit of celebrating the Chinese New Year with a pig head.* Every household would make it into cold dishes which went well with alcoholic drinks for friends and relatives. Before the New Year, pig heads were difficult to buy. People who had connections with the food company would try to buy one through the back door. To ease the pressure, the retail department sold ten pig heads to every member of the company, who could then sell them to friends and relatives.

Naturally, Zhu Zhongxin, the Manager sixth in line, who had just transferred to the company, also got his share, but this instantly became a headache for him, for he had nobody to sell them to. Zhu had always led the simple life of a veteran Eighth Route Army man. Following the rules in whatever he did, he was sincere and honest with everybody he dealt with. So the back door had nothing to do with him.

But what was he going do with the pig heads? He thought of returning them to show his disapproval of the common practice of taking advantage of whatever is within reach. But Sun, the department head, had informed him that the deal had been approved by the manager and the first three assistant managers. "If we don't sell them to the staff, we could be accused of breaking a promise." As a

---

* *Translator's note:* The place in the story is fictitious: there is no place in China where every household wants to buy a pig head for the Chinese New Year.

newcomer and the least powerful manager, Zhu just could not go against everyone else.

Of course, he could give the pig heads away, but to whom? He would not even give them to his own relatives and close friends. "What kind of official would I be if I placed myself above the public! Right! I might as well sell them to the people waiting outside."

What a crowd he saw in front of the store! Several erratic queues of shoppers were waiting to buy pig heads. His eyes sweeping across the queues, Zhu started to pick people who he thought belonged to the most disadvantaged group.

"Granny, you are too old to wait in such a long line. Come over here. I'll sell you a pig head."

"Grandpa, don't squeeze in. You can't beat the younger guys! Let me sell one to you, all right?"

"There, there, there! My dear sister with a baby in your arms, it is no fun waiting in line like this just to buy a pig head!"

In this way, Zhu finally picked ten customers for various reasons.

"Our company hasn't done its job well. It's ridiculous to wait such a long time just to buy a pig head," he said, pointing at the fat pig heads in his two baskets. "I'll sell these pig heads to you," he added. "Just take it easy. There's one for each."

To his surprise, after a long wait, none of them would take the pig heads. Instead, they became skeptical about Zhu's sincere offer and started to ask questions.

"Is there anything wrong with the heads?"

"Do they have a parasitic disease?"

"There's got to be a problem," said an alert customer, turning them over to check them out. "Otherwise, why would you move them out and sell them here, when they are so hard to buy?"

"My goodness!" Zhu cut in and explained. "I have just taken them out of the freezer. They are perfect heads. Believe me!"

The more he assured them, the less they trusted him.

"Are you making a profit? No? Then why are you selling them?"

"That's right! If the fat heads are good, and if you aren't making money, what the heck are you doing it for?"

Interrogated this way, the manager, who was now rather desperate, thought he had better tell them the truth. "The company has given me these pig heads to sell to my 'connections.' I thought you were having a hard time lining up out there. So I decided to sell them to you. I am a manager of the company, so I must always think of the public first, mustn't I?"

More and more people crowded around. Their sharp questions and comments made Zhu's chosen customers even more suspicious.

"Now, now! Doesn't that sound beautiful? But who would ever believe him? What a decent manager! Why not bar the back door then?"

"He could be a crook. You never know!" said an impetuous young man who had come forward to challenge him. He glanced over Zhu's rather old and unstylish clothes, and said, "I'll go check if the company has really sold pig heads to its staff."

As quick as he could be, in less than three minutes, the young man returned to announce the result of his investigation: "I checked with Sun, head of the retail department. He told me they have never sold any pig heads to the staff."

The ten customers roared with triumphant laughter, sounding like they were celebrating their alertness.

"Jeez!" Zhu heaved a deep sigh of disappointment, not knowing how to convince the sarcastic crowd.

Invisible Label

By **Jiang** Zilong

Jin Liu was dumbfounded, looking idiotic and confused. He stood near the flower bed in the middle of the compound of the Education Bureau where he looked like a fading narcissus that had been frostbitten. This stupefied man was by nature weak, and seldom had ideas of his own in difficult times.

How he wished to bump his head against the marble and kill himself now! The other Rightists* in his village had all been vindicated and had returned to the city, while his problem remained unsolved. As nobody had given the least attention to his case, he came to where he had once belonged, namely, to the Education Bureau, to find out why. After looking through the files, the Personnel Department informed him that all the Rightists of the Bureau had got

---

* *Translator's note:* Rightists are those who were accused of opposing socialism in 1957. In April 1957, the Central Committee of the Communist Party of China gave instruction for rectifying its work. At this moment, some people, mostly non-members of the Communist Party, came out to demand positions from the Communist Party, asking it to give up its power. Such people were considered "Rightists," or people against the Revolution, a criminal title. (Leftists were considered good revolutionaries.) Regarded as harmful elements to the Revolution, the Rightists were sent to work in the country or in remote places (usually at labor jobs) or punished in some other ways during the Anti-Rightist Movement. Many innocent people were wrongly accused and unfairly punished, usually with a label of "Rightist" kept in their files. The Rightists had their names cleared only after the Cultural Revolution (1966-76) ended and when Deng Xiaoping returned to power.

their labels removed and had returned to the city. They told him that he had never been given the label of "Rightist," and that since his name could not be found on the old list of the Rightists, he had to return to the country.

"But, God! Isn't it clear that I was condemned as a Rightist? Otherwise, why did they force me to go to the countryside?"

"We really don't know why. Those who gave you trouble don't work here any longer."

For more than two decades, this label of "Rightist," which he hated so much, had been haunting him, but now it had become precious and vitally important to him. It was like an auspicious bird and the God of Wealth. Why had it disappeared at this crucial moment? Without it, his criminal title could not be removed; nor could he return to the city. Where could he recover the invisible label which he had been wearing all these years? The sympathetic man working in the reception room walked over to him, patted him on the shoulder and said, "Go find Lao Sui. Ask him to be your witness."

Good advice! Lao Sui had been the Party secretary of the Bureau when Jin Liu was being condemned, eventually to hard labor in the countryside. Surely he would witness that Jin Liu had been a Rightist.

After asking scores of people and trying dozens of places, Jin Liu at last found Lao Sui in the small meeting room of a luxurious hotel. Their conversation had hardly started when Lao Sui recognized his visitor—this fool before him had been reported as a Rightist for approval, but the higher authorities had rejected it. However, treating him as a Rightist, Lao Sui had still sent him to the country. But how could Lao Sui admit it now?

"Jin Liu, I never condemned you as a Rightist when I was the Party secretary of the Education Bureau," he said categorically. "You can check it on the files if you want to."

Jin Liu was furious and wanted to reason with him, but Lao Sui waved him away and said, "I have an important meeting to attend now. I have made it clear to you: the implementation of the policy for

Rightists has nothing to do with you. You'd better forget about it and go on with your work in the country." With this, he took his measured steps toward the inner room.

Jin Liu could not but leave the hotel, mumbling, "Label! My label! Where's my label?"

Tigers Don't Eat Humans

By **Ru** Rongxing

There was a hill, known as Jingyang Hill, in the southeast suburbs of the administrative town, Yanggu County, Shandong Province. Tigers on the hill had long been notoriously dangerous. Ever since Wu Song, as narrated in the classic novel *Water Margins,* killed with his bare fists that fierce-looking beast with a white forehead, its descendants had taken the human race as their enemy. From generation to generation, they had been bent on revenging themselves on humans. That is why anybody who passed through the hill would encounter hostile, bloody tigers that had savaged many human lives, leaving piles and piles of human bones all over the weeds and in between the rocks.

However, in the 1990s, news suddenly spread that tigers on Jingyang Hill did not eat humans anymore.

On hearing the news, Mr. Mou, the well-known contemporary tiger expert, was not only surprised but elated. "Why not go for an on-the-spot investigation?" he said in a happy mood as he calmed down. "If it is true and if I can find out the real reason why tigers do not eat humans anymore, the Swedish Academy will have to create a new prize, just for me! Then I would have lots of money and could join the most honorable rich in today's society!"

Seeing a bright future awaiting him, Mr. Mou started packing that same night and set out in the starlight. After traveling hundreds of miles, changing from buses to ferries, eventually he got to the Jingyang Hill.

What he saw and heard confirmed that tigers on the hill had indeed

16

changed. People passing through the hill day or night no longer had to go in groups. Neither did they have to arm themselves with sticks or swords. Everybody just went straight through, free of fear. From his interviews, Mr. Mou learned about what had happened to the last victim: One night in early summer two years before, a self-employed peddler from Zhejiang was eager to negotiate a business deal with his partner, so he ignored the warning of the owner of the hotel at the foot of the Jingyang Hill. After a good drink, he tried to cross the hilltop. As a result, his body was found in the messy woods. The wound on his throat showed clear tiger's tooth marks; the ten thousand yuan on him was not touched.

Mr. Mou was puzzled: why did the tiger kill the man without eating up his flesh? Strange, strange, strange!

Then Mr. Mou thought of meeting the tiger himself. "The common saying goes, 'Nothing ventured, nothing gained.' This is my only way to demystify the case in order to join the rich."

After much painstaking effort, Mr. Mou finally found the haunt of the tiger. Looking up, he caught sight of a listless giant cat lying next to a jagged rock. It was so skinny that one might even doubt if it was a real descendant of the tiger killed by Wu Song. Stranger still, it took several steps backward at the sight of Mr. Mou.

Seizing the opportunity, Mr. Mou started talking with the tiger.

"I hear you don't eat people anymore. Does it mean you have changed?"

"A leopard never changes its spots. You know that. Besides, the human race killed my ancestor. How could I ever forget that?"

"How come you don't eat humans anymore, then?"

"There is a strange odor in human flesh these days!"

"What odor?"

The tiger was silent, but Mr. Mou could not wait for the answer. His dream would come true soon. Just a step away!

All of a sudden, the tiger's ears stuck up as it opened its eyes wide. Then it walked up to Mr. Mou, seized him by the shoulders with one paw, reached into his upper pocket with the other and drew out a stack of banknotes. Dropping the notes onto the ground as if it were fire, the tiger frowned, wrinkling its nose at the terrified Mr. Mou. "There, it's the smell of this!" it said.

Then it dumped the dumbfounded Mr. Mou on the ground, returned to where it was lying and pretended to doze off, sighing angrily, "Humph! If your flesh didn't smell of that odor, I would have eaten you up long ago!"

Premonition

By **Teng** Gang

When Mr. W. got up in the morning, a horrific thought flashed across his mind like lightning: "I may be struck and killed by a truck today!" It was a surprise for him, but Mr. W. thought it had come for some reason. It was a premonition—people usually have them before they die. Previously, Mr. W. had not really believed that there were premonitions of death, but what had happened recently had made him a true believer.

In the same morning, the day before yesterday, two accidents had taken place in front of his house, resulting in two deaths—a gardener and a teacher. Both victims were run over by trucks, their bodies left battered beyond recognition. As Mr. W. learned later, the gardener looked deathlike and didn't say a word when he woke up in the morning on his last day. Stranger still, after he got up, he even took a bath, clipped his fingernails and put on brand-new clothes. It had never been heard of and was simply unimaginable in that locality that someone would ever take a bath after he got up in the morning. The gardener's odd behavior showed that he had had a premonition of death.

The teacher's case was more bizarre. He was said to have started burning his diary, letters and other manuscripts one month before his fatal accident. He had even written to his friends, asking them to return his letters to him. In short, he had destroyed practically everything he had written in this world. That morning, he had just started to cross the asphalt road when he saw a truck, which had lost control, chasing him. He kept screaming as he ran madly for his life, but he was still hit and killed.

Mr. W. believed that the gardener and the teacher had lost their lives because they had not taken their premonitions seriously. "If you have a premonition, you should do everything possible to prevent it from happening. You can't just let it take its course." Mr. W. therefore decided not to leave home that day: it was unlikely that a truck would run him over in his own house.

After brushing his teeth and washing his face, he told his wife, "Today, I'm not going to work and I won't leave home, either. I'll be reading in the backyard. Do not call me no matter what happens. If anybody comes to look for me, tell them I am not home. This is very important, but don't ask me what it is. Even if you ask, I don't have an answer for you, anyway. That's it." With this, he grabbed a book and a few pieces of bread and hid himself in the mud-brick hut that had been used as a storage room.

Mr. W.'s mysterious remarks confounded his wife; she felt as if she had lost her direction in a thick fog. He had been working 365 days a year, had never been late for work and had never come home early. He went to work even when he was ill, but why, all of a sudden, had he decided not to go to work? Why would he be reading in the mud-brick hut? That was a place he had never been in. She thought of asking him several times, but she dared not, for he was one who always meant what he said. Then she went to her own employer to ask for a leave of absence, and hurried back home. Whatever the case, she should not leave him home alone. She thought that he must have something too difficult to tell her.

Between 8:00 a.m. and 4:00 p.m., fourteen people knocked on the door, asking to see Mr. W., but his wife admitted nobody. At 4: 15, Mr. W.'s manager came to his house, asking him to return to work immediately to deal with some extremely urgent matters. Since it was his manager, who had urgent matters for him to attend to, Mr. W's wife could not but take him to the backyard.

"No! I won't go. I won't go anywhere today," said Mr. W., stern in voice and countenance. "You don't need to tell me anything more. Even if you fire me, I still won't go. And don't ask me why. I have something very, very important. You will know it later on. Please leave now." He waved the manager away, sweating all over from anxiety. "Having urgent matters to deal with at this moment is just an evil omen, a call of death!" he said to himself. He could not tell his manager why he behaved that way; he could not tell him about his premonition. For, once revealed, it would surely bode ill, not well. He would tell him everything only afterward.

The manager was mystified, telling Mr. W.'s wife before he left, "Watch him closely. If he gets worse, call for a doctor." She nodded, in tears.

At about seven o'clock in the evening, near a fork on the asphalt road, a heavy, fast-moving truck had to make a swift turn in order to avert a head-on collision with a coach that was driving in the wrong lane. The truck flew into a small lane by the road, finally coming to a halt after it crashed into a fence and a mud-brick hut.

When Mr. W. was pulled out of the debris, he showed no signs of life.

Mr. W.'s death shocked everybody. This astonishing incident then turned into a strange tale among the locals. From then on, whenever somebody questioned if premonitions of death existed, they would cite Mr. W. as an example. If he did not have a premonition of death, why would he have locked himself up at home for a whole day? Why did he hide in the mud-brick hut waiting to be crushed? And why did he say all those strange things?

Tiger Skin

By **Yi** De Er Fu

This is a story about a pair of sandals and tiger skin.

That summer, after I was transferred to civilian work in the city from my mountain frontier pass, I decided to buy a pair of sandals. As it turned out, it was rather difficult to find a pair that fit me. I am a small man who naturally has small feet. Small feet, needless to say, require small sandals. I wear size 6, which wasn't available everywhere. After trying various shoe shops and department stores, on one sunny Sunday I finally found what I had been looking for in the state-owned Saibei Department Store: a pair made of cowhide. Happily surprised, I immediately made the payment and left with the merchandise. I always trusted the government-owned stores and never really checked what I bought when I shopped there.

I started wearing my sandals as soon as I returned home, but hardly had I put them on when a friend came to visit me. We were friends in the army, from which both of us had been transferred to the local Public Security Bureau. He used to be a scout, so he always looked at things carefully. No sooner had he seen my new sandals than he burst out laughing, asking why one sandal was bigger than the other. I looked at them closely myself, and found one was really larger than the other. Immediately I removed them from my feet and measured them against each other, only to find that the larger one was also longer.

As soon as my friend left, I rushed back to the department store for an exchange. Remembering the number on her work clothes, I walked up to the saleswoman, placed my sandals on the counter, and told her that I had discovered something wrong with the sandals I bought in the morning and that I wanted an exchange. Instead of checking my sandals, with examining eyes she coldly swept over my faded Dacron army clothes from top to bottom, then from left to right. "No returns!" A dark cloud suddenly gathered over her chilly face.

"There's something wrong with the sandals—why can't I have an exchange?" I reasoned.

"It's our policy: All sales are final. No exchange. No refund."

I continued to reason with her, but in vain.

After dinner that evening, I sat chatting and drinking water with my old neighbor Lao Qiao under the tree in front of our houses. Lao Qiao, who was the assistant manager of a restaurant, told me funny unheard-of news and stories. Since I had nothing much to tell, I told him about the bad service in the stores—how I had failed to exchange my sandals. After hearing my story, he asked what clothes I wore on my two trips to the department store. It was Sunday, I told him, so I was wearing the same casual old army clothes I was in.

"You went to exchange your sandals, but why didn't you put on your police uniform?" he asked, pop-eyed.

"Would it make a difference?"

"Of course. Go again tomorrow. Put on your police uniform. I guarantee you will bring back a new pair."

I dressed as Lao Qiao suggested the next day and went to the store again with my sandals. It was the same saleswoman there. This time, when I walked up and stood by the counter, she quickly came over to ask what she could do for me. I handed my sandals to her, making more or less the same request as I did the day before. She gazed gently over my uniform and, without a word, exchanged them for a top-grade pair with exactly the same widths and lengths.

After telling Lao Qiao about my success, I asked him why the saleswoman exchanged the sandals for me when I wore my police uniform but not when I was wearing my casual clothing.

"You've been in the army living in the mountain valley for over ten years, and have become a real mountain guy," Lao Qiao roared with laughter. "You've just been given the job in the city and you don't know the peculiar ways of the city people. Some will just treat you according to your coats and caps. With a coat of 'tiger skin' you'd find it much easier when you deal with them."

Lao Qiao's words started a funny feeling in me. "How come the police uniform has become tiger skin?"

New Poems

By **Zhou** Daxin

Accompanied by his secretary Xiao Liang, Director Chang of the Bureau was chauffeured throughout his inspection trip to the various counties. Wherever he went, he was entertained by local officials with sumptuous dinners full of rare delicacies, all paid for by public funds. Every time the Director offered to pay for their food, his hosts would shake their heads smilingly: "Forget it! What times are we in now?"

After visiting all the places, they started their trip home. Night fell when they were halfway through, so the Director suggested that they stop at the roadside restaurant for dinner. The driver pulled up accordingly, and they soon ordered a whole table of food.

While the waiter was writing the bill for them, the Director said, "Throughout this trip, we've been eating free meals—all paid for by taxpayers. We should pay ourselves tonight. Please don't stop me. I earn more than you, and I want to be your host for tonight." The secretary and the driver found it difficult to accept, so they drew out their wallets, fighting to pay. Seeing that neither would give in, the Director smiled, "Now, how about this? Each of us will make up a poem. It must contain the following words: 'round, round, round,' 'sharp, sharp, sharp,' 'hundreds and thousands,' 'thousands and hundreds,' '. . . have . . .?' and 'no.' Whoever fails will pay. How's that?"

"Great!" answered the secretary and the chauffeur.

"Now, since I'm not very well educated, I'll go first," said the chauffeur after a moment of thinking as he looked down. "Here's my

25

poem."

> *My car's lights are round, round, round;*
> *My car's front is sharp, sharp, sharp.*
> *I have traveled hundreds and thousands of miles;*
> *I have driven thousands and hundreds of people.*
> *But have I ever had an accident?*
> *No.*

The Director nodded at him, "Pretty good poem. It's acceptable. You don't have to pay for this meal."
Then came the secretary's poem:

> *My pen is round, round, round;*
> *Its tip is sharp, sharp, sharp.*
> *I have written hundreds and thousands of "reports";*
> *I have summed up thousands and hundreds of cases of*
>   *"experience."*
> *But have I ever written an honest sentence?*
> *No.*

The Director nodded again, "Pretty good, too. You don't have to pay for the meal, either. Now listen, you two. Here's mine."

> *My mouth is round, round, round;*
> *My teeth are sharp, sharp, sharp.*
> *I have been invited to hundreds and thousands of banquets;*
> *I have hosted thousands and hundreds of dinners.*
> *But have I ever paid a penny?*
> *No.*

The secretary and the chauffeur clapped their hands, "Good poem! Good poem!"

"We have all made up a poem," the chauffeur then shouted with a smile, "and every one is good, so who should pay for the dinner?"

"All right, then," sighed the Director. "In such a case, we can only use public funds. Xiao Liang, go pay now. But don't forget to get a receipt so that we can have it reimbursed when we return home!"

An Art Lover

By **Xia** Xueqin

Ma Chao was an active art lover living on Ziling Alley. He had enjoyed daubing pictures ever since his childhood. In grade 5, when his teacher took the class to an art show, Ma Chao was fascinated by a traditional Chinese painting entitled *Autumn*. He stood there staring at it without blinking. The serried woods painted in deep colors, the lasting appeal of the blending of ink and wash, and especially the woman with a happy face showing joy at the autumn harvest reminded him of his dead mother. Clearly a motherless child seemed to understand more than the average. Only when the teacher called them together did he wake up and tear himself away from the painting. He caught the artist's name, Shi Banqiao, when he was turning about to join his class.

From then on, he started to dream of being a great painter one day. Later, Ma Chao learned about Zheng Banqiao, who turned out to be Shi Banqiao's teacher. Their names were the same except one word, thought the teenager.* Like a seed, Shi's name took root in Ma's heart. Occasionally when he came across Shi's paintings printed in the newspapers, he would cut them out and stick them in his favorite notebook. He loved Shi's paintings so much that he hated to leave them out of his sight. Ma Chao himself did not know why he did that. Was it because of his dead mother, or was it because of the weird name, Shi Banqiao?

There is always a gap between one's ambition and reality. After

---

* *Translator's note:* To be more accurate, Zheng Banqiao was a renowned painter of the Qing Dynasty (1644-1911), after whom Shi Banqiao named himself.

graduating from high school, Ma Chao tried the examination for admittance into the College of Fine Arts, but failed. He was very disappointed in himself, but despite this setback, Shi remained as important as ever in his heart.

After he became a factory worker, Ma Chao continued to worship Shi in the same way, and he continued to enjoy painting as before. Then, gradually, he even thought of owning one of Shi's paintings. Ma Chao mentioned this when he was chatting with a friend who worked for the city's Fine Arts Association. "That's easy," said the friend. "I have his address and phone number. Go to his home and beg for one. That's all." His helpful friend paused, then added, "But why do you have to own one of his? His paintings aren't that great."

"In one of his paintings there's a woman who looks like my mother," Ma Chao blurted out.

His friends all said he was an idiot, but the artist friend still promised to help him by contacting Shi.

With his month's income, Ma Chao bought two huge boxes of tonic drinks for Shi. He went to Shi's home with the nervous feeling of going to visit one who was his senior. Through humming and hawing, he told Shi the purpose of his visit.

"How come I don't know you?" said Shi, looking at Ma indifferently.

"I know you don't, but I know you. I have known you for twenty years."

"Who are you then?"

"I am nobody. Just one of your super fans."

"I have plenty of fans; how can I give each one a painting?"

"Of course not. Of course not. But—"

"You must know that each of my paintings can be sold for ten thousand bucks."

Ma Chao hung his head in silence. A little while later, he bade goodbye to Shi and departed, leaving the gifts for him.

Three years later, Ma Chao came to Shi's home again, this time with plenty of cash.

"Looking for me?" Shi asked, glancing at Ma Chao.

"Yes. I want to buy a painting!"

Shi's face instantly lit up with joy. Smiling, he invited him into his home. "Now, here. These are all new paintings. Pick any one you like."

In the most careless manner, Ma Chao picked one, paid Shi and started to walk out.

Shi showed him to the door politely, saying repeatedly, "Come again—you're always welcome. Come again—you're always welcome."

"Thank you!" said Ma Chao, tearing up the painting.

Shi flushed at what he saw. "You—you—you—how dare you tear up my painting!"

"It's not your painting. It's my money. I can do whatever I want with it," said Ma Chao as he walked downstairs.

Later on, Ma Chao quit his job in the factory and opened an art gallery on Ziling Alley, named Ma Liang's Art Centre. His business boomed from the day it opened. Before long, it became the best-known and busiest art centre in the city. Many of his friends—painting and calligraphy lovers—loved to come there to sit or to chat about art and life and to exchange anecdotes within the art circle. Of course, their hottest topic was still Ma Chao's art gallery.

"Ma Chao, what tricks do you have?" one of them asked. "How come your gallery boomed from the day it opened?"

"I have no tricks," Ma Chao smiled. "Don't take paintings too seriously. Just treat them like carrots and greens in the food market. That's all."

Everybody present became speechless. "Aren't you blaspheming art, Ma Chao?"

"Yes, art is priceless. But anything that has a price and can be sold is merchandise, or it has to be a bill, don't you agree?"

Again his friends were stupefied, but soon they were whispering to one another.

Doctor Song

By **Ling** Junyang

For some reason, the suicide rate of Hilly City had been climbing with no signs of declining. Finding it a pain in the neck, the municipality decided to create a Suicide Prevention Committee to bring it under control. Dr. Song, an expert in suicide prevention, was appointed chairman.

As the common saying goes, "A new official works hard for his name." In the beginning, by racking his brains, Dr. Song worked out many measures that effectively stopped the rise, then reversed its trend. However, his success was short lived: a few months later Hilly City's suicide rate quickly rebounded to its original level.

Sandwiched between his superior's chiding and the cold looks of his subordinates, Dr. Song felt extremely hurt. Coincidentally, as he discovered he had heart trouble, the stock market crashed and nearly wiped out all the savings the experienced stock speculator had accumulated during the previous few years. Doubtless, this dealt him another insufferable blow. Soon after, his wife decided to divorce him, and while he was fighting for the custody of their son, he was struck by a bolt from the blue once more—his son was killed in a traffic accident.

This series of misfortunes crushed Dr. Song, who now looked like a frost-bitten eggplant; he finally thought of death.

"The chairman of the Suicide Prevention Committee wants to commit suicide?" He found it rather ridiculous himself, but it did reveal some kind of desperation.

Dr. Song started to browse through information about suicides on the Internet, coming upon a headline, "Our Suicide Club Welcomes You!"

"I've never known there's such a club!" sighed Dr. Song. Reading it carefully, he learned that the club was located in Lakeside City, not far from his own. In the Suicide Club, members could enjoy all the pleasures of living in the world before taking their own lives. More ridiculous still, the establishment of this club was even approved by the local municipality. "I simply don't know what the officials are doing there!"

In the end, Dr. Song did register as a member after all.

Finally came the day when Dr. Song was invited to the activities of the Suicide Club. Entering the club, he found that its decor could be described only as luxurious. Led by a waiter, Dr. Song started to enjoy all sorts of services: he rode in a Mercedes Benz, stayed in a villa and was entertained with sumptuous dinners, all of which he had never dared to think of enjoying. He was also dressed in clothes that he had never dared to touch in fashion stores. In short, Dr. Song indulged himself in a luxurious life he could not even afford to dream of.

"Sir, your time is up," the waiter said in an indescribable tone while Dr. Song was lost in such joy and pleasure that he had simply forgotten the purpose of his visit. "Choose your method of suicide, please!" With this, the waiter gave him a pamphlet that described the various methods available for suicides.

"Wait a minute! I—I—I don't want to die yet!" Dr. Song suddenly found a strong will to live. "Is it all right if I don't commit suicide?" he stuttered as he found himself in an emergency.

"Of course, it is all right, sir," smiled the waiter, giving him a bag before ushering him out of the club.

Too anxious to wait, Dr. Song opened the bag as soon as he stepped out. It turned out to be a book on psychology, attached to which was a slip of paper with a Web address on it. He visited the Web site when he returned home, discovering it was the Web page of the Suicide Club, which published the number of its visitors, all of whom said, "I can't live any longer!" when they came, but few of whom really committed suicide in the end.

As he read on, Dr. Song suddenly seemed to realize the real function of the Suicide Club in Lakeside City. Shrugging his shoulders, he decided to follow suit and be a worthy chairman of the Suicide Prevention Committee.

Money for Bottles

By Li Yongkang

Without the lawsuit, he might never have known the real cause of the accident.

At noon that day they had a blackout with no water supply, so he took his son, daughter-in-law and grandson to the Flies Restaurant for lunch. While his son had Chinese wolfberry wine, he ordered a bottle of beer—drinking beer was a habit he had developed after retirement. When the waiter brought over the beer, his grandson seized it and said, as if he were an expert, "Let me see if it's a fake." He began to shake it in the way his father usually checked out his white spirit. The grandfather was about to stop him when the bottle suddenly exploded. The grandson was unhurt, but the grandfather could not open one of his eyes anymore.

He wanted to take it as an unfortunate accident and endure the loss of his eye himself, but his son would neither forgive the brewery nor let it off easily. He not only took the matter to the Consumers' Association, but also went to the law office. The brewery, though, made a wise decision, readily promising to compensate fifty thousand yuan for the old man's injury. At this point, the old man had learned that eight or nine of ten beer bottles that exploded were ones that had been used repeatedly. He felt guilty when he accepted the money, for he had sold numerous such bottles himself.

From then on, whenever he had beer bottles, he would simply break them and dump them into the garbage can.

As reasonable young people, his son and daughter-in-law said, "Since Dad paid in blood for that money, he should spend it in whatever way he likes."

"The beer bottles," he said to himself, "even if I don't sell them, others will. The breweries will still buy them back and reuse them anyway. Why not use the fifty thousand yuan to open a small shop just to buy back people's beer bottles? Besides, I can still sell the broken glass to the glass plants after they are smashed." He told his son and daughter-in-law about his idea, but neither supported him, saying that he would be looking for trouble and torture for himself, and he was a bit too naïve.

But he had a peculiar habit he had developed throughout the past thirty years or so: once he had decided to do something, and once an idea had taken root in his mind, even the power of ten oxen could not stop him. Thus, his Recyclable Materials Buy-Back Shop opened as scheduled.

In the beginning, it was the garbage pickers who shuttled through the streets and lanes by bicycle who sold bottles to him. Gradually, other people brought bottles to him. Some who knew about his story did not even want to take the money, which would move him to tears. Yet he would insist that everyone accept the money, even if it was just a dime or two. Whenever somebody refused it in deadly earnest, he would say sincerely, "Come on! Just for your legwork!"

With his business run this way, its income, of course, could not cover the expenses. You can just imagine: he paid three dimes for a bottle, but after he smashed it, he could sell it for only a few pennies to the glass plant. Nevertheless, he felt that every penny lost was worth it—every accident he prevented would count. "I'm old, and that's what I can do," he said.

"I'll close it down when I have used up all my money," he told his son and daughter-in-law.

One day, almost nobody brought bottles to him. Individual household bottle sellers were out of sight, while garbage pickers who bicycled by looked into his shop with strange eyes. At first, he thought he did not pay them enough, so he raised the purchasing price by several pennies per bottle. He wrote the notice on a piece of red paper and posted it on the wall, but it did not help: nobody came for days. Then he raised it again, but again no one came to sell bottles to him. He was baffled— "It's the hot season for beer consumption right now!"

When he returned home in the evening, he began to drink in dejection.

"Dad, will your business boom soon?" his son and daughter-in-law teased him.

He shook his head, sighing. His daughter-in-law then quietly handed him a newspaper. Opening his eyes, he discovered that after learning about his shop, the brewery which had paid him for his injury had got in touch with the newspaper and claimed that they would commend and award him for what he was doing. It also said that it would offer him a position as special adviser and that it intended to start a joint venture with him. He was outraged, his face turning blue.

"People in my office said we will become rich soon," said his son.

"Dad, I think—" The daughter-in-law tried to sound him out carefully, but he interrupted her by striking the table with a firm fist.

"It's killing without a knife!" he said furiously.

An Old Model Worker

By **Ye** Dachun

From the day he became an apprentice until the days preceding his retirement, Lao Mo fed coal to the boiler, for almost forty years. He made the boiler room his first home and seldom took a day off, so his wife deserted him and his daughter did badly at school until she had to drop out, while his son, who was left without guidance, misbehaved and finally ended up in jail.

Lao Mo, though, became a Model Worker* of the province, thanks to his devotion to the boiler. His certificates of merit inscribed on boards and in frames covered the walls in his home. His numerous medals of merit crowded the walls of his cupboard behind its glass door. Based on an eight-hour day, somebody added up his unspent holidays and overtime and found that Lao Mo had rendered more than twenty years of extra service.

Shortly before his fortieth anniversary as a boiler feeder, it was rumored that the factory was going bankrupt and would soon be sold to a business owner. The anxious Lao Mo became worried and restless. If he had not been tied to the boiler, he would have gone to his co-workers to find out what was going on days ago. But he was a man with a cool head full of ideas. He knew that the boiler could not

---

* *Translator's note:* A Model Worker was somebody who worked tirelessly, doing an outstanding job, while being loyal to the government and without asking for anything in return for overtime work and so on. An honorable title or equivalent of a hero among workers, it was a popular title for many years, especially from the 1950s to the 1970s.

operate without him and that the factory would come to a halt without the boiler. If the boiler exploded, it might even cause deaths. Furthermore, he was a Model Worker of the province who could not lower himself to the level of the common workers. "Whatever happens, I should have confidence in the government and the local leadership. I should only help, not meddle."

Then one day the factory director, who had not shown up for a long time, unexpectedly came into the boiler room, looking wan and sallow. Offering a cigarette to the exhausted old worker covered with black sweat, the factory director felt grieved and guilty.

"Lao Mo, please stop feeding coal to the boiler from today on," he said slowly. "Take a good rest yourself." Then he wrote a few lines on the cigarette box and gave it to Lao Mo. "From tomorrow on, the state-owned factory will become a private business. Today is also my last day as the factory director. I haven't really cared for your well-being throughout the past years. I owe you so much at the personal level. This is also the last time I am exercising my power as factory director. I am granting you a Model Worker subsidy. Please go and get your money without delay."

Lao Mo was trembling when he received the thin slip. It showed a sum that was neither big nor small, but enough for his son to start a small business when he came out of prison. As soon as the factory director turned and left, Lao Mo threw it into the fire. "I not only shall share happiness with others, but mishaps as well. Now that the factory is closing down, how could I have the face to go and cash the Model Worker subsidy?"

Lao Mo stopped the fire in the boiler, but he still stayed by the boiler around the clock, for he feared that infuriated workers would do foolish things—they might steal the parts or smash it and sell it as scrap.

It is hard to know people's hearts when catastrophes are befalling them. In such crises, every character shows his or her true colors. Indeed, in the small hours of one night, several shadows sneaked into his boiler room, waking him up.

"What do you want?" he shouted in a stern voice.

"None of your business. Be a smart man and just go on sleeping," said one shadow. "Otherwise, we'll have to tie you up!"

"Don't you dare to lay your hands on the boiler!" Lao Mo roared in rage. "I've been staying with the boiler for so many years and I love it more than my wife. If you dare to smash it, don't blame me for being rude!" The furious old man swung his sledgehammer in the air, scaring all the shadows away.

After the new factory director assumed office, one way or another, he learned of Lao Mo's heroic deeds, for which he awarded him a big sum of money. When Lao Mo received it, he gave it to the needy unemployed workers and his sick workmates. One or more of those who benefited were among the shadows that had wanted to smash the boiler.

Lao Mo attended to the boiler as before, still as self-motivated, still working hard and overtime. He just felt dejected—a feeling beyond description—when he thought that in the past he was contributing to the state but that now everything he did was for an individual owner. Though he was much better paid than when the factory was government-owned and his benefits had also improved, he always found an indescribable cloud of melancholy clinging in his mind. As it weighed on him, he would sigh and mumble to his old pal, the boiler, and weep sometimes.

One evening, the new factory director, who took pride in his success, strolled by the boiler and was surprised to see the sweaty Lao Mo covered with coal dust from head to foot. "Why don't you wear your boiler suit and your gauze mask and gloves?" he asked. "And why didn't you go and get an electric fan?"

"I'm an uncouth worker. Not that delicate!" chuckled Lao Mo. "Does a boiler man really need any of these? I've been working like this for forty years. I'm quite used to it."

"No. That won't do. The new factory has its new rules. Our labor safety rules must be followed strictly. The boiler room is no exception. It must not drag down the whole factory," said the new factory director. "If I see you working bare backed or without wearing a mask again tomorrow, you will lose your bonus and I will suspend you from work as well."

Lao Mo was dumbfounded.

"How many people work in the boiler room?" the new director continued.

"Only me," said Lao Mo.

The factory director was stupefied. "I will send two more people here tomorrow," he then said.

Sweeping his hand, Lao Mo said, "Don't send anyone here. I can look after the boiler all by myself. I have been doing this myself for so many years—"

"Nonsense!" The new director became angry now. "You work overtime day after day, year after year, without even taking a day off on festivals and holidays. It's against the Labor Act. Do you want to get me into legal trouble or topple me?"

Lao Mo felt a shiver in his heart, uncontrollable tears trickling down his old cheeks.

Lost Voice

By **Ah** Zhu

Soiled by mud mixed with sweat, TV A's journalist Lu Bin and his photographer Wu Sheng, both working for *Voice,* finally finished their interviews in Dagou Village. Immediately, they came to its upper township administration compound to interview the township leader, Wang Fuchang, who was playing mahjong with his other officials.

"*Voice* or noise, what do you want? Speak out," Wang said without raising his head.

"Mr. Wang, we'd like to know how you have been collecting money from the villagers for the building of your roads. " Lu Bin pushed the microphone close to his mouth.

"Several TV stations have interviewed me on this. We have ready answers for you." Again he did not raise his head.

"Could you please tell us what has happened in Dagou Village, then?"

This time, Mr. Wang did raise his head. "Go and ask the county government about it. I have nothing to tell you," he answered rudely. "*Voice!* Who cares! I don't buy it!" With this, he signaled his people to turn the journalist and his photographer away. Instantly the hallway became chaotic as Wang's officials tried to manhandle the two intruders.

Meanwhile, two breathless men emerged from the stairs. One was Director Zong of the Public Communications Department of the county government, who had been trying to locate Lu Bin ever since he had learned of his arrival. Zong was all smiles as he swept over the ID card the journalist was carrying. "Oh, dear! Mr. Lu, why didn't you let us know ahead of time? I'm sorry we are late. Won't you forgive us? Now come over to the meeting room. Please." Zong's unexpected hospitality took Lu Bin by surprise, and he did not know how to respond.

The township's secretary and Zong's assistant immediately picked up their guests' equipment, leading them to the simple meeting room. Zong himself went into the mahjong room, or Wang's office. About ten minutes later, he came to the meeting room with Wang.

Wang seemed to have changed to a new person as he approached Lu Bin. "I'm sorry," he said, holding Lu Bin's hands. "I was lost in playing and must have offended you."

Next came the interview, which went very smoothly, beyond Lu Bin's expectations. Undeniably, Wang tried to avoid answering some of the questions directly, but generally speaking, he answered whatever he was asked. When the interview was over, Lu Bin told Zong that he also wanted to interview the Party leader of the county.

"No problem," said Zong. "In fact, Secretary Zheng is also inviting you to dinner tonight."

In the evening, the whole team proceeded directly to the best hotel in town, where Mr. Zheng Ran, Party leader of the county, had been expecting them for quite some time.

Zheng, a not-very-tall man in his fifties, looked like a practical man to Lu Bin's mind.

"I want to make it clear: I'm not entertaining you with a sumptuous feast in order to seal up your mouths today," Zheng said as he welcomed his guests at the entrance to the restaurant. "It's just that I've long heard your big names and seen you on TV many times— I'm honored to have the opportunity to meet you in person and to make friends with you. Today, we'll talk friendship only, not work."

Food began to arrive and wine glasses were filled, with Zheng proposing the first toast to So-and-So for such-and-such reasons, then the second, followed by the third. After gulping down a few glasses, as expected, Zheng started his conversation topics around *Voice*. He knew the program well, telling how the Party secretary and the mayor of a certain city, the director of a certain bureau and so on and so forth, one by one, got caught, lost their jobs and were found guilty, all after they were exposed by *Voice*. Some of his stories were new even to Lu Bin, which nearly terrified Wang to death.

"I wanted to do a good job quickly when I came to Q County," continued Zheng as he skillfully shelled the large shrimps, then put them onto Lu Bin's plate. "But I've gone too fast, so I have displeased some people above me and some under me. Nowadays, you can't get anything done without money. If we don't collect money from the villagers, where can we find it?" Zheng nearly broke down, so he pacified himself by gulping down a glass of wine. "Today, we won't mention titles. I'm older than you, so I am your elder brother, and you are my younger brother. You won't topple your brother because of this, will you?"

Lu Bin became a little soft-hearted, regretting having met such a county Party leader. "As journalists," Lu Bin said, "we follow instructions from our supervisors, who follow theirs. We report the truth, but it is the head of the TV station who decides what to broadcast."

Zheng sighed a breath of relief, saying, "But you are still the most important 'kings' without crowns."

When they had drunk and eaten their fill, Zheng accompanied them back to the hotel as if they were distinguished guests. No sooner had Lu Bin and his photographer entered their room than the doorbell rang: it was Zong. "Mr. Zheng has prepared this special material for you," he said, leaving a large, bulging envelope on their bed.

Seeing Zong off, Lu Bin opened the document bag, finding several stacks of hundred-yuan bills, totaling sixty thousand yuan.

The next morning, as scheduled, Lu Bin interviewed Zheng in his office, after which he told him, "Mr. Zheng, we have looked through the documents, and are returning every one of them to you. Here you are."

Upon his return to the TV station, Lu Bin buried himself in the editing. The morning of the third day saw him emerging, with black eye sockets—a sign of lack of sleep—from his office with his finished news report ready to deliver to the supervisor who had sent him to Dagou Village.

"Someone from the department above the TV station has called our head. Our head has decided not to broadcast your news report," said the supervisor.

"What?" Lu Bin flew into a rage. He was stupefied, his mouth wide open. "No way! Even if I can't topple these dirty officials," he cursed to himself, "I must win something for the villagers!" Then an idea struck him.

He managed to get in touch with Zheng and Wang, who had slipped into a nearby hotel and were looking for connections to kill his news report. Lu Bin gave them a private preview. The ten-minute program was just too much for them. Wang's feet started to shake uncontrollably and sweat oozed from his forehead.

Finally, Wang broke the silence, "We have collected over 300,000 yuan this year from the villagers, but we've thrown away more than 200,000 on this trip, without seeing even a ripple. Now—"

"Mr. Lu," interrupted Zheng, "what do you think we should do?"

"Your county was hit hard by natural disasters last year, and the villagers really don't have the money for you. Why not give them a break this year? Also, the two arrests you made were illegal. I think it's better to release them."

Zheng thought for a moment and said, "It makes sense."

Soon another three days had passed. At last, a representative from Dagou Village called to thank Mr. Lu. "Our money has been returned and the two people they had arrested were released two days ago. But could you do us another favor—could you ask them to return the money to the other villages as well?"

"What?" shouted Lu Bin. "You aren't telling me they've returned the money only to your village, are you?"

"Yes."

Lu Bin hung up, for he could not stand another moment. Immediately he dialed Zheng's phone number.

Zheng answered the phone himself. "Honestly, we knew even on the day we met that your report wouldn't be broadcast," he told Lu Bin.

"Why did you still return the money to Dagou Village, then?"

"We are friends after all. I can't afford to offend you, can I?"

Hearing that, Lu Bin felt something blocking his throat. He wanted to swallow it down, but could not. He wanted to shout, but found no voice. Finally, he flung the receiver on the desk and roared, "F—f—f—k you!"

Human Harmony

Celebration Ceremony for the Day When Wars Are Eliminated

By **Zhou** Daxin

Location of ceremony: Outside the headquarters of the United Nations
Starts at: At 9 hours, 9 minutes and 9 seconds in the morning
Attended by: Heads of all the countries and representatives of every country and nation
Presiding: United Nations Chairman of the Preparatory Committee (hereafter, "presiding master")

Procedure and activities:
1. Presiding master declares: "Humankind's celebration of the elimination of wars now begins." Ten thousand guns start firing; each fires a salvo of ten rounds, each round representing one year. The 100,000 shots fired symbolize that the human race has been dreaming of this day for 100,000 years.
2. The band plays "Song of Peace." Everybody present sings in his or her own language the following verses:

    The plague of war is gone from every place;
    A lasting peace arrives on earth with grace.
    We'll point no more guns at each other's face;
    Humankind shall remain a happy race.

3. United Nations Secretary General speaks. In his speech, he announces the following figures:

- Ever since the first war broke out within the human race, there have been x million wars.
- These wars have killed x hundred million lives.
- These wars have left behind x hundred million handicapped human beings.
- These wars have wasted x billion of hours.
- The monies spent on these wars are worth x billion tons of gold.

4. Showing the remains of those who died fighting, unearthed from each and every one of the old battlefields in the world. The two score giant TV screens set up along the four sides of the gathering simultaneously show the excavations and heap after heap of remains.

5. Playing the horrifying screams of those wounded in battles and the desperate crying of those who lost their relatives, which have been recorded by reporters of different ages.

6. Destroying all weaponry in stock. As the presiding master announces it, a little planet appears on all the giant TV screens around the gathering. The planet is covered with all types of weapons made by different countries, ranging from nuclear missiles and hydrogen bombs to tanks and cannons. A boy and a girl walk up to the platform, and together they push the button to destroy the weapons. In a twinkling, the weaponry and the planet, which may otherwise bump into the earth, explode, burning into ashes instantly.

7. Freeing the peace doves. On hearing the presiding master's announcement, the thousands of children release the thousands of peace doves from their bosoms. In the blue sky, the doves gather together to form a giant word, "LOVE."

8. Cleansing the earth of the bloodstains left by the wars. The gigantic globe placed in front of the platform slowly starts turning. Everyone sees clearly that every continent was stained with red

that resembles blood. A representative from each nation, hose in hand, shoots at the globe. In two minutes, the "bloodstains" are cleansed.

9. Over three thousand actors and actresses from every corner of the world start a huge group gymnastic performance. Waving their wreaths, they form a line of large words: "WE ARE ALL BROTHERS AND SISTERS."

10. Giving away anger management devices. The presiding master says, "Now that the world is rich in material products and fully democratic, it is primarily emotional rather than economical and political factors that cause human conflicts. Accordingly, everybody will be given a free anger management device. Those present will be the first to receive this device." With this, he pushes the button beside him. "Bang" comes the sound as numerous little rubber balls start to fly down from the sky. Everybody at the ceremony finds one in his or her arms. Written on the ball is, "Please hit me when you are angry!" A curious man hits his, and out jumps an almost-real beautiful girl. The girl bows at him politely and says, "I am sorry, but please do vent your anger at me." Meanwhile, she gives out some kind of extremely elegant fragrance. When a woman strikes her ball, out jumps an almost-real handsome young man, who bows politely at her and says, "I am sorry, but please do vent your anger at me." At the same time, he gives out some kind of elegant fragrance mixed with a light odor of men's sweat.

The ceremony ends in the soft music entitled, "How Nice to Be Alive."

What Scares the General

By **Lin** Ruqiu

When the general set foot in his home village again, his hair was all gray. On his chin was a visible scar, which he said was a souvenir from the Civil War. He used to have two sets of relatives, but they were all killed by the enemy. The older generation of the village had all died and none of the younger generation could really recognize him, except his childhood friend Brother Cang, with whom he used to find river snails, collect bird eggs and pick mountain pears. A hospitable host, Cang accompanied the general when he went to pay respects to his parents at their tombs. He also walked him around the places they had frequented in their childhood years.

At night, Cang set two beds in an "L" shape, saying, "When we were young, we used to sleep on the same bed. Now that we are old, I'm afraid you won't enjoy it as much. So let's separate ourselves into two beds, instead." The old pals chatted into the night until they fell asleep. But in the small hours, the longer the general stayed in bed, the less sleepy he became. He got up quite a few times, unintentionally waking up Cang as well.

"So you can't sleep on the strange bed?" yawned Cang.

The general shook his head.

The following night the general also got up quite a few times. Very puzzled, Cang asked, "What happened? Anything wrong with you?"

"I've heard crying, children's crying. It's soft babbling," said the general.

Cang put his ear to the window lattice and listened attentively, but heard nothing. "Hey, you've been fighting in battles for half of your life," he smiled at the general. "You aren't telling me you're afraid of ghosts!"

Giving a bitter smile, the general shook his head again.

The third night also saw the general tossing and turning in bed. He got up, then lay down, again and again, repeating that he had heard children's crying. Finally, Cang got off his own bed, opened the door and went out to listen, first to the east, then the west. He shook his head as he stifled his laughter. Stepping in, he closed the door and said, in surprise, "Strange. How come I can't hear anything?"

Again, the general just shook his head.

On the fourth day the general decided to leave, despite Cang's insistence on keeping him for some more time, so Cang walked him to the bus terminal. When they reached the village entrance, the general found a little girl crying by a ridge* adjacent to the rice-fields. Looking nervous, he strode over and held her in his arms, drawing out a handkerchief to dry her tears. Stroking her head, he coaxed her into stopping. "Why are you crying?" he asked. "Are you hungry?"

The girl shook her head.

"Do you want to have a bun?" he asked her.

She shook her head again.

"Want some bread then?"

Again, she shook her head.

Cang who was listening the whole time could not help laughing. "People in our village are not yet rich, but they have plenty to eat. Nobody has to go hungry anymore! You can buy buns and bread in the village's small restaurant or the convenience store. The children

---

* *Translator's note:* Approximately fifty centimeters wide and forty centimeters high, the typical earth path in the story retains water and fertilizer for the crops. Farmers also use it when they carry heavy loads to and from the fields.

are all tired of such food."

The general then asked the little girl, "Do you go to school?"

She nodded, saying she was in Grade 3. The general pulled out a big gold pen and gave it to her. She giggled when she received the fountain pen. Then she twisted away from him and ran away. The general laughed as he gazed at her receding figure.

"Stop running. Stop running," he shouted, waving his hand. "Or you will trip and fall!"

"The old and the young!" Cang sighed. "When you get old, you not only behave like a child, but get along with kids easily."

"You are right. You are right," the general nodded. "I just love children, but I am really scared when they cry."

Cang watched him uncomprehendingly. The general offered him a cigarette, lighting one for himself. Drawing a deep breath, he spoke slowly as he blew out the smoke:

"One day during the Civil War in 1948, I was taking a group of children, seven of them, out of the enemy-controlled zone. But on our way, I found that our roads had been sealed off by the enemy. Unable to break through the blockade, we could only hide ourselves in the reed marshes. After starving for five days and nights, we had to fill our stomachs with reed roots. It was winter and the roots were bitter and hard to chew. The kids could not swallow them. They kept crying and crying because they were so hungry, but they dared not cry loudly in fear the enemy would discover us. The hungry kids' suppressed, helpless and desperate crying cut my heart like a knife, simply tearing me apart. How miserable I was! But we were surrounded by the enemy, and we did not even have a gun. Besides, they were only eleven- and twelve-year-olds, no match for the enemy soldiers. So we could only stay hiding quietly there. Sobbing feebly, three of the kids were starved to death right under my nose. It was five days and nights! The kids' hungry sobbing plunged into my brain like a dagger. Several decades have passed, but I still cannot wipe out the painful memory. That's why I'm very sensitive to children's crying. I cannot stand children's crying. I'm most scared of their crying. I couldn't sleep well these few nights, because I heard children crying every night."

Cang did not respond for quite a while. "If kids ever cry today, few of them really cry because they are hungry," he eventually broke the silence. "So, brother, you don't have to take it to heart all the time!"

For a long time, the general looked impassive but finally nodded in agreement, "Mm."

Su Seven

By **Feng** Jicai

In the early years of the Republic of China, Dr. Su, whose full name was Su Jinsan, opened a clinic in Xiaobailou in the city of Tianjin. He was known all over the city as the best expert in treating bone problems. Even foreigners who broke their limbs racing horses would come to him for treatment.

Dr. Su, who wore a long robe, was a tall man in his fifties with skinny but strong hands. He had red lips, white teeth and bright, shining eyes. He had a shiny black goatee that seemed to have been soaked in oil. When he spoke, his words seemed to have come straight from his chest carrying *dantian qi*.* Whether heard far or near, they were always loud and clear. Should he have joined the theatrical troupe those days, he would have become a real rival to Jin Shaoshan. Still more impressive was what his clever, quick and neat hands could do. When somebody came to him with a sprain or a broken bone, the clear-minded doctor with sharp eyes would easily find out the exact problem by probing their skin and pressing the flesh underneath with his fingers. All of a sudden, like lightning, his hands would turn up and down around the limb like two white birds. The patients heard only cracking or snapping sounds, and before they could feel any pain, their fractures had been set. Then he would cover the area with salve and secure the bones with splints. The fractures would heal and no second visit would be necessary. If patients ever returned, they mostly came to give him a deep bow or to express their heartfelt

---

* *Translator's note: Dantian qi* is deep breathing controlled by the diaphragm.

thanks verbally or through a flat board with grateful words inscribed on it.

Talented people with special skills often have peculiar ways. Dr. Su was one with a rule that could not be broken: every patient who came for treatment, be they rich or poor, friends or relatives, must first put seven silver dollars on his counter. Otherwise, he would not see them. What kind of rule was that? But that was his rule!

"He cares for money, not his patients," people sniffed. "He is just worth seven silver dollars." Accordingly, out of disrespect, they nicknamed him "Su the Seven Silver Dollars," or "Su Seven" for short. They called him Dr. Su in his presence, but Su Seven behind his back. Thus, nobody knew his real name, Su Jinsan.

Dr. Su loved playing cards. One day he had nothing to do, and two card-player friends had come to play with him. Since there were only three of them but four were needed, he asked Dr. Hua to join them—Dr. Hua's clinic was north of his, not far away. When they were deep into the game, a passenger tricyclist* named Zhang Si rushed in and stopped against the door, his right hand holding his left elbow. Sweat was streaming down from his head, his small gown showing a wet ring around the neck. Obviously, he was in unbearable pain caused by the injured arm. But how could the tricyclist, who lived on whatever he made on a daily basis, afford the seven silver dollars? Zhang Si said he could not pay Dr. Su up front, but promised to pay him later on, as he groaned in pain. Yet, playing in the same old way, Dr. Su paid no attention to him and continued to pick his cards, check them and calculate them. Appearing happy one moment, worried the next, then shocked, then pretentiously calm, Dr. Su concentrated fully on the cards at the table. One of the players who could not stand it anymore pointed toward the door, but Dr. Su's eyes were still fixed on the cards. Su Seven had shown the real meaning of his name!

---

* *Translator's note:* A passenger tricyclist makes a living by pedaling passengers.

Dr. Hua, who was well known for his kindness, excused himself by saying he had to go to the washroom. He walked to the backyard, snuck out of the door at the back and found his way to the street. From a distance, he quietly beckoned Zhang Si to come over, then drew seven silver dollars from inside his pocket and gave them to him. Before Zhang Si could express his thanks to him, Dr. Hua hurried back to the table by the same route, and continued to play his cards as if nothing had happened.

A moment later, Zhang Si staggered into the room again and placed his seven silver dollars on the counter. The crisp sounds from the silver dollars worked better than the bell this time. Before Zhang Si raised his head, Dr. Su was already in front of him, sleeves rolled up. Dr. Su placed Zhang Si's arm on the counter, squeezed its bones several times, then pulled it to the left and pushed it to the right, before he pressed it hard from the top as he supported it firmly from underneath. Zhang Si shrank his neck and shoulders, gritted his teeth and closed his eyes, readying himself for some rough acts, when he heard Dr. Su say, "Done." Dr. Su immediately covered the area with some salve and secured the arm with splints. He also gave Zhang Si several doses of medicine to relieve his pain and to improve his blood circulation. Zhang Si said he had no more money for the medicine.

"You can have it for free," said Dr. Su, returning to the card players.

Everybody lost some games and won some that day. They all indulged in playing until dark, when their empty stomachs kept groaning. Only then did they leave the clinic. When they were about to step out, Dr. Su stretched out his skinny hand to stop Dr. Hua, asking him to stay. After the other two card players had left, Dr. Su took seven silver dollars from the pile in front of his seat and thrust them into Dr. Hua's hand.

"There's something I need to tell you," he said to the stupefied Dr. Hua. "Don't mistake me for a stone-hearted man. It is just the rule I have set that cannot be broken. That's all."

Dr. Hua took these words with him and pondered them for three days and three nights, but he still could not understand him thoroughly. Yet from the bottom of his heart, he admired Dr. Su for what he was, what he did and what it meant.

The "Government's" Assassin

By **Sun** Fangyou

On Shangwu Street in south Chenzhou there lived a man by the name of Qiu Ying. Qiu was a well-known "government's" assassin, who would chase and kill only prominent political offenders, notorious robbers and other people the local authorities had listed for execution.

As the story goes, with no brother and sister, Qiu became an orphan at the age of five. At six, he started to learn *gongfu* from his uncle, later acquiring a perfect set of martial art skills. His light martial art was second to nobody's; he could leap onto roofs and vault over walls as adeptly as walking on the ground.

Thanks to his reputation, whenever the local government failed to catch a criminal, it would ask Qiu to assassinate him.

That year, east Chenzhou was frequently harassed by a great robber named Gai Tian. Gai was a "lone thief"—he acted all by himself, never co-operating with anybody. Such thieves were usually daredevils, difficult to chase and extremely dangerous to deal with. In fact, Gai had been captured by the local authorities several times, but each time he escaped due to negligent guarding. The government had long since issued a document declaring that he deserved death, for he had been robbing nobody but the local government. Accordingly, the prefect invited Qiu over, offering him two thousand taels of silver for Gai's head. Having seen Gai before, Qiu did not need his portrait, so he just set out with his sword.

After over a month of inquiries and private investigation, he finally learned of Gai's whereabouts. As it turned out, Gai was a very tricky man. He knew that the local authorities were trying to catch him wherever he was. In such a situation, you might never think he would dare to sleep in his own home, but that was exactly what he did. Taking advantage of people's disbelief, he simply snored under the nose of his enemy. In the depth of one night, when Gai disappeared into the dark after another robbery, Qiu chased him closely until he got to a small village, where he slipped into a deserted yard. Knowing it was Gai's home, Qiu jumped over the fence and hid in a corner. The yard was not big; within it there were three shabby thatched rooms and a small kitchen. It was pitch dark, so it took Qiu a while to figure out his directions.* There, Gai stood still in front of his door for some time. Finally, when he was about to enter the room, he suddenly turned about, looking around on full alert. Only when he found nothing suspicious did he open the door and go in. Qiu was about to move forward when he heard Gai's door open again. Out came Gai, jumping from east to west as if facing a forbidden enemy. Holding his breath, Qiu said to himself, "Gai is really no ordinary robber."

After a while, Gai seemed to have calmed down and stepped in again quietly. Deciding it was time to act, in a flying motion Qiu tiptoed over and clung to the wall by the entrance, deliberately making some noise. As if he had been waiting behind the door, Gai suddenly opened it and thrust out his sharp sword, a black shadow gushing out instantly. Qiu thought Gai had come out with his sword and was about to kill him, but immediately suspected it might be a trick. In the twinkling of an eye, while Qiu was still wondering what to do, Gai had already shot out through the window. With no way out, Qiu cleverly lay down on the black object, a quilt Gai had thrown out.

Gai searched every corner, but failed to find Qiu. Qiu lay there breathing noiselessly, waiting for the moment of assassination. As he expected, after finding nothing suspicious, Gai decided to pick up

---

* *Translator's note:* It is said that masters of *gongfu* (kung fu) can sense objects in the dark.

his quilt and go back into his room. At this moment, Qiu raised his sword, removing Gai's head instantly.

Qiu frowned briefly when he smelled the hot blood, then he drew out a wrapping cloth and wrapped up the head. He was about to leave when somebody inside called out "Tian'er." He looked in the direction of the voice. A shivering old woman was groping her way out of the room. "Tian'er," she called out gently, feeling her way forward along the wall as if touching the body of an elephant.

"So she must be Gai's blind mother!" Qiu thought, stupefied. Then he put down the wrapping cloth and moved away Gai's remains gently before he entered the room and lit a candle.

"Tian'er, what have you done again?" asked the old mother on hearing the noise.

Qiu dared not answer, but opened the parcel Gai had brought home. In the parcel, besides silver and gold, there were several hot steamed buns. Qiu walked up and gave the buns to the old woman, who ate them up like a hungry wolf. "You have sworn several times that you wouldn't do it again, so why did you?" she reproached her "son," looking stone cold and sober.

Qiu remained speechless.

"Speak out!" The trembling old woman pressed harder for an answer, as she "stared" at her "son."

Overcome by grief, Qiu said after a long while of silence, "Aunt, I'm Gai Tian's friend! Gai Tian has left home for a faraway place. He won't be home for some time, and he wants me to look after you."

Terrified for some time at what she had heard, the old woman finally sighed, "It's all my blind eyes' fault. I have blamed my visitor by mistake! Gai Tian lost his father at the age of nine. It was with painstaking efforts that I brought him up, but unexpectedly he took to evil ways. How sad and disappointed I am!" With this the old woman wiped her tears, then continued, "Please do persuade him to quit stealing and become a good man again!"

Finding his eyes somewhat moist, Qiu promised to do whatever he could, adding he would ask somebody to send food and drinks to her from the next day on. Saying goodbye to the old mother, Qiu carried Gai's remains and buried them somewhere among the unmarked burial mounds outside the village. Then he knelt down to comfort Gai's spirit in heaven, promising him that he would take good care of his mother.

The following day, Qiu received his reward after presenting Gai's head to the local authorities. After that he hired somebody to send food and drinks to the blind mother every day.

One evening, while he was chasing another prominent criminal for his head, he passed by Gai's village. It was already dark, so he decided to visit the old woman instead. Gai's mother was overjoyed, thankfully grasping his hands, which she fondled for quite some time. Groping around, she made the bed for him, saying, "My child, Gai Tian hasn't been home these days. Luckily, I have you around!"

Qiu lied to her that he and Gai were sworn brothers who had long since completed a ceremony before the celestial beings, so he was her younger son now. After that he said emotionally, "Aunt, I lost my mother when I was a small child. Now you are just my own mother." She burst into tears, and did not stop crying until quite a while later. Then she asked Qiu, "May I touch your sword?" Qiu pulled out the double-edged sword and gave it to her. Receiving the sword, she felt it with her hands, swayed it in front of her eyes, then sniffed at it. All of a sudden, she jumped, flying into the air. Landing in a fighting position, she accurately cut off the wick of the candle in a simple stroke and turned the room into a patch of darkness.

Qiu was stunned—he had never imagined that she could use the sword so skillfully. He quickly slipped under a cover, dodging the dazzling sharp sword that gleamed in the dark. Like raindrops that could fall on Qiu any time, her sword created a net that encased him tightly, leaving him no way to escape. The tip of her sword would accurately touch him in the chest, then lift up his coat. Qiu's chest suffered so many cuts that bits of cloth flew like snow in the air. The terrified Qiu was trying to escape when the sword landed right on his neck. As if she were exerting a thousand pounds of force, she pressed him so hard that he dared not exhale.

"I know everything," the angry old woman blasted at him. "It was you who killed my son! Although he was not a lawful man, he was a good son to me. Though he was a robber, he never harassed the common people. And you, you help the wicked do evil—you try to kill the innocent for the local authorities. How could I spare you!"

Qiu closed his eyes in agony.

The sword then fell loose gradually. Withdrawing her *gongfu,* the old woman put down the sword, lit the candle, felt her way to the bed and sat herself up. "Go away," she said exhaustedly. "Knowing you lost your mother when you were young and that you are a brave man with some conscience still, I'll spare your life." With this, she drew out a new robe, throwing it to him.

Seeing the robe that the blind old woman had sewn for him stitch by stitch through feeling and touching, Qiu seemed to be engulfed in motherly love for the very first time in his life. Unable to hold back his tears, he threw himself on his knees, calling her, "Mother, mother, mother!" Then he put his sword back into the case and said emotionally, "Mother, from today on, I am your own son."

The old woman broke down, crying her heart out.

Walking out of the village in dejection, Qiu could not but look back, only to see Gai's house engulfed in flames. Startled, he dashed back, climbed over the fence and tried to run into the thatched rooms.

But the doors were all bolted. Howling thunderously, he broke open one of them. In the light of the fire, he saw the neatly dressed old woman sitting straight, hands closed. Qiu kept crying "Mom" as he rushed over, intending to carry her out of the fire, but she was as firm as a rock.

Knowing his martial art was not as good as hers and that he could not remove her, he pulled out his sword, knelt before her and cried, "Mom, please give me the pleasure of death!"

"Go away!" she said coldly, refusing to take his sword.

"If Mom doesn't go, your son will stay with you until we're burned to ashes!"

Moments elapsed. Finally the old woman took Qiu over and held him in her arms. Mother and son burst into wails that did not stop.

Surrounding them were flames ...

Identifying the Suspect

By **Tao** Ran

He was half asleep, thinking that he was participating in the TV program *Millionaires*. When he woke up, though, he realized the man in front of him was not Chen Qitai, but a detective in plain clothes. *I am positive. But if I really single out that man, will I get into great trouble?*

"You need some more time?" asked the detective.

He nodded. *In "Millionaires," you get help from the "Loving Counsel," but I'm all alone. Yes or no, the choice is all mine.*

It was that man; he could never forget his cruel eyes. Even if the man's face was covered up, as long as he could see one of his eyes, he could still recognize him without difficulty. That man had a pair of terrifying eyes that had more white than the average. When they rolled up, they gave out a chilly, murderous threat. That man's husky voice echoed in his ears all the time: "Smart boy, watch what you say! Or I'll skin you alive. Even if you escape to the end of the world. You can try if you don't believe me!"

That man had broken his legs, and he had become a cripple, subsequently deserted by his girlfriend. A flame of hatred burned in his heart.

If I could, of course, I would have this son of a bitch persecuted. He deserves a taste of what it's like behind bars. Hong Kong is a place ruled by law. How could we simply blink at these gangsters who have been tyrannizing lawful citizens! But if this tyrant escapes punishment and retaliates, who could protect me? I have neither money nor power.

"So? Is it a fifty-fifty?"

Fifty-fifty! His heart was throbbing. *Pick out the suspect or claim memory loss?* Passion and reason lost their balance in the conflict.

Everybody knows this guy is a heinous criminal. He knows that the police also know it, but the rule of the law is that you would rather set a criminal free by mistake than convict one wrongfully. Even when they know he is guilty, if they lack hard evidence they still can't do anything about him. No wonder he claimed loudly before the TV camera, "I have confidence in the police. I believe the police will protect lawful citizens. I am an honest businessman and taxpayer! Why wouldn't the police protect me?"

He believed the bastard had carefully premeditated whatever he had done in such a way that he would not appear involved. "Man, you'd better be careful. I hear he had discussed his plan with his lawyer in detail before he hired the thug to hit you," somebody had reminded him. "They were sure that it wouldn't involve him. That's why he had given the order. He is no simple man like Li Kui in the novel *Water Margins*. He's one who lives by his brains. Otherwise, how could he have gone scot-free like this despite all his crimes?"

"Do you want to call somebody? Or talk with anybody who was on the spot?"

What's the use of calling somebody about this. Anybody . . . on the spot? But there wasn't anybody on the spot. I've got to face it myself. It's easy to answer yes or no. It's just the consequences that I'll have to face in the end.

"Are you afraid? What are you afraid of? This is Hong Kong. We police won't allow thugs to be at large. As long as you tell the truth, we will send officers to protect you, like bodyguards, twenty-four hours a day. What are you afraid of?"

What am I afraid of? I am afraid of many things. Protect me? But could you protect me all my life? Even if you could, I would be living in the shadow of death every day. I would be under close watch even when I had some intimacy with a woman. What joy would I have, to live a life without privacy? Then a moment of your negligence might result in my death in the street . . .

"Come on! We aren't making a movie here! It's real life. It can't be that horrifying!"

Maybe you are right, but I am not that optimistic. A gentleman might wait ten years to revenge himself, but who knows what a thug will do?

"All right now. Be sure of yourself. Can you recognize him?"

Separated from him by the one-sided mirror were about ten "players" lined up in a row. He could easily identify the assailant, but the moment he picked him out he would have no way to escape himself, while the assailant could continue to live a happy, free life.

Forget it! A step backward will mean a bright future. I can't change the fact that I'm a cripple anyway. What good will it do even if I vent my anger?

Staring at the detective with a blank expression, he said, "I can't recognize the man."

People who participate in "Millionaires" can still get a check even if they quit halfway through. I have wasted so much time, and I don't know how many brain cells I have lost, but I am empty-handed. He seemed to hear the detective suddenly dropping a sentence at him: "We'll play it again next time!"

Fruits

By **Yi** De Er Fu

His name is Zuo Wenge, a colleague of mine I got to know not long ago. One day, when he dropped by my house and saw the two luxuriant trees in my yard covered with fruit, he gasped in admiration and asked how I had become engaged in fruit culture.

"I know a pomologist," I said. "It is he who has been teaching me about grafting, lopping, fertilizing and pesticide spraying."

"When did you plant these trees?"

"In 1980."

"They are bearing fruit only eight years after they were planted! My tree was planted in 1970. It's eighteen years old now, and, damn it, it just doesn't bear fruit!"

"That's impossible."

"Come see it yourself if you don't believe me."

One Sunday, I really made a trip to see Zuo's fruit tree. Situated in the southern suburbs of the county town, his was a detached house with a large yard. In the yard there was only that tree Zuo had told me about. I stared at it for a long time and thought it wasn't like a fruit tree. It was unhealthily swarthy and wrinkled; its trunk was only as big as a cup. The skinny, crooked branches made it resemble a *longgua* scholartree. The few leaves that had all curled up were a sign its survival was threatened. I told Zuo that it was definitely not a fruit tree, but he strongly disagreed, telling me that it was a gift from the orchard, planted by its employees.

To prove me right, I went with Zuo to the home of the pomologist, Mr. Du Yinong, intending to ask him to come and check it out. Mr.

Du, who was busy writing a paper when we arrived, burst out laughing when I told him the purpose of our visit. Then he grasped Zuo's hand and asked, "Don't you remember me?"

"You are . . ." Zuo looked a little nervous.

"I am Du Yinong, one of the 'ten black gang members' in this county, denounced and condemned by you, the rebellion commander,* eighteen years ago!"

Zuo flushed.

Mr. Du continued smilingly, "Don't forget that while you were condemning me, you said, 'When you take the correct political route, even a non-fruit tree will bear fruit.' Your fruit tree has been growing for eighteen years without bearing fruit. It looks like you have taken the wrong route, eh?"

The red-faced Zuo was really embarrassed.

Finally, Mr. Du told Zuo that the tree in his yard was not a fruit tree, but a wych elm.

When we were saying goodbye to him, he told Zuo, "When I was carrying out your order, I did ask the orchard workers to send you a fruit tree seedling, but instead they sent you a wych-elm seedling without telling me, so as to take revenge on you. I didn't learn about this until later on. I should apologize. Next spring, I will ask the workers to send you a few real fruit-tree seedlings."

On hearing that, out of guilt or gratitude, Zuo made a deep bow to Mr. Du, tears welling up in his eyes.

---

* *Translator's note:* When China went through the chaotic period between 1966 and 1976 known as the Cultural Revolution, factory workers and other blue-collar workers, backed by the military led by the late chairman Mao Zedong, ruled the country. High school, college and university students turned into "Red Guards," rebelling against anything traditional or conventional or against any scholar or professor they did not like, under the pretext of following the correct political line set by Mao, who said, "It is right to rebel." Zuo Wenge in the story was a local leader of that rebellion, crowned "Commander," with absolute power to deal with the "reactionaries" in any way he felt fit.

Boatman

By **Wu** Jinliang

The dark, skinny-faced man had been following Wang Si and his girlfriend from the bus terminal to the harbor, a distance of at least half a kilometer. Wang had tried several times unsuccessfully to keep him away.

"We want to find a hotel and take a rest before we tour the lake," Wang told him.

"I can help you find your hotel first, and I won't charge you anything. Whenever you are ready, I'll come pick you up," said the man, stooping forward with a bent back. He followed Wang closely in quick short steps, wearing a pleasant, flattering smile.

Wang's girlfriend, leaning against him, walked in silence as she looked the man pestering them up and down. Hidden under the man's sort of faint smile was some kind of obsequiousness. On her side, she loved to see him follow Wang and continue in a flattering tone to beg them for business. She found her superiority sufficiently satisfied as she thought of Wang's unfavorable position as owner of a clothes store in the city. Though he was the "big boss," in order to sell something he often had to go out of his way to curry favor, nod and bow at the customers, which she would rather not watch. Now she thought Wang had finally gotten an opportunity to show his superiority.

"Don't you worry about us," Wang said with a stern face. "What we came for is fun, but we might not have to hire you. Please stop following us!" He was losing patience with the man.

"Of course, of course." The man smiled mockingly and refused

69

to leave. "You can tour Baiyangdian in anybody's boat, but I can assure you one thing: nobody's rate is better than mine. You can try if you don't believe me."

"Do you think I want it cheap?" Wang said, holding his step. "If I wanted to save money, I would have stayed home. I can tell you, I care about everything except spending money. Money I have plenty of!"

"I believe you, but nobody would simply throw away money for fun. The standard rate for a one-day tour on the lake is fifteen to twenty yuan. If I asked for one hundred, I am sure you wouldn't want to pay. For example—"

"One hundred yuan will buy one hundred yuan's service and fun," Wang interrupted him, looking fearfully serious now. "If I really paid you one hundred, could you satisfy all my needs?" His girlfriend smiled in delight with closed eyes at Wang's peculiar habit of preferring to lose money rather than face.

The man was dumbfounded for a moment. Then he said, "If you do pay one hundred, I wonder what mischief you would get into. Come on, don't talk foolishly. Let's be serious—"

"Talk foolishly? Now, get in the boat." Wang straightened his neck, leading his girlfriend down to the pier. The boatman followed him in quick short steps, stealing a glance at his face.

Their boat left the pier, took a turn and immediately entered the watercourse. On both sides, cogongrass stretched to the horizon. Wang became himself again, leaning against his girlfriend at the prow, sipping soft drinks. It was a typically cloudy day, breezy and cool on the lake. He conveniently pushed his light-sensitive glasses up on his forehead. The watercourse widened as they rowed along; several bamboo poles had been planted alongside its edge, bordering the cogongrass. Something resembling a net appeared faintly around the poles from time to time.

"What's that?" Wang asked the boatman.

"It's a fishing trap."

"A fishing trap?" repeated Wang. He bent forward, intending to touch the trap. The boat rocked, and Wang's light-sensitive glasses dropped into the water.

Wang's girlfriend screamed, and the boatman immediately stopped the boat. "Man, you can't get one hundred yuan without doing something," smiled Wang calmly. "Now fish up my glasses." He squinted at the boatman, who frowned at the muddy water.

"What are you going to do? They cost me five hundred Hong Kong dollars. If you fish them up for me, I'll give you another hundred yuan!" Wang stared at him provokingly.

The boatman swallowed, his Adam's apple moving up and down. His face was none too pleasant to look at. A little while later he gave a hesitant smile. "You said you want to pay me one hundred yuan, but how can I take it? Our county government has this old rule: anybody who overcharges customers will be fined. For your lake tour, I will charge you just twenty yuan according to the limit, not a penny more. The water here is at least four or five meters deep, and the glasses are so small. I'm afraid I may not be able to find them for you." Then he started rowing again.

"Now, you—" His girlfriend was about to blast at the boatman when Wang interrupted her with a gesture. "That cheap pair of glasses," Wang smiled coldly, "cost me only five hundred Hong Kong dollars. Forget it. I'll leave them here for a cuckold."

The boatman dared not respond anymore. He kept paddling with all his strength.

As he promised, when they returned to the pier in the evening, the boatman asked them for only twenty yuan. Then he took them to the nearest hotel. Because of the loss of his glasses and the feeling that his superiority was somewhat dampened by the boatman, Wang was dejected and grew much quieter. Seeing this, his girlfriend dared not speak much, either. After they checked in, the boatman said goodbye to them and left.

The following noon, when Wang and his girlfriend returned from

71

another boat tour, the attendant asked them to see the manager of the hotel. Wang went at once by himself and was soon back, his face red.

"What happened?" asked his girlfriend.

"He dove into the water and found them this morning." He drew out the light-sensitive glasses. "He also made a special trip to bring them back to me. We were not in, so—" His face looked strange as he spoke. His girlfriend was dumbfounded for a while; then she gave a sigh. Lying on bed, Wang said softly, "The boatman wanted the manager to tell us that he did not help us find the glasses because he thought our words were none too pleasant. Also because there was a female on the boat and he had only a pair of shorts with nothing to change into."

At this Wang's girlfriend also blushed, giving another sigh, followed by silence.

The Old Man and the Pickpocket

By **Ma** Baoshan

After traveling a long distance, a coach pulled up at a small town for a noon break. At the tea stand nearby, a young man encountered an old passenger who had just descended from the bus. While the senior passenger was paying for his tea, the junior caught sight of a large sum of cash that he was carrying. Immediately the young man started to follow at his heels.

The young man was a pickpocket dressed in a T-shirt and with a canvas backpack on his shoulders. When the driver started his engine, the pickpocket followed the old man on board, helping him onto the bus at the door.

Not long after they resumed traveling, it started drizzling. The drizzling turned the open country into a vast haze, sending every passenger into a doze. The thief was standing close to the old man, waiting for the right moment to act. A little while later, when the old man closed his eyes like others, the thief tried to reach into the right pocket of his coat, only to hear a loud cough. He quickly withdrew his hand, but the old man did not open his eyes after all.

Out came evenly deep breathing from the old man's nostrils. The pickpocket tried again, reaching into the left pocket of his coat. This time the old man did not seem to notice anything, though a faint smile emerged from his face, but again the thief found nothing.

Where could it be? While helping the old man on board, the thief had tried his pants pockets. Right! The old man must have hidden his money in his shirt pocket. With the dwindling glow of his eyes, the young man swept across the bus, seeing the lethargic passengers mostly sleeping. The suddenly emboldened thief tore open the old man's coat, dipping straight into his shirt pocket. Wasn't it more like robbery than pickpocketing? Yet again he found nothing.

Meanwhile, the bus pulled up at a small place where a passenger next to the old man had to get off. The young man immediately occupied the vacant seat. As the bus roared forward, quiet on the outside, he kept wondering: Where did the old man hide that coveted money?

The drizzling stopped at dusk, and so did the bus at its destination after a long day's traveling. "Wake up, young fellow." The old man gave him a gentle push. "The bus has reached the terminal."

Descending from the coach, the old man grabbed the young man's hand without asking if he wanted to go and dragged him straight into a hotel room he had booked. Then he drew out a hundred-yuan note as if performing a magic act, saying, "Our friendship started with today's traveling. Here, my friend, I contribute the money and you do the legwork. Go get some food."

Before long, the young man returned with quite a bit of food and two large bottles of whiskey. Turning the hotel's teacups into whiskey glasses, they sat at the desk face to face and began to drink. The alcohol was soon working on them.

"Young man, so that's what you do?" asked the old man all of a sudden, making a gesture of pickpocketing.

"Sir, but how do you know?" The young man flushed.

Sipping his whiskey, the old man answered, "I knew it the moment you appeared at the tea stand in the small town . . ."

"So you knew it every time I tried to search your pockets on the bus?" The young man frowned.

"Of course, I did. And I also knew that you'd follow me all the way here and drink with me." With this the old man gulped down another cup.

"But what made you so sure that I'd follow you to this place?" The young man was puzzled.

"Your greedy eyes and that little stubborn character shown on your face."

The old man's mysterious look earned him great respect from the junior, who immediately rose to refill the senior's cup. "Dear sir, " he said, "it seems you are an expert in this business. Do you mind telling me where you have hidden your money? As a green hand, I just want to know. I'll never dare to bother you again, sir."

"It's right in the canvas backpack you've been carrying!" He laughed, seizing the bag from the bed. Then he opened it and showed the young man a stack of notes, taking him by surprise.

"I put it into your bag at the moment you were helping me onto the bus in the small town," said the senior. "All the way, you kept searching my pockets, but forgot the little trick I had played—the 'cicada' that had sloughed off its skin was hiding in you."

Throwing himself on his knees, the young man begged, "My master, could you please take me as your disciple?"

The somewhat saddened old man stared at his junior pitifully for some time, then asked, "Do you really think that'd mean a bright future for you?"

The young man hung his head in silence. The old man helped him up to his feet, then refilled the two cups with whiskey, saying, "When I was young, I made the same living as you. After 1949, the government rehabilitated me and also gave me a job. But I just could not quit my bad habit: my fingers were always so itchy whenever I saw money in people's pockets. The government had tried to help me quit several times, but I just could not. I knew what I did would only lead me to doom and death, so one day I made a painful decision and cut off the forefinger and middle finger of my right hand. Later on, I started to work for the police, catching only pickpockets, until I retired at the age of sixty. These days, I help businesses and offices deliver cash from one place to another. That is to say, I am still making use of the remaining years of my life."

All ears, the humble, respectful young man kept refilling the old man's cup with whiskey while listening to his story. Now much impressed by the junior's manners, the old man sighed, "What a nice young fellow! But how could you have picked the job of stealing!"

The next morning, the old man woke up only to find the young man missing. Left on his night table was the following note: "I learned a great deal from you yesterday. Many thanks for your advice and the tricks you told me."

It was signed, "A trainee detective from the Police School."

Flowers in Full Bloom

By **Xie** Zhiqiang

The thin drifting smog that irritated my nose just would not float away.

We local residents had a hobby of growing flowers, but recently word had spread that the potted flowers of every household, which should have been in full bloom, had all withered. Only those—a great variety of them—in the yard of my eccentric neighbor, a retired gardener, were in dazzling bloom.

I regretted that I had not tried to associate with him. I have had many opportunities which I have deliberately missed, for by instinct I have an adverse reaction to eccentricity. Now I could only enjoy seeing his flowers from behind our tall fence.

How happy he was, I thought, to have so many blooming flowers to enrich his life! I saw him carrying a watering can, watering the flowers once in the morning and once in the evening, always carefully, always attentively. I had even given two loud dry coughs to attract his attention, but obviously he did not hear me, or perhaps he was lost in a no man's land where he cared about nothing except his flowers.

I raised my head and looked at the smog hanging over our small town, whose streets and roofs were all misty. I was puzzled that his flowers had survived the badly polluted smog. "Isn't it a wonder? Flowers are the most beautiful but also most tender and fragile plants," I said to myself. Often, with rapt attention, I would watch him watering his flowers from beginning to end, hoping he would notice me on the other side of the fence.

Finally, I grasped the opportunity one evening when he had closed his door without latching it. He was carrying his watering can and must have been out of his yard—I had seldom seen him on the street. His door was otherwise always latched.

Being a gardener for half of his life, and an expert at dealing with flowers only, would he associate with people at all? Why not try my luck anyway? Having prepared many compliments for him, I gently pushed open his door, which gave a dry screech.

"What are you doing here?" He stared at me in astonishment, as if discovering an intruder in the Garden of Eden.

"I just want to ask you a question," I smiled.

"Well?" He stood there holding his watering can.

Seizing this opportunity, I went over to him. "Our flowers have all withered. Could you kindly tell me some tricks for flower growing?"

"Tell . . . tricks?" he seemed to ask himself.

His can suddenly dropped to the ground, splashing some water about. I strode over quickly and picked it up for him before he could. As I bent down, I was shocked to see some plastic flowers. Then I found that his whole yard was covered with plastic flowers.

"They don't wither because they aren't alive," he murmured.

"I'm sorry," I said.

I don't know how I got out of his yard, but somehow I had grown sympathetic toward him.

As I saw, he did not water his flowers the next morning.

The smog was thickening; my throat seemed to be suffering some kind of attack. Breathing this air, I could not but feel like vomiting. I tried to hold my breath, but not for long. I had to breathe.

Loving Parents

The Mice Are Getting Married

By **He** Peng

After twenty-one months of confinement by the "masses" for his political opinions, my father finally returned home on Chinese New Year. To celebrate the New Year as well as my father's release from captivity, my mother went to the market and bought half a kilogram of pork—we were definitely going to have dumplings!

As a custom, we had vegetarian food on New Year's Day, so we could have dumplings only the next day. Actually, I had no idea at the time what they tasted like, so ever since my mother had returned home with the meat and told us we were going to have dumplings, my little sister and I had been so excited that we would not go out to play again. We were waiting for the moment the dumplings would be served.

In the evening, my mother chopped the pork until it turned into minced meat, then she mixed it with the carrots she had chopped into tiny pieces. My father kneaded the dough, then cut it into smaller lumps and rolled them out into wrappers. With tender care, my mother put some filling in the centre of each wrapper, lifted up both ends and pressed them tight as she held them between her hands. "This is a dumpling," she said. Our family was poor at that time, so I could not find the word "dumpling" in the vocabulary stored in my memory.

When all the dumplings were done, my mother placed them neatly on the chopping board, took a final look and smiled happily. My father cleaned the flour off his hands. Then he lit an Economical cigarette, a package of which cost nine *fen*, sucked it with a deep breath, then slowly sent up rings for me and my sister to catch. We tried to catch them as we laughed. We laughed as we tried to catch them. Yet we could not but look at the dumplings on the chopping board from time to time. We wished the night could pass faster and morning come sooner.

It was late at night, but my sister and I were too excited to fall asleep. We kept pestering our father for stories, so he told us some fairy tales, including many yummy things to eat and adding that in the years to come we would have deep-fried cake and dumplings with all-meat filling on every Chinese New Year. He kept talking to us until we happily fell asleep. That night, I also had a sweet dream, dreaming of my mother cooking all-meat dumplings for us. They smelled delicious, but they tasted like steamed corn buns, which I just could not swallow. Finally I refused to eat them. Then I stood by the stove, inhaling the delicious smell instead. It smelled so good that I kept laughing, laughing until I woke up.

When I woke up, the delicious smell was gone. I was really disappointed.

Then I crawled up quietly to look at the dumplings on the chopping board, hoping that I could see them with the help of the faint moonlight coming through the window. "Why, where are the dumplings?" I rubbed my eyes very hard, but still saw nothing. In the dim light, I only saw a bare chopping board lying quietly by itself. I found it very odd, so I nudged my mother gently to let her know. When she saw all the dumplings missing, she immediately gave my father a push and woke him up. My father got up anxiously and at once lit the oil lamp for fear he would not see well without it. Without covering himself with a coat, he got off the *kang* with his lamp and carefully examined the area surrounding the chopping board, from left to right, from front to back. Then, with the oil lamp, he followed the traces to the end of the wall, where he squatted down and stared at the large mouse hole for a long time.

"God!" he finally gave a deep sigh. He then blew out the lamp and went back to the *kang** without saying another word. When my mother asked him if they had all been taken away by the mice, he gave a gentle nod in the dark without saying anything.

My sister and I did not know what had happened, so we wanted to get up with daybreak. We kept asking our mother to get up and cook the dumplings for us. My father quickly pulled my sister and me under his quilt, holding us in his arms, fondling my head, then my sister's little face. "What day is it today?" he asked me.

"Second day of New Year," I answered without thinking. "It's the day we have our dumplings." But he said I was only half right.

"It's not our day. It's the mice's day," he said. "The second day of New Year is the day the mice are getting married. The dumplings we have made are for their wedding, so the mice will have dumplings today."

My sister was all confused. "Why don't the mice make their own dumplings since they are getting married?" she asked.

"The mice in our house wanted us to do it for them, so that they could just take them away," said my father. "Then they can enjoy their wedding. It's a great, happy day. We ought to be happy."

Though the mice in our house were getting married, I just could not find joy or excitement. My sister buried her head in my father's arms without saying another word. Then all of a sudden she burst out crying, "I want dumplings, I want dumplings—"

My father held us close and tight and told us in a soft voice, slowly, "The mice's wedding is also an important event. After their wedding today, we'll make some more dumplings for ourselves. Is it okay? Now let's cheer for the mice and celebrate with them. Otherwise, they will be upset and will steal our dumplings again when we make more." So my sister and I jumped out from under the quilt, and clapped our hands as we shouted, "Oh, the mice are getting

---

* *Translator's note: Kang* is an earthen bed that is heated in wintry nights, mostly found in the cold regions.

married! The mice are getting married!" My sister's tears jumped with her in the air before they finally landed on my father. My father felt her tears on his hand, then sat up and joined us in cheering for the mice, "The mice are getting married! The mice are getting married—" He clapped his hands too, but his voice sounded somewhat strange.

We didn't want the mice to steal our dumplings again, so we wanted our mother to join us in our cheering. But she did not seem to hear us. We didn't know when she had covered up her head with the quilt. My sister tried to lift it up, but she just could not. Also we heard faint weeping from inside. My father asked us not to disturb her. "Mom is busy inside," he said. "She's sending her best wishes to the mice."

Women Bandits

By **Sun** Fangyou

The 1920s saw a band of bandits frequently appear in eastern Shandong Province. This gang consisted of girls from poor families, except their chieftain, who came from a big, noble family. Nobody knows, or can find out, why the noble girl became a bandit. These bandits killed the rich to help the poor, never bothering the common people. In most cases, they only robbed rich households and kidnapped members of wealthy families.

Unlike their male counterparts, the women bandits engaged in "civilized" robberies and abductions, seldom using their guns and knives. They would first pick a smart bandit and make her up, then send her into a rich and powerful family as a maid. After a few months, when she had familiarized herself with the layout, they would pick a date, and through close co-operation between the maid inside and the other bandits outside, take away a child from that home. Afterward, they would ask a go-between to bring a letter to the master of the family, demanding a ransom.

That fall, they kidnapped another child, the only son of a wealthy businessman in Chenzhou, the richest man in town with seven wives. He hadn't had a son until the seventh wife gave birth to his heir. The seventh wife, a learned woman, was desperate for the return of her darling son. After careful thought, she wrote the bandit chieftain a letter, saying,

I am willing to kneel praying for mercy in front of you
for as long as it takes. For God's sake, please return my

child unharmed to me so that I won't have to endure such unbearable suffering. In the name of a mother and a member of the same female sex as you are, I am asking you to think carefully about the harm you have inflicted on our whole family by taking away our child. I want my child back more than anything else in the world. I am willing to do anything for you in exchange for my child. Please tell me your conditions.

Much impressed by the touching letter, the bandit chieftain, who was in a terrific mood, wrote back to her immediately:

I don't want to kneel in front of anybody; nor do I want anybody to kneel in front of me. I only ask you, for God's sake, to send to me safely what I need so that I don't have to suffer the pain of life. In the name of a member of the female sex, I want you to understand that my life is different from yours. As one philosopher said, no one wants to be led by fate, but in the end, it is fate that rules so many of us! The god of fate has forced me into banditry, so I want survival and revenge on all the rich more than anything else in the world. I am willing to keep your son safe and unharmed for you, but please bring along three thousand silver dollars to a place I will tell you any time in exchange for your son on this *x* day of this month. For safety reasons, you'd better not tell anybody about this!

The mother was surprised at the bandit chieftain's letter, for she had never expected her to be so knowledgeable and reasonable with the ability to write so beautifully. Somehow, she yearned to see the learned woman, and she immediately readied the three thousand silver dollars. When word came from the bandit chieftain, she took a boat to the reed marshes east of Chenzhou.

The bandit chieftain did not miss the appointment. Seeing that everything around was safe, with a conqueror's air she emerged from a small boat. Her bright red cloak, which fluttered in the wind, looked like a large red peony against the dark green curtain of tall reeds, setting off her beautiful eyes and good features. The seventh wife was taken by surprise. Only when her moment of surprise had elapsed did she find the maid who used to work in her chamber playing with her child. Totally relieved, she told her helper to show the silver dollars, asking the bandit chieftain to verify the amount herself. Smiling, the bandit head gave a whistle. In no time a small boat shot out of the reed marshes with two bandits in it, each armed with a gun and a knife. They took the money, counted it, then shot back into the depth of the reed marshes, disappearing into the vast green. At this moment, the bandit chieftain made a gesture for the two boats to close up. She handed over the child to his mother, but most unexpectedly, he did not want his own mother, clutching to the bandit chieftain's shoulders, wailing non-stop.

The mother was shocked, sad tears rolling down her cheeks. "I never knew you had first kidnapped my child's heart," she told the bandits. "It makes me shudder."

"A child is a child," the chieftain laughed. "When any woman shows him motherly love, he will feel it and enjoy it. My respectful madam, that's something money cannot buy. The common saying goes, 'Birth parents are second to adoptive parents.' Have you ever thought about my sister here? How would she feel when you take away your son?"

The mother raised her head only to see the young bandit crying heartbrokenly, as if she was sharing the same misery she herself had.

Much touched, the mother begged the chieftain, "Allow this little sister to return to our chamber and work as our maid again."

"I don't think it's appropriate, because she has revealed her identity," she said as she glanced at her. "If you want your son to return home a happy child, and if you want to win back something

86

money cannot buy, you are welcome to stay with us for a few days."

The mother knitted her beautiful brows, hesitated a moment, then with determination climbed into the bandit chieftain's boat.

Renting a Son for New Year

By **Zong** Lihua

His eyes brightened up at the ad.

The content of the ad was unique: "Looking for a loving boy who likes relatives to spend the New Year's Eve with us." It was signed by "A Senior Couple."

He laughed—doubtless that was the best place for him for the time being. So he called the old couple to express his interest. At the other end, the woman was exceptionally excited. He overheard her saying, "Old man, we have finally got a call!"

He knocked on the door as soon as he found the house at the address he was given. It was a common small *siheyuan** house in a remote town. The couple who received him appeared to be older than he had expected. Their hair was all grey, and they walked very slowly.

He was wondering how to address them when the red-eyed hostess called out, "My child, you are finally back home!" He saw the corner of her mouth twisting when she spoke.

He felt as if somewhere inside his body had been struck by a heavy blow, his eyes becoming wet. "Mom, I'm home!" He called out uncontrollably, thinking of his own mother.

As a matter of course, he was flanked into the house by the parents. Once inside, he found himself in the atmosphere of a home filled with family warmth. His "mother" dusted his clothes for him, while

---

* *Translator's note:* A *siheyuan* is a compound with a traditional one-story Chinese house built with grey bricks and tiles covering the four sides of the courtyard.

88

his "father" quietly handed him a bowl of brown sugar water. He started to play his role. The mother led him by the hand, saying, "We've had your room ready for you for a long time. It's all the same as before. The washroom is on this side and the kitchen is over here. Wash yourself first, then we'll make dumplings together."

After washing his face, he dried it with a towel as he walked into his room. An unexpected, enlarged photo of a young man, twenty years old or so, came into his sight.

"That's our son." The young man turned about and found the old man standing behind him; the old man kept his mouth shut after saying that.

At this moment, the mother shouted from outside. "Have you washed yourself? What are you doing in there, you slowpokes?"

"Yes. We'll be with you right away," he said, as his face instantly changed into a smiling one.

The dumpling filling had been long prepared. The mother was rolling out the wrappers now. The rolling pin under her hands was making happy sounds. Rolling up his sleeves, the son sat down to knead the dough. That was what the family had done in the previous years. The father was in charge of boiling the water, which was an easy job. All he did was fill the pot with water, turn on the stove and that was it. After that he sat by the side, quietly watching mother and son happily making dumplings. The mother started to talk about some trivial matters, which the son was not interested in, but knowing the mother liked them, he listened. Occasionally, he would ask her a question; she would stop working to answer as she stared at him.

It was their custom to set firecrackers before they got the dumplings out of the pot.

The mother's excitement reached its peak at this point. As she stood under the eaves watching the colourful fireworks in the sky, her face beamed with happiness. "Now we can light our firecrackers, too," she commanded. So he did. She walked to the courtyard clapping

89

her hands, jumping like a child at the sounds of the exploding firecrackers.

After that, together they ate their dumplings, chatted, laughed and watched the "New Year Eve's Party" on TV, until she was tired. "I am really overjoyed, but I am very tired now," said the mother.

"You should take a rest now," said the father after he came over to her.

That night the son had a sound sleep, which got rid of all the fatigue he had had during the past few days. The next morning, he woke up all of a sudden when the sun shone through the window. Only after sitting up for quite a while did he realize what had happened.

Today the old couple appeared to be in poor spirits. The old lady walked over to his bed, buttoned up his coat and said, "My child, I know that I can't replace your mother in your heart no matter what. Remember, even when you are living a wandering life away from home, you should still find time to call your parents and go visit them . . ."

He felt heat circling the rims of his eyes, seeing the old lady's tears rolling down her cheeks. So he raised his hands to wipe them out for her. "I know." He nodded.

Walking him out of the house, the old man quietly drew out a bill. "Thank you very much indeed," he said. "This is your pay. We can't afford more than this."

He resolutely refused to accept it. "I have learned about so many things from you," he said.

The old man kept saying thanks, "You have made our wish come true. Your auntie, in fact, doesn't have many days to live. She's got cancer, and her dream is to have another New Year Eve's dumpling dinner with her son, made by herself. But our son—he—he would never have another dinner . . ."

He did not hear clearly what the old man said after that, but instantly he felt he had changed to a new person.

Saying goodbye to the old man, he ran all the way to the phone booth to call his own family. Even before he heard his old mother's voice, tears were running down his cheeks. His mother immediately called out his name! She did not hear him speak, but she knew it was her son!

After a long silence, he cried, "Mom, I want to go home."

The girl who collected fees in the booth stared at the mysterious caller. Of course, she did not and could not know that he was a murderer at large.

A Snow Statue

By **Xu** Xing

It was a summer night. The street lamp dropped silvery light over the road, on which people were chatting, and playing chess and cards. There came a woman holding a man's jacket, looking for somebody.

"Let's go home now," she said to a middle-aged man who was watching people playing chess. "Yuanyuan has finished his homework." Then she spread the jacket over his shoulders.

So the man went home with her.

Their home, with a floor space of about fifteen or sixteen square meters, was crowded but cozy. It was furnished with a double bed, a single bed, two trunks and a student's desk, on which Yuanyuan put his textbooks and exercise books. The desk was for Yuanyuan only. Fortunately, the couple were not intellectuals, so they did not need a desk themselves.

Theirs was a family of three. Yuanyuan's parents were factory workers, and life was not easy for them. They had lived in this place for more than ten years, with Yuanyuan now in his third year in middle school. The older their son got, the smaller their home became. They found it almost too small to house them now.

His father was rather disappointing; he had been suffering from tracheitis, a common disease in northern China. He coughed from morning till night. Once he started coughing, he shook everything in their small home. Unavoidably, that disturbed Yuanyuan, who had to concentrate on his homework. Consequently, he often had to calculate his math problems several times. Yuanyuan had a hard time, and so did the father, but what could they do? They had no better home to move into, nor could the father's disease be cured. People could just be so helpless in life!

Whenever the father felt his throat start to itch, he would immediately run into the kitchen, but the kitchen did not even have a door to keep away his noise. Sometimes he would simply lie down there and cover himself up with a quilt, but all the same, his coughing was still heard everywhere at home.

God, why did he ever get that trouble? Bottle after bottle of cough drops and package after package of antibiotics all failed to bring it under control.

The son was very understanding. "Daddy, please just cough!" he said. "It doesn't bother me. I can still do my homework."

"Oh, my child, Daddy's sickness has affected your—" An illiterate man with no schooling, he knew how important it was to study. He was afraid of ruining his son's future.

Now, the father would leave home so as to cough outside when his son had to do his homework after dinner. This had become a rule, a habit.

But the father was a patient with tracheitis, after all, and he had to wear a large mask when it was cold.

"Please don't go out, Dad," Yuanyuan stopped him.

"I have to. Dad has something to do."

What did he have to do? Why always at this time? Yuanyuan knew it well. He loved his father, but could not keep him at home. He knew that his father would do anything for his studies. Whenever the sensible child thought of this, tears would flow inside.

Winter in the north came early. There was this day when Yuanyuan's father said after dinner that he wanted to play a couple of games with a chess friend in the opposite building. It was near the end of the semester, when Yuanyuan had a lot of homework that would all be due soon. In this quiet and cozy little home, he buried himself in his schoolwork. When he finally finished it, he suddenly realized that it was already late at night. He was starting to relax when he unexpectedly heard faint coughing from outside the window. He looked out and saw that snow had been falling in big feathery flakes for quite some time. In the snow was a person in a cotton-padded overcoat, wearing a large mask. He was all white, looking like a snowman!

Yuanyuan was as shocked as if he had touched a live wire. Tears streamed down his cheeks as he ran out shouting, "Daddy, oh, Daddy—!" Yuanyuan burst out sobbing before he could speak.

"My child, you've done your homework?" asked the father with love and concern, looking up at the desk lamp that was still on.

"Yeah. Daddy. Oh Daddy—" He clutched his father in his arms.

The silent snowflakes, white as silver, soft as cotton, immediately covered up both father and son who were in each other's arms, creating another white statue in the middle of the tranquil street.

Winter Scenery

By **Mo** Bai

Ye sat on the snow, looking back at the hospital she had just left behind. "How I wish I could make a huge snowman!" she thought to herself. "But where could I make one? Back home? After they divorced, Mom went to a city in the south, and Dad has also gone to the south for a big business deal. Home is cold like winter now." She looked blank as she raised her head, lost in thought. "Where could I make a snowman?"

She put out her tongue to lick the snow, which had become watery. Slowly she closed her eyes and seemed to see a white, open country. She saw her grandma, supported by her walking stick, standing in front of her house near the village entrance, looking into the distance. Ye felt two warm streams of tears on her cheeks, but she did not wipe them. She kept her face skyward to feel the falling snow.

There was this afternoon when the snow was coming down thick and heavy. In a street in the city, an eight-year-old girl by the name of Ye, skinny and pale, boarded a long-distance bus that was going to the countryside. The conductor, who was wearing a red down jacket, felt sorry for the tiny girl and did not ask her to buy her ticket. The bus took her straight to the place called Qiushu. Only after seeing the bus disappear into the distance on the road did Ye turn about and walk into the village. Very few people were out walking in the snow, and Ye looked all the more forlorn and frail on the quiet country road. Finally, after trudging down the road, she came to a yard at the edge of the village, fenced up with many dry twigs and branches. Ye stood before the wicker gate, looked across the yard and saw the house beyond. Then she burst out, calling, "Grandma—" as she ran toward the door. While running, she saw the dark brown door opening. Standing by the door was her trembling grandma, who was holding a walking stick.

"Ye, is it you?" said her grandma.

Forgetting about everything, Ye ran straight into Grandma's arms. Fondling Ye's icy cold face with her old hands, Grandma said repeatedly, "Darling, is it you? Darling, is it really you? Grandma was about to go see you. I have just cooked the eggs for you, but I can't walk and I am also bus sick." Finally she asked Ye, "And where's Daddy?"

Tears were trickling down from Ye's eyes.

"He left you in the hospital alone?" said Grandma. "That son of a bitch! Darling, don't cry. Tell me, are you feeling better?"

"I overheard them whispering between themselves that I have leukemia," said Ye. "Grandma, is leukemia easy to cure?"

The old woman clutched Ye in her arms, tears welling in her old eyes. "Easy, it's easy," she said. "My poor child—"

"I want to make a big snowman," said Ye, pushing away Grandma slowly.

"Darling, rest a bit. Let me do it for you," said Grandma.

"No, Grandma. I want to do it myself," said Ye.

"Great. You do it yourself, and I'll cook for you, is it okay?" said Grandma.

There was this winter evening when the snow was falling thick and heavy. In front of her grandmother's poor eyes, an eight-year-old girl by the name of Ye was piling up snow with painstaking effort to make a snowman. Her face was getting paler and paler. When it got darker, she felt exhausted; the shovel slipped from her hands and she sank to the ground.

Grandma came over to help her up and said, "Darling, go in and rest awhile. You can go on tomorrow." Supported by Grandma, Ye went back into the house, lay on Grandma's warm shakedown on the floor and soon fell asleep.

It was daytime when Ye woke up. She could not find Grandma on the shakedown, or anywhere else in the house. When she opened the door, she was dumbfounded at the sight. She saw a huge snowman sitting in the yard smiling at her. Then she saw Grandma next to the snowman. Grandma was sitting with crossed legs, looking very, very tired. Together with the area around her, she was covered with a thick layer of snow. Ye ran calling out to her, but Grandma did not respond or move one bit. It looked like she had fallen asleep. Ye didn't want to disturb her, so she sat next her quietly, and she sat there for a long, long time. The scenery of white snow had turned into a timeless picture in the little girl's mind.

Red Umbrellas

By **Jiang** Han

Yu Fen knew well that her mother had been born with a foul mouth. Thanks to her father, a factory worker, her mom improved her status from country resident* to non-country resident, feeling superiority over others. Whenever she opened her mouth, with saliva spraying all around, she poured out words that disgusted her listeners.

After giving birth to two sons and a daughter for the Yus, she prided herself as a winner with outstanding achievements, washing her hands of the raising and education of her children. Since they all took her husband's family name, she swore that she would not take care of them, and she kept her word.

When Yu Fen found she was with child, she thought of her mother all the time, hoping that she could help her make the necessary preparation before her baby was born. At least her mother could give the son-in-law some advice so that they could avoid repeating chores or making mistakes. She had written her a letter, but never received a reply. When she finally got through to her on the phone, her mother gave her a solid reason: "We didn't help our first two children when they had babies, so we won't treat you differently." Only when the old woman learned she had got a grandson did she agree to come,

---

* *Translator's note:* Citizens in China cannot move freely. If they are permanent residents dwelling in the countryside, they may not be able to move at will to a city or town. If they do they will face all types of inconveniences, and their children may have no school to attend. Those living in the countryside are accordingly called "country residents."

98

persuading her husband to come along too.

So they came finally. Yu Fen's father, who had been buried in the deep mines for half of his life, was glued to the TV every day. Her mother, on the other hand, devoted all her attention to her daughter instead of the newborn. Upon her arrival, she complained that Yu Fen was too skinny, babbling about what Yu Fen should and should not eat in the month after giving birth to the baby. As the saying goes, "A lady talks, not works." She meant every comment for her son-in-law, seeming to complain that he had treated her daughter ill.

"It doesn't really matter whether it's a boy or girl," said Yu Fen's mother.

"Everyone tries to have a boy by all means these days. It drives everybody crazy," Yu Fen smiled. "In fact, I prefer a girl myself."

"You do," said her mother, "but he may not." With this she threw a cunning glance at her son-in-law, whose look was indescribable. Then she laughed in contempt and seized the opportunity to tell her a story.

There was a couple who dreamed madly of a son. When a baby girl was born, they would kill her. One after another, they killed seven of them. Finally they got a son, who they feared would melt in their mouths, would drop from their hands, would be eaten by the cat on the bed. So they took turns guarding him. Then the corn in their fields was ready for harvesting. When the man wanted to go, the woman was worried that it would tire him out. When she wanted to go, he was worried that the work was too hard for her. If they both went, nobody could look after their son. In the scorching sun, they could not take the baby with them, so they put him in a basket and secured it onto the bed with a rope. It was a perfectly safe place, so they left the baby sleeping in it.

The couple then went to the fields and started to pick their corn. They would stop working every few minutes and look at their house. One hour later, the woman said she had to feed the baby. When she looked up, she saw several people, each carrying a red umbrella, walking toward their house. "We have visitors," said the woman. The man looked up and saw them too. "Strange," he said. "Why are all the visitors carrying red umbrellas?" "The door is still locked," said the woman. "I'll go now." So she did. The man picked up his load of corn and followed her home.

When they got home, their door was open, but they found no visitors. They quickly went over to look at their baby, and both were stupefied: several pythons as thick as bowls had twined themselves around their son. They counted and found exactly seven of them. Seeing the dead baby, the woman screamed desperately, "My son's father, it is our daughters who have come back—"

"Mom!" shouted Yu Fen in shock, passing out. Her mother held her up, finding her face blue and white, her lips turning pale. The old man stared at his wife angrily for her loose tongue. "Still believing in such things? What times are these now?" said the mother. Yu Fen revived, but with a strange disease. Even when she was in hospital, she was still tortured by nightmares, screaming in horror at night, waking up the other patients and those looking after them in her ward. Neither did her mother who was taking care of her have peace night or day.

"Loose tongue! Why that story?!" The old woman slapped her own face on the quiet.

Before her son could be weaned, Yu Fen died.

Grievous news!

After she was cremated, the widower wanted to send his parents-in-law back home.

"My poor daughter, it must be the poor care and lack of rest in that first month that killed you!" the old woman shouted in a frenzy, with her grandson in her arms, blaming it all on her son-in-law, who was just about to explode. The cool-headed old man gave her a pull, but she just did not want to leave. "I want to avenge my daughter!" she screamed hysterically.

"On whom?" the son-in-law clenched his teeth.

"You!" she said. "You are the killer!"

Her son-in-law was suddenly choked. How could he say, "Old woman, you were the python who killed your daughter! Do you know that in order to have a son, she . . . ." But he could not tell her that. "God!" He just struck down his fist in anger.

Seeing this, the old woman ran up to him and said, "Here I am. Hit me now! Hit me! Now!" She was like a red umbrella charging at her son-in-law.

Coming Home for New Year

By **Ma** Duangang

At the marketplace, Er Die,* a farmer from the impoverished Kaoshan Village, finally sold his two pigs before sunset.

New Year was approaching and the streets were all decorated with lanterns and streamers. The village was bathed in jubilation. The day before, Er Die had received a letter from his two sons, who were studying at the university in the provincial capital, saying that since they had missed their last New Year, they would come home to join their father for a great celebration this year.

Er Die's wife had died at a young age, leaving two small boys behind. Through aches and pains, Er Die had brought up his two children all by himself. Co-operative and understanding, his sons had always done well at school. All the villagers in Kaoshan said that he was a fortunate man and that his sons would become important officials one day.

The year before, his two sons had passed the national college entrance examination and both were admitted into university. It took the village, the township and even the county by surprise. The elders said it was unprecedented in their village. The county governor, in particular, made a special trip to the sparsely populated Kaoshan Village from the county town some one hundred miles away, just to congratulate the brothers upon their admittance into the university. Needless to say, Er Die was overjoyed, but he hung his head the

---

* *Translator's note:* In the story, "Er Die" literally means "Second Father," namely the younger brother of one's father.

102

moment he heard that university tuition fees cost about thirty times as much as the local high school. Well, what could he do? Where could he find the money? The income from his whole year's hard work could not even cover the sons' tuition fees, not to mention food for himself. Finally, one way or the other, Er Die managed to cobble together the money for his sons which enabled them to go to university.

His children did not let him down. Half a year later, the elder son became something like the chairman of the students' union. The university administrators, according to their policy, reduced the tuition fees for the brothers after learning about their financial difficulty. The brothers studied extremely well and won scholarships from the university. Sometimes when Er Die recalled the small details, he felt guilty for having let down the two children, for not fulfilling his fatherly duties.

It was after a whole day's waiting that Er Die found a buyer for his pigs. Whenever he thought of a reunion with his sons on New Year's, he was simply overjoyed. Actually, Er Die didn't really want to sell the two pigs, but it was for his sons' new tuition fees that he had made that difficult decision. He did not want them to worry about their money again.

Though he had not eaten for a whole day and his stomach kept groaning, Er Die did not even go into the roadside restaurant for a bowl of noodles. He wanted to save every penny of his hard-earned money. Instead, he bought two much cheaper steamed buns and began to munch them as he hurried home.

Er Die was in a very good mood today. The buyer, who wore a dog-fur hat, was really nice. He didn't bargain over the price and didn't even want the twenty yuan change from him, which he said was for Er Die to use on his way home. Er Die said to himself, "How could there be such a good person on earth!" as he murmured a popular tune.

It was pitch dark by the time he arrived home. Er Die decided to fry an egg and enjoy a drink. He was busy cooking in the kitchen when he heard his dog bark.

"Is Er Die home?" he then heard someone calling out. He peeped out through the window and saw the village head, accompanied by several young men, holding something which he could not identify.

"My dear Er Die, where have you been all day? What a time we've had looking for you! You haven't paid your *tiliu* money* this year, have you?" said the village head angrily.

"Suozhu, you know that we've been hit by the drought and have lost all our grain this year. You and I are eating our leftover grain from last year. Where could I find the money for you?"

"I don't care about this. Sir, I only hope that you know that whoever understands the times is a wise man. We are from the same village, and I hate to hurt our feelings. If you don't pay, we can only take away your pig as substitute payment."

"Suozhu, you can't work against your conscience. You know that Dawang and Xiaowang haven't come home for a whole year. It is this pig that will bring them home to join me for New Year."

"Which is more important? Money for the state you are supposed to pay? Or your sons?" With this, the village head handed over a slip of paper full of words and numbers. In the light, Er Die saw more than twenty fees, including "road construction fee," "family planning** fee," and "immunization fee," totaling 890 yuan.

"Suozhu, could I delay my payment? I'll find the money for you after New Year."

"No more excuses, Old Sir. Pay now!"

---

* *Translator's note:* It is a variety of fees demanded by the local government.

** *Translator's note:* Family planning—or rather, "population control"—has been a fundamental policy of China for decades. Late marriage and late childbirth are encouraged. Generally speaking, couples in the cities and towns are allowed to have one child only, while those in the countryside may have a second one if the first one is a girl.

"But where can I find the money now?"

"In that case, you mustn't blame me for being rude!" The village head waved to the group of young villagers standing by, who immediately rushed into the pigsty and started to tie up the pig. Er Die tried to stop them, but was clutched by the village head, helplessly seeing his pig dragged away.

The smell of fireworks filled the morning air the next day, two days before New Year. While people were indulging themselves in the jubilant atmosphere, sad news shocked Kaoshan Village: Er Die had hanged himself. In his home, people discovered the following note:

> Dawang and Xiaowang:
>   I am sorry that I have left you so early. Please give this three hundred yuan to our village head. It is the required payment our family must make. I hope you can ask a favor of the village head. Pay him a ransom to get back our pig so that you can sell it for some money for your tuition fees. From now on, you two must look after each other and study hard. You mustn't be a good-for-nothing like me. Sons, I really have no other way out . . .

Hearing the news, the village head knelt down in front of Er Die's temporary memorial tablet, crying, "Why were you so silly? The county government knows about our financial difficulty and has exempted us from the required payment. I was just about to return the pig to you . . ."

Another letter from Dawang and Xiaowang arrived on New Year's Eve: "In order to save our traveling cost, we have decided not to come home for the New Year. We hope Dad will not be offended."

A Little Bird

By **Lu** Fuhong

When the retired man walked into the park every morning, he would pace around Old Blindman for quite a while. Old Blindman had come to play with his little bird, of an unknown species. He was holding a walking stick in one hand and an exquisite birdcage in the other. It was a very, very beautiful bird with a fine coat of bright, shiny feathers. Its jet black eyeballs kept rolling as it looked around. Its chirping was very sweet. What's more, the bird was called Jie'er, which would make the retired man's heart pound fast. Whenever Old Blindman intimately called it Jie'er as if calling his own son, and when he tried to teach it some words, the retired man would become restless, as if a strong earthquake were rocking his heart.

The retired man was a very peculiar man. Ever since his retirement, all he had done was stroll in the park early every morning. He could not play chess or cards, and he showed no interest in growing flowers and plants or in keeping a dog or a bird. But ever since he had seen Old Blindman's bird, he had longed for it, no matter the cost!

With that thirst rooted in his mind, he would try to be close to Old Blindman wherever possible. Old Blindman turned out to be a kind-hearted and open-minded man, so they soon became good friends. Old Blindman, who had no relatives to take care of him, lived in solitude, so the retired man would go to the park right on time to accompany him every morning, and then they would play with the bird together.

The retired man cared for the bird more than anything else. Every two or three days, he would buy a lot of bird feed and take it to Old Blindman's home. There he would enjoy watching the bird eat while chatting with the owner, often becoming absent-minded and losing control of himself. Fortunately, Old Blindman could see none of this.

Then came the day when he could not help telling Old Blindman that he wanted to buy his bird. He asked him for a price, sounding very sincere, but apart from feeling surprised, Old Blindman just shook his head. "No. I'll never sell this bird."

"I'll pay you good money," he said impatiently. "Eight thousand yuan or ten thousand yuan, whatever, I will pay. I won't bargain."

"If you really want one of these birds, I can ask somebody to get one for you," said Old Blindman, who was just as sincere.

"I only want this one."

No matter what he said and what he offered, Old Blindman would not sell it. But the retired man just would not give up. He tried to change Old Blindman's mind a few more times. Yet the answer he got was always, "No. I won't sell it." He became embittered by his repeated failure, which then seemed to block something in his heart. Soon he fell ill, fully aware of the root of his own illness. When his children and grandchildren asked him to take medicine and wanted to send him to the hospital, he would not even listen.

It was not until a few days later that Old Blindman learned about the retired man's sickness, which he knew was caused by his yearning for the bird. Old Blindman, despite his love for the pet, took it to the retiree's house with one hand carrying the cage and the other holding his walking stick.

"Old chap, since you love this bird so much, I'll give it to you."

From his bed, the retired man saw him with the birdcage. On hearing his offer, the retired man almost burst into tears. Instantly his health started improving. He seized Old Blindman's hand, still holding the walking stick, and would not let it go.

"Old chap, in fact, this is not a rare or expensive bird. It's a very common one that cost me even less than twenty yuan. But, throughout these years—"

"Brother, don't tell me any more. I want this bird, not because I think it's a rare one, or expensive one."

Several days later, Old Blindman groped his way with his walking stick to the retired man's house again, this time to visit him and the bird as well. But when he entered the house he heard no bird chirping.

"Where is the bird?" he asked at once, "Where's Jie'er?"

The retired man remained silent for a long time. "I set it free," he finally said, looking away from his visitor. But he could imagine his surprised look.

"What? You set the bird free? How could you set Jie'er free?" As expected, Old Blindman sounded extremely agitated.

"Yes, brother. I set the bird free. You don't know this. I have ruled on various cases for thirty-some years. I feel I treated all lawbreakers equally, whether they were common citizens, important officials or noble lords, and I made my judgments with a clear conscience, believing I convinced people by reasoning. Now when I think back carefully, I made just one wrongful ruling in my life. By the time I learned all the facts, it was too late to overturn the original conviction, for he had already died in jail. I have retired now and nobody really knows about this, but ever since I saw your birdcage and heard you call your bird Jie'er, my soul could no longer rest in peace. Brother, the young man I wrongfully convicted was also called Jie!" Tears were trickling down his cheeks as he spoke. He saw that Old Blindman was stupefied at hearing him. Tears too welled in Old Blindman's sunken eyes, then streamed down his cheeks, but he remained silent.

Several years later, Old Blindman died. His now bosom friend, the surviving retired man, looked after his funeral personally despite his own old age. After the funeral, while sorting out the things Old Blindman had left behind, the retired man found a photograph inside a notebook. In the photograph was a strong young man. He looked at

it once, then again. He could not believe his eyes. The young man in
the picture resembled the Jie in his memory in practically every way.
The retired man was not sure whether it was the same Jie. Or could it
be just a coincidence?

Holding You

By **Ma** Shaoxian

Jay, Mom is holding you in her arms!

I am sitting on your bed, facing southwest—my arms are wide open, my heart is saying, "Mom's holding you, Mom's holding you . . ."

It's midnight and Mom is lying in your bed, still thinking that I am holding you in my arms.

I can't sleep, I just can't sleep. So I sit up, still facing southwest, holding you in my arms. If I don't hold you this way, I can't stay alive!

At the spot where the demon stole your life, I was almost paralyzed—my feeble legs just could not carry me. At that moment—over one year ago—I didn't know and still don't know what I wanted to do when I was trying desperately to jump at you when you were within my reach. Was I going to carry you home? Or into the other world? Was I going to hold you to satisfy a mother's love for her son? Or to regain life? I could never lose my dear son . . .

This, all this, was not within my consciousness. My mind was blank, all blank. I was just fighting desperately to jump at you. That required no thinking, no consciousness—it was a mother's instinct. You were part of Mom's life after all.

Our relatives were holding me and my wheelchair. They were

Translator's note: This story was written one year after the author's son died at work at the age of twenty-three. Like what happened at his funeral service, the mother in the story tried desperately to hold the remains of her son, but never succeeded.

110

pushing me towards you—but God! Oh, God, they simply pushed me away! Oh, God forbid! How could they have done so! I wanted to hold the real you in my arms, and forever. That is why I had the courage to come to you!

I started stamping my foot. It was the first time I had ever done so. I don't know why. I stomped desperately, repeatedly, wanting to smash the wheelchair so that I could jump at you, wanting to kick away the wheelchair so that I could run out to hold the real you in my arms. I stamped, I stomped, I wanted to smash the earth, there, the real you, my life—oh, I don't know. I didn't know what I wanted to do—oh, but I still wanted to take you away. Yes, Mom wanted to take you home!

Yes, in the emptiness of desperation, my only consciousness and movement was holding you. Mom kept calling you; I was holding you with my open arms. I was carrying you away, to anywhere, even to the place where no shapes and sizes exist. There, you would return to my life. Forever and ever! Only in this way would I be free of grief, free of hatred, free from all the unbearable pain and suffering. Free, free, free!

But I was too weak. Our relatives just tore me away, away from my flesh and blood that used to be part of me. What a cruel fact it was!

Jay, why are you so peaceful, so perfect a son? You love your mom dearly; you've always understood her and supported her. That's why you've been such a good child who has left your mom in a vacuum where I know nothing.

Son, it would have been normal if your mom had gone before you, not you before me. You are the continuation of her life. It is through this pattern that human life continues on earth from generation to generation.

Son, you haven't left me, really. Although I had mostly lost my memory during the two days when I flew to you and back home, as your eldest aunt told me later, I was holding you in my open arms, calling your name all the time.

Ever since, I have been holding you in my arms right in your bed, in your room, every night—always.

Caring Children

Birthday Diary

By **Ling** Dingnian

Thursday, February 6, 1997
Cloudy

Today is Chinese New Year's Eve. It is supposed to be a day for family reunion, the happiest day of the year. It is also supposed to be the happiest day of the year for me, because it is my birthday. But how could I be happy?

Look at our neighbors. They are all busy celebrating the New Year. Everywhere else is filled with the festive air. In their homes, people go in and out. In their homes, people are busy cooking in their kitchens. The delicious smell of their New Year's dinner fills the whole residence, upstairs and downstairs. It has drifted into our home, and it's making my empty stomach groan.

Our family is the only one that is not celebrating. Not at all! Over the slightest, worthless trifles Dad and Mom have started quarrelling again. I don't remember how many times they have quarreled this month. One fight after another, then another and another. We are one family; what do they have to quarrel about? I don't understand.

Mom curses Dad: "You can't make money. You can't even provide for your wife and child—do you call yourself a man?"

Dad raises his voice and shouts back, "You lazy woman, you want good food and good clothes. Where do you get them? Dropping from the sky? Such a lazy woman, who cares so much for eating, you deserve to be a prostitute—"

Crash! Mom starts to smash things again!

114

"Go ahead, smash whatever you like. Don't you think I dare not do the same! If you don't like me, we don't have to live together." Dad starts to smash things too.

A once happy family has been ruined by quarrelling. A happy New Year is turned into a sad "No Year."

Mom is crying, crying heartbrokenly.

Dad is smoking, smoking sulkily, fouling the air in the whole room.

As a last resort, Mom grabs some clothes, rolls them up and leaves for her mother's.

"Take the child with you!" Dad shouts in a frenzy of rage.

"Beibei belongs to the Wangs. I don't want anything from the Wangs." Mom considers me a thing belonging to the Wangs. How hurtful it is!

It looks like Mom won't come back within a week or two. This New Year will surely be a miserable one.

How could I have been born into such a family?

Other children's fathers and mothers love each other. They are so nice and friendly to each other. Why do my parents fight almost every day?

Is there a way to stop their fighting? It's my fault I am not eloquent enough to help them make peace. I really should slap myself for having a useless tongue.

If only there was medicine that could eliminate anger and rage! I would try to buy it for Dad and Mom, no matter the cost, so that after taking it they would stop fighting, speak to each other and laugh with each other. Even if it meant I had to go without candies, cookies and new clothes.

But where could I find that miraculous medicine?

Tuesday, January 27, 1998
Cloudy

Time flies! Another year has passed and I am already in grade 6. I used to love New Year more than anything else. I used to have good food—a whole table of it—and new clothes. I used to fire firecrackers and fireworks, and receive lucky money. Maybe because I was born on New Year's Eve, I was always given lots of lucky money. But now I hate New Year. I hate my birthday. Other families are all celebrating New Year happily, but my family quarrels through New Year. No New Year is better than New Year.

After their quarrelling escalated, Dad got addicted to drinking, to drown his sorrows. He drinks when there's food on the table. He drinks when there is no food on the table. Every time he drinks, he gets drunk. When he is drunk, his eyes become red and he looks ferocious as he howls and pounds on the table.

Mom doesn't care about him, nor does she fear. She even deliberately provokes him: "What a hero you are! To pop your eyes and shout at your wife! I tell you, I despise you from the bottom of my heart!"

Before long, their trivial quarrel turns into a full-scale fight, with one striking the table and the other smashing things.

"Dad, Mom, won't you stop quarrelling?" I said in tears. "I beg you for a little bit of peace. Could you give me a tiny bit of warmth, please?"

Dad pushes me aside while Mom lectures me: "You know none of this, little girl. Don't interrupt."

"If you don't want to live with me, we'll divorce."

"Divorce! If you don't do it, you are a rotten bastard, son of a bitch!"

I've heard the word "divorce" so many times that it has deafened my ears. I am scared that Dad and Mom will really divorce. I love Dad and I love Mom. I want Dad and I want Mom. I want a whole family, but Dad and Mom won't listen to their daughter's heartfelt wishes. You both are so selfish. So selfish!

Many times I have miserably thought about this: if Dad and Mom really divorced, should I live with Dad or should I live with Mom? Tears wet my pillow, as I think and think.

Finally Dad and Mom divorce, ending their protracted fights. Dad is dejected and Mom is exhausted, yet I am the most unfortunate one. Beyond my imagination, Dad doesn't want me, and neither does Mom. I seem to be an unwanted person. Am I not their own daughter?

It's hard to understand at first, but not really. If Mom wants to marry another man, I will become her burden and get in her way.

Dad hurts me even more when he says, "God knows which bastard is your father. Do you look like me? Tell me, in what way, even the slightest way?"

Finally, I understand everything. It was all because of me. Mom, you shouldn't have given birth to me fourteen years ago, but why did you? Why?

My happy days in the past have become memories, getting more and more distant and blurred.

For other children, New Year's Day follows New Year's Eve. And me? Where can I find my happy days?

Dad and Mom, do you know what your daughter is thinking?

Sweet Dirt

By **Huang** Fei

The northeast wind was whistling, blowing up the remnants of snow on the roads. Though spring had begun, it was still very cold.

She stood against a poplar near the school gate, as still as a snow statue.

The swift bell's ringing brightened up her dull eyes, which instantly glowed with eager hope.

A group of children walked out of the school gate, singing, but none was her son. Another group came out chatting and laughing, then went into the street. Again she did not see her son. Fewer and fewer students came out until nobody was in sight.

The iron gate creaked closed, locking up the quiet school.

She felt dizzy and almost collapsed. She ran staggering toward the gate, seized its iron bars and began to shake it frantically.

"What do you want?" asked the displeased old man who was guarding the gate, as he walked out of his office.

"Liang, my boy, Liang!" She sounded like she was gasping and also crying.

"The children have all gone home for lunch."

"I—I know," she muttered with dull-looking eyes. She hung her feeble head and let go of the bars slowly. Putting her hand into the pocket of her *dajin* cotton-padded coat,* she drew out a tightly wrapped package of sweets that still carried her bodily warmth.

---

* *Translator's note:* It is a coat buttoned on the right, likely home made.

118

"Sir, could you—please kindly give it to my boy," she said.

"What's his name?"

"Wang Xiaoliang."

"Which class, and which grade is he in?"

"He has just turned eight today."

"I am asking which class, and which grade he is in!" The old man was obviously a little annoyed.

"Oh—maybe he—" But she began to shake her head, looking perplexed.

"Who are you, then?" said the surprised old man, looking the neurotic woman up and down.

The only answer he got was a pair of tearful eyes and the back of a figure staggering away from him. The confused old man sighed, now seeming to understand a thing or two.

Eventually, in the afternoon, the surprise sweets were passed to Wang Xiaoliang, a second grader in Class 2. He was thrilled: they were his favorite toffees, which he had not eaten for a long time. Rubbing his little hands against his clothes back and forth, he thought for a little while, smiled, then gave one to everybody in his class. His best friends got a second one. In the most respectful way, he gave five to his teacher. "Come on. Eat it." He jumped and screamed happily till his torn, shabby shoe fell off his foot. His classmates shared his happiness, laughing with him merrily. Only the teacher turned around quietly . . .

Xiaoliang was still indulging in joy when school was over. He was bouncing homeward, but stopped all of a sudden. Terror struck him as he touched the toffees he had spared in his pocket. He seemed to see it again: New Mom raised her thin eyebrows and whispered something in Dad's ear. Dad looked fierce, seized a wooden stick and was walking toward him. Xiaoliang was lost in a daze, not knowing what to do.

He beat his pocket as hard as he could. "Nope. It just bulges out no matter how you look at it." He hung his little head, sucked his finger and thought for quite a while. Finding nobody around, he quickly buried the toffees in the snow by the roadside, then planted a little wooden stick there.

Xiaoliang had an exceptionally sweet sleep that night. He dreamed that Old Mom had come back home and that New Mom had left with a hung head. How happy he was!

He got up very early the next morning. As always, he emptied the waste jar for the whole family and brushed it clean. Then he washed the rice in the pot, added water, and gave the stove a poke before he placed the pot on it. After that, he put on his schoolbag, picked up a cold steamed bun and slipped out of the door. He was dying to dig out his toffees.

To his surprise, the temperature had risen overnight. The snow had melted and the syrup of the toffees mixed with the water had seeped into the earth. Left on the wet ground were the wrinkled wrappers and the little stick marking the spot.

Xiaoliang kept blinking, tears rolling down his cheeks. He squatted down, heartbroken, gazing at the spot with a blank look on his face. After a while, unable to restrain himself, he stretched out his little cold-chapped fingers for a bit of wet dirt and put it on the tip of his tongue.

There, the dirt was sweet! He was smiling again.

A Fearless Experiment

By **Zhang** Jishu

Jun was a good boy well known in the county town. He was eager to do well at everything, and was particularly fond of studying. Indeed, he was often the top student at school.

When his parents moved to the city for their new jobs, he came with them, switching to No. 1 Middle School. In the new school, Jun became a very ordinary student, well below the average. "If I don't reach the top, how can I ever enter Beijing University or Qinghua University?" He felt dejected.

Jun's strong desire to be the top student started to burn him like fire until he could neither eat well nor sleep properly. He wanted to catch up with the city kids and surpass them. Though he also studied during mealtime and at bedtime, he still could not catch up with them. What had happened? Why had he become such a low achiever in the city?

One day, while reading a magazine, Jun came across an article written by a certain expert, entitled, "How to Become a More Clever Person." It said that "people who have experienced death but have managed to survive are the smartest. These people can also do wonders." A skylight seemed to open up over his head. He thought that that must be the same idea as the Chinese saying, "If you survive a great disaster, you are bound to have good fortune later on."

That night, he conceived an idea to experiment with death. He wanted to experience the struggle of death, but he must survive. When the decision was made, he started to choose his method.

Jumping from a tall building? No. If he didn't jump properly, he could become handicapped.

How about braving the waves in the sea? No, for he could not swim. If nobody was available to rescue him, he would drown.

None of the methods he thought of was good, but how could he achieve his goal then?

When Jun was watching the TV show *Prime Minister Liu Luoguo* one day, he was enlightened. In the show, the emperor granted Heshen the privilege of hanging himself; this struck a chord in the child's tender heart. A sparkle flashed across his eyes. "That's a good idea." So he decided to use the same method to conduct his experiment.

Jun had heard that a person usually died only after seven minutes of hanging. That being the case, he decided to hang himself for just five minutes, merely to be tempered by death yet to survive death. With this plan in place, he felt as pleased as if he had just had a bowl of sugar water. After this struggle, he would become the smartest child in the city and would score first among all the students at the municipal level.

When should the five minutes be, then? He thought and thought. Finally, he decided to do it before his mother came home from work. He knew she was a punctual person and always returned home at 6:30 p.m. With his father on a business trip out of town, besides her job, she worried about nothing more than her darling son. So recently she had been coming home even more punctually than ever before.

Eventually, Jun picked Friday afternoon for his experiment. Their now two-day weekend actually started on Friday. On the weekend, his mother loved to take him to the Xihuchun Restaurant for Western food—to let him experience foreign life. "It would be interesting. If I go there for my Western food after being tempered by a unique experience, the food will definitely taste different."

So he secretly wrote down his plan in his diary. Only after his experiment and when he became the smartest child in the city would he show his diary to his parents. That would be a happy surprise for them.

He left school at four o'clock on Friday afternoon. First, he went to the store to buy a beautiful nylon rope. He had to choose one carefully, for it would be an important souvenir afterward.

It was five o'clock when he got home. He tried to do some reading, but just could not. Then he stared at the clock on the desk. It seemed to smile at him, calling him a good boy with lofty ideals. When six o'clock came, Jun became really excited. He thought the experiment would surely make him the first "crab eater"* among the middle-school students of the new era. His name could even be included in the *Guinness Book of Records!*

At this moment, he thought of calling his mother to ask her to come home on time, but he changed his mind. "It doesn't make sense if I call!"

At 6:20, he tied the rope to the bar above the lintel behind the door. That was a place his mother would not miss. The moment she opened the door, she would see him and do whatever she could to revive him. Then he would have succeeded in his experiment.

Now he was just waiting for the arrival of 6:25, which was five minutes before 6:30.

"Tick-tock, tick-tock . . ." The second hand was running, and the minute hand moving. Finally, it was twenty-five minutes after six o'clock. Without hesitation, Jun got on the stool, put the loop around his neck, then kicked over the stool!

At this point, dear reader, like me, I believe you are anxiously waiting for Jun's mother to return home. But she did not come home on time that day. As coincidental as it could be, when she had almost finished work, the company received an unexpected assignment and her boss wanted her to work overtime. She called home at 6:30 to tell her son she would be late. The phone rang for a long time, but nobody answered. "My son must still be at school," she thought. At 7:00 she

---

* *Translator's note:* It refers to the first courageous adventurer.

called again, and again nobody answered. "Maybe my son has gone out to eat by himself," she said to herself.

When she finished work at 8:00, she rushed home immediately.

The moment she opened the door, she was stupefied by what she saw! Her son was hanging from the bar, much of his tongue sticking out. He had long gone to the other world.

She clutched his legs and passed out instantly.

Dentures

By **Zhong** Zimei

When Ying Wei woke up, his throat and lips were dry. In the ghastly dim light of the white ward, he recognized his son's face as the son moved closer to him.

"Dad! Dad!" his son called out, exposing a set of neat white teeth.

Ying Wei tried to smile but could not. He felt that one corner of his mouth was flat. It seemed to have caved in. In fact, he had forgotten to wear his dentures, but what had happened seemed like a remote event.

He had been in his own home near the Litchi Lake in Shenzhen. All of a sudden he had started to tremble from head to foot: the pain was too hard to endure. His 85-year-old mother was sitting at the head of his bed, grasping his hands. "Wei! Wei! Don't scare me!" she cried repeatedly.

Their neighbor, by the name of Zeng, called an ambulance for them. The doctor came with a stretcher, but nobody was able to carry Wei to the ambulance. The anxious neighbor was spinning around, not knowing what to do, and Wei did not know what had happened after that.

"We are in the Prince of Wales Hospital in Hong Kong," said Wei's son, who could read his father's eyes. "I rushed to Shenzhen yesterday. An ambulance from the People's Hospital there sent you up to the Wenjindu Customs. Then a Hong Kong ambulance picked you up from there and brought you here."

"Good, good," Wei uttered with great effort.

Only then did the son discover that his father was not wearing his dentures. "Dad, I'll go back to Shenzhen and pick up your dentures from home tomorrow," he said.

Wei knew that he had cancer of the liver in the advanced stage, so in order not to disturb his son's work, he had moved back to his own home in Shenzhen, where he stayed with his old mother. Though his mother could not move freely, she was still in good health. Yet she did not know that her unhealthy son, who had just turned sixty years old, was suffering from an incurable disease.

Wei thought of his home in Shenzhen, then of his old mother. Breathing with difficulty, he uttered, word by word, "I don't have many days left. After I die, go get the dentures and tell Grandma I can eat now. Don't tell her about my death. Keep it from her, as long as you can . . ." Then the sleepy Wei seemed to be sitting in his mother's arms. She opened his small mouth and cried in joy: "My little son has teeth now!"

A Gift from McDonald's

By **Ye** Qingcheng

I returned home for the weekend before Christmas when I was in my first year of university. Sipping the sparerib soup my mother had prepared for me only, I kept wondering, "Should I ask Mom for the money?"

Dad passed away when I was young, and I had since got used to seeing Mom's hard life, but I had never asked her for money for non-essential things. But this time was different, because of Zhu Ying.

Quite often, I would pace up and down on the campus paths with Zhu Ying. Without our knowing it, we had been to every corner of the campus, and I had run out of ideas how to keep time with us. My roommates started to offer me advice, saying I should strike while the iron was red hot by giving Zhu Ying a romantic Christmas Eve. Most of the Chinese restaurants were noisy and distasteful, but the few tasteful ones were too expensive for me. Finally I chose McDonald's.

"But how should I ask Mom for the money?" I kept thinking, the hot soup choking my throat. The room was quiet except for the noises I made while I drank the soup. Mom was sitting in front of me, gazing at me in silence. "Two days ago, we had a meeting at the factory," she suddenly said. "A group of people will be laid off."

I stood up uncontrollably and stared at her in terror. "Mom, you have been laid off?"

Mom was dazed for a moment, then she laughed. She laughed lovingly, with boundless tender affection. "See how scared you are! I said a group of people will lose their jobs. I didn't say I am one of them. I have been doing very well."

I breathed a sigh of relief, thinking that Mom must be in a pretty good mood. Biting my lips, I made my request. "Mom, I have to go on a field trip to a factory next semester, and need to pay two hundred yuan for the materials."

"Oh—" Mom uttered, clearly disappointed. "More money to pay—"

"Or, I'll tell my teacher—" I dared not look her in the eyes. She turned around and opened the drawer.

"I will give you two hundred-yuan notes. Make sure you won't be pickpocketed."

Mom looked through the drawer for a long time and found only one hundred-yuan bill and one fifty-yuan bill; the rest were all ten-yuan notes. She smoothed out the corners of the bills, counted them again and again, then folded them two times into quarters. Finally she cross-folded them into a small square. After that, she carefully put it all into the inner pocket of my satchel, then secured the double zipper for me. When she was seeing me off at the door, she told me again and again, "Be careful when you are on the bus. There are thieves everywhere these days."

"I will," I said, but I could no longer control my feet. I started to run. The more I ran, the faster I ran, dying to be with Zhu Ying at once.

It started snowing on Christmas Eve, making the holiday atmosphere more distinct and luxurious. McDonald's was filled with customers. We had to wait for a long time before the people at a table got up and left. I dashed over and seized the seats. Zhu Ying waved at the attendant. "Miss, clean up the table."

An attendant started walking toward us quickly. In the distance, I saw a somewhat frail figure walking with her upper half bent slightly forward. How familiar it was! "Mom!" I was dumbfounded.

"How could it be Mom? She—she is supposed to be working in the factory now." Suddenly, I remembered seeing her cheerless face in the dim kitchen back home. "Could she—could she have been hiding the truth from me? Could Mom have been laid off?"

Mom also spotted me in the crowd. Instantly, her eyes opened wide, staring at me furiously without blinking. I saw endless violent waves of fright, doubt, disappointment and pain surging from her eyes. I saw her body shaking gently.

Yet Mom said nothing. She just lowered her head and quickly started cleaning up the messy cups and plates on the table. I wanted to call her "Mom," but perhaps because of shock or the noisy crowd around, or merely because of Zhu Ying, I could not utter a word. I just stared at her, dumbfounded.

She did not look at me again, but went straight to the next table. While she was dumping the garbage into the waste can, she paused and put her hand against her forehead. When she walked past me again, I saw the obvious, long tear stains on her arms as clear as burn scars.

"God, did Mom mean to tell me she had been laid off that day? Did she change her mind because she couldn't bear to see how panic-stricken I was at that moment?" I clutched the bills inside my pocket, knowing the importance of money for the first time in my life.

Memories of growing up welled up in my mind like turbulent waves. I could not hold back my tears. Tearfully, I saw Zhu Ying's beautiful eyebrows, her slim waist shown under the elegant black leather jacket. Suddenly I realized, "Dating is too expensive a game for me."

Shortly after my second year in university started, I placed a stack of banknotes in front of Mom and said, "Mom, I can pay my own tuition fees next semester. I have the money now: I have won a scholarship, I work as a tutor as well as a laborer. So please don't work so hard yourself from now on."

Mom stared at the money for a long time. Then she covered her face with her hands. She was crying.

129

Should I Stay or Go

By Harry J. **Huang**

"Mom, you are busy, eh?"

"Yes. What's up?"

"I have three—"

"Three what?"

"Boyfriends—oh no. Candidates only."

"So many? Who are they?"

"I won't tell you their names yet."

"Then tell me what they are."

"Candidate A is the son of a vice-provincial governor. If I could marry him, his father would be a great help to you."

"And Candidate B?"

"Candidate B is a businessman who owns a company himself. If I could marry him, you would never lack money, Mom."

"And?"

"And Candidate C is emigrating to the United States. His father owns a restaurant in New York. If I could marry him, you might have a chance to go to the United States. Mom, should I stay or go?"

"Silly girl, go away."

130

Interpreting the Will

By **Ma** Baoshan

After lying unconscious on his deathbed for several days, the old man suddenly opened his eyes, which were still shiny eyes. The three sons, who had been keeping a bedside vigil, thought it was the last momentary consciousness their dying father had recovered, so they all moved close to him.

The sons were waiting for his last advice on how to behave themselves and how to deal with others.

The old man had lived an unusually successful life. At the age of eighteen, he had worked for Longchang Business Firm as a junior accountant. When he was twenty-two years old, he became the manager representing the private business owners of a giant business firm jointly owned by the state and individual investors. In the 1950s, when the state paid special attention to secondary school teacher education and when he was not quite thirty years old yet, he was appointed vice-principal of a teachers' school and concurrently director of the Teaching Affairs Office. Later on, he was promoted to be education bureau director of the city, then director of the municipal finance department. During the Cultural Revolution, when every official, big or small, suffered in various ways, he only had to leave his post for a few days until he was integrated with the three-in-one leading body of the Revolutionary Committee of the municipal finance department. He had a smooth sail for years and years. The old man retired at the age of sixty, resigning with honor from the position of vice-chairman of the Political Consultative Conference of the city, and was guaranteed the benefits of the head of a prefecture until death.

The old man, who had led a peaceful life full of promotions, rising step by step, must have had a trick or two unknown to others. Since he was leaving this world, he ought to leave the legacy to his own sons, if not to outsiders. Looking solemn and earnest, the three sons were all ears, ready to hear the last words from their father.

The old man's eyes showed no sign of liquid, but were still clear. Sweeping across the sons' faces, he slowly opened his mouth, which exposed no teeth, only bumpy gums. Like a crawling eel, his tongue was running along the gums and licking the lips.

The sons all held their breath, awaiting some philosophical sayings from him that could benefit them for the rest of their lives, but all they heard was a long sigh, after which the old man shut his eyes.

The old man passed away peacefully without leaving a word.

They held a grand funeral for him, after which the sons started to recall the old man's looks and little movements before he breathed his last. The three brothers all agreed that by opening his mouth, stretching his tongue and licking his lips, he meant to tell them, "At this moment, silence is louder than words."

The eldest son, who was the office director of a large company, concluded that through the three little movements, his father wanted to tell him that his teeth were sharp, but it was exactly their vigor and sharpness that had led to their early loss. His tongue, by contrast, remained alive and vigorous thanks to its smoothness and flexibility. Wasn't it his father's warning that a staunch man would fall but a docile man would rise? He admired his father earnestly.

The second son, who worked as a secretary in the municipality, gathered that by opening his mouth, rolling his tongue and licking his lips, his father was telling him, "Least said, soonest mended. Watch your mouth and mind your words. Better still, keep your mouth shut." The second son engraved these words on his heart.

The third and also least successful son, who had worked for a store as a purchasing agent but was not being paid though he retained his job, was now making a living by finding customers anywhere for a fundless company that speculated on price differences. His interpretation of his father's little movements was simple: "A man needs nothing but food and clothing." That was a shrewd old man!

Later on, when their mother learned about this, she scolded them all. "You bastards, what last words were they? Wasn't your old man asking for a drink of water!"

Dumbboy Ah Tong

By **Wan** Qian

Ah Tong, called by his family name, had a stubborn character well known in town, where everyone called him Stubborn Dumbboy.

In fact, Tong used to speak, until he was fourteen years old. That year, a young woman in the neighborhood—or a "big" girl, as he saw her—lost her favorite bra when it was drying in the sun; she said she had bought it from a specialty store in the big city. She claimed Tong was involved—out of mischief, saying she had spotted him strolling on the sunning ground all by himself. It was a disgrace, and naturally Tong denied it.

"There are so many people in our town. Why didn't she single out somebody else?" said his father. "You must have done wrong one way or the other."

Again, Tong flatly denied it, but the more stubborn he was, the more insistent the girl became.

What followed was corporal punishment for Tong, but that only hardened his position. His father beat him up until he was bruised and lacerated, and did not stop until he was torn away by onlookers. Then the stubborn Tong simply remained where he was, looking like a stone statue on the brick ground outside his old house. For three days and nights, he did not eat, drink or go to the toilet. Finally he collapsed in a rainstorm because his body could not sustain any more.

Tong fell ill for several days. When he eventually recovered, he did not speak again. His eyes were now blank and hostile, as if everybody he saw was his enemy. So nobody dared to provoke him.

Tong, a dumb boy now, dropped out of school. His teachers came to visit his family repeatedly, but all in vain. Tong, who had no school, never played with anybody anymore, day or night. He would just eat, then sleep, then eat again and sleep again. For this his mother would cry her heart out.

Tong's father knew it was all his own fault, fully aware that he had made an uncorrectable mistake. So he kept Tong with him at work, hoping that he could learn some carpentry skills which could earn him a living in the future.

Tong was already a tall and sturdy man at the age of twenty, so his parents began to look for a wife for him through a matchmaker. But every girl who heard of his dumbness would just shake her head and say no. Advised by whomever it was, Tong's parents took him to the specialists in the large hospitals in the big city. His parents did not really understand what the specialists said, but they did remember that it could do him good to let him leave home and try to make a living by himself—the earlier the better. Tong's parents agreed to give him a try.

After much consideration, his father decided to put him on the town's construction team so that he could experience life in the city by himself, which might help. Thus, Tong came to Suzhou with the construction team to build big buildings in the developmental zone. At the work site, like before, Tong would work quietly and eat in silence. After the last meal of the day, he would just go to sleep. When he woke up, he would work like a horse again. His workmates knew his peculiar ways. Everyone was scared by his hostile, blank eyes, so they just left him alone. Nothing unusual ever happened, and two years seemed to have passed peacefully in the twinkling of an eye.

Then came that day when all the workers were given a day off. Tong's workmates all went window-shopping, so Tong went with them. Unexpectedly, at some point the muddled man lost the team by getting on the wrong bus, not knowing where it was going. The moment he got on the crowded bus and found himself alone, he wanted to get off, but it was too late: the bus was moving. It was about to pull up at the next stop when a passenger suddenly shouted, "Someone has stolen my purse!"

The bus fell into chaos, as some people wanted to get off while the owner of the missing purse did not agree. Somebody suggested that the driver drive directly to the police station. At this chaotic moment, the purse was found, right at Tong's heel. All eyes were fixed on him like sharp knives. Tong's blank eyes counterattacked with hostility. All of a sudden somebody shouted, "It's him. Beat up the thief!"

People began to charge at him. Tong saw numerous fists and feet flying at him from all directions. Some were cruel, aiming straight at his private parts. Tong fought back by instinct, but was quickly struck down with both hands twisted behind his back, so he could no longer defend himself. Blood was running down his face.

"You can easily tell he is the thief just by looking at his eyes!" someone said as his fist landed on Tong.

At the moment of desperation, Tong saw a beautiful young woman elbowing her way through the crowd, shouting at the top of her voice, "Stop it! He's not the thief. Stop it! He's not the thief." Then he saw fewer fists and feet.

"I am a reporter for the evening newspaper," she added. "I assure you based on my profession."

Then she waved something in her hand. Tong could not see it clearly, for his eyes were covered with blood. Soon they all stopped hitting him. "We can still trust a reporter," said one of them.

The bus pulled up at the bus stop. She got off, and Tong followed suit. She drew out some facial tissues and handed them to him to wipe the blood.

He did not wipe the blood. Instead, he made a deep bow to her and said "Thank you!" like a baby learning to speak.

Tong returned home the next day and called his Dad and Mom. It didn't sound like a big deal, but it rocked their hearts. His mom clutched him in her arms, as she burst into tears. "My dear child, I knew you would speak again!"

From then on, Tong was not dumb anymore, though nobody in his hometown knew what had happened to him.

My Home, My Family

By **Xiu** Xiangming

Whenever I quarreled with my wife, our son would beg us to make peace, but how could a ten-year-old boy make peace between his fighting parents!

Things changed later on. It was not that my wife and I stopped fighting, but that once our fighting started, our son would not try to beg for reconciliation between us anymore. Instead, he would pick up his brush and begin to paint on his paper.

He would paint a two-bedroom apartment, carpeted in red with its walls sprayed with bright, vivid colors. It was furnished with Simmons mattresses and leather sofas. On the balcony were potted plants, such as scarlet Kafir lilies and asparagus ferns. In the goldfish aquarium, goldfish with open fins seemed to be flying. In the washroom, the shower head connected to the water heater was sprinkling water that looked like flowers.

And these were exactly what my wife and I had been quarrelling about. The three of us lived in a room with a floor space of twelve square meters. Next to the street was our kitchen, with only enough room for two people to stand. It was built from a few boards unprofessionally nailed together, looking like a broken outhouse. Three-fifths of our room was occupied by the bookcase, the cupboard, the wardrobe, the loveseat, the tea table, the desk and the bed. It is not difficult to imagine how little room was left.

Naturally, we experienced a lot of inconvenience in life. My wife and I were as scared as thieves when we were making love, for fear our sleeping son would wake up and see us. We three could still endure this room in winter, but in summer, after being scorched in the sun for a whole day, our small home was just like an oven. We would lie in bed sweating all over. Sleeping in the same bed, we three felt as if we were being boiled in a kettle. With no other way out, I tore open the cardboard TV box and put it on the floor to make another bed for myself. This was where I slept throughout the miserable summer nights.

In the beginning, my wife blamed me for the hardship. Then she started quarrels, followed by scolding.

"I've married such a good-for-nothing who can't even give me a place to live!

"I am already forty-five years old and will retire in five years. Am I going to live in this cowshed all my life?

"This is a shed for a migrant laborer, and you call it a home!"

In fact, I was very frustrated myself. I wanted to live in a bigger place too. If I could buy a decent apartment by cutting out three pounds of onions or two pounds of chives, I would definitely tighten my belt. The reality was that even if I sealed up my mouth, ate nothing and drank nothing, and saved every penny I earned, I still could not afford a decent apartment.

So when I could not endure my wife's endless cursing and scolding, I fought back. There was not a single day of peace at home anymore, and that terrified our son.

I knew he was painting to kill the miserable time while my wife and I quarreled. The tears he had once shed when he tried to stop us quarrelling had turned into thick and shiny engine oil. This oil had soaked a pair of attentive eyes that radiated with eager prayers and hope. And I admired our son's imagination and his talents in painting.

Strange to say, he did the same picture every day, so pictures of a two-bedroom apartment with a living room covered the walls all around our bed.

Once after a quarrel with my wife, I guiltily walked over and tried to enlighten him. "Son, painting a picture is like writing a book,"

I said. "You should only do things you are familiar with. Just paint our own one-room bungalow. Only in this way can you do good pictures."

"Daddy, I am also familiar with two-bedroom apartments," he said. "My classmates Nannan and Yuanyuan both live in two-bedroom apartments. I have played in their homes. Because Nannan's father is the factory head and Yuanyuan's father is the manager of a company, their homes are very beautiful."

He swallowed his saliva, his lips quivering, as if thirsting for something very delicious.

I could not hold back my tears, which started to roll down my cheeks. I was grateful to him. I thanked him, even wanting to hold him in my arms and kiss him. He had seen those beautiful homes, yet he had never complained or blamed me like my wife did.

As always, once my wife and I started quarrelling, he would start painting that two-bedroom apartment, showing an idiotic look like that of an obsessed painter at work.

Perhaps my son's good faith touched God. At long last, I moved into an apartment with two bedrooms and a living room, which my factory had bought for me for 110,000 yuan.

But my wife and I had divorced one month before that.

My smart son chose to live with me. To show my gratitude to him, I decorated the bedrooms, the balcony, the washroom, everything in exactly the same way he had been painting.

I occupied the bigger bedroom, and he, the smaller one.

"My child, now you are living in an apartment that really belongs to you," I said to him the night we moved in. "I am sure if you continue to paint the same picture, you will do much better."

The next morning, I found him sleeping at the desk when I wanted to wake him up. He had not slept in bed at all. His desk was covered with more than ten pictures, different from his previous ones. They were all pictures of the old, small one-room bungalow we used to have.

140

I woke him up and said, "My child, why didn't you paint the same picture? Hasn't the dream in your old paintings come true?"

His eyes looking rather tired and blank, he glanced at the beautiful new home, then at the pictures he had done overnight. Finally, he burst into sobs, throwing himself into my arms.

Wolf Path

By **Meng** Meng

When I was a child, the adults often said, "There's a wolf path north
of the city. It's like a wolf. The wolf has a drooping tail that looks
like a broom. It runs quickly on its skinny legs that look like cotton
stalks, from inside the earth in West Sky to every corner of the *kang*
in every house. It eats up any child in any family who is naughty,
mischievous, and cries. Sometimes, it also eats children on the path.
It has three tricks before eating a child. First, it cries. It cries
heartbrokenly, like a woman whose child has been snatched away,
until you feel sorry for it and won't be wary of it. The second trick is
confusing you. Like four turning wheels, its paws keep digging the
earth rapidly, to thicken the air and confuse your eyes. The third trick
is hooking. Like two iron hooks, it fixes its green eyes on you. It
hooks away not only your soul, but also your organs. Then it eats
them."

The adults also said, "The wolf eats a child in three steps: first, it
bites your mouth; second, it claws at your chest; third, it gnaws your
thighs." So children dared not cry when they went to sleep; neither
dared to kick off their quilts or touch their parents. Otherwise, they
would be eaten up if the wolf knew it.

I went to check it out for myself one day. Really, the path was
narrow and winding, looking like a broom or a cotton stalk. In winter,
it was bare with no sign of water, yet it was also an object of the
scenery in the deathly white wintry days. Thick weeds that could be
woven into ropes covered the road, stem upon stem, patch after patch,
creating a cottonlike pad all over the wolf path. The goatee weeds

that had lignified on the outside were yellowing, though their cores were still green. They reminded me of the wolf's eyes that could hook away people's souls. I got scared when a gust of wind blew thick dust, thinking it could be the wolf digging the earth. Occasionally, when I looked closely, I found places of wolf droppings inside the weeds. The gleaming droppings that showed some bone fragments were extremely smelly. It was very frightening, but I did not see any wolf crying like a woman. "In the daytime, wolves don't snatch babies from women, so women don't cry, and wolves don't cry like women either." Seeing nothing there, I felt pretty hollow inside myself. I gazed along the wolf path into the distance, from West Sky to the lanes to the moat of the city. It connected the villages with the other places like a pitch arc. Now I became confused: "Why does the wolf path run through the village, but the villagers don't even use it?"

One day in the fall, I went to the valley to cut some grass. It was getting late, so I took a shortcut through the wolf path. On both sides of the path were corn fields. The cornstalks, so tall and thick, nearly covered up the wolf path, blocking the view of the fields.

All of a sudden, in the evening mist, I saw a wolf digging earth, hooking a child's soul and imitating a woman's crying. Terrified, I dropped the grass basket from my shoulders and lay behind it for a close look.

The wolf was really eating the child. First, it bit the child's mouth, then clawed at the chest, and finally gnawed the thighs. My heart was pounding fast when I saw the wolf push down the child and about to finish a life! Suddenly, I discovered the child was as big as the wolf. Their eight legs entangled, they started to shake the wolf path. The child was not eaten up at all, but was giggling with the wolf. I did hear crying, but not the wolf's imitation of a woman's. It was joyful crying. I could not be more astonished when I squinted at them—jeez! They turned out to be a male wolf and a female wolf. More terrifying still, they even got up and walked upright!

When I got back home, I told the children, "The grown-ups are the wolves. The wolf path was opened up for them." After I told them my strange encounter, nobody was afraid of the wolf path anymore. Less likely would anyone believe that a wolf would lie at the corner of the *kang*. Though adults still kept talking about wolves when they tried to stop us from mischievous doings and crying, we did not care. We made mischief when we wanted to, and we cried when we had to cry.

Sweet Romances

My Wife's Hands

By **Gao** Weixi

I found myself busy writing at the desk again. I had made up my mind to water, with my life, this beautiful flower of literary prose. I treated it with the care of poetry; my fountain pen, soaked in enthusiasm, inked out words, page by page. I rose early and retired late, devoting every minute of my spare time to nothing but writing.

"Good God!" my wife cried. Her chopping board became silent.

Dropping my pen, I dashed into the kitchen, only to find her pressing her left forefinger with her right hand. Her mouth closed, she frowned at the wounded finger. Blood was oozing from its tip, then running along the back of her hand before it dripped onto the cement floor.

"God! My wife got a cut when she was chopping her vegetables," I said to myself. "God! My wife, who's got a cut, is scared!"

"Easy!" I shouted. "Press it harder and raise it a little higher up. I'll find the medicine for you."

After a quick, frantic search in the drawer, I found the ethyl alcohol, mercurochrome, cotton balls and bandages. I lost no time in bandaging up her finger with tender care.

When all was taken care of, I held up her hand and led her into the bedroom. We sat on the bed. I safely put her hand over my large palm, placed it against my chest and started to fondle it. I kept fondling it as if to soothe the long years of hardship it had gone through, as if to pacify the pain of the cut. Only when my wife's face lit up with a faint smile at the corner of her mouth did my tight, wrinkled heart start to expand to its own shape. Yet I did not stop fondling her hand.

146

All of a sudden, I seemed to discover a new continent: how had her once tender, smooth hands become so rough? Where were her ten small, slender fingers now? My! The upper knuckles of her fingers had turned purple, the bottoms covered with button-like calluses. Her skin had also become very loose, no longer as springy and tight as it used to be.

I raised her hands for a close look and found them pale and covered with wrinkles, her veins bulging out under her skin. I was even more shocked at seeing the spots, like bruises, on the back of her hands, which I had seen as a child on the skin of the older generation. Age had eaten up its youth; hard work had aged it too early. Feeling a surge in my heart, I found moisture in my eyes; it flickered in the light, then slowly turned into tears, falling onto the back of her hands.

Seeing what was happening as she turned around, she gave me a gentle stroke with her shoulder and said in a soft voice, "Now there! Aren't you being silly! You are not a child anymore." With this she put her chin over my shoulder as she used to do when we were young . . .

Memories of the misty past, somewhat bitter-sweet, welled up in my mind. When I heard a light waltz, I summoned my courage, walked up to her with a courteous bow, making a gesture of invitation. She smiled shyly but accepted my invitation at once. Thus, for the first time in my life, I was holding her hands, dancing merrily around.

I tried to be graceful throughout the dance, politely holding her four closed fingers with my left thumb and three other fingers, while my right hand gently touched her back. However, being a greenhorn, I found it rather challenging and danced out of step in no time. Barely surviving the first dance, I lowered my head and apologized earnestly: "Do excuse me, I am no dancer." But she answered me with a forgiving smile. Then we each found a seat and sat down.

There were plenty of dances in the university, and practice made me a good dancer. As we danced, we became more and more familiar with each other. Perhaps it was during one of the early dates that I suddenly found her hands so tender and soft, just like a little mass of warm dough. I almost wanted to call them "as fair as jade," as they are often described in classic novels. Later on, our relationship took a leap forward, and I could, without restraint, bring her hands over to my knees and enjoy viewing them closely. Only then did I discover that my wife-to-be's hands were so charming—smooth, slender and youthfully energetic.

"Aren't they neat and delicate hands?" I said in admiration.

"Aren't all girls' hands like these?" she replied in a soft, sweet voice.

"Perhaps they are, but I've never found out." Then I started to laugh, proud of the witty reply I had carelessly uttered.

She pouted, throwing a glance at me. "And there, when you were first dancing with me, you squeezed my hands so hard."

"What? Me squeezing your hands? Oh, that's unfair!" I protested. "I was just learning to dance. I was concentrated on my steps. I took care not to step on your feet. I was afraid of making mistakes and was nervous all over. That's why I squeezed your hands. Honestly, my hands were numb, and I never knew I was squeezing yours!"

"But what proof do you have?" she naughtily provoked me.

"Proof? There, there. But am I still doing that now?"

"Now?" She turned sideways as a sparkle flashed in her eyes. "Now you can have them any way you like." With this she thrust up her tender hand toward my chest.

Happy but nervous, I simply led it up toward my lips and . . .

In those days, her hands were engaged in note-taking and writing. The tip of her pen kissing the blank paper rustled like a silkworm feeding on mulberry leaves—it was melodious. I was surprised that her hands were even more nimble and more clever than my much larger and stronger hands.

Her hands also took over the duties of my washing, sewing,

knitting, everything, even before we got married. I thought that hers must be the most beautiful and most clever hands in the world.

Later on, after we got married, I simply forgot about her hands.

Unbelievably, more than twenty years have passed as if in the twinkling of an eye, and her hands have become so rough.

Nonetheless, the long years have witnessed that she possesses a pair of hard-working hands that can do wonders. Throughout the years, at work, they have been a social asset, producing high-quality food for the minds of numerous readers. At home, these two hands run almost everything, from household financial matters to raising a lovely son and a beautiful daughter to doing tedious household chores as well as grocery shopping, cooking, cleaning, clothes mending and sewing. These hands even spare time for writing, often until midnight. The result is that a family which is pretty hard up has been operating in an orderly way, with all its members happy and harmonious.

Hardened by the years of life, her hands have become more and more clever. Now by taking some rough measurements and through a few cuts by the scissors, then by pressing through the sewing machine, they magically turn an oddment of cotton print into a dress for our little daughter. A perfect fit, simple but elegant, it makes the girl look gracefully quiet—just beautiful! Our girl was once so excited that she threw herself into her mother's arms, dropping kisses on her lovely hands.

Several cabbage leaves, chopped into threads, poured into the hot vegetable oil in the heated wok, then stirred with a handful of dry shrimps, some milk, cooking starch and other ingredients, rapidly turn into a fine dish that not only looks tempting and smells savory, but also tastes delicious. There, the dish looks bluish white, dotted with dozens of red stars; she has named it "Clouds Over the Sky." Every visitor who tastes it praises the hostess for her creative mind and clever hands.

Once leaving her hands, an article of two or three thousand words written by an inexperienced writer would have its theme clearly sharpened in a carefully crafted structure whose language would flow like water. That is why writers have comments like, "That editor has miraculous skills that turn hopeless manuscripts into print."

She is a faithful, devoted wife who appreciates my rigorous attitude to life: I am a hard-working professional who never rests on his achievements, a husband who devotes all of himself to his wife, a modest and amiable man who lives a simple life. She encourages me to incorporate this in my literary works, contrasting herself with those who criticize me for my outdated way of life and literary concepts. Indignant at such criticism, I once even wrote a lengthy letter to defend myself. Seeing what I had written, she gave a winsome smile, and with a pen in her clever hand that had borne long years of hardship, she crossed out the unneeded words for me, finally keeping almost nothing except "Thanks!"

Open-minded, patient, modest, generous and forgiving—that is her all over. She will not fight over trifles, right or wrong. The guiding principles she follows in dealing with herself and others often enlighten me. Whenever I think of this, heartfelt thanks emerge from the bottom of my heart. I keep fondling her hands, as we smile at each other.

The only disappointment I feel is that her hands have handled too much extra work. As we originally agreed, we have to bring up our children to be self-reliant and hard-working, and that they should wash their own clothes as they grew up. Yet whenever one of them, like a spoiled child, refuses to do it, she takes over—these hands of hers busily finish it up for them instantly. According to our agreement, our little son is in charge of dishwashing, but once he shows signs of disliking it, that pair of hands immediately gets involved again— picking up the bowls and chopsticks, washing and drying them on his behalf. Yes, those are my wife's hands, a mother's hands. Indeed, every mother loves her children. Every mother is generous and forgiving toward her children. How could she possibly distinguish her work from her children's?

I have been told that my wife is getting old quickly, more quickly than I am, suggesting that she is no longer a perfect match for me. No way! With such a pair of hands, which have brought about a happy life and family for me, she is forever young, forever beautiful!

At this moment, as I am fondling her now old-looking, rough hands, an insuppressible feeling of virgin love is surging all over me. That drive is just like that of a young lover's, or even stronger . . .

I cannot but hold up her hands toward my lips again . . .

"Love your wife, love your wife forever! Do look at your wife's hands should distracting thoughts ever bother you. Hers are a diligent pair that has been working day and night, creating a happy life together with you, through thick and thin!"

I am in boundless love, so I am fondling her hands with boundless joy.

I love work, so I love my wife's hands.

I worship creativity, so I worship my wife's hands.

I praise the true, the good and the beautiful, so I praise my wife's hands.

I have a wish: may my wife's hands, which have contributed greatly to humanity, never be forgotten! For this purpose, I have decided to write a fine piece of prose, and to entitle it "My Wife's Hands"!

Hand-Pulled Noodles

By **Xu** Xing

He loved noodles and was never tired of them, even if he had them for breakfast, lunch and dinner every day. They were not the type of noodles sold in the grain store.

When he was a child, his mother had made noodles for him. For his noodles, she would also prepare some thick sauce mixed with eggs and a plate of tender green onions or cucumbers, or pickled radish, or some other side dish. What a delicious meal he would enjoy then!

His wife found out about his favorite food soon after they were married, and put even more effort than his mother did into his noodles. She not only rolled out noodles, she also hand pulled them. She could hand pull her dough into noodles of whatever size she wanted, thick or thin. Her noodles were even better done than machine-made fine dry noodles. They were kind of chewable and stringy, with good texture, and they even felt better in the stomach.

Unfortunately, his wife died before him. Though he was well past sixty, he was still in great health, with good teeth, and he still loved hand-pulled noodles. Then he married another woman, in her early fifties, who only bought dry noodles for him from the grain store. How tasteless they were!

One Sunday, when his daughter came to visit him, she found him frowning at the noodles in his bowl, refusing to touch them. She took over the bowl and said, "Dad, just wait awhile." With this she put on the apron and went into the kitchen, immediately starting to mix some flour with water to knead the dough. Then she let it stand and soften before hand pulling it into noodles.

About half an hour later she brought him a bowl of hand-pulled noodles. He was surprised. "When did she learn these skills from her mother?" This time, though the noodles tasted delicious in the mouth, he felt bitter at heart. When he thought of his first wife, tears welled up in his eyes.

His second wife had seen everything and felt really bad about herself. After breakfast the next day, a gift box of fine pastry in hand, she went to see a hand-pulled-noodle chef in a restaurant, asking him to teach her the tricks. There she learned to mix flour, knead the dough, control its softening, then hand pull it into noodles. The last step was the hardest. Somewhat clumsy, she was too old and too weak for the job. No matter how hard she tried, she could never be as skilful as the cook. Her noodles would either stick to each other or break. She was sweating all over well before she could pull a kilogram of dough into noodles. Giving up, she bought five hundred grams of such noodles at a higher price from the cook instead.

When the retired old man, who had been working on a book of historical records in his office every day, returned home for his lunch that day, he saw a bowl of hand-pulled noodles placed before his seat at the table.

"Oh, did Xiao Feng (the daughter) come today?"

"No. I did it for you."

"You can pull . . .?"

"Don't look at me with strange eyes!"

The noodles were almost the same as what his first wife had made. The old man enjoyed them to his heart's content. "I never knew you were so good at this. It tastes just like what she made in the past." He was so happy that he was somewhat carried away.

His wife was not too happy to hear his comments, thinking, "This old man never forgets his first wife!" But it was a compliment, after all. What did it matter to compare her to his first wife anyway? So thinking, she became quite happy too.

The next day she made still greater efforts to practice noodle-pulling. First she went to the restaurant for her instructions, then she practiced hard at home. She tried again and again, but just could not pull out the noodles properly. "It looks like it will take some time," she said to herself, "at least ten or fifteen days."

Realizing it was time to cook lunch, with no hand-pulled noodles made, she could not but run to the restaurant to buy some. Only after much tactful flattery did she manage to buy five hundred grams of hand-pulled noodles, charged by the bowl.

"Oh?" She saw the door open when she returned upstairs. The old man was home.

The cat was out of the bag now.

"Oh dear! I didn't know my food had got you into such trouble!" The old man felt quite guilty as he learned of the game.

This time, he only ate half of the noodles she had cooked for him. Deep down in his heart, somehow he found the noodles did not taste right.

"Let's just have *laobing* (flapjacks) instead from now on!" he said.

The old lady's tears quietly wet her pillow for half that night.

It was another Sunday when the daughter came to visit her father. Again she wanted to make hand-pulled noodles for him, but the old woman stopped her quickly and said, "Let me do it!"

The old man and his daughter stared at her with their eyes wide open as she skillfully pulled her dough into noodles.

That night, the old man was very excited. He had two cups of whiskey and was naturally aroused. In bed, he clumsily helped his wife remove her clothes, but he was astounded when he removed her shirt. "God!" Her arms were swollen like leavened *mantou*!* Finally, he learned about all her pain and suffering. His heart quivering, he held her tightly against him as he fondled her arms with tender affection. Loving tears filled his eyes.

"Jesus! Those goddamned hand-pulled noodles!"

---

* *Translator's note: Mantou* is plain steamed bread or buns.

I Don't Know Who I Am

By **Xu** Xijun

"Who are you?" his wife suddenly asked him as he sat at the dining table.

"Who am I? Don't you know who I am?" He glanced at her in bewilderment. "Why are you asking?"

"I am asking you. Now answer me. Who are you?"

Looking at her serious face, he was baffled, not knowing what had happened.

"Who are you?" She continued to press for an answer, looking more serious.

Could something have happened today? he thought. His wife was a teacher of psychology. He had never seen her losing her temper in her life. Whatever happened, she would reason carefully and patiently until her counterpart was fully convinced. Never had he found her so serious. Could she have heard of that little gossip about Yan and me? No. That's absolutely impossible.

"Now answer me. Who are you?" His wife looked inwardly angry now.

Terrible, he thought. It's terrible. Perhaps she knows about the 1,000 yuan the Training College of China Bank paid me for the two lectures I gave to its students. I didn't hand in the extra income to her, but have sent it to my old father today. Does it mean she knows it? But how could I explain it clearly!

She kept pressing him for an answer.

He remained silent.

"Who are you?!" she seemed to roar in anger now.

Knowing he could not get away with his silence, he said, in a soft voice, "Let me think."

"You even have to think about who you are. Looks like you are anything but a decent man!"

Terrible, he thought, absolutely terrible. She must have learned about everything.

Trembling with fear, he said, "I'm not ready yet. Give me some more time to think about it."

"I am just asking who you are. Why don't you answer me now?"

"I really don't know how to answer your question," he said in a begging tone. "I really don't know who I am."

"Tell me then, who am I?" she said, switching to an upbeat tone.

He raised his head and stared at her with wide eyes. He was even more confused. Her face simply looked like a labyrinth which he dared not enter, or, rather, which he feared he would not be able to get out of once he got in.

"Come on! Who am I?" She looked even more amiable.

He became even more uncertain of himself. She, too, was staring at him with eyes wide. Their eyes met, but he immediately retreated. Many people appeared in his mind instantly, yet he just was not sure who she was.

"Answer me now. Who am I?" She pressed him again.

He was getting more and more confused.

Every time she repeated the question, his heart shivered.

His uncompromising wife insisted that he answer the question, and so he did.

"I'm sorry," he said, shivering in fear. "I really don't know who you are."

Their child who was eating beside him laughed, "Dad, you are my father, and she is my mother. Did you forget? Why couldn't you answer?"

"What game are you two playing today?" said his mother-in-law who had finished eating and was cleaning up.

"Mom, I've done it!" his wife laughed as she picked up the thread of conversation. "I have been doing a psychology test to prove the thesis of my paper. I've done it, and can hand it in now."

A Sudden Choice

By **Liu** Gong

We still had to wait half an hour before boarding the plane. I would not have been able to sit still if it were another day, but today I had no intention of moving around.

The woman sitting in front of me was a real beauty. When you walked into the waiting room, especially when you are a man like me, you would find your feet filled with lead, simply too heavy to drag forward. Your foolish eyes would fly to her as if attracted by magnets.

When your gaze became prolonged, of course, she would be annoyed. From her eyes, I knew she was feeling annoyed and was ready to protest. Before long, I fixed my eyes on her again, though subconsciously. I could see that she could not suppress her anger anymore, so suddenly she got up from her seat and left.

Soon a polite police officer came and asked me to go to the security office. "Do you know her, sir?" he pointed at her with his mouth. I saw her sitting, lying against a sofa, looking at me disdainfully out of the corner of her eye.

"No," I said.

"This is Li Lili. She was the gold medalist of the National Fashion Models' Competition held in Dalian last year. She is flying to Paris to participate in the Venus International Invitational Models' Competition. She has complained that you have been blinking at her in a flirty way. Is it that true?"

God damn her! What a fuss she was making! I would not have been offended if they did not mention my eyes. Now I was really furious that they did. Who would not want a pair of bright and healthy eyes?

It was deep winter when I first arrived in the northwest, a season when the winds were whistling day and night, blowing up the fine sand everywhere. My eyes unfortunately got infected. My swollen eyes looked like peaches then. It took more than a month to bring my unendurable pain under control, but after that I got the blinking habit. God damn her! I really wanted to scold her, but remembering who I was, I managed to control myself.

"Officer, please allow me to explain myself," I said. "I have been serving in the army in the Gobi Desert for nearly ten years, and have been suffering from the sandy winds. My eyes have been infected and that is why I have this blinking problem. You can call my unit to verify this." I showed him my identification card.

The police officer looked at my ID card and called my army unit to verify my eye trouble. After that he apologized politely. "Sorry. It is just a misunderstanding." He rose to see me out of the security office. Before stepping out, I uncontrollably cast a sidelong glance at her. She looked down quickly. Outside the office, I heard a faint but clear voice drifting from behind— "I'm sorry." Her apology lifted my bad mood a little.

As odd as it could be, after boarding the Boeing, I found my "foe" sitting right next to me, on the right. Though the elegant fragrance of her perfume lifted my heart all the time, my somewhat excited mind just could not burst into wild joy. My embarrassment lingered in my mind.

Less than twenty minutes after the departure, we suddenly felt the plane rocking. It appeared to be an ill omen. The passengers looked at one another.

"Ladies and gentlemen, please fasten your seat belts," said a comforting flight attendant. "There is a little mechanical problem with the airplane, and our technician is doing his best to fix it. Please remain calm and do not leave your seat."

Every passenger, as at the moment of life or death, was panic stricken. Some were screaming, and others burst out crying. Instantly the airliner was in an uproar. The attendant shouted at the top of her voice, "Please remain calm. Please remain calm." But it did not help at all.

I could not stand it, so I stood up and shouted, "Fellow passengers, your emotion directly affects the pilot who is flying the airplane, and also the technician who is fixing the problem. As a result, it will threaten our own safety. So will you please calm down!"

Finally, the passengers calmed down. According to the attendant's instructions, to prepare for the worst, every passenger was asked to write a will and draw out his or her valuables, which I collected and kept in a traveling bag on her behalf. When I walked up to Miss Li, she just kept sobbing. "Where's your will?" I asked her.

"I have no will. I have let down my coach," she said as she held back her tears. "I can't complete my mission. I can't participate in the Paris competition."

"Hurry up, sir!" The attendant urged me from behind.

I put all the small valuables and wills in place quickly. Meanwhile, parachute in hand (the only one allowed on the airplane at that time), the attendant walked up to me and ordered, "Put on the parachute. Quick!"

Habitually, I put it on my shoulders and fastened the belt around my waist. The attendant then handed to me the traveling bag that contained all the passengers' love for their cherished ones. "Get ready to jump!" she continued. The atmosphere in the passenger cabin was frozen. All the passengers fixed their eyes on me at the same time as if I was their hope.

But I said to myself, "No, I can't be a runaway. No, never! The airliner needs me, and the passengers need me more. I shall suffer with the other passengers. I shall live and die with them."

My eyes sweeping across the passengers, I caught sight of the well-known model Li Lili and suddenly felt strong compassion and respect for her. I opened my mouth and spoke to myself haltingly. "No. She mustn't die. She must never die. I can die one hundred times, but not her!" I nearly spoke aloud. "She is the pride of the fair sex. She is going to Paris to show to the world the beauty of Miss China."

The plane was still rocking and descending. The situation was deteriorating, leaving me no time to think. I took off the parachute and, without her permission, tied it to her back as if by force. I repeated the key points she needed to know about how to open it up and how to land. She kept nodding, seeming to understand me.

Supported by the flight attendant, she started to walk slowly toward the cabin door. Then all of a sudden, she turned round and came back to me. Trembling, she presented to me a photograph of her beautiful self, held between the thumb and the forefinger of both hands.

"For you," she said tearfully.

I received her picture respectfully and said, "Go now. Quick!" Her cheeks covered with tears, she looked back at me with each step.

Silently, I wished her a smooth landing and success at the competition.

Suddenly, all the women passengers burst out sobbing, creating a painful scene.

About ten minutes later, the technician showed up, waved his hands, a little oil stained, at us and shouted in mad excitement, "Stop crying! The problem has been fixed!"

This sudden, life-saving news instantly turned tears into laughter, applause, and hurrahs, which, mixed with the noise of the engines, resounded in the sky. At this moment, the eager airplane also climbed up to its normal height.

Time zipped by, and suddenly I found my two-month wedding leave almost over. When I returned to the barracks, I received a stack of letters from the messenger. Most of the letters seemed to have come from one single pen. Carelessly, I opened one of them and found the following words, ". . . Could I call you 'Darling'? You are the most lovable man in the world. I want to give you everything I have, without the slightest reservation! I yearn to hear from you." It was signed, "Li Lili."

My heart throbbed as I read these emotional love letters. I quickly opened the other letters. They were more or less the same. Facing these letters soaked in sincere feelings, I tossed and turned in bed all night, unable to fall asleep. Should I write her back? If so, what should I write?

Be a Young Man Again

By **Ling** Dingnian

Tao Yeming was not surprised when his wife passed away. She had had lung cancer that had not been diagnosed until its advanced stage. Tao was so heartbroken that he could not cry anymore.

He sat there stupefied, speechless. The calm manners he once used in dealing with difficulties and his airs of a supervisor were nowhere to be found. He was now wan and sallow, looking as if he had changed into a different man.

Fortunately, he had the assistant director of the Mining Company's office to take care of the funeral arrangements. Huang Xinghong did such a perfect job that even the smallest detail was attended to. What a hard but good job she had done!

Huang was a competent woman, Tao thought. He did not thank her, but from the bottom of his heart he was grateful to her, though she had done everything in the name of the company.

After his wife's death, Tao's life became peacefully quiet, so quiet that he felt somewhat lonely. When his wife was in the hospital, he had to visit her, look for certain medicine through his connections and cook special food for her, besides receiving all types of people at home or in the ward who claimed to have come to visit her. At least, this was all over.

Sometimes he did not feel good about the peace and quiet at home. Recently he had even had a mysterious premonition, but what was it? He did not know.

It was not until months later that Tao heard, through twists in turns, the shocking rumor that, forgetting about his age, he was

163

scheming to marry Huang. Of course, there were others who said that Huang was trying to seduce him.

Huang was a spinster in her late thirties. "Huang hasn't been married. There, they've finally let the cat out of the bag. Perhaps they had started an affair long before this," one gossip said. It was unknown who had started the gossip, but the wider it spread, the worse it became.

Throwing himself on the sofa, Tao simply could not believe his ears. How could there be such rumors! He and Huang only had business contact and had never crossed the line, though he always thought well of her. Besides, he was already fifty-five, fifteen something years her senior. A relationship with her was out of the question.

Huang had really been wronged. She was a woman, after all. He was not sure if she had heard the sizzling rumors. He felt very bad, thinking it was unfair to her in every respect.

"Refute the rumor?" he said to himself. "No, that would be silly. People may take it as 'a clumsy denial that results in self-confession.'"

"Transfer Huang to another place so as to cut off contact with her? No. That's even worse." He suddenly felt ashamed of himself, and guilty of even thinking of this. "Huang has been doing a perfect job, why transfer her?"

There, Huang had just come to see Tao. She stood silently in front of his desk, her eyes revealing some kind of sadness.

Tao knew that since she had come, she must have something important to tell him. He wanted to ask her what it was but dared not. He just stared at her in silence. The assistant office director before his eyes was no longer a girl in her golden years, but her full breasts, her maturity, her temperament, her manner seemed all the more appealing to him than those of a young girl.

Finally, Huang drew out a document, solemnly placed it in front of him: it was a request for a job transfer.

164

The reason for the request could not be simpler. "I can't stay here any longer."

Why? She did not explain. Was it necessary?

"I know you've been wronged. I will do my best to help you . . . if you really want to leave. Anyway, perhaps your decision is right. Gossip kills!" Tao gave a deep sigh.

Suddenly, Huang burst out crying as if to pour out a whole body of grievances. Tao did not know what to do, clumsily drawing out a handkerchief as he walked up to her in an attempt to stop her crying. At this moment, he heard someone opening his door. When he turned about, the unknown person was long gone.

This had thus become something for Tao to worry about.

Not unexpectedly, another wave of gossiping swept across the office. This time it was more specific and descriptive, saying Tao was harassing Huang in his office. Huang cried until her eyes were swollen.

Then came the director of the independent Commission for Inspecting Discipline, who interviewed Huang privately to find out what had happened.

Huang was shocked, then furious. The anger that had been suppressed within her uncontrollably burst out at him. "Director Tao has lost his wife, but does it mean he cannot date again and marry again? Does it mean I don't have the freedom to date and marry? What's inappropriate, even if we really do date and get married?"

"Oh, that's great. That's great! We are waiting for your 'happiness sweets.'* Please don't be offended. What you have told me clarifies everything, doesn't it?" The director changed his tone.

Workers in the first few offices that heard the news immediately started pooling money for a gift for the Mining Company director's

---

* *Translator's note:* "Happiness sweets" refers to sweets or candies that are offered to friends or visitors who come to somebody's wedding ceremony or party.

wedding.

"What's going on?" Tao was so impatient that he just wanted to break things.

Tao knew that he could not resist the temptation of the charming woman. Since the public had started to tie him with the image of Huang, Huang's image had got into his heart and life.

Tao heard knocking on his door. When he opened it, he was shocked at Huang's presence. He invited her in but dared not close the door.

They sat face to face, staring at each other. Finally, the red-faced Huang broke the silence. "I have been thinking about it for a long time. Let's get married."

Tao felt a current of youthful blood surging inside his blood vessels, but he calmed down quickly. "I'm old now, but you are still young—"

"Be a young man again!"

"Be a young man again!" What a temptation it was!

Tao decided to "be a young man again!"

Instantly, he felt he had endless energy, as if his youth had returned to him.

A Soldier's Wife

By **Liu** Wanli

Xia, whom I called Sister Xia as a respectful title, became a village schoolteacher, while my brother joined the army and went to Tibet. Now thousands of miles apart, they could exchange their feelings only through letters.

Sister Xia's face would beam with happiness whenever she received a letter from my brother. Her happy beams aroused my curiosity. "Let me read your letter, Sister Xia," I said.

"Little boy, it's grown-ups' stuff. You know nothing about this," she said, flushing.

"I have a girlfriend, too," I told her. "At least I can be counted as a grown-up."

She chuckled. She looked really charming when she chuckled.

Sister's Xia's elementary school was close to my home. When she finished work every day, she went directly to my home, did the laundry for us and helped with our farm work. At that time, my father was paralyzed and my mother was in poor health. It was Sister Xia who helped my family carry through until today.

Sister Xia and my brother had agreed that they would write to each other once a month, but there was this period of three months when she received nothing from him. During that period she looked really fragile. Every time she met me she would ask, "Has your brother written to you?"

I would say no and she would look disappointed.

Sister Xia would go and wait for the postman at the village entrance. When he appeared, she would go up to him, all smiles, and ask, "Is there any mail for me?" He would say no.

She kept asking him in the same way, and that kind of embarrassed him. So when she asked him again on a later day, he said, "You don't have to wait here. If there is any letter for you, I will send it to you right away."

That day Sister Xia was teaching Wang Wei's "In Memory of My Brother in Shandong on September 9;" tears rolled down her cheeks quietly when she was reading "I'm a lonely stranger in a strange place; / I miss my loved ones more on holidays." At this very moment, she saw the postman waving a letter at her outside the window.

Sister Xia's heart pounded as she received the letter. As soon as class was over, she rushed back to her dormitory and locked herself in. When she came out, she looked like a peach blossom, and her students said she was very beautiful.

When she finished work that day, she hurried over to my home to announce breaking news: my brother was coming home for the Chinese New Year. My whole family was soaked in joy. Taking out a pen, Sister Xia drew a circle on the calendar, which I knew was the day my brother was coming home.

New Year was approaching, and Sister Xia was happily busying herself with the holiday shopping, washing the quilt covers and clothes, and so on. New Year was arriving, but my long expected brother was not home yet. On New Year's Eve, it started snowing. Sister Xia stood at the village entrance waiting for my brother until midnight, when she finally turned into a snow-woman.

"Sister Xia," I said, "let's go back. My brother must have received some special task that keeps him from coming."

"I'll wait a little while longer," she said. In the quiet of the night, I could hear the sounds of her tears falling onto the snow.

In the end my brother did not come home. His letter arrived later, explaining that he had received an unexpected assignment. By the time he finished it, it was already New Year's Eve. He still wanted to come home so eagerly that he decided to set out on New Year's Day, but a heavy snowfall buried all the mountain paths, so he just could not get down the mountains.

My brother said he was coming home for the Chinese New Year every single year, but he never did. Five years passed without our knowing it. Then he became a volunteer instead, but still he never came home. He still had to communicate with Sister Xia through letters.

Later, I was admitted into a military academy after an examination, so I had to say goodbye to Sister Xia.

When I returned home for my first winter vacation, Sister Xia told me, "I'm going to the army. Your brother and I are going to get married. Your brother has picked the date. Are you willing to take me there?" I had long wanted to go to the army for a visit, so I said yes without hesitation.

"We'll set out tomorrow so that we can get there before the snow seals the mountain passes," she said.

Our family members gave us a warm send-off the next day. We first took a train, then changed to a coach, until we got to Mount Tangula. Snow was blackening the sky when we arrived at the foot of the mountains. We were warmly received by the chief, who said my brother was on a mission up on the mountains. Immediately he got a jeep to take us up there, but instantly, the roads all disappeared in the heavy snowfall.

"It's getting dark," said Sister Xia. "It's dangerous to drive ten miles on the mountain roads in such weather."

"But it's your wedding day today," said the senior officer. "How could we let you stay apart?"

"I have been waiting for eight years," said Sister Xia. "Why would I mind another day?"

The best room in the barracks was turned into Sister Xia's wedding chamber. All the soldiers swarmed in to tease the bride and the bridegroom, who was still on the mountains. The senior officer

169

arranged a phone connection for the young couple, with Sister Xia holding a receiver on one end, my brother on the other.

The chief shouted to the receiver at the top of his voice, "The wedding ceremony now begins! First, the bride and the bridegroom kowtow to heaven and earth!"

Sister Xia kowtowed to heaven, then to earth.

"Second, the bride and the bridegroom kowtow to their parents!"

Sister Xia kowtowed to the senior officer, for her new home was the barracks.

"Third, the bride and bridegroom kowtow to each other!"

Sister Xia kowtowed to the top of Mount Tangula.

The senior officer then pushed the button on the cellphone and asked my brother, "What's the first thing you wish to tell the bride right now?"

"I want to thank her for understanding me," said my brother.

"Something more exhilarating than this!" demanded the senior officer.

"I'll love my bride forever!" said my brother.

"Louder!" said the soldiers. "We can't hear you."

My brother repeated his words. Then I saw fat tears rolling down Sister Xia's cheeks. The senior officer handed the receiver to Sister Xia and said, "Take your time and enjoy your whispering." He swayed his hand and the soldiers soon disappeared.

It was Sister Xia's sleepless night. She did not doze off until daybreak, but just then she heard snow shoveling outside. She got up and opened the window only to see the soldiers shoveling the waist-deep snow off the road. Sister Xia was deeply touched. She felt she was the happiest person in the world. Picking up a shovel, she joined the soldiers. She kept shoveling single-mindedly until blisters appeared on her hands. Her blisters broke, and like flowers, the red blood dropped all over the white snow.

At the other end of the road, with a hung head, my brother was also shoveling the snow. He had been doing it throughout the night and he did not raise his head even when the two teams almost met. At this time, Sister Xia could already see my brother. They were only some thirty meters apart. Sister Xia wanted to call out, but tears streamed down her cheeks instead. Now my brother looked up and caught sight of Sister Xia, too. He saw the red scarf on her head flapping like a flag. It was the silk scarf he had bought for her in high school with the money he had saved penny by penny.

My brother rushed through the snow over to Sister Xia, as she dashed toward him. They flew into each other's arms in the waist-deep snow . . .

An Excuse for Love

By **He** Baiyuan

Huada Developmental Corporation was a newly established business.

To save time by improving efficiency, Mr. Ou, the general manager, decided to buy six motorcycles so that his officials who had to go out on business could each ride one. Accordingly, the six men and four women from the different departments and offices who could not ride a motorcycle were required to learn the necessary skills in their spare time and to obtain their license within two months.

One month later, the ten young people all had good news for him: they had all passed the written test.

After another ten days or so, one after another, the four female officials came back with more good news; they had passed the road test and would soon obtain their license. Yet none of the six young men had made it. In other words, they had all failed their first road test.

Shaking his head with a wry smile, Mr. Ou said to himself, "The ancient saying goes, 'Women aren't inferior to men.' Now it looks like it isn't just a matter of not being inferior—they are superior to men!"

After two weeks of hard practice, the young men went for their second road test. To pass the road test, you had to drive not only on flat and straight roads, but also on figure-eight- and snake-shaped roads. The most difficult part was the bag-shaped road after the uphill driving, where many people were thrown clear off their seats.

As it was reported to the company, all the six young men failed the second road test.

172

Mr. Ou was shocked, wondering why, while the roads, however they were shaped, were equally difficult for everybody, the women all passed the first test but the men had failed repeatedly.

Before the third test started, Mr. Ou secretly went to the test field, where he hid himself, hoping to find out the answer.

Nothing looked out of the ordinary. He saw the six young men doing the test one by one. Those who were waiting went on with their last-minute practice.

What puzzled him was that nearly every one of them went down with his vehicle as soon as he entered the bag-shaped road after climbing up the slope. Thus, they all failed the road test for the third time.

Mr. Ou thought, "Since the key difficulty is the slope and the bag-shaped road, why not just practice that particular part afterward?"

He turned round and was about to leave when he found something rather strange: despite their fresh failure, instead of looking dejected, the young men were all very happy. Then he discovered a girl coaching them. He walked up to find out what was happening.

Naturally, he never knew what she looked like, but the moment he saw her, his eyes brightened up. Indeed, she was very beautiful. She was a tall girl who had an oval face with two lively eyes that seemed to speak when they blinked. She had a perfect figure with beautifully permed shiny black hair tied at the back. Under her straight nose was a little smiling mouth. Soon he learned that she was one of the examiners, called Miss Jin.

Miss Jin attracted the six young men like a magnet. Listening to her instructions as she demonstrated driving skills, the men all looked eagerly attentive but appeared to be in fear and trepidation. Obviously, the young men and Miss Jin seemed to know each other quite well.

A ray flashed across Mr. Ou's mind. He was aware that the six young men were not really that stupid. Neither were their driving skills substandard. It was all for more opportunities to meet Miss Jin that they had failed the road test repeatedly.

Mr. Ou called the six young men to his office the next day. Looking nice and kind, he told them the following story.

While he was in university, a beautiful girl would teach him and a couple of other male students how to dance at the weekend dance. He loved this girl very much at that time, so, in order to receive more help from her, he always pretended to forget what he had learned. Before Mr. Ou finished his story, he suddenly changed his topic, saying, "That girl never fell in love with the moron in the ballroom. Likewise, perhaps a beautiful woman would not love a fool who cannot even pass the motorcycle road test, would she?"

His final words that highlighted the point shocked and impressed the young men. Their mouths open in surprise, they thought that the general manager really had a unique talent for reading people's minds.

Five of the six young men eventually passed the fourth road test. Only Xiao Dong suffered another failure. Learning about the results, Mr. Ou smiled, "It's not hard to understand. As the common saying goes, 'It's human to err.' Xiao Dong outdoes others in practically everything. In some aspects he may be a little slow. This may have something to do with his disliking activities. Never mind. Just keep learning."

On a holiday several months later, Mr. Ou was shocked when he saw Xiao Dong riding a brand new Honda motorcycle at full speed to the beach swimming pool. Sitting behind him was that charming Miss Jin.

"When did you pass the road test?" Mr. Ou asked Xiao Dong afterward.

"Just recently," said Xiao Dong.

"You picked up everything easily," said Mr. Ou. "Why did you fail the road test again and again?"

"Didn't you see through it right in the beginning? If I passed the first test, how could I have had the other opportunities to go to the other road tests?"

Looking at the naughty young man, Mr. Ou started laughing until out of breath. "At that time," he finally added, "a female student didn't love a moron in the ballroom, but today a beautiful woman has fallen in love with a fool who just could not learn to ride a motorcycle. It looks like my story is out of date."

Going to Town

By **Zhang** Ke

Last summer, the producer of the TV station learned that a 120-year-old woman in the South Mountain Village was still healthy and active. He therefore asked me to go there for an interview with her. Unexpectedly, when I inquired about her at the village, I was told that she had passed away a month ago. I left empty handed, taking a small bus back home.

The bus I boarded zigzagged along the mountain road, stopping frequently to allow group after group of passengers to get on and off. At one small stop, it picked up a teenage girl. Her eyes swept across the seats and found one in the first row by the window still unoccupied, except by a parcel wrapped in cotton print. Next to it sat an old man with a wrinkled face, whose age was difficult to judge. The girl went up to him and said politely, "Sir, is the parcel yours? Could you please move it away?"

"Someone's sitting here."

"What? But it's a parcel!"

"My—" He stopped as soon as he opened his mouth.

Seeing this, the conductor, a motherly-looking woman, also spoke out. "Sir, could you please move away the parcel so that the young lady can sit?"

"No, no!" said the old man as he threw himself over the parcel. "Girl, be kind to us. How about me buying another ticket for the seat, then?" He stared at the girl anxiously, clutching the parcel with care.

The girl was about to say something when the old man suddenly got up and said, "Or, you can have my seat."

"Well—" Instead of insisting, the girl walked away and stood by herself.

Now the passengers started making remarks.

"What right does the old man have to occupy two seats while she is standing?"

"He must have small valuables in that parcel!"

"He must be an idiot!"

The old man hung his head in silence as the uproar continued. Gradually, the bumpy mountain road rocked the passengers to sleep. Only the old man was fully alert, guarding his parcel all the time.

"Isn't it awful! It's our first trip to town, and you had to hear all that. I'm really embarrassed, but—" the old man said to himself.

The bus was driving at full speed; the scenery came flashing by.

"We are at the Green Hill Cliffs now," shouted the excited old man as he patted the parcel. "We'll soon be out of the mountains."

The slopes along the road were covered with persimmon trees loaded with red fruit that signified a year of bumper harvest.

"Look! Aren't those persimmons like the red lanterns we hang up for the New Year?" The old man talked on and on.

"Wake up now, everybody!" called out the conductor. "We'll be in town soon. Anybody want to get off in the suburbs?"

"Wake up, my girl's mother! We'll be in town any moment!" The old man could not refrain from his excitement. He raised his head and looked out. "My big niece, is it the town?" he asked the conductor. "How come there are no tall buildings?"

"We are still in the suburbs. Where do you want to get off, sir?"

"Anywhere with tall buildings."

"Is it your first trip?" smiled the conductor.

The bus had reached downtown, where the old man was getting off. His hands trembled as he opened the parcel, showing a picture of a smiling granny inside a black picture frame.

"Come on, my girl's mother! See that tall building!" said the old

177

man as he got off the bus, holding the picture against his heart.

He walked away, leaving silence behind him. In the silence was a crowd with me staring at him. If any human classic is ever heard of, it has to be the old man's guarding of his love.

Sea Burial

By **Yin** Quansheng

The sky was blue and the sea was blue. At the end of the blue sea and the blue sky were heaps of gleaming white clouds, under which there was a still, bluish-grey sail.

The boat had reached the area where they were supposed to cast the net, but the five people on board remained as still as the sea. The three fierce-looking old fishermen were smoking silently inside the cabin, while Ah Gen and Dove sat on the deck, exchanging their perplexity and worry through their eyes.

They had not come for fishing. It was a plot!

Dove's grandfather was the chief plotter. At the age of fifty, he had picked up Dove, a deserted infant. Picking up Dove meant picking up untold hardships, though it also meant ending the widower's loneliness. It was with his salty sweat and blood that he had brought up his darling. In order for her to have one tear less and one smile more and to buy another dress for her, he fished even in storms, once nearly struck to death by a bolt of lightning. Also, his ribs were once struck and broken by the tail fin of a black shark.

Dove was nineteen years old now, and like a mermaid. Her grandfather's old life had been soaked in smiles, but gradually he found that Dove no longer acted like the spoiled child who used to stick to him like a kitten. Instead, she started an intimate relationship with Ah Gen. This unwanted change worried the old man as it confused him. Never had he thought that Dove would fly away from him one day. If Dove really did fly away, how could he live by himself? Besides, in his eyes Ah Gen was no match for Dove, not in the slightest way. Also, Ah Gen's family name was Wei! For this he had warned Dove and tried to persuade her and even begged her to leave him, but all in vain.

"Grandpa, don't you worry about me," Dove would flush and say.

"This goddamned Ah Gen has really dug away my Dove's heart!" he said to himself. Then he asked his two younger brothers to come and help him work out countermeasures. Inside the old cottage in the fishing village, they drew the curtains over the windows, lit the candle, then poured whiskey into large bowls and drank until their eyes were blood red.

"That son of a bitch is breaking my heart!" Dove's grandfather said, wiping the two streams of thick tears from his cheeks.

"Our family name is Yu. How could we tolerate their relationship! Why not feed him to the fish?" The second brother's eyes were burning in a panic.

"Break them up!" The third brother struck his fist on the table.

The three brothers, whiskey bowls in hand, worked out an evil plot: "Ask Ah Gen to help us with our fishing. When we get to the deep sea, force him to break up with Dove. If he refuses, dump him into the sea for the fish! If we are ever caught, and have to go to jail or be hanged"—they smashed their bowls at the same time as they howled in one low voice— "it's worth it!"

They also decided to bring along Dove. Women were not supposed to go to sea, but they were not really going fishing anyway, so they should let her . . .

The sea was quiet; the sky was peaceful; the clouds and the sail were still.

Dove's grandfather blew out a mouthful of thick smoke from his lungs as if it had come from a stove where a fire was being made. "Come down here, Ah Gen."

The panic-stricken young man walked into the cabin, staring at Dove's grandfather's feet. Dove quietly followed Ah Gen, staring at his heels.

A strong wind suddenly started blowing on the sea, rocking the boat momentarily. Dove's grandfather started: "Boy, you are not allowed to seduce my Dove from now on!"

"But we—" Ah Gen blushed.

"—get along well." Dove completed his sentence, rubbing the toes of one foot against the other's.

"Your family names subdue each other!"

"We don't believe in fate!" they said simultaneously.

Waves were surging turbulently while dark clouds were gathering rapidly. The sea and the sky were now engulfed in black flames. The boat was burned by the sea, so it jumped up into the sky, but when it got burned by the clouds and became scared, it retreated to the waves. Securing his body, Dove's grandfather shouted at Ah Gen, "Boy, as long as I am alive, you will never have it your way!"

"I'll never change my mind," they said in one voice again.

"Whether you change your mind or not, you will just have to break up!" Dove's granduncles slapped their own thighs.

The boat took a sudden plunge as if it were trying to somersault. Ah Gen caught the falling Dove just in time. The old fishermen could not stand it anymore.

They sprang up and shouted in one voice, "Feed him to the fish!"

"Me too!" Dove covered Ah Gen with her own body.

The torrential rain was spreading closer to them; deafening thunderclaps were crashing toward them. Over the roaring sea the spinning sky was crumbling down upon them. Giving in to the threat and assaults, the sail betrayed the fishermen by working together with the windstorm. It bent like a bow, sending the stern into the waves and pulling the prow skyward. Soon it bent the other way. The raging waves, which wore a villainous smile, crashed into the cabin.

Stopping their almost-finished threats, the old fishermen shot out of the cabin, grabbed their axes and cut down the mast with all their might. Yet the many holes in the wooden boat caused by the pounding, bumping and crushing were unstoppable. In a desperate attempt, Ah Gen managed to seize hold of the last two lifebuoys hanging on the gunwale. He thrust one at Dove and handed over the other to her grandfather.

Dove's grandfather sniffed at him in contempt, snatched the lifebuoy, then gave it to his two brothers, but his brothers pushed it back to him as they shouted amid the roar of the stormy waves, "Brother, take Dove away with you. Go—"

The grandfather, bug-eyed, swept his gaze across the four people and finally fixed his eyes on Ah Gen, his veins bulging out on his forehead. The clouds were coming down; the waves were surging high; the boat was sinking. Blood was boiling . . . Suddenly the lifebuoy was put around Ah Gen's neck. Dove's grandfather's voice drowned the roar of waves and thunderclaps: "You son of a bitch, take good care of my Dove—"

His two brothers were astonished, but only for a split second. Then the three pairs of old hands together wiped the tears from the two young faces. The same old hands together pushed the two young people who had knelt before the elders off the boat with a last shout: "Go home, Dove! You two—"

The six light beams that gleamed with hope pushed the two lifebuoys toward the invisible shore of life. Then, eyes closed, they fell into the cabin with the turbulent waves and locked the cabin door. They sat down in the waist-deep water, opened the whiskey bottle—what excellent, strong aged whiskey it was! With a few cups down, their lofty sentiments overcame melancholy: "We are all men with many children and grandchildren anyway!"

"My Dove will live a happy life now!"

Bold smiles, old smiles, contented smiles! No storms could hide them. No thunderclaps could drown them. No waves could bury them!

Though only the blue sea and the blue sky remained after the windstorm.

Oh sea . . .

Call Me "Ai"

By **Liu** Liqin

When Hao Wen climbed to the mountain pass, a breath of air from the slope swept against him. He felt something abnormal, as if the tip of Shanniu's hair had carelessly touched his face. He looked back, and there she was, walking toward him. The wind that blew in his face now smelt of her fragrance. He felt faint pain in his heart as if it had been gnawed at by ants.

Hao Wen was an elementary school teacher who came from the city. He had studied in a teachers' college, and upon graduation the government had assigned him a teaching job at the local school. Time flew; suddenly he had taught here for several years. His former resentment and other hard feelings had all disappeared with the powder of the chalk he had used. What remained in his memory was the honest smiling faces of the children and the calls from their tender voices. Those smiling faces and tender voices had turned into a net that kept him inside. When he was struggling to get out of it, Shanniu entered his life. Shanniu had recently finished high school in the city and had just returned to the mountain village. Her quiet, faint smiles and her sweet calling of *laoshi** had further tied up his hands and feet, so he could not but plunge into her eyes, which were filled with words that could drown him.

Soaked in her eyes, Hao Wen found himself indulging in such pleasure that he just would not want to get out. At such a moment,

---

* *Translator's note: Laoshi* is a respectful title students use when calling teachers.

183

Shanniu would uncontrollably smile and call him *laoshi*. Her voice was very sweet and her smiling face charming, but Hao Wen found her calling of *laoshi* outrageous. In his daily life, he loved to be called *laoshi,* which suggested a close relationship with his students and which made him happy, but when he was with Shanniu alone, he hated being called *laoshi*. But what should she call him? He did not know, so all he could do was be upset himself about nothing when she was not around.

After many joyful moments and lots of unenjoyable ones, Hao Wen finally hit upon an idea: invite her to see the Qingyun Temple. There were no Taoist priests up there, and the statues of Buddhas and gods had all disappeared. With no more joss sticks or candles burning in the temple, Qingyun Temple was the most remote and the quietest place they could go to. There he would not bump into his students or their parents. "Nobody will call me *laoshi* there," he said to himself, "so Shanniu ought to call me something else."

However, on their way to the Qingyun Temple, Shanniu never stopped calling him *laoshi*. His happy moments were killed by her calls, one after another. Finally he was so upset that he left her and *laoshi* far behind him, climbing straight up to the temple all by himself.

As they stood on the green slab stone in front of the temple, he saw her face covered with tiny drops of sweat and heard her breathing heavily. He felt so sorry for her that he almost called out "Shanniu," but when he thought of that damned *laoshi,* he held his tongue in fear that she would return and use the word *laoshi* again. Gradually, Hao Wen's anger disappeared. Then Hao Wen, who was not angry now, really wanted to do something a man ought to do, but he did not. He turned and walked away. He felt he was afraid of her, afraid that she would call him *laoshi*.

But this time she did not. She did not call him for quite a while, but then he felt a little lonely, as if he had missed her. When he turned around, he saw her giggling.

"Why don't you call me *laoshi* now?" Hao Wen could not help asking.

"No. I won't," she said.

"Why not?" he asked.

"My grandfather says you must not call out people's names in the graveyard or in the temple," she said, "for anybody whose name is called will have their soul hooked away by the mountain god or the wild ghosts."

"Oh—" said Hao Wen, in happy surprise. "What would you call me then?"

"What do you think?" she lowered her head.

"Call me 'Ai' for once, all right?"

She blushed at his words. That was what a woman in the mountain village would call her man for the rest of her life! Her face reddening, she raised her head, only to meet the sincere teacher staring at her eagerly. She opened her mouth and said "Ai" very softly. Hao Wen heard it, and returned a much louder "Ai."

The soft voice and the loud voice startled the birds around them and happily stirred up the two young people's hearts. The sun was hiding behind the mountains as it stole glances at them who had drowned themselves in the sounds of "Ai."

Warning

By **Yi** De Er Fu

Retired factory director Jigemude came to his young successor's office. "Aoribu, you've got to watch what you're doing! People are complaining about you," he warned the young man in the most solemn manner.

"Sir, what about? My work—"

"No, no, no. It's not about your work," the ex-director interrupted him. "No one can ever find fault with your work. After you took over my job, our once hopeless factory started to pick up steam. Our near-bankrupt factory that had been losing money for years is making a profit and has now become one of the business leaders in the city. All this is attributed to your courageous reform. Nobody can deny this."

"Since they can't find fault with my work, what are they complaining about then?"

"You have an intimate relationship with the technician Tuoya, am I right? I want to know."

"Yes."

"People said there is something wrong with your relationship."

"Nothing abnormal has ever happened to us, and we are very happy with each other."

"Aoribu, I'm talking to you seriously as your senior and an old Party member, out of responsibility. I'm earnestly trying to help you. For it was me alone who picked you as my successor. I don't want to see you trip and fall; you can't afford to make mistakes. I want you to be honest when you answer my questions."

"Sir, to tell you the truth, Tuoya and I really have a very good

186

relationship. It's perfectly normal and there's absolutely nothing wrong."

"Tell me, what relationship is it?"

"We are friends."

"Isn't there a problem between you two?"

"What do you mean?"

"Isn't it clear? It's a relationship between a man and a woman. Have you started an affair with her?"

"No."

"But people have seen you hugging and kissing each other in the park. Isn't that more than a relationship between two friends?"

"We are deeply in love with each other. Can't we hug and kiss each other?"

"What! You are dating Tuoya?"

"Yes. We share the same ideals and principles: our minds are joined by one thought and our hearts are tied by one soul."

"You know it well. Though Tuoya is as beautiful as a rose and an outstanding worker, she has a problem with her way of life. She had an abortion when I was the head of the factory. She is an indecent woman. How could you be dating someone like her?"

"I disagree that she is an indecent woman. I think she is a good person. As for her pregnancy before marriage, it wasn't her fault. It was . . ."

"It was what? Speak out!"

"There was something to do with you."

"What? She didn't behave herself, and you want me to share her fault?"

"Yes. Because you didn't educate your son properly. Your son Bagen took advantage of your position as factory director: it was he who raped her and ruined her virginity."

"What? Did Bagen really rape her?"

"It is true."

"But how come I didn't know?"

"For the sake of your reputation, Tuoya has been enduring the shame all by herself and has never told anybody the truth."

Jigemude was stupefied, his mouth wide open. "God!" he uttered. Then he sat there speechless.

Slippers

By **Ling** Dingnian

In a city where more than ninety-nine per cent of the households went straight into their living rooms and bedrooms without removing their shoes, Ah Nong was nicknamed "Slippers." His nickname, in fact, came from an unusual experience.

Ah Nong was a popular person, good at making friends, and he had many friends. His wedding chamber was completely fixed up and decorated by his buddies. On his wedding day, group after group of well-wishers swarmed into his home to congratulate him. To put it in the Shanghai dialect, the wedding chamber was so crowded that not one single crab could crawl in.

The day after their wedding, his wife, Xiaojie, purchased six pairs of slippers and placed them at the door, announcing a rule for everybody: "From today on, whoever enters our home must change into slippers."

Ah Nong was baffled, for many of his friends were careless, easygoing people. How could he tell them about her rule? On the other hand, he loved Xiaojie dearly and did not want to disappoint her, or spoil the joyful atmosphere of their honeymoon, so he observed her rule anyway.

Ah Nong's friends were good at behaving themselves; seeing the whole row of slippers at the door, they would take off their shoes and change into slippers before he had a chance to ask them to. However, a few closer friends would sometimes tease him with a few naughty words in an almost serious tone, such as "Ah Nong, bring over the vacuum cleaner so that I can have a better cleaning,"

189

"Ah Nong, are you competing for a three-star award for your home?"
"Ah Nong, my feet smell when I take off my shoes, please give me some French perfume."

Ah Nong could only turn a deaf ear to them, or simply take it as tonic.

On several occasions, on seeing the slippers lying neatly by the door, his visiting friends hastily withdrew their feet before they landed on the other side of the threshold. Instead, they stood outside the door, quickly exchanged a few words with him, and said "Bye-bye."

Ah Nong felt that he had let down his friends. They were on one side, his wife on the other. He did not know with whom to side.

Gradually he began to lose his friends, sincerely feeling he owed them something.

Then one day, when Xiaojie was away from home on a business trip, Ah Nong invited a few friends over for a get-together, as if to make up for something. No sooner had they appeared at the door than he told them, "Forget it. Forget it. You don't need to take off your shoes."

His friends were puzzled, but soon understood him. Taking things easy, everybody had a terrific time, leaving a great mess behind.

After his friends left, he first swept the floor, then mopped it. He also made use of his vacuum cleaner. It took him quite some time to clean the room and restore it to its original state.

"Isn't it wonderful to be clean?" he said to himself.

Unexpectedly, Xiaojie discovered that people had come into her home without taking off their shoes. Ah Nong naturally had to reproach himself and apologize.

After this incident, whenever friends came again, Ah Nong would take the initiative, saying something like "Do me a favor. Change to slippers," "I'm sorry . . .," "Excuse me . . ."

It was unknown who was the first one to call out "Here comes 'Slippers'" when Ah Nong met his friends one day, but that was when his nickname "Slippers" came into use, and it soon became more popular than "Ah Nong."

Ah Nong missed the days when he had had no slippers at home, but he also enjoyed a home with slippers.

He wanted to raise the issue of slippers with his wife several times, but each time she gave him a gentle kiss, dispersing every word on his lips. All right, all right, Xiaojie had not done anything wrong. Whatever she did, she did it for her home, but—what was Ah Nong supposed to say? Several times he simply stood stupefied as he stared at the slippers by the door.

Red Bundle

By **Liu** Fengzhen

Hong Baofu, or Red Bundle, who passed away quietly not long ago, was buried with her real name, Ai Lan, and all the happiness she had once enjoyed and whatever shame she had endured.

Hong Baofu was an open-minded woman who sometimes behaved like a lunatic in others' eyes. She had the guts to provoke a group of men into talking about the secret of what they did with their women in their arms on the *kang* at night after they blew out their lamps. Then she would listen to their coarsest and most primitive chatting, which often sent her into hearty laughter. "Hey, Lüju, you stole an ass last night, didn't you?" she provoked him while working in the fields one day. "There, you droop and stoop!" With this she threw a lump of mud at the foot of the earthen wall against which he was resting.

"If you excite me again, I'll have you in your cave tonight," the sleepy man shot back at her.

"You droop and stoop. You can't even please your own wife, what else can you do to me?"

"Now you! You'll know what kind of man I am when you have me!"

"Dirty Lüju, how dare you!" She charged at him and started tickling his armpits. Both rolled over the slope of the valley, while the men and women working with them all started laughing.

She loved her man more than herself. "It seems as if she has never seen a man in her life!" the villagers would chide her. Her man was a cattle keeper for the production team, and he had to stay with

192

the animals every day until midnight for the last feed. She would go out to find him whenever he was late. With no moon, night was pitch dark, and she had to strike matches to light the road. Worried that he might have been seduced by another woman, whenever she failed to find him in the cattle shed she would run straight to the straw stacks in search of him, striking one match after another—it seemed as if the straw stacks were the best place for extramarital affairs. One night she failed to find him and accidentally started a fire on the wheat straw instead, turning it into a mountain of flames that spewed thick smoke surely higher than the mountains nearby. After this incident she stopped looking for him with matches in the dark. Then she would stand on a knoll not far from home waiting for him every day.

In her eyes, he was the best man on earth no other women could find.

"Fuyuan, my sweetheart, is there anything wrong with me?" she would say as she cuddled up in her husband's arms at night. "I'm never tired of looking at you, and I'm simply beside myself if I don't see you for a day. I always think I love Mom and I love Dad, but I love you more."

"Silly woman." He would drop a kiss on her forehead.

She had given birth to seven sons and two daughters, a great result of their love relationship. She prided herself on this all her life, knowing it was directly attributed to her man's competence and her own efforts. She would, among a crowd of women, animatedly describe the different feelings she had when she bore each and every one of her children, from conception until delivery. Whenever she got excited and found it too difficult to describe, she would demonstrate the acts with both hands and feet, starting a roar of laughter in her audience, who had to hold their sides.

"I was forty when I gave birth to my ninth child. My bones were hard and they nearly took my life. Luckily, Third Granny had a pair of calloused hands that dug out its head then quickly dragged it out! What a breathtaking act!" When she said the word "dragged," she

193

spoke with animation as if her hands were really pulling something out of her vagina.

"Does your mom call your dad 'sweetheart?'" Hong Baofu would sometimes ask other small children after calling them over.

"I don't know," they would say. The anxious children preferred playing to talking, but she would not let them go. She would coax them into saying yes by promising to give them tomatoes to eat. When the children repeated the negative answer, she would murmur to herself, "I know it even if you don't tell me. I'm sure they do, you've never heard it, that's all."

That was the way she was: wanting to know, through the little ones, if other wives also loved their husbands in the same way as she did, and if they also kept calling them sweethearts when they cuddled up in their arms after blowing out their oil lamps at night.

"That wife of Niu Baosheng's often keeps a straight face with her eyes looking upward," she thought. "She pays no attention to anybody, looking so serious as if she were a top-ranking imperial concubine who's just come out of the palace. Doesn't she do it with her man? I would be surprised if she did not! Were those boys and girls of hers born out of the blue? Hypocritical!"

She thought, "Women must be more or less the same, all loving their men and wanting the men they love to love them. Then I've done nothing wrong, but why have people despised me and mocked me? Why wouldn't Dad allow me to live with the man I love? Why wouldn't he marry me to my man in an honorable way with wedding music played? Dad refused to come to see me all his life!" Hong Baofu had been looking for the answers all her life, but had found none.

When her father died, the messenger broke the news only to her sister, also informing her that her eldest brother would not allow Hong Baofu to attend the funeral service, saying that it was their father's will. She was not far from her sister when the message was being delivered, so she overheard everything. She pondered throughout the night and finally decided not to go. Knowing her dad had a temper, she did not want to see him going to the other world with an unhappy feeling because of her presence. The next day she went to a remote valley with joss sticks and paper money; there she cried for the whole day, crying for her dad and her long-dead mom.

That year, she was sixteen years old and was as tender as a haw whose sweet juice would drip with just a gentle squeeze. When she was helping her sister in the month she had given birth to a baby, Hong Baofu unexpectedly fell in love at first sight with her brother-in-law's younger brother Fuyuan, who also fell in love with her. Their relationship developed until she sneaked into Fuyuan's bed in broad daylight when her sister and brother-in-law were working in the fields.

"You shameless brat," Fuyuan's mother scolded her, lifting open her cotton-padded quilt. "Where are your manners!" She then got her out of the bed.

After that, Hong Baofu would come to visit her sister frequently. Once she had come, she stayed, not wanting to return home. Even when her sister got upset and told her to go home, she still did not want to.

The story goes that it was a snowy day when her dad beat her nearly to death. He hit her so hard that the handle of his shovel broke into several pieces. He would hit whomever tried to stop him, so nobody dared to get close. The girl was rolling like a mud-ball in the yard, screaming in excruciating pain . . .

Then there was that day when a crippled girl carrying a red bundle unexpectedly emerged from the slope of the West Valley. The whole village poured out to watch her. From then on she became Fuyuan's woman, thus earning herself the indecent name Hong Baofu, or Red Bundle.

A Buck's Love Story

By **Wu** Wanfu

Qiulin bumped into a girl on the street that day. She was a beautiful girl with a fine temperament, extremely sexy with a slender figure, hilly breasts and slim legs.

Qiulin was uncontrollably attracted to her after that unexpected glance at the elegant curves of her perfect body. Though he had lived for so many years, he had never known that the Creator could have made such a perfect thing on earth. Every move of hers had the power to drag him along.

She crossed the intersection, and so did he.

She walked through the lane, and he was right behind.

She entered a modern luxurious building, and he followed suit.

The girl was aware that he was following her, but she did not want to embarrass him, that was all. Whatever he did came from a mysterious subconscious state of mind.

Before he could locate the girl, who had disappeared from his sight, Qiulin heard a sweet voice floating in the air: "Sir, do you want to deposit any money?"

Raising his head, he realized he was inside a savings office. He looked at the speaker closely and found her to be the girl he had been following; she wore two white butterfly bows on her ponytail. The girl, beaming with joy, cocked her head and smiled at him, radiating enthusiasm and appreciation. At this very moment, Qiulin wished he could sink through the floor. "God, how could she ever know I am a poor wretch!" he thought. "I can't even afford to find a wife! How could I have savings? But if I don't deposit something here, why am

196

I here, anyway?"

After halting his words for quite a while, he finally uttered, "Mmm ..."

Qiulin started groping in his pockets. A thorough search in all his pockets produced one yuan and thirty-five *fen*.

The girl kept on smiling while she waited for Qiulin to get his money ready. She gazed at him in a caring manner that made her look well cultivated, patient and tolerant with a refined personality.

Qiulin's heart throbbed, as he held the ten-fen banknotes in both hands and said, "I have only one yuan and thirty-five *fen*. That's all I have. Could I deposit it?"

"It's fine, sir," she said with a gentle smile. "We'll open an account for you, as long as you have one yuan."

Hesitantly, Qiulin handed over one yuan to her.

Receiving his money, the girl drew out a green bankbook from her drawer, and asked for his name, address and other information, as she buried herself in the paperwork. After carefully writing down his name and account number and everything, she pushed the bankbook toward him in the most business-like manner.

He picked it up, put it in his pocket and left without delay. No sooner had he got out of the savings office than he started running like a runaway.

Qiulin felt really embarrassed about his one-yuan savings. If it had not been for the girl who had struck a chord in his heart, he would never have gone there to deposit it in the first place.

He swore to himself that he would save lots of money. Only when he saved money there could he have a good reason to talk to the beautiful girl.

In the days to come, Qiulin went all out to make money, and he really made a lot. Whenever he had some money, he would take it to the savings office and deposit it with the girl.

A few years later, the former pauper became the richest man in his town. The girl had filled up for him one bankbook after another.

By now their relationship had developed from acquaintances to lovers, till they eventually walked hand in hand into the sacred wedding hall.

The girl was called Xiao Han.

On their wedding night, holding Han in his arms, Qiulin kept groaning, "Han, Han, Han—" as fat happy tears rolled down his cheeks.

Han's face reddened all over, as she buried herself in his chest.

Then Qiulin murmured as if he were talking in his sleep, "Han, do you know? If it wasn't you who received me that day, or if you didn't take that yuan as my initial deposit, I might have felt painfully dejected forever, and I wouldn't have this day."

"Honestly, anyone else would have done the same . . ." she smiled shyly.

They held each other in their arms tightly, as their happy life began.

Love in the Air

A Snooperscope

By **Chung** Ling

The blockhouse was hidden inside the huge crags on the seashore. On the flat plastered roof above its third floor was a woodshed. Inside the shed stood two large telescopes, each sitting on a tripod. One was used in the daytime; it could enlarge objects by fifty times. The other was a snooperscope, used at night.

Ah Hsiung, who had been busy looking through the daytime telescope, suddenly raised his head and shouted, "Two people are kissing!" On hearing this, the ten or so soldiers who were eating on the first floor all dropped their bowls and chopsticks, fighting to get onto the narrow wooden ladder of the blockhouse.

This telescope not only served as a coastal security device, it also provided the best entertainment for these bachelors. The desolate sea and the rocky coast surrounding their blockhouse meant there was little fun for them. Yet, as the story has it, there was a little pavilion under the cliff half a kilometer away. On the other side of the cliff was a park. As the pavilion lay at a dead end, lovers who frequented it all thought they were far away from the human world, thus often performing the thrilling scenes they would usually perform only in private.

Thanks to the outstanding performance of the telescopes, they showed not only the lovers' acts, but even their facial expressions. It was just like watching that kind of videotape on TV. Often the poor soldiers could not see a single woman for two weeks in a row. You couldn't blame them for fighting to see lovers kissing.

They crowded behind Ah Hsiung for a look, but he would not

give up his seat.

"Ah Hsiung, you're going to have sties!"

"If you don't want to give up the telescope, 'report what you have discovered' immediately!"

Ah Hsiung then reported: "They are kissing now. He holds her in his arms. No fondling. No caressing. Oh, God! She pushes him away. He charges at her again, but she pushes him away again. Now he sits by her like a good boy, holding her hand! What? The woman even throws away his hand! What a disgrace he is!"

"Shame on him! Are they high school students?"

"High school students? The man is in his thirties! I can only see the woman's back. She has a really slim body. Strange. Now they sit by themselves without touching each other. Maybe the man is listening to her lecturing. What a fool he is! I don't want to see it anymore."

Another soldier took over the telescope. He saw the average-looking man dressed in a grey suit with a light blue shirt. The woman had a slender waist and long hair touching her shoulders; she was wearing a long black skirt with a cream-colored blouse. They sat talking face to face. Two other soldiers took over the telescope, but the couple's positions never changed. Finding it rather boring, the bachelor soldiers, except Ah Hsiung, all left the telescope in a hubbub. Ah Hsiung swept his telescope across the evening beach as he continued with his duty of guarding the coast.

He led her by the hand to the centre of the pavilion, where he sat her down. Then he sat beside her. Turning round, he looked at the path through the rocks by which they had come, and found nobody in sight. On the right-hand side was the vast sea with its roaring waves. On the left were the desolate crags. They were the only two in this world now: the moment he had long waited for. Eagerly he stared at the woman, who had lowered her head. He had not seen her for five years, but she still looked the same to him. The only difference was that she was now wearing a pair of sunglasses. She didn't wear lipstick, but the long walk here had made her lips a lively red.

Her lips, which were marked by clear contours—the soft and beautiful lips he had kissed numerous times, and the human bud that had started his warm exploration in life—roused him. Suddenly he circled her in his arms and kissed her. Unprepared for this sudden act, she was at first panic-stricken, then she started to tremble all over. Under his gentle pressure, her lips began to open up a little bit. He squeezed her against his chest, moved his face closer to hers. Plop! Her sunglasses dropped onto the cement floor, exposing two dead grey eyeballs permanently fixed in her face.

She pushed him away with all her might while he stared at her eyeballs in painful astonishment. The pair of eyes that used to give him joy when he saw them now looked like the plastic balls glued in the eyeholes of china dolls.

She had refused to see him ever since her glaucoma had started to deteriorate, so he had never seen her artificial eyes. Seeing her mouth twisting, he knew the pain in her heart. He picked up the glasses quickly and put them back on her face with care. Then, hurrying forward, he stretched out to hold her again. This time he was not urged by sexual excitement. He just circled her gently in his arms, but she pushed him again. "Please don't," she said. "I told you we shouldn't do this even five years ago, let alone now that you are married. I wouldn't want to be a burden to you."

"Hsiao Hong"—he called her by her childhood name, moving his body away but still holding her hands tightly— "does it really matter if I hold your hands? It's perfectly all right for me to do so."

"Perhaps it is for you," she said in a low voice. "I don't know how much you love her . . ." She paused, her lips quivering a couple of times. "I don't want to know, but I can't—can't stand it when you hold my hands. Will you please sit away from me? All right?" With this, she quickly drew her hands back from his.

"You forgot why I agreed to come," she continued. "Ever since I became blind, I have been imagining what it looks like at sunset."

He turned to look at the sea. Yes, the setting sun had a dazzling charm. They had once—five years ago—picked sunset viewing as the first activity for their honeymoon. How should he describe it to her?

"The sunset glow is dark red, the same red as the color of the Black Pearl wax-apples you love to eat. The sky is covered with thin clouds that look like fish scales. It's purple, as purple as—as the skirt I bought for you. The sky is blue. I'm sure you can capture these colors with your paint brush." He stopped suddenly.

"It's all right, as long as you describe it for me. What about the waves? I hear the noise, but what color are they?" A tear rolled down her cheek.

"The sea is..."

Night fell. Ah Hsiung turned on his snooperscope instead, sweeping across the beach. Thinking of the two lovers he had seen earlier, he focused on the little pavilion. His night-vision telescope was able to condense light, so what he saw was not dark, but dark green pictures, the same color as that of the firefly. The two people were still sitting in the same place without touching each other. Surrounded by weird-looking coral crags, they looked like two statues on another planet in outer space. The man was still facing Ah Hsiung, speaking to the girl carefully.

"Rookie!" Ah Hsiung could not help cursing.

"Are you happy?" she asked him.

"It's just a home, a place where I go and rest when I finish work and social activities."

"What—what is she?"

"A vocational high school graduate, a short and small person, but her—her facial features look just like yours." He thought, in fact it was her eyes, it was her eyes that were like hers. "Otherwise, no matter how my father forced me, I wouldn't have married her."

He took her hands again. This time, she did not reject him . . .

203

Kindman

By **Gui** Qianfu

For more than ten years in a row, a man had stood under the ledge of a building at the corner of the street. He was not well proportioned: his legs were abnormally short and had to bear the weight of his large torso, making him waddle like a duck when he walked. He was not an attractive man, but a day of his absence would disappoint many— "We can't have delicious *shaobing** cake today now."

His name was Kindman, without a last name. He did not know who his parents were, not even their family names. Many kind people had offered him the necessities and given him money which had enabled him to survive until he was able to look after himself and, finally, to own his present old shabby handcart and clay stove. For this reason, he called himself Kindman. In his memory, the best food was *shaobing* cake. What he got was sometimes not too fresh, but he would make a fire and bake it until it was golden brown. He must have eaten at least a hundred flavors of *shaobing*. So when he baked his own, he was really into it: he would treat everything with the best care, from fermenting and kneading to baking. As he wished, he succeeded in making a delicious type that had an exceptional chewy texture. He did not know how to describe it, but whoever ate it would give him thumbs up. Thus, Kindman did not feel lonely and dejected anymore: he had become a useful person in the world.

Most of Kindman's customers were peddlers, passengers passing by and people without a routine life. One day, whose date he couldn't

---

**Translator's note: Shaobing* is a thin cake usually covered with sesame seeds.

remember, a beautiful woman joined his customers. When she reached out for his *shaobing,* he found her hands were so tender and slender that he froze.

"One *shaobing,* please," said the woman, tossing her black hair as she swung her head. "I hear you make the best *shaobing.*" Her large, glassy eyes were fixed on him.

"Well," he said without knowing what he was saying as he received and put into another pocket a twenty-*fen* bill with a special scent. He was very excited that day, for he had never seen such a beautiful woman buy his *shaobing.* Yet you may not know that when he returned home, he suddenly thought of his parents and started to admire people with families, and followed it with a good cry. Then he started to hate himself.

The woman came frequently, and told Kindman that her name was Liangliang. She had come to this city with her parents when they fled the famine in her early childhood. She said she was a fussy eater, but she loved his *shaobing* most. She must have said something else, but Kindman did not remember. What happened next was that when he raised his head, he saw her still standing in front of him. She was as bright as the rising sun. The cake she was holding was already cold, so without asking her, he snatched it from her and heated it up for her in the stove. "Whenever it's cold, I heat it up for everybody," he said, lest she misunderstand him. "When you eat freshly baked *shaobing,* you should eat it slowly. Otherwise, your mouth will get burned," he added.

"You have such a kind heart."

Those were the most touching words people had ever said about him. Tears began to roll down onto the burning charcoal, wisps of white mist rising instantly. They became special friends. Every day they would meet and exchange a few words, or just remain silent until she finished her *shaobing.* Every morning, rain or shine, even when he was sick, he would come pulling his heavy handcart and arrive at the same place at the same time. Immediately, he would busy himself baking *shaobing*. At least, he had to make about a hundred pieces before people went to work.

A day when she did not show up was a day of sadness for him.

She was a university student, but she never told him about it herself.

"Are you a university student?" he asked her.

"Mm."

"Why do you have to hide it from me? Tell me everything." He tried to make it sound like joking between two acquaintances.

She chewed her *shaobing* slowly, her throat bobbing up and down as she swallowed bit by bit. His hands were busy choosing *shaobing*, which he would throw into the air, then turn a circle to catch it and put it in the stove for baking again. In the red-hot charcoal, his *shaobing* would swell up instantly.

"I have a boyfriend," she said.

His *shaobing* dropped onto the ground. She picked it up and gave it back to him. He took a deep bite, which released the steam from inside, leaving two bright bubbles on his lips.

"Kindman—"

"Bring him over," he interrupted. "And then, on a rainy or windy day, you can just ask him to come get it for you." His joking tone was now rigid.

So her boyfriend came, a tall man with an impressive bearing. Kindman suddenly felt he was a dwarf, like a tree stump that had just lost its trunk.

"When are you going to stop selling *shaobing*?" the tall man asked, eyes glowing. Kindman did not know how to answer him, for he did not know what else he could do.

"I want to tell you, from now on, Liangliang will not eat your *shaobing* anymore. Stay away from her!"

Kindman gazed at the large receding figure, tears rolling down uncontrollably. Compared with his past insults, it was not the worst, but it was the most hurting.

Liangliang returned, with tearful, swollen eyes that looked like freshly picked peaches. She said she still wanted to eat his *shaobing,* asking him not to take her boyfriend's words to heart.

For several days in a row, Kindman had been teaching the junior newcomer on the other side how to make *shaobing.* He taught him every small detail, from mixing the flour, adding the ingredients, fermenting, and kneading and rolling the dough to baking. The newcomer did not sell his *shaobing* until after Kindman had tasted it and given it the nod. One day, Kindman bought one from the man opposite him and gave it to Liangliang.

"Try this," he said.

"Hey, why did you teach him your skills?" she asked after taking a bite.

"I happen to be Kindman," he smiled reluctantly. "If I am gone one day, you can have his."

"Why will you be gone?" She pressed for an answer.

"Maybe because of sickness, or because a relative has come—"

"Didn't you say you have no relatives?" she interrupted him.

"Oh." He patted his head. "One way or the other, there will be something. Something will happen so I can't come, right?"

As confusing as his words could be, she nodded in hesitancy. After that, she saw him no more.

She stopped eating *shaobing* altogether.

My Wife's Pearl Necklace

By **Zhang** Jishu

My wife has a pearl necklace. Whenever I see it on her, a funny feeling comes over me. Is it sweet, or is it sour? What's more, it is a memory I can never forget.

When I was in my fourth year of university, I madly fell in love with the university flower Xin.* Like her name, her beauty connoted many other things. I knew that at least twelve boys were courting her. She had not made her choice, but she liked three or five of them. Honestly, I didn't even know if I was one of the three or five. So I tried to be more aggressive by sending her something from time to time, things such as a tube of toothpaste, a cake of soap, a bunch of flowers, and finally a pearl necklace. She accepted everything else, but not the necklace, no matter what. She told me she already had a similar necklace and would wear it if I did not believe her.

The next day was Valentine's Day, and she really wore a pearl necklace to class. Later I learned that it was a gift from Xi, our class president. Xi was an introvert who never showed off anything he did. At that time, I was not only jealous of him, I hated him. He was more handsome than me and he outdid me in every course.

I don't know how many times I had cried to myself, until I secretly made up my mind to outdo him in all the subjects in order to show Xin my competence. "Before you get your marriage license," I said to myself, "there is always a chance Xin may throw herself into my arms."

---

* *Translator's note:* Xin in the story means "strong and pervasive fragrance."

Unlike before, except for showing diplomatic concern for Xin, I tried not to be overly enthusiastic toward her. Like a thermos bottle, I was hot on the inside but cool on the outside. I had learned this from my rival. Xin seemed to prefer boys of this type. She smiled at me more often even though the eagerness on my face had disappeared. Each of Xin's smiles was like a tulip that would bloom in my dreams. Perhaps that is what "distant beauty" means.

In the summer, the university arranged a trip to Mount Tai for us students. Xin remembered me and personally asked me if I wanted to go. If so, we could go together, she said. With great pleasure I said, yes, of course, but to my surprise, I saw Xi before we started out the next morning. What was more, Xin was wearing his pearl necklace. That really gave me a pretty sour feeling. Wearing his necklace meant that Xi remained her first choice.

I was so upset that I almost decided not to go, but then I thought, "If I don't go, doesn't it mean I give her up altogether?" Finally, I buried my anger in my heart and started smiling instead. On the way, whenever Xi was not glued to her, I would offer to do whatever I could for her.

When we were going down the mountain on our way back, something happened which foreshadowed our love story. The sun was setting when we passed by the Zhongtian Gate. It grew dark before we got to the foot of the mountain. We kept talking and laughing in order to dispel our fatigue. All of a sudden, Xin shouted in surprise and everybody stopped talking and laughing. Somehow, the string of her necklace had broken and the pearls had fallen all over the place. Immediately we switched on the flashlights and started picking them up for her one by one. Before long, we found a small handful, including five I had found. When I handed over my pearls to her, she smiled at me, which, as I read it, seemed to have a hidden meaning. A moment of frantic searching found all the pearls but two as Xin counted them. We continued to look for them. Suddenly, Xi said he had found another one, so only one was missing now.

"We may as well forget it," said Xin.

"All right, we can forget it," said Xi.

But, flashlight in hand, I continued to look for it in the crevices of the rocks. Everybody was going down the mountain, but I refused to leave. When Xin came over to drag me along, I said, "You go first. I'll look for it for another moment." When she tried again, I declined, saying, "Please go down yourselves. After I relieve myself in a minute, I'll catch up with you."

The next morning, Xin came up to look for me. When she saw me, her cheeks were soaked with grateful tears.

"So you stayed here all night," she said. "I was so worried about you!"

When I presented the last pearl to her, I was rewarded with two more strings of pearl-like tears trickling down her cheeks. She threw herself into my arms and did not speak for a long time. "Why did you?" she finally said.

"I was worried somebody might pick it up in the morning," I said.

I don't really need to tell you much about what happened next.

After we went down the mountain, my love relationship with Xin took a real leap forward. Still later on, she broke up with Xi.

Xin and I got married right after we graduated from university. On our wedding night, I recollected my memory of the trip to Mount Tai. She would have thrown away that necklace if I had not given her that cunning smile, but she kept it anyway.

Now, here are a few words just for you folks, words which I have never told my wife. In fact, I found the last pearl even before they went down the mountain. I just hid it and did not want to give it to Xin. That's all.

Another Kiss

By **Wang** Kuishan

When Mangzi returned to the army, Xiao'e went to the city to see him off.

When they got to the railway station, the booking office was not yet open. Since it was too early to buy a ticket, Mangzi and Xiao'e squatted down in the square outside the station and started chatting. A moment later, Mangzi suddenly stopped talking and gazed at Xiao'e blankly.

"Will you stop staring at me in that foolish way," said Xiao'e. "You look so greedy!"

Mangzi burst out laughing, "If you hadn't been staring at me in that foolish way, how could you have seen me staring at you in that foolish way?"

"Aren't you ashamed?" she spat at him.

Then, Mangzi abruptly said in a low voice, "I really want to kiss you again."

"Are you crazy?" said Xiao'e, rising to her feet. Since she had stood up, Mangzi had to follow suit.

After he stood up, he began to walk back and forth on the same spot. Then he said, as if he had made up his mind, "I won't take the next train!"

"Why not?" asked Xiao'e.

"I won't take the next train," he said. "I will take the night train. There's a train after ten o'clock."

"You have made all the arrangements, and now you say you won't take it. One idea after another!"

"I'll wait for the night train," he smiled bitterly. Then he added in a low voice, "When it's dark, I can give you another kiss. If I don't kiss you again before I go, I won't feel good when I leave." With this, without waiting for her reply, he strode toward the avenue. Knowing his stubbornness, Xiao'e could only catch up and accompany him.

They went window shopping. While window shopping, Mangzi saw city lovers walking hand in hand, and several times he wanted to do the same, but he fell short of stretching out his hand. Later on they went for a stroll in a park. In the park, lovers sat leaning on each other or snuggled up in each other's arms. Some simply hugged and kissed each other on the lips in broad daylight. Seeing all this, Xiao'e, scared, turned and hurried back to the entrance. When Mangzi saw her leaving so quickly, he did not know what to do. "Xiao'e, Xiao'e! Stay! Do stay!" He shouted with the accent of a mountain villager and in such a loud voice that he sent all the tourists nearby into hearty laughter.

Worn out by the slow passing of time, they returned to the square outside the railway station in mid-afternoon.

"There's a five o'clock train," said Xiao'e. "You might as well take that one."

"No. I definitely won't take it!" Mangzi said angrily. "I will only take the one after ten o'clock!"

"But what should I do after you leave? It's going to be midnight," she said after she thought for a moment.

"Can't you stay in a hotel?"

"You make it sound so easy," said Xiao'e. "A night in the hotel will cost at least eight or ten bucks."

"No big deal. We can afford it anyway," he said.

"What a swollen head!" She threw a supercilious look at him, and he started to laugh.

Suddenly they heard someone calling, "Mangzi! Mangzi!" When they looked in the direction of the voice, they saw Mangzi's father.

Not knowing what had happened, Mangzi asked at once, "Dad, why are you here?"

"Didn't you say you were taking the nine o'clock train? Why are you still here?" asked the father.

"I couldn't get a ticket," Mangzi said, his face reddening.

"Your mom thought it was already late, and Xiao'e hadn't returned home," his father said. "She was worried that something might have happened, so she asked me to come and pick her up."

Mangzi immediately lost his temper. "It's daytime! What could have happened?"

Knowing his son was upset, the father said haltingly, "Your mom insisted that I come. I also said everything would be all right. But she insisted."

"Go back!" Mangzi was none too friendly.

"Why go back?" said his father. "Since I'm here, I'll see you off and go home with Xiao'e."

Hearing that, Mangzi knew his plot had fallen through. Fuming with anger, he rose to his feet and went straight to the booking office. Xiao'e immediately caught up with him.

Seeing the booking office in noisy disorder while Mangzi was lining up for his ticket, Xiao'e offered her little hand to him under the pretext of thrusting a handkerchief into his hand. Unexpectedly, he rejected it, brushing it far away from him. Smiling, she poked him in the stomach and gave her hand to him again. This time, he took it, clutching it tightly and firmly for a long time. Her hand hurt so much that she started to take deep breaths, but instead of withdrawing it, she allowed him to grasp it that way.

Mangzi eventually took the five o'clock train.

Shortly before he boarded the train, he suddenly said, "Everything is so hard for us country folks!"

"What's hard?" his father threw a questioning look at him. "The bus takes you from our village to the city, and the train takes you

directly from the city to the army. What's hard about that? If—"
Xiao'e threw a secret smile at Mangzi.

Wind-Bell

By **Liu** Guofang

Bing was on leave, visiting relatives in his hometown. When Qi came to see him with a baby in her arms, his bustling house suddenly quieted down. The roomful of excited people soon streamed out, leaving them and the baby alone.

Bing and Qi sat face to face in silence.

Qi finally spoke. "I've let you down."

Bing was silent.

"It was my mom who forced me to marry Dagou," she said. "He is rich. He gave my family 20,000 yuan. I didn't want to marry him, so my mom tried to kill herself by jumping into the river twice."

Bing was silent.

"I loved you, and I always will," she said. "I know you love me, too. If you agree, I'll divorce him and marry you."

Bing was silent.

Hearing no response from him, she left his house, but she soon returned. She was back not only with her child, but also with a wind-bell.

"This is the wind-bell you gave me two years ago," she said. "I've always hung it on my door."

Seeing the wind-bell, Bing finally spoke out, "So you are returning it to me, is that right?"

She shook her head and said, "I've just told you—if you agree, I'll divorce Dagou and marry you. You don't have to decide it right now. Think about it carefully. If you agree, hang the wind-bell on your door. When I see it, I'll come to see you." She left the bell with

215

him and went back home.

There was nobody in the house except Bing, who looked vacant for quite a while until he picked up the wind-bell and started to shake it. Jingling was heard from his house, so Qi, who lived next door, ran out to look at his door, but saw no wind-bell.

She stood at her own door, tears trickling down her cheeks.

Bing did not hang the wind-bell up on his door, either, before he left for the army. Instead, he brought it with him and hung it on the door of the barracks. The northwest was very windy, so the bell jingled all day long. When he had nothing to do, Bing would stare at it blankly and say, "Qi, I've hung the wind-bell on the door. Can you see it?"

In the beginning, the soldiers found it fun, but after some time, they grew tired of it. They said the bell was too noisy, so they asked him to take it down, and he did. Instead, he kept it in a safe place, and whenever he had some free time, he would take it out and go to a place with nobody around, where he would sit and shake it before his chest. "Qi, I have hung the wind-bell on my heart. Can you see it?" he would say as it jingled.

Qi did not see it. She could not see it whether it was hung on the door of his barracks or on his heart. She could only see his door next to hers, and she saw no wind-bell there.

Two years later, Bing was discharged from military service and returned home. This time, Qi did not come to see him. "Where's Qi?" he asked people around him. "How come I haven't seen her?"

"She stays home all the time and doesn't want to go out," they said.

"What happened?" he asked.

"Her husband has found a younger woman and divorced her," they said.

Bing became silent. He hung the wind-bell on his door the next day, but Qi did not come. Staring at it with a dazed expression, Bing said to himself, "Qi, I have hung the wind-bell on the door. Can you see it?"

When the wind began to blow, the bell started jingling. Bing heard it and said to himself, "Qi, the wind-bell is jingling. Can you hear it?"

Qi had heard it and seen it, but she sat still in her house with the child in her arms and did not come out.

The next day Bing went to see her instead. Before he went, he took off the bell and hung it over his chest, shaking it with his hand. Jingling accompanied him into her house.

Qi hung her head when she saw him. "I'm a deserted woman now," she said. "What have you come for?"

"I've come to tell you I have hung the wind-bell not only on the door, but also on my heart." With this, he started to shake the bell again.

The child in Qi's arms, who was four years old and could speak now, stretched out his hand when he heard the jingling, and said, "Mommy, I want it."

A Katydid on Her Head

By **Zhang** Kaicheng

About thirty feet apart, Xiu and Cai had almost reached the top of the Nanling Peak. Xiu was leading the way to the township administration for a divorce.

The exhausted Xiu was sweating heavily when she had climbed up the peak. The sun on this clear September day was still very hot. Of course it was. Otherwise, how could the crops ripen? She sat in the shade of an old persimmon tree by the road, drew out a small handkerchief folded into a square, and wiped her sweat. From where she sat, she could see the scenery on both sides of the mountain. In the south was their home Liang'ao Village, and in the north, Nanling Town, the well-known big centre of their township, where the township administration was located. Two years ago, she and Cai had gone through the same route for their marriage certificate, but today, gosh!

In the east was a cotton field. The cotton leaves were still green, but the bolls were already bursting into bloom. The field was dotted with white, looking like there had been a snowfall in between the green leaves. Seeing the fluffy cotton, Xiu's hands itched. She wanted to pick a bunch, but unfortunately it was not their own. The slope in the west was covered with Chinese sorghum—heavy, fire-red sorghum that weighed down the stalks. Nearby were a few patches of corn and soybeans. The soybeans' green leaves, many of which had tiny worm-eaten holes, were turning yellowish. Somehow there were so many katydids in the soybean field. Xiu was really bothered by the contest-like continuous chirping of the katydids that was heard from one

218

spot before the other had quieted down.

Cai had climbed up as well, but he did not feel tired. Picking up a broken tile, he threw it at a persimmon that looked like a red lantern. How accurate he was! The "red lantern" fell, and he caught it in the air. It was not damaged, so he gave it to Xiu and said, "Here. Quench your thirst. Take a break yourself. I'll go relieve myself over there."

Xiu took a suck on the persimmon. It was very sweet. She wanted to finish it up, but remembering what they had come out for, she simply threw it away.

She was angry with him. After their marriage, he had bought a tractor and started carrying cement from the county town to the village building-supplies factory. He got up early in the morning and did not return home until it was pitch dark. He was so dirty that even the children in the village chanted this doggerel when they saw him: "The tractor chugs by; a grey mouse comes in sight." She was infuriated whenever she heard it.

She told him to change his clothes and wash his hair, but he simply turned a deaf ear to her and countered, "How can a farmer be clean. If you want somebody clean, why didn't you marry a big official in town?" This was too much for her. She admired other young couples in the village who dressed themselves neatly in the latest fashion. The affectionate couples would often go window shopping together in town, or go to the temple fair in their local township. They would chit-chat, whisper and tease each other with loving words, but Cai gave her none of this.

Once, when he was cranking up his engine, the bar slipped, flew out and struck his mouth, knocking out one of his front teeth. She immediately brought over a bowl of water for him to rinse his mouth. "You love the tractor, but it doesn't love you," she said to herself. "Now you've got to rest a day, won't you?" But to her surprise, he just spat out the blood, then jumped onto his tractor again and chugged away without even saying goodbye to her.

Not long ago, she had caught a bad cold. She was running a fever and was feeling extremely weak. She asked him to cancel one trip so as to take her to the hospital in the township, but he surprised her by saying, "Drink some unhusked-rice water. When you sweat it out, you will be all right. I've got to carry the cement." Then off he went. She slept at home for two days all by herself. Tears welled in her eyes whenever she thought of her life. "What's the point of living with someone like this?"

Suddenly, she felt an itch on her head. She was about to touch it when a katydid suddenly started gurgling on the itchy spot. She looked over her shoulder and saw Cai holding a fresh cornstalk to her, laughing with his mouth wide open, showing his missing tooth.

"Don't move," he said. "If you touch the katydid, it will bite you."

Xiu knew that katydids had two razor-like teeth and that their clips were painful. She was helpless, saying to herself, "Now, you naughty devil! You are finally having fun with me!" Somehow, the originally full balloon in her heart started to deflate as if it had been pricked by a needle.

"Now, naughty devil, get it off my head quickly. I don't want it to soil me."

"No, no, it won't. It's standing on your hairpin now," he continued to laugh. "Don't move. Wait, it'll chirp again."

He closed his fingers and rubbed his fingernails to make the katydid chirp, and it really did. Xiu could not hold back her laughter. She laughed happily, something she had missed for more than a year.

The moment Cai clapped his hands, the katydid stopped. When he moved the sorghum stalk against Xiu's head, the katydid jumped back to its top. He conveniently tied it there by fastening its neck with some sorghum skin.

"I won't play with you anymore," Cai said. "Let's go. Otherwise, the office will be closed."

Xiu did not move. She was still lost in the chirping of the katydid, in the joy of a happy couple.

"You can't walk anymore? Let me carry you on my back."

"Finally, you care about your wife. Only now do you more or less look like a man."

"What was I like, then?"

"A machine that only knew how to make money."

"Okay, then, I won't be a machine anymore. We won't go now, all right?"

"We'll go." She rose to her feet.

"Still want to go?"

"We'll go have a canine tooth made for you!" she said, poking his forehead with her finger.

Touching the Wrong Chin

By **Xu** Xijun

Commended by the bureau director, Section Director Lou was overjoyed. Now that he was elated, he wanted his wife to share it with him, so he hurried home as soon as he finished work.

Finding his wife not yet home, the excited Lou decided to do something. He discovered that the garbage can was full and took it out to the garbage station. He met his wife on the stairs when he got to the second floor. Though the dim stairs were not lit, he could still tell that her graceful bearing, enhanced by the smart, long hair that covered her shoulders and by her well-tailored woolen windbreaker, could easily excite any man. Thanks perhaps to his terrific mood, when his wife brushed past him the usually serious Lou surprisingly stretched out, aimed at her chin, and gave her an intimate and romantic flirter's touch. She ignored him, but he still enjoyed the little pleasure. After emptying the garbage, he had a great chat with his neighbors by the roadside.

When he was walking back to the apartment building, Lou bumped into his wife.

"What are you going to do?" he asked her, garbage can in hand.

"I forgot to close the windows when I left the office. I have to go back to close them," she said.

"Were you home just now?"

"I haven't gone upstairs yet."

Lou felt there was something wrong as he walked on. "Since my wife hasn't gone upstairs yet, then who—?" Now he broke out in a cold sweat. All of a sudden, Lou felt terrified and rushed up the stairs.

When he got to the fourth floor, his neighbor, Yun, a woman who worked for him in his office and who lived across the corridor, was coming downstairs. Yun, a good friend of his wife's, wore the same woolen windbreaker and had the same long hair as Lou's wife.

Lou felt an explosion in his head. He staggered into his apartment and collapsed on the sofa, shivering all over.

Upon her return home, his loving wife found him looking queer, so she asked if he was all right. Lou said he had a little chill. Seeing sweat oozing from his forehead, she thought he was ill, so she helped him to bed. The nervous Lou then asked her, "Did I pat your face when I was going upstairs just now?"

"Pat? No." She smiled sweetly.

"It was not you—" Lou was more frightened now, and he started to shiver again, muttering something his wife could not make out.

When he saw Yun at work the next day, Lou blushed like a thief who had been caught red-handed. He dared not look at her. Shivering, he tried to explain to her when nobody was around, "I'm so sorry, Yun. I mistook you for my wife—"

"Mr. Lou, will you please stop it!" she cut him short, as she found his behavior rather weird. But he continued, "I'm really sorry. Last night—"

"What's the matter with you?" said Yun in surprise, running out of the office, terrified.

For two days in a row, the agitated, red-faced Lou would try to apologize to Yun and to ask for her forgiveness whenever they were alone. The more he tried, the more weird he seemed. Thinking he might end up causing trouble, Yun told her good friend, Lou's wife, what had been going on.

So when he returned home, his wife reproached him severely, "What a husband you are, Lou! You are trying to start an affair with someone! She has complained to me about you."

Lou knew he was in trouble, aware that Yun had told her all about it. He felt too ashamed of himself to face anybody. After five days of mental turmoil, he eventually collapsed. While he was being taken to hospital, he still kept saying, "Sorry, Yun."

Yun came to visit Lou, dressed in the same woolen windbreaker. He saw Yun and his wife, who was caring for him, wore the same clothing, their hair done in exactly the same way as the day he met Yun on the stairs. Hardly able to distinguish one from the other, he suddenly felt guilty, which urged him to repent again. "I'm sorry, Yun. When I was emptying the garbage that day, I mistook you for my wife."

"What are you talking about? I don't understand you!" Yun was at a loss.

"So, it's all for that!" Lou's wife giggled as she joined in. "It was me you touched that day! Aren't you being funny?"

Lou shook his head and frowned, still looking guilty. "You both know I am ill. So you gang up in order to comfort me. But please believe me, Yun. I didn't do it on purpose. I am not that kind of man."

His helpless wife could not but move closer to him and say, "Now, silly old man! Touch me again if you don't believe us!" Lou stretched out to touch her chin and gave it a pinch, his face lighting up instantly. He stared at Yun, then at his wife, before bursting into uncontrollable laughter.

The shine in his eyes that had long been lost started to radiate again. "I have good news for you," he told his wife. "I have been commended by the bureau director!"

Nearly Said

By **Gao** Weixi

Melancholy emerged in my mind as if it were a ghost. Day after day, I tried to shake it off, but it clung to my heart; I tried to kick it out, yet it lingered in my soul. It seemed as if it would accompany me throughout my life. I was lost in astonishment—what had happened?

In the barracks, men always outnumbered women. Beautiful as a rose, you had a slender figure with a tender temperament, just like a phoenix standing in a flock of chickens—a rare treasure. Many eyes stared at you with admiration. There was that short section director who would stand by you whenever we had to line up, whether it was morning drill, meal time or evening roll call. Everybody felt surprised, but your generosity allowed you to ignore everything, treating him with courtesy.

Perhaps he had somebody bragging to you about him—a tall, big man often came to visit you openly. I did not take it to heart when I first saw you two sitting on a tricycle heading for town, but soon I sensed something wrong there. Some said he exploited the crisis of a relationship; others said you invited a wolf to your house.

By chance I once saw his coquettish look almost sparking a line of self-conceit in you. Then I thought, perhaps you really had made your choice.

You and I were only colleagues in language teaching, that's all. We might have more common conversation topics. We did often have

225

little disputes over Confucius,* the literary merits and blemishes of Pushkin and Chekhov, and the importance of Sherlock Holmes's detective stories in literary history. But those were just academic issues, weren't they?

At dusk in May, the pomegranate blossoms were bright as fire. I leaned against the tree trunk as you sat on the fork, opened your red lips, and in a low voice began to sing the "Song of Mei Niang." When you finished singing, we were lost in silence. We each embraced the evening wind, and did not want to leave. Then what did I decipher from the dancing freckles of moonlight on your face which crept through the flowers when the moon appeared in the east? It was a poem written without words. It was a three-dimensional picture. It was holy teaching that exposed human secrets. My heart began to tremble.

Then it was another May, when the earth was covered with pomegranate blossoms again. Our old wounds had just healed, but we ran into each other again. You whispered to me when nobody was around, "Everything's been pre-arranged. I never knew I would marry him." Didn't your words spoil the scenery? "What do you mean?" I asked. You looked down, lost in thought for a moment. Instead of answering me, you gave a sad smile and tripped away, leaving behind a lifetime mystery.

Always dim and vague, now visible, now invisible, you never faded in my mind during those long years. In May when petals fell in riotous profusion, I often walked back and forth under the tree, cherishing that little feeling you had left in me, picking up the fallen leaves and chewing on the days that had passed. Using that drifting

---

* *Translator's note:* Confucius (551-476 BC) was a sage in ancient China, born in the feudal State of Lu, or today's Shandong Province. He advocated a system of morality and statecraft that would preserve peace and afford the people stable and fair government. The influence of his doctrines has spread from generation to generation and far beyond China itself.

train of thought, I tried but never succeeded to draw your clear figure: it was always like one drawn in water—once you wiped it, it was gone. Yet just like a spirit lingering around, momentarily you would appear in my mind again. As our ancestors said, hardly had I closed my eyes when I saw you again.

May God be our witness: we never said or did anything that lovers would have done. Perhaps because of this, it invites more guessing and provokes more thinking. And probably because of that, our relationship has reached such a lasting state that it takes shape after our thinking and creates kindred spirits. It was God's will that this piece of blank paper be created, ready for a most beautiful and ingenious human picture to be painted by a clever hand, brushes, paints and ink lying by, ready for use.

The last words I heard from you were forwarded to me by another person: "Tell him I wish him good luck!" You asked someone to forward your message even though today's means of communication are so advanced that nobody really needs anyone's assistance. May I ask, you cunning woman, what are you really up to? What message do you intend to convey?

You wanted to say it, but you did not. You wanted to say it, but you never did! It seems you just wanted to create a broken relationship that is not totally broken. Several decades have flown by. Indeed, it is that "last wish," like gossamer, now drifting away, now clinging around me, that has been resounding in my ears up till today.

I was told that you still live in my remote home city. Human feelings change day in, day out. Time can turn out tragedies, but wonders more so. I sincerely hope that you live better than I do. I am sure you do!

Missing the Heart

Mung Bean

By **Zong** Lihua

On a sunny afternoon, joining her two elder sisters, Sorghum and Buckwheat, a girl was unexpectedly born into Granary's family.

Bending close to the soil, the father, soaked with sweat, was busy working when somebody started shouting to him, "Granary, Granary, your wife is in labor now." A handful of mung beans in hand, Granary rushed home like a tornado. Hardly had he stepped through the front door when he heard an unearthly cry. The midwife Second Widow, who held a baby with two tiny feet dangling in the air, came out and said, "Congratulations! It's another girl, Granary."

"F—k," Granary cursed, without moving his feet.

He named her Mung Bean.

Mung Bean cried a lot, and she would cry non-stop. The annoyed Granary once smashed his porridge bowl, yelling, "Crying and crying! But can you cry a teapot spout out of your mother's butts for me?"

The situation facing people who had broken the family-planning rules was grave. Witnessing heavily fined violators, Granary's wife suggested to him, "I may as well go for a tubal ligation,* what do you think?"

Looking out, Granary sat on the threshold that divided his buttocks into two. After a long silence, when he had blown out a cloud of smoke, he sighed. "All right. Every man has his life!"

Inside Granary's head an ambitious plan was then conceived. He

----

* *Translator's note:* Women are urged to go through this sterilization procedure once a couple have had the number of children they are permitted to have.

229

was going to bring Mung Bean up to be a child who could provide for her parents. In other words, he had assigned the task of son-in-law to Mung Bean.

And the following is a commonly heard touching dialogue between father and daughter:

"Mung Bean is a good child, isn't she?"

"Yes."

"What should she do when she grows up?"

"Look after her parents."

"Why would Dad find a husband for her and keep him home?"

"Dad needs him to buy wine for him."

He would tighten his face to the shape of a peach, looking very pleased, while innocent Mung Bean giggled.

Mung Bean's growing up fully demonstrated the bean's true ability to resist drought, to stand vile weather. Though she was raised with simple food and cheap clothing, Mung Bean grew like a Lombardy poplar and turned out to be an outstanding peasant. She could push carts and carry heavy loads, just like an able man. Then a few men, all charlatans, secretly worked out a scheme. "Who will be the one to subdue her?"

The job of subduing Mung Bean was soon undertaken by a young man from another village. After rejecting a series of Granary's intended arranged marriages, Mung Bean started her own love affairs.

The young man was the only son in his family, an obviously unsuitable candidate to look after the parents-in-law. Worse still, Mung Bean did not want him to live in her own home.

Thus, a protracted war started between Granary and Mung Bean.

One day Granary raised a wooden stick and struck at her back. The stick sprang back forcefully with a "pop" sound. Tears instantly filled his eyes. "God damn you," Granary cursed. "Why didn't you dodge it? Why didn't you dodge it?"

Granary suddenly realized that his daughter had grown up and that he could not hit her that way.

Instead, he went on a hunger strike, lying on the *kang,* covering himself up with his quilt. Mung Bean did not ask him to get up, but cooked him two or three delicious dishes and placed them at the head of the *kang* with a pot of heated wine. The first day, Granary refused to eat, so Mung Bean finished the food like a hungry wolf in front of him. It happened again the next day. On the third day, Granary jumped out of bed, cursing, "Damn it, the urine alone will kill me!"

Mung Bean and her mom laughed outside the window.

Finally, Mung Bean married her sweetheart, accepting her parents-in-law as her own. The young couple went all out at work, and within a few years they built a row of redbrick houses with red tiles.

"We should invite my parents to live with us now," Mung Bean said to her husband one day.

"Isn't it the same for me to live in their house and look after them there?"

Mung Bean raised her eyes at him. "Don't you know the difference yourself? Just go and pick them up. Don't babble."

"I'm just teasing you," he smiled. So he went to pick up his parents-in-law. On their way back, he also bought a barrel of rice wine. For he knew his father-in-law just loved a sip or two in his leisure time.

A Woman Hostage

By **Sun** Fangyou

He kept playing with the revolver, skillfully. When he had had enough, he drew out a bullet the size of a peanut. After putting it in his mouth for a second, he glanced at it in the bright sun, then threw it up into the air and caught it firmly.

"It will depend on your luck," he said as he looked at that woman with hill-like breasts, at the moment when a breeze swept across her, blowing up her *qipao* dress and exposing her sexy thighs. The white light seemed to have burned his eyes. He stayed stunned for a moment, feeling fire burning all over his body.

"Isn't our boss thinking of fun?" Out came lewd whistles from the depth of the reed marshes.

The woman saw the stubborn corner of his mouth pulled up by the quivering on his face, deforming his young face momentarily. He raised his revolver, whose magazine looked like a small wheel, or a beehive, that could hold six bullets. The magazine could turn freely counter-clockwise, but when the trigger was squeezed it could also rotate clockwise. She saw him loading it with that bullet. After that he turned it counter-clockwise several times, saying, "It depends on your luck. It's only loaded with one bullet. If the chamber happens to be empty, I will take you as my wife."

She stared at him in contempt.

"You know, we bandits don't kidnap women. Women are not worth much. Rich men play with women like playing cards and will never pay a big ransom for you." He raised his gun as he spoke, but suddenly he put it down again, adding, "I'll let you know this before

232

you die. We wanted to kidnap your husband, but my brothers got you by mistake. We aren't lustful bandits and will not keep a woman to bother us. However, if I take you as my wife, nobody will bother you. But I don't really want to marry a rich man's third mistress, either. So heaven will decide everything for us." With this, he rotated the magazine a few more times before he slowly raised his gun.

The woman closed her eyes calmly.

The slope of the island in the middle of the lake was quiet. Only a water bird that had landed beneath the woman's feet was shaking its head and fluffing its feathers. The hungry eyes hidden throughout the reeds were fixed at this spot.

Gritting his teeth, he fired his gun.

Nothing happened!

"I beg you to fire another shot," she said after she opened her eyes at him.

He shook his head. "No. I said I would fire only one shot," he said as he walked over to her. "It happened to be empty. That means you are lucky, and it also means we are meant for each other."

"Isn't it too good for you?" she smiled bitterly.

"What do you want then?" he asked, surprised.

"I wanted death, but didn't die. I want fate to decide for me, too," she answered as she glanced at him, gently shrugging her shoulders and combing her messy hair with her fingers.

"How?"

"I'll fire one shot at you, too!"

He was stupefied, staring at her unbelievingly for quite a while. Then he burst out laughing, "Awesome! It's damned awesome! No wonder that old guy Chen Youheng liked you! I have finally met a real match. It's worth it even if I die." With this he gave her his gun, drawing out another "peanut."

Upon receiving the bullet, she pushed it into the magazine and rotated it expertly before walking toward him.

She raised her gun, with a graceful posture.

233

He was shocked, his mouth wide open.

"Big Brother, we hear she is an expert shooter!" shouted the people in the reeds in chorus, their voices filled with worry and fear.

Smiling, she rotated the magazine again and said, "If there's no shot, I'll be your wife." With this she raised the small revolver again. Her hand a little shaky, she aimed at him for a long time, but suddenly put down her gun in dejection. "I won't accept what fate decides anymore," she finally said. "I only beg you not to be a bandit anymore and to start a new life with me."

He was stunned, staring at her blankly as if making up a dream.

"You were born with a bad life, but I'm willing to be your wife and suffer with you," she said, tears mysteriously welling up her eyes.

Perplexed, he walked over, picked up his gun for a look, and was dumbfounded.

"I rotated it two times, but each time the bullet landed at the breech," she cried. "At that moment, I really wanted to kill you, but when I thought of your miserable life, I felt a little sorry for you. You don't know, but I also have had a bad life."

Out of rage, he fired his gun. The shot broke the silence with a clap of thunder inside the Reeds Lake.

Dejected, he lowered his revolver, saying to her, "All right then. I will listen to you. I will take you out of here and start a poor life with you."

Deafening shouts were heard from all directions. Out came numerous men, who knelt in front of him, begging in one voice, "Boss, you can't go."

"It's a blessing for me, Ma Fang, that I've got Bao Niang today," he said calmly. "Brothers, forget about me!"

Those who had money began to draw out money for him. Before the new couple was a patch of radiance. Looking at the radiance, Ma Fang knelt down to bow with one hand clutching the other and said, chokingly, "I'll never forget your kindness, brothers, but you risked your life for every dollar you've got. I won't accept one single penny." With this he respectfully drew out the revolver and placed it on the ground.

She walked over to help him to his feet. Then she picked up the revolver, saying, "You have been a chieftain. You may get into trouble, so you'd better keep it for self-defense, just in case."

He started crying.

They both went down the mountains.

Can't Live Without Love

By **He** Baiyuan

Zhuang Liyi was in her forties, with a daughter in middle school. Her figure was still perfect, her hair luxuriantly black, and she had no crow's feet at the corners of her eyes yet. Often she would look in the mirror for a long time, lost in a trance.

Her husband was a pastry cook working for a big hotel. Every morning he had to get up at four o'clock to go to work, so he had to go to bed early every night, leaving Zhuang and the daughter watching TV in the living room with the volume low. Mother and daughter were really glued to the TV, especially when there were love stories and stories about family morals and affectionate relationships. They would fix their gaze more firmly where lovers exchanged vows, followed by "explosive" scenes. The daughter enjoyed it out of curiosity, while the mother watched it out of admiration as well as doubt about the existence of love. "Except on TV, there can't be true love in the world," she thought.

"How would a woman feel when she is being loved?" she would wonder when she looked in the mirror.

She had never felt loved. No man had ever courted her in her forty-two years of life. No man had ever written her a love letter, or said "I love you" to her. After graduating from high school, she had settled down in the countryside for six years and did not return to the city until 1978. That year, matchmakers came to her home to propose to her on behalf of three men. After careful comparison, her parents picked for her an honest and kind man with a clean political background who was working for a state-owned business—today's husband. Unfortunately, no love relationship ever really developed between them.

On their wedding day, their employers held a joint celebration for them. Noisy good wishers from both sides kicked up a fuss, asking the bridegroom, Tong Jiaman, to say "I love you" to the bride right in front of the crowd, and kiss her. But he stood there like a tree trunk and would not do it, no matter how people booed and hooted.

Her memory was still as fresh as yesterday's. More than a decade had passed, but she had never tasted the happiness of love or experienced the excitement of trembling caused by the touching of two hearts. Never had Jiaman said to her, "I love you." They were just a couple who had married for the sake of marriage. She began to understand that love might differ from marriage.

She often thought that being courted and loved must be a very happy experience. If she could be truly loved by a man once, it would be worth her life.

One day, she suddenly thought of Mr. Zhang, the medical practitioner of the state-owned farm where she had worked after high school. All of a sudden, she realized that perhaps Zhang had been in love with her. Once when she was seeing him in the clinic, she carelessly mentioned she was interested in the novel *A Dream of Red Mansions*. After that, despite the great risk, Zhang managed to borrow a copy from someone, and started to hand copy it for her. At that time, reading this novel was branded by the government as "chasing the sentimentalism of the rich landlords and capitalists," so Zhang could do this only secretly in the wee hours behind closed windows and doors when everybody had gone to sleep. He did not stop copying even on the hottest summer days. One must know that he did not even have an electric fan at that time. Zhang was still copying the novel when she returned to the city. Soon after that, Liyi and Jiaman became engaged and then got married. She thought she should not receive anything from anybody other than her husband, so she wrote to tell Zhang to stop his copying.

Now she came to know that the devoted Zhang had been risking his life when he was secretly copying the banned novel for her. That was love and devotion. Throughout the years past, Jiaman had never shown the slightest feeling of that type for her. But why didn't Zhang tell her his feelings at that time?

From then on, she would think of Zhang when she looked in the mirror.

She longed for a love letter from somebody in her lifetime.

But life lingered on in the same dull way without the uproars of a couple's quarrelling or the dizziness of love.

Suddenly, she thought, "Why not let my imagined lover write me a love letter then?"

So she sat at her dresser and started to write, stroke by stroke, one word after another. She filled the two-page letter with all the words she had learned from films and television— "love," "for life," "until death," "sweet," "sour," "tears." The letter was signed Zhang Ke, the full name of the medical practitioner.

Tears rolled down her cheeks as she read the letter.

From then on, whenever she could not stand her loneliness, she would bring out the letter and read it. Tears would accompany her throughout the reading. When she finished it, she would lock it up in her elegant dressing box that she had bought for her own wedding.

Now she felt she had a secret a woman should have.

Now she felt the joy of being loved.

Buttons on Her Back

By **Zong** Lihua

A sparkle flashing across her eyes, Zhuhui caught sight of a silvery grey blouse.

Yizong spotted her moment of happy surprise just in time, asking, "Do you like it?"

She nodded, then added, "But look at those buttons!"

"What's wrong with the buttons?"

"They are at the back."

Indeed, the uniqueness of this blouse was where the buttons were placed.

"I won't be able to button them myself," she said, her shiny eyes flashing.

"Are you sure you like it?" Yizong smiled.

Zhuhui nodded again.

"Buy it, then. I'll be happy to button it up and unbutton it for you every day."

It was that fashionable blouse she wore when she went to the government office with Yizong for her marriage license.

How happy she felt! Every morning, when she turned her back to Yizong like a spoiled girl, he would understandingly come over and do up the buttons for her, one after another, from bottom to top. At night, he would unbutton them from top to bottom. Sometimes Zhuhui would intentionally fall against Yizong's body. Yizong would then circle her with his arms. Then she would close her eyes and spread out her arms like wings, as if standing on the *Titanic*.

And how proud she was! She indulged herself seeing her

239

colleagues staring at her blouse. They kept praising her for having such a devoted and loving husband.

For these reasons, she truly loved this blouse and so she wore it frequently, but she had never thought of touching the buttons herself. Time flew in this daily activity of buttoning and unbuttoning until she became a mother.

After she became a mother, Zhuhui seemed to like that blouse even more, but slowly Yizong grew tired of this job. After he got married, he had more obligations to fulfill, and more banquets to go to. Sometimes his pager or cellphone would ring when he was excitedly chatting with his fellow drinkers. Zhuhui would tell him that she could not undo her buttons. Yizong would smile, but after several times, he stopped smiling, feeling a little bit annoyed.

"You may as well stop wearing that blouse. You've been wearing it for so many years anyway," he told Zhuhui one day.

Zhuhui looked at him mysteriously. "Are you tired of it?" she asked.

"No. How could I be tired of it?" He smiled in embarrassment.

Then there was that day when Yizong was astonished that she did not need him to button and unbutton the blouse for her.

It was the day when she had to write an examination in another city where she had to stay in a hotel overnight. She badly needed a good mark on this examination, so although she knew it was not the right thing to do, she had copied some answers, which could best be covered by her favorite blouse.

Thus, Zhuhui went to the examination in that blouse. She returned home in that blouse, too.

Shortly after she returned, Yizong discovered what she had worn.

"Well, how did you unbutton your blouse in the past two days?" he asked.

"Would the earth stop turning without you?" Zhuhui glanced at him.

Yizong found it inappropriate to ask any more questions, but he felt really reckless, especially after he learned through other people that Zhuhui had gone to the examination with a rather handsome colleague.

In the following days, they had several quarrels, neither small ones nor big ones, until one day when Yizong could not hold back anymore. "I'm just not sure how you buttoned up your blouse when you were away from me," he said.

"So you think I couldn't do it myself?" Zhuhui laughed coldly.

"Show it to me then," said Yizong, his eyes brightening.

She stared at him as if he were a stranger.

He looked away. "Somehow I still don't believe it."

"Why do I have to prove it to you?" she said.

"Are you guilty of something?" he asked. "I know somebody did it for you."

"Since you know it, why are you asking me!" Tears instantly welled up in her eyes.

What followed seemed to be a venting of uncontrollable anger. Yizong broke a glass into pieces on the floor, startling Zhuhui with the unexpected noise. Quite a while later, she grabbed a cup within reach and smashed it onto the floor. Then she packed, picked up her child and slammed the door behind her.

She flung the blouse on the bed before she left.

"Okay, you go. Go. And don't ever come back!" he roared.

Yizong felt extremely bad in the days that followed. When he calmed down, he began to ponder, "Could she really have unbuttoned the blouse herself?"

He had a younger sister with a figure similar to Zhuhui's, so he called her over.

There, in front of his doubtful but surprised eyes, his sister easily buttoned up the blouse, then unbuttoned it, all by herself.

He stood there speechless for a long time. Then he called and got through to Zhuhui.

"Zhuhui, that blouse is truly very beautiful. I want you to come back and put it on right away. I will do and undo the buttons for you like before."

At the other end of the line, Zhuhui was silent for a while. "Yizong, I don't want to wear that blouse anymore," she finally said.

Her Husband's Mistress

By **Lin** Ruqiu

Meiwen climbed haltingly to the seventh floor step by step with a bunch of vegetables in hand.

She had overworked herself in the past few days. Her husband's aunt's family had come to visit them from Singapore, so all day long she had busied herself cooking delicious food for them, boiling, frying, and stewing. As the common saying goes, "The host is at peace only when the guests are gone." Meiwen had some time for herself only after their relatives left last night. This morning, she slept in before she started to tidy things up. After that she went to the market to buy her water spinach.

Eventually, Meiwen got to the top floor and soon found herself inside her apartment. She had just changed to her slippers when a stranger shot out of her bedroom. Dressed in the latest fashion, the stranger had the classic beauty of an attractive woman: peach-like cheeks and almond-shaped eyes. In shock, Meiwen was about to ask who she was and how she had got into her home, when the stranger confronted her, seized her collar and roared, "So you are Yu Meiwen, aren't you? There you are! Your husband is a liar after all. He told me he is not married and wanted to marry me. I wanted to come and see his home several times, but he always had an excuse to keep me away. What an unfaithful man! He is married, but he has been looking for mistresses and hides everything from his wife. Indeed, you can see a man's face, but never his heart. That bastard has cheated me!" After shooting off a series of accusations, she burst out crying.

It struck Meiwen like a heavy blow; she almost collapsed. What

243

was going on? She had been married to Xiaohua for two years, and there was nothing out of the ordinary about their marriage. The only thing suspicious, if anything, was that Xiaohua had seldom returned home before midnight lately. He told her he had so much to do that he could not finish it during regular work hours. "You can't see someone's heart after all. The popular saying goes, 'A useless man keeps only one wife; a capable man changes mistresses every night.' Has it really come true?" Meiwen's jealousy started to burn inside her. Pushing away the stranger, she shouted, "Where are you from? I shall take him to task when he comes home!"

"Why worry about where I come from!" said the woman, wiping her tears. "If he hadn't got me with child, I wouldn't have been able to steal his keys. And why would I have come here in such a hurry, anyway? I hear he has two more girlfriends. That's why I became more careful. If I hadn't seen your wedding picture, I wouldn't have known you were married." With this she burst into wails again.

"What? He has two more girlfriends?" To Meiwen, this was like adding oil to a fire. "This faithless man has gone too far! No wonder he didn't try to entertain his aunt when she was visiting us. Instead, he was indulging himself with those women! That is why . . ." Meiwen was so furious that she did not know how to vent her anger. She gnashed her teeth, cold sweat oozing from her palms.

The strange woman continued to sob by herself. "This cheater Xiaohua has ruined—ruined my life. That son of a bitch, what am I going to do now?"

Seeing her weeping in uninterrupted choking sobs, Meiwen felt somewhat sorry for her. She drew out a tissue and gave it to her. "Here, wipe your face first. I'll get you another hot towel." With this, she walked into her bathroom.

"Never mind, Meiwen. I really appreciate it. I'm leaving now. Just don't tell Xiaohua I have been here when you see him, please."

Meiwen heard every single word clearly from the bathroom. Unable to make up her mind, she was wondering whether she should ask her to stay or see her off.

Bang! She heard the door slam.

The strange woman had gone. The angry Meiwen walked out of the bathroom. Greatly confused, she walked several circles in the living room until she clenched her teeth and uttered in hostility, "That faithless man, I will choke him to death when he comes back!"

At noon Xiaohua finally returned home. He entered the apartment only to hear Meiwen shout, "You faithless man!" and charge at him grabbing for his neck.

He tried to push her away as he shouted, "What are you doing, Meiwen!"

"What am I doing!" laughed Meiwen bitterly. "You keep several mistresses outside, and you think I don't know it!"

He denied it resolutely.

"You don't have to swear to heaven or God; you got her pregnant and she came just now. You still want to deny it!"

After all, women are no match for men. After a fierce fight, Xiaohua managed to conquer her. Meiwen wept and wailed in the sofa, and the infuriated Xiaohua started to smash cups on the floor. Their neighbors who heard their fight came to knock on the door to find out what was happening, but Xiaohua only told them from behind the door, "Nothing. I just broke two cups accidentally."

After their neighbors left, the couple started a cold war. The sulky Xiaohua buried himself in smoking until he suddenly thought of something. "Did that woman get into our apartment by herself? Or did you open the door for her?"

"If she hadn't stolen your keys from your pocket, how could she have got in here?" said the unfriendly Meiwen.

Hearing this, Xiaohua dashed into the bedroom without saying another word. He opened two drawers in one breath. "Where are the five thousand Singapore dollars and the gold necklace and bracelet my aunt gave us?" he shouted after a moment of frantic searching. "Where did you put them?"

"What?" Meiwen screamed as she felt fear on her head. She ran into the bedroom and started turning over the things in the left drawer and the right drawer. Then she pounded the dressing table with her fist and howled, "That goddamned thief! What a cunning and vicious woman she is!"

Bragging

By **Zhong** Zimei

Whenever Dr. Lap thinks of the human race today, he bursts into laughter, even in his dreams. Now that he is suffering from severe insomnia, he laughs all the more. After one or two more technical breakthroughs, his invention of a super bragging machine will be completed. He just has more difficulty falling asleep!

With an abundance of materials, the worry-free human race simply goes the opposite direction to what prophets have predicted. An abnormal phenomenon of "well-fed and well-clad humans longing for bragging" has occurred. All day long, men and women do nothing except brag. Bragging has thus become the only criterion to judge the worthiness of every human being. Anybody who brags wittily and beautifully becomes superior to others. Even the election of the Global President is no exception.

Due to excessive bragging, people unavoidably find their mouths and lips dry. So, as it happens, the clever human race has invented a bragging machine. It looks just like a tiny black spot stuck at the central point above the upper lip. Interacting with the human nerve cord, it brags at the owner's will. Simple and convenient, it also serves as an ornament.

Inventor Dr. Lap has decided to upgrade the bragging machine so that it can brag automatically all day long. If it can brag without requiring the slightest thinking of the owner, and if it can still be used as an ornamental sticker, won't the human race love it more?

The ridiculous thing is that when Dr. Lap first mentioned his idea, his wife, Hua Zi, started to laugh until she had to hold her sides.

"You?" she said. "I'll tell you what! I thought of this invention when I was only seven years old." Dr. Lap shrugged his shoulders, taking her words as bragging only.

In the Bragging Age, honest words are nowhere to be found. Whatever little honesty remains may be found only in the few people like Dr. Lap. An inventor's strength lies in his or her talents, but at a crucial moment it may be a sudden inspiration flashing across the inventor's mind that triggers a breakthrough.

Dr. Lap has almost fallen asleep when a flash of light occurs in his mind which completes his invention of a new bragging machine.

Not surprisingly, Hua Zi becomes the first person to try Dr. Lap's upgraded bragging machine. His bragging machine, now yellow, is also like a talking machine. As soon as it is stuck to the central spot over the upper lip, it can turn itself on and off automatically. The tiny yellow sticker is a real success. It makes Hua Zi a superior bragger nobody can match.

"My dream has come true!" the overjoyed Dr. Lap laughs as he listens to his wife. "I will become the most important inventor in the entire human race."

After he calms down from his excitement, Dr. Lap enjoys a daylong sleep. After he wakes, stretching out his body, he opens his eyes only to see his wife wearing an unusually radiant face. She sits at the edge of his bed with the bragging machine talking non-stop: "This first human bragging machine has been invented by me, Hua Zi. I wanted to invent this machine when I was as young as seven years old. This bragging machine makes twelve contributions to the human race. First, it saves all the mental work of the entire human race. Secondly, it enriches the imagination of humankind . . ."

"Wonderful! Wonderful!" the self-content Dr. Lap chuckles at her bragging.

"Accordingly, I have taken out a patent to protect the invention of this bragging machine under my name," says Hua Zi.

"Were those words from the bragging machine, or from you?"

Dr. Lap is taken by surprise.

Isn't it a shame that the human race can no longer directly distinguish falsehoods from truths!

"They came straight from my vocal cords, so they've got to be mine," Hua Zi says solemnly. At a critical moment of interest, she needs to tell the truth.

What apparently follows is that Hua Zi becomes the third Global President of the Bragging Age, while Dr. Lap remains the same ordinary doctor who is now a divorcee.

Midsummer Lotus

By **Liu** Liying

The bright moon appeared in the sky, covering Lotus's courtyard with a layer of frost. It was at this time that Lotus, entering her courtyard, heard a loud cough from Dad.

"Fooling around. You just keep fooling around!" Dad spat heavily on the ground.

"I've been sitting and chatting with Xiu'er at her home. That's all."

"Sitting and chatting." He spat on the ground again. "I've brought you up to such a big girl, and now you just sit and chat!"

"I've carried the water and filled the jar, and I've carried the firewood for the stove, too," said Lotus.

Dad then busied himself smoking his pipe. Having smoked tobacco this way for more than half of his life, he would huff and puff non-stop throughout the winter. It rent one's heart to see his bony chest working like a bellows. Once her mother bought him a carton of cigarettes instead, asking him to stop smoking his pipe. "It's harmful for you," she said. Her father snatched it from her, smashing and trampling the cigarettes until the floor was covered with broken tobacco fragments.

"Bad woman. Bad woman! You could use up a mountain of gold and silver if we had one, you cheap woman! What a great wife you are! You are buying cigarettes for your man. You want me to smoke this family to bankruptcy, huh?"

Lotus's mom remained quiet as a mouse.

"Mom," said Lotus, "sooner or later, you will be beaten to death by Dad."

"But you must know the husband is as important as Heaven. With your sick father around, we are a complete family with everybody alive."

Tears filled Lotus's eyes. "When I have the money, I'll buy a whole truckload of cigarettes for Dad to tread on. He's got to stop when he's tired out."

"Don't think money is easy to make! It's not free for you to pick up. It's called fate."

In the bright moon, Dad's pipe bowl glowed up and down with sparkles, looking like a small fireball. "Your marriage with the man in Nanling is a done deal."

"Done?" asked Lotus.

"Done," Dad repeated.

Lotus's mother stood in the central room of the house, her hands resting on the door frame with one leg inside the threshold and the other outside. Mom was only forty-something years old, but she had so much grey hair.

"No father-in-law and no mother-in-law; no brother-in-law and no sister-in-law. The day you are married, you'll be the hostess of the family," Dad said. "They have sent over the money this afternoon."

"Really?" said Lotus.

"Really," Dad said.

"I've just talked to Xiu'er," Lotus said. "She said the good thing about this marriage is he is a lazy good-for-nothing, fond of food but not work."

Dad's face suddenly seemed to be covered with frost. "You know it all?"

Lotus glanced at Dad, then Mom.

Then she caught sight of her elder, crippled brother limping in the yard. Whether the moon lit the yard in part or in full did not matter to him. Pushing away his rice bowl, he would drag along his lame leg, limping back and forth in the courtyard. Her brother's

251

footsteps were rhythmically uneven, with one heavier than the other. They seemed to cut the hearts of the whole family like a huge, dull saw, causing permanent anxiety. At this time Lotus would hear Dad's deep cough. "I know a three-legged toad is nowhere to be found, but I don't believe we can't find him a two-legged woman."

Lotus knew what was in Dad's mind—he was waiting for her nod so that he could pick a date for her wedding and start to buy material to make her new clothes, but Lotus just would not open her mouth. She said to herself, "I don't have to read the looks on your face like Mom. You won't knead me as you like."

At this moment, her mother tumbled out of the door, throwing herself on her knees in front of Lotus. "My good child," she said, "here I am, kneeling before you. Mom will tell you the truth. They have sent over a big stack of bills, enough for your brother to find a wife and build a new house. But I know you'll suffer from this marriage, my poor child. Mom has let you down."

No sooner had Lotus's father's flying foot landed on her mother's face than blood started oozing from her mouth. "A high mountain cannot cover the sun. She fed on your milk. How could you kneel before her!" said Dad.

"If you ever dare to touch my mom again, I'll go straight to Nanling to tell them I have broken off the engagement!" The blood from Mom's mouth dyed red a large spot on her bluish-white flat-collared blouse. The blouse had been given to Lotus's family when the county government had been helping the needy last spring. In the spring, her mom did not really want to wear it, lest people feel jealous of her. Only later on when she found everybody in the neighborhood wearing clothes given by the government—some even made of better materials than hers—did she dare to wear it out.

"Mom, I'll take it," said Lotus. "I'll take it. That's all." With this, Lotus kicked the folding stool her father had just sat on in the courtyard, and it flew out of the front entrance.

One day, when Lotus was a small child, she went to cut grass on

252

the slopes with her brother, but on their way home, they encountered two dogs engaged in a fierce fight. The sickle she was holding provoked them. The dogs thought she was going to harm them, so they turned about to attack Lotus. Her desperate brother stopped them by throwing his basket at them. The dogs then started to come back at him. His sickle was in the basket, so he shouted, "Lotus, cut the dogs. Quick! Cut the dogs. Quick!" Lotus quickly went to his rescue, but she missed the dogs. Instead, she cut her brother on the leg. Blood was gushing out of his leg. She tried to stop it with several handfuls of soil, but it kept gushing out. Later on, one of her brother's legs became lame.

In the summer of the following year, Lotus was married to the man in Nanling. After marriage Lotus seldom visited her parents.

Once when Xiu'er was visiting her parents in Nanling, she saw a noticeable scar the size of a red date right on the cheekbone of Lotus's face. When Xiu'er enquired about it, Lotus said her husband had hit her with a brick. One year later, when Xiu'er went to visit her again at home, she was told that Lotus had become the head of a fruit-processing factory in the town and that she was now busy from morning till night.

"Is her husband still hitting her?" Xiu'er asked.

"He's now one of her employees," the villagers told her. "Everybody knows he's a violent man, but in the end, he has to listen to Lotus. It's called brine touching bean curd: everything has its vanquisher."

Xiu'er breathed a deep sigh.

"Croak, croak, croak." Xiu'er heard the clear croaking of frogs, as she saw the lovely lotus flowers in full bloom on the lake in front of the village.

The Noble Lady

By **Shen** Zulian

Her husband had left her a house, a large sum of money and a car before fleeing China with his young secretary. The wife found little to regret—what did she have to regret, anyway? He had owed more debts than he could ever pay, but he had had more money than he could ever spend. Naturally, fleeing the country was the best choice for him. As for her, though she had lost her husband, she had gained the custody of three sons, living an easy life. In the world she knew, there weren't that many women who were blessed with three sons.

Accordingly, she started to consider herself a noble lady. Just look at her: she visited the beauty parlor once a day; her hair was worn in a bun at the back and a high curve in the front; her ring, necklace, bracelet and earrings were all made of pure gold. Wearing a pair of noisy high-heeled shoes, she looked like an out-and-out arrogant and overbearing woman, as her breathing could almost be heard from heaven, her airs filling the sky. As one could expect, she could not get along with her relatives; nor could she share conversational topics with her friends. And since she did not like playing mahjong, she ended up being a loner, accompanied only by her shadow. Every day she would watch TV and play with her little dog. Luckily, she had a peculiar habit of sightseeing, so when she grew tired at home she would go out to enjoy the scenery. Outdoor activities were easy for her because she owned a car. The moment she gestured, her chauffeur was at her service.

The chauffeur was a tall, strong and simple man who loved his job more than his life. Since he was hired to drive her around, he

254

would follow his lady's lead all day long. Whenever he saw her step out of her house, dressed up with her jewelry on, he would immediately walk over to the car, opening the door with one hand and covering the entrance overhead with the other. Only when his lady had taken her seat would he get in through his own door, start the engine and ask, "Ma'am, where are we going?"

Only then would she tell him where she was going. Usually she uttered only one or two syllables, for example, "Fangcheng," "Beihai," or "Nanning," never telling him one extra word. In the car, she would also say two words only— "Let's go" and "Stop now"— or just one— "Go" and "Stop." When she got to the destination, she would get out of her car without saying anything to him. Her smart driver, though, would wait for her patiently, even if it meant waiting from morning till afternoon. During her absence he would busy himself polishing the car until it was shiny, without a speck of dust. When she got back to the car, he would again open the door for her and protect her head as she got in. Then he would sit still behind the wheel, usually silent. He would start the engine only when she said, "Go." After they returned, he would see her to the mansion, and only when all was safe and sound would he drive the car into the garage then go home himself.

She had given him a pager and would call him whenever she needed him. That is the way the boss used her employee, and nothing out of the ordinary had ever happened between them.

Then there was a morning when the chauffeur, after she got into the car, noticed from his rear-view mirror a faint smile on her face which was a little rosy.

The chauffeur again asked her where she was going.

"Where do you want to go?" she said. "Any place is fine with me. I just feel so bored at home."

"Asking me? Has the sun risen from the west today?" The chauffeur smiled to himself. "How about Dongxing then?" he suggested.

"Up to you." The chauffeur found his lady clearly more talkative than before. When they got to Dongxing, she told him that the border was a bewildering place, so she wanted him to accompany her. Having had a great time, on their way home she also broke the rule by sitting in the front seat next to the chauffeur. Smiling, she would look at his hands on the wheel from time to time, or watch him step on the gas pedal, or stare at his eyes that looked into the distance.

"*Shifu,* * is it difficult to learn to drive?"

"What? You want to drive yourself?"

"Yes. I want to learn. Could you teach me?"

"Doesn't that mean I will lose my job?"

"Take it easy. I've never said I don't want you. You are such a good driver. I'll have you for the rest of my life."

"For the rest of your life!" His jitters made the car shake, causing her to fall onto his right arm.

"I'm sorry, Ma'am. I didn't do that purposely."

"Does it matter even if you did?" She gazed at him with wide-open eyes. How beautiful her eyes were, the surprised chauffeur found!

"I really didn't mean to do it."

Only then did she reluctantly sit up straight.

When she returned home, in the same way, the chauffeur opened the door for her and saw to it that she got out safely. When he was about to drive the car into the garage, she suddenly said, "Could you stay for dinner with me tonight?" She sounded as docile as a domestic cat.

"How could I say no when my lady says yes, but—"

"But what? Can't you just call home and tell them you are still in Dongxing and won't be home tonight?"

Thus, for the first time, he entered her magnificent dining room. When he wanted to go home after dinner, she stopped him by saying,

---

* *Translator's note: Shifu* is a polite term for "driver" in the Chinese language.

"Didn't you say on the phone that you are in Dongxing tonight? Also, I have some more work for you to do."

"Whatever you want me to do, please just tell me."

"I have something to move around in my room. You are strong, so I want you to help me."

"You just need my strength? That's easy." So he followed her into her bedroom. Inside, his eyes popped at the furniture. What a bedroom—he could never have imagined it! The walls, the floor, the bed and the other furniture—everything dazzled his eyes as if he had entered a royal palace. His lady was smiling at him.

"What should I move?"

"This," she pointed at herself. "Come over here."

Understanding what she meant, he shuddered. "Ma'am, you are such a noble lady. I'm just a driver, I dare not."

"What's wrong with being a noble lady? Isn't a noble lady a woman too? You don't like me—" She began to sob. "You don't know how miserable I am."

An impulse backed by bravery that he had never had emboldened him to stride toward her and hold her up in his arms tightly.

Reading of Love

By **Xu** Huifen

It is difficult to control one's life. "Those who are always sick may not necessarily live a short life," a doctor once told me. "A slightly cracked vase, for example, may stay intact if you take care of it. On the other hand, a perfect china bowl may break into pieces if it falls by accident." What happened to him and her confirmed these statements.

After they had lived together for thirty years, despite her near-perfect health, she suddenly died, while he, a long-term patient, lived on. Yesterday, she went to the funeral of an old gentleman who stayed in the same cowshed with her during the Cultural Revolution.* On her way home, she suddenly fell to her death.

He just could not accept the unexpected mishap one way or the other. Kneeling before her, he grasped her bloodless hands and repeated again and again, "We agreed that you would see me off. How could you have gone yourself! How could you have left me behind!" She seemed to have heard him: her dull eyes flashed, and her closed mouth opened, uttering some kind of whispering that sounded like "I am sorry, I am sorry—" The man's wailing was heartbreaking.

Finally, the daughter tore away her father, who had been rooted

---

* *Translator's note:* The "Cultural Revolution" is short for the Great Proletarian Cultural Revolution, which was started in 1966 by Mao Zedong, then chairman of the Communist Party of China; it ended in 1976.

258

to the ground.

After her funeral, he and his daughter started to sort out the things she had left behind. For her different hobbies, she had collected many things, including books, paintings and a stack of stamp albums. Everything he saw recalled his wife: her quiet smile, her soft voice, her occasional mild temper and her rough hands that had been bringing him food and herbal medicine soup; her hands no longer looked the least like those of an well-educated woman's . . . Again, uncontrollable tears started streaming down his cheeks.

He kept fondling the pile of books and notebooks she had used, turning over the pages one by one. Suddenly he found one notebook he was browsing to be a little abnormal. After a careful look, he discovered that the pages inside were glued in pairs along the edges.

Finally, with great care, he separated the pages. Before his eyes emerged more than thirty blue letter sheets, each of which contained long lines mixed with short lines. They were thirty-some love letters a man had sent to a woman. The poet was that old gentleman who had passed away recently. These poems had brought to life a secret love relationship of over twenty years.

He fell into silence as if he had become a statue, with the daughter gently resting her hands on his shoulders. Seeing her grey-haired old father, she spoke chokingly as her hands started trembling, "Daddy, please forgive my mother. She is gone, so be generous and—"

He seemed to have fallen asleep and did not open his eyes until quite a while later. Then he said slowly as he looked at her, "My child, the one who should ask for forgiveness is not your mother, but your father—"

"But my mother has cheated you for so many years after all—" she said in shock and bewilderment.

"Listen to me, my child," he wiped her tears. "Don't use the word 'cheat.' If you cover something up for a day or two, or for a year or two, that is cheating. But you can't call it cheating if it is a matter of over twenty years. Who would have cheated me by sacrificing more than twenty years of life? Don't you agree such cheating is love? My child, I have been a happy man. I have had more than twenty years of your mother's love. If she were alive, I could enjoy much more. But it's a shame that I got to know this too late. I haven't given her a happy life—"

"Daddy! My good daddy!" The daughter's wailing rent the air.

Broken Strings

It's Late

By **Xing** Qingjie

The train had not yet pulled into the station when the nervous man ran onto the platform with the woman he led along. He had just heard from a worker on duty who was holding a walkie-talkie that the train would be late.

"Late again!" said the man, depressed. "Why is it always late?"

It was a small station, with only a row of four or five single-storey rooms. The paint on the walls had mostly peeled off, exposing the bare cement, which made them look almost like abstract oil paintings.

Thirty years had passed, and many changes had taken place around the station. The new dazzling structures, featuring top-grade, well-decorated exterior walls, further humbled the small, shabby old station.

More than ten passengers were patiently waiting for the train. They walked back and forth on the platform.

It was late fall, and the wind was chilly. Pulling up her collar, the woman said to the man, "No. Let's go back. I don't feel comfortable waiting here."

"Take it easy," the man said. "No one will look for you this time. You are not what you were thirty years ago."

"Not anymore," said the woman. "I'm old now."

Thirty years ago, they were both young. They had met in a mass labor campaign of the county, where they fell in love with each other. Nonetheless, the woman's mother wanted to exchange her for a daughter-in-law.* The man had two brothers who were also bachelors. He had neither a sister for the woman's family nor acceptable betrothal gifts for her parents. Needless to say, marriage between the man and the woman did not look very likely, but the man believed none of this. Then he asked the woman to run away from home with him and she agreed after much hesitation.

As planned, they left home for this small station one night. It looked the same thirty years ago, but in the young lovers' eyes, it was a great, strange structure. They were very excited when they met at the station, for they would soon be together and nobody could ever separate them. As agreed, they would flee to his aunt's in Heilongjiang.

The man had enquired about the departure time of the train and had bought two tickets before they had come. They arrived almost at the time the train was supposed to pull into the station. It seemed like a perfect arrangement: soon, they would be in tandem, belonging to each other.

But the train played a cruel joke on them—it was a full hour late.

The woman's family, more than ten members in total, came looking for her as the man and woman were leaning against each other to keep themselves warm. They beat up the man badly, and they tied up the woman with her hands behind her back and carried her back home with the rope looped around her neck.

The injured man had to be carried home by his own family and could not work in the fields for a month. By the time he had recovered, the woman's parents had already married her, through hasty arrangements, to another man.

The man remained unmarried for a few more years until his

---

* *Translator's note:* In rare cases in which a man cannot find a wife for various reasons—such as poverty, unpleasant appearance or the like—his parents may marry his sister to a man who has a sister in exchange for a wife for him. In other words, two men marry each other's sister, creating a double relationship between the two families.

financial situation improved thanks to the individually farmed land he was assigned.* Though he was now a relatively older bachelor approaching thirty, because he was tall and strong, helpful people still came to offer willing women for his consideration. Turning them all down, he surprised the whole world by marrying himself as a "live-in" son-in-law to a woman in another village, which meant living in his parents-in-law's house and allowing his children to carry on his wife's family name. In the countryside, no man would ever want to be a "live-in" son-in-law unless he had no other way out. He would be despised as a good-for-nothing who had lost his family name—a great disgrace to his ancestors. But this man chose to break up with his family and willingly became a "live-in" son-in-law.

People understood him only when they learned later on that the woman he had married lived in the same village as his old sweetheart, Chunping. The villagers started to worry that their love relationship might revive, but for many years it never did. They each had their own children and never started an extramarital affair as feared.

Thirty peaceful years went by in the twinkling of an eye, and both had become old. As it happened, the man's wife died of lung disease and the woman lost her husband in a traffic accident.

After that, when they met on the street again, the glow in their eyes that had disappeared for decades was rekindled. According to generational seniority in the clan,** he should call her "aunt," but in order not to arouse suspicion among the villagers, they had never exchanged a word during the past thirty years or so.

Seizing the last opportunity in life, the man plucked up his courage and set up a date with her, proposing a reunion. After much hesitation, she accepted.

But their love relationship was again fearfully opposed, this time

---

* *Translator's note:* Land used to be cultivated collectively.
** *Translator's note:* A clan is part of a village population that shares the same family name, belonging to the same family tree.

by their own children. It was not because the children were uncivilized, but because the woman was one generation senior to the man. Should they really get married, people would gossip about them.

They fought with their children for more than six months, but failed to change their minds. Then they decided to flee from home again, just as they had thirty years before.

In the distance, the train was hooting, stirring up the passengers on the platform.

Holding her hand, the man said excitedly, "The train is pulling in."

"It is, finally," sighed the woman, glancing at him. "It was late last time, so it has made us late for half of our lives."

No sooner had the train arrived than the woman's son and daughter, daughter-in-law and son-in-law appeared in front of them. They seized her and took her away by force. Before they left the station, her son threw a hostile look at the man—it was a vicious look.

The train dropped off some passengers and picked up some new ones. Then it started moving again, sounding its siren. The man stood still on the platform for a long time, gazing into the distance as the train disappeared, foot-long spittle dangling from his lips. A good while later, he murmured, "This time, I'm late for my whole life!"

From then on, the man came to wait for the train every day, though he never really wanted to board it. He just wanted to find out if it was on time. He would gaze into the distance where the rails came from, anxiously glancing at his watch. The workers at the platform had driven him away dozens of times, but he would always return immediately. In the end, nobody cared about him anymore.

The man had thus turned into a permanent, mobile scenic object on the platform.

Also a Toxic Drink

By **Xie** Zhiqiang

This time I invited him out instead, to a very unattractive restaurant. He who frequented luxurious restaurants asked if I wanted to go to another restaurant. I said no, since we had sat down and I was used to such places.

I knew he thought it was too small and simple to match his social status. We had been separated for six months, and I could see he felt rather awkward. After a long year of battling for a divorce, I finally felt it was time we parted, though I had flatly rejected his idea in the beginning.

He asked me if I had any other conditions. He would accept any condition I would raise. "After all, we have been husband and wife!" He thought financial compensation would entice me to end our relationship. Yes. He had offered me a large sum. I filled both glasses with red wine and raised mine. He thought I was still dreaming of a reunion.

"If you have any other conditions, just let me know," he assured me again. "I don't mind." I had heard those words many times.

"Come on!" I said, raising my glass once more. "We married happily and shall end our relationship happily, too."

Instantly he looked relaxed and said, "Please don't blame me."

"Here, another glass!" It was a dry red, as red as fire, as red as blood. My stomach was burning. We started to help ourselves to the food. He looked me up and down from time to time as if expecting me to say something.

My difficult period was over. I remembered that we had also sat face to face in the same way as we did now when we had started dating. The only difference was that we had had tea instead of wine. During the past six months I had found that the liquid was capable of cleansing worries from my head.

"Let me tell you a story," I suddenly said to him. "Perhaps you haven't heard it yet. It's about wine."

"No, I haven't," he said.

"In that case, you'll more likely find it a strange story, though it's not a new one," I said.

He blinked at me like a child. I laughed and began my story.

"A young man who had graduated from high school answered the call of the government and went to a remote village. Following the local customs, he married a country girl there. Later on, as the trend started, city youths began to return to where they came from. Every other educated young man or woman who had no relatives in the countryside went back to the city, leaving him behind as the father of one. But he missed his home city very much, so he planned secretly for his return home. One day when he was going to visit his relatives in the city, his father-in-law held a farewell dinner for him. At the dinner, he offered him wine. The son-in-law found that it tasted strange when he drank it. When the old man saw him onto the road, he told him that he had to come back within a month. Otherwise, the toxin in the drink would turn lethal and kill him. The son-in-law had drunk toxic wine brewed by the local villagers. Nobody could detoxify it except the brewers themselves."

He gazed at me, wanting to know what happened to the son-in-law. I told him that he returned to the village on time. His father-in-law detoxified it for him at a welcoming dinner. He asked me what happened still later. I said that he forgot about the idea of returning to the city and became an out-and-out villager.

"Come on, drink up the last glass," I said. He hesitated, refusing to lift his glass. I paid the bill, then told him that we could go to get our divorce papers the next day. "But—" he nearly called out.

I rose and said, "That's the way to go."

"Now listen," he said.

"I know it," I said. "We have talked too much already."

"But—"

"Won't you be free then?" I said. "I know you have been waiting for this day."

He called me in the evening and asked if we could postpone it a little bit.

"What's the matter?" I asked him.

"I'm not feeling too well," he said.

"I've never been feeling well," I said.

"But—I've never wanted to harm you," he muttered and mumbled.

The next day, his mistress came to my home to beg me, "He has been suffering from poisoning. Could you go see him?"

"How could it be?" I said. "What has he eaten?"

"You know it," she said. "You drank together."

"We had a dry red. That's what he always enjoys drinking."

"He shows symptoms of poisoning," she said. "A very strong reaction."

"What did the doctor say?" I asked calmly.

"The doctor could not determine the cause," she said. "We beg your help."

"You can check with him yourself. I only told him a story," I said.

"He told me you can save him."

I held up my open hands and said, "I can't. I haven't done anything to him. The trouble is within himself."

Almost one month later, supported by a walking stick, he came to see me.

"We are going now?" I asked.

"Don't talk about that for the time being," he said. "You've got to help me."

"What can I do for you?"

"The story you told me," he said, "You can detoxify me."

"That was just a story." I burst out laughing. "All you drank was wine. That was it. You've been so suspicious yourself, suspecting it was a toxic drink."

Eventually we divorced. I was told that he had quit drinking, but his health deteriorated day by day. She came to me for help several times, fully convinced that he had been poisoned. She retold the story about the toxic drink to me.

"He truly believes it," she said.

"I never knew he was such a weak man."

Farewell Breakup

By **Yan** Chungou

The moment Yiyi got on his motorcycle, her arms would circle his waist tightly. That is how she sat behind him. Then she would scream as the vehicle sped up to full speed.

Today, however, she was quiet. From time to time she would squeeze his stomach as if to test his sincerity. Often, Yiyi would do something out of the ordinary. Once when she saw him yawning as she was going out with him, she simply turned about and returned home, complaining that he was not sincere.

Sincerity was a matter of principle to her, but what has a man's yawning got to do with it?

Anyway, he had got used to her peculiar ways. Sometimes he would just smile, "Look, you just act on your emotions. Aren't you behaving like a child?"

"If I am really like a child and do not grow up, do you still want me then?" she would pout.

"Of course, I do," he would assure her quickly. "If I didn't, wouldn't another man be profiting?"

Their joy in exchanging such banter did not really last long, especially after they had slept together. When he was able to copy the birthmark on her belly without looking at it, their banter occurred no more than once or twice a month, and it would happen only when they were in a good mood.

As a matter of fact, they had been in a cold war for several months. For weeks they had not even called each other. Whenever his phone rang, he thought it was Yiyi, but it never was. Every time he was

270

about to call her, he would hear a voice stopping him: "Don't spoil her. If it continues this way, you will lose all your self-respect."

No man dates a woman for the purpose of losing his self-respect, but men often end up losing self-respect when they date. Whose fault is it? It is the man's.

He thought, "I've had enough! Already like this, even before we get married! What would she be like if we really got married? How could I stand it, if I have to live with her from morning till night for the rest of my life?"

If a man has to hang his head before his wife, how can he raise it in front of his boss? Or before his foes in a competitive society, who would never hesitate to trample him to death?

But she still kept calling him and annoying him every day until about three weeks ago: "Where did you go today? Who did you meet today? What did you talk about? Who paid for the meal? Did you get a ticket from the police?"

Sometimes when he was upset, he would tell her, "You don't know so-and-so, anyway. What's the point of telling you?"

"The point?" she would say. "When I hear more about it, I'll have a better idea. At least I can watch out for you and help you with the crucial issues. You men are always simple-minded. You may be cheated, but you may not even know it yourself."

"Should I suffer you to watch everything I do, I'd be a good-for-nothing!" he thought. "Now you deserve a breakup!"

Yet Yiyi would come over and conquer him by soft tactics afterward. She would talk and talk until his anger melted. When he went her way, whatever he did, she would say smilingly, "That's a good boy!"

But every time, he would regret his weakness deeply. If it continued this way, he could even lose the minimum self-respect of a man!

He had not really made up his mind to break up with her until after the most recent cold war. He thought, "A man has to be decisive if he has to. It will do no good if such a relationship lingers on." This time he gave neither him nor her a second chance.

The motorcycle pulled up at the mountain pass near a slope, a remote place they had frequented. A cool breeze was gusting. They sat quietly in the tree's shade for a long time.

He thought she was going to cry. Her tears were like anesthetics, and he was afraid of them. He was afraid she might plunge into his arms and create a pitiful scene with her trembling shoulders. He was afraid that his heart would soften when he held her in his arms and that they would start all over again.

But she did not cry this time. Instead she said angrily, "Emotionally I have invested so much in you. I miss you day and night. When I have breakfast, I wonder what you eat for yours. When I lie in bed, I wonder if you ever dream of me. Think for yourself, have you got so much feeling for me?"

He thought about it and had to admit that he did not. Men are always careless, though they are covetous. Before he had gone out with her on their early dates, he would only think, "Should I kiss her tonight? Should I make love to her?" Men all want something practical, while women want romance as if they have watched all the touching love stories.

"Give us one last chance, all right?" she suddenly begged him. "If we really cannot get along, I won't insist."

Without giving it a thought, he said resolutely, "When I say no, I mean no." She kept pestering him, sometimes using soft tactics, sometimes hard tactics. She even threatened suicide, but he was not moved. When a man makes up his mind, he can be stonyhearted.

Afterward, he decided to take her back to the city, thinking it was her last ride on his motorcycle.

A thin drizzle was falling. He felt Yiyi's face touching his back, her body trembling. She was sobbing softly. Suddenly, she started pounding on his back, as she clenched her teeth. "Now, you remember how you have treated me! You—"

All of a sudden, she twisted his arm with great force. His motorcycle started swerving to one side. He was just about to brake when it flew off the road, then into a tree on the roadside.

Before he passed out, he saw Yiyi rolling down the slope. She had curled up, looking as if she was determined to roll down the valley. She bumped into a protruding stone and sprang up a little bit. Whenever he thought of this scene afterward, he would agonize as he seemed to feel Yiyi's once live body in his hands. It was a perfect body, gentle and soft.

But more often would he think of her words, "That's a good boy."

It was all right if he wanted to leave her, but why would he have ridden a motorcycle? It was all right if he rode a motorcycle, but why did it rain? All right then. They had an accident, but why was she the one killed?

A Buddhist Convent

By **Ma** Baoshan

There were bamboos over the mountains; they were purple bamboos. There was a convent below the mountains; it was a Buddhist convent.

There were two nuns in the convent: the fifty-year-old mistress and the sixteen-year-old disciple. Every day, they read and recited scriptures, accepting the donations of the limited number of pilgrims and worshippers. They started their morning by striking the bell and ended their afternoon by beating the drum, spending their time in a leisurely way day after day, month after month.

There was a river in front of the convent; by the river stood a thatched cottage. In front of the cottage was a newly opened-up field. A young couple sowed the field in the spring and harvested it in the fall. Time spent its days and months in the happy laughter of the couple.

By the oil lamp, the lonely young nun was often interrupted when she was reading. "A man farms while his woman weaves—isn't it a wonderful life!" she thought.

The young nun often came to the little river for water, so she often met the young couple. As time went by, they got to know one another. On a windy or rainy day, the young couple would carry water into the convent for her. One day, when she came to draw water from the river again, the young couple working in the fields happened to be taking a break by the river, so there came the following interesting dialogue.

"Young mistress, what are you doing in the nunnery every day?" asked the farmer.

"Reading the scriptures, cultivating myself according to the doctrines, praying for my next life—"

"Praying for a happy marriage in your next life?" interrupted the farmer.

"A nun has a pure heart with no desire for such."

"You want to be an important official and make lots of money then?"

"We monks and nuns have a rule: neither money nor power."

"Then you want glory and wealth?"

"We care for a quiet life—tranquility and leisure."

The farmer burst into laughter. "Does it mean you are cultivating yourself so that you will be a little nun again in your next life?"

Now the young nun's eyes were filled with more perplexity. She looked at the chilly convent at the foot of the mountains and heaved a sigh. "I've been cultivating myself," she thought, "but if I'll be a little nun again in my next life, then what do I need to pray for today?"

Gently wiping the tears from her cheeks, she carried her water back to the convent.

On the riverbank, the dialogue between the couple continued, only sounding more bantering.

"If you really have a next life, what do you want?" the man asked.

"Guess," answered the woman.

"Want to be an important official and make lots of money?"

The woman shook her head.

"You want glory and wealth then?"

The woman shook her head again, waving her hands as well.

"Oh, I see," said the man. "For sure, you want to be a quiet nun in your next life."

"What a bad man you are! Bad man. Bad man!" The woman stroked him on the chest with her little fist.

Seizing her hand, he pressed for her answer again, "Tell me, what do you want?"

The woman blushed rosily, saying, "Neither money nor power, neither glory nor wealth, I pray only for a happy marriage in my next life. I want to be your wife again." With this she threw herself into his arms. Soon the playful couple were rolling over the flood land in each other's arms.

The dialogue on the riverbank and the couple's fun playing on the flood land struck a chord in the young nun's heart. No longer could she concentrate on her reading; nor was she serious about cultivating herself now. Seeing that the Buddhist discipline had long left the agitated young nun, the mistress showed her out of the convent.

Having no relatives and friends, the young nun had to stay with the couple who lived in the cottage on the riverbank. They did not call her a young nun anymore. Instead, they called her "Nunny." Following the young couple, Nunny started farming at sunrise and did not stop until sunset. The farmers' simple food and plain tea turned her into a more healthy and charming girl. Elegant, beautiful hair gradually grew on her head. Now she had really become a beauty.

Naturally, a woman who has resumed secular life will have an ordinary person's feelings. With an ordinary person's feelings, a woman will create ordinary people's stories. People's stories are more or less the same, so I will not waste time telling them here. To cut it short, there came a day when the bright sun was shining on the earth, when happy fish were swimming in the river, when the birds were singing sweetly on the trees. The landlady of the cottage, who had just been to the marketplace, returned home with her salt. "Good heavens!" she screamed as she entered her cottage, and there followed a burst of crying. The crying accompanied an almost mad woman staggering all the way to the river. She wanted to kill herself by jumping into the river, but it was too shallow. She then staggered up the cliff. She wanted to jump down, but it was not high enough. Instead she ran straight to the convent at the foot of the mountains.

By the oil lamp, the old nun who had been rather lonely for some time wanted to know at once what the woman she was seeing wanted for her present life and her next life. "Do you intend to stay in my convent temporarily or permanently, Miss?"

"Permanently, Mistress. Please take me as your disciple."

"Do you want to be a nun so that you can be an important official and make lots of money?"

The woman shook her head.

"You want glory and wealth then?"

The woman shook her head again.

"You want a happy marriage in your next life then?" No sooner had the nun finished her last word than bitter tears began to roll down the woman's cheeks.

There were bamboos over the mountains; they were purple bamboos. There was a convent below the mountains; it was a Buddhist convent. There were two nuns in the convent: an old nun and a young nun who had just arrived. Every day, they read and recited scriptures, praying for their next life . . .

Bread and Roses

By **Liu** Guofang

At that time, Yi was yearning for a bunch of roses from somebody. Roses symbolized love, so what she really longed for was the arrival of love. On Valentine's Day that year she really got a bunch of roses from Ping.

Knowing it meant love for her, Yi was very excited and almost shed tears. Ping read the excitement on her face, and asked, "Do you like them?"

"Yes, I do," she answered.

"From now on, I'll send you a bunch of roses on Valentine's Day every year."

"Can you keep your promise?"

"Yes, I can."

Yi was in love now. For more than six months they frequently appeared by the water on the riverbank, amid flowers and in the moonlight. That bunch of roses indeed had started a romantic love relationship for her.

However, good times do not last long enough. Six months later Ping went abroad. Yi looked worried and gloomy when she was seeing him off at the airport.

"Cheer up," Ping comforted her. "Though I'll be abroad, we are still together."

"How can we be together when you are abroad?" she said.

"Our love has no boundaries. It travels across all mountains and oceans."

Yi gave a listless smile.

In the first few months, Ping called her whenever she missed him. Then she would feel so excited, seeming to see him in front of her. Soon came the first Valentine's Day after Ping's departure. When her doorbell rang early in the morning, she opened her door to see a bunch of fresh roses before her eyes.

Like the first time, she was so excited that she almost cried.

"Have you received my roses?" Ping asked when he called soon after.

She nodded and said, "Yes. But you are abroad now. How did you still remember to send me roses?"

"I promised you that I would send you roses on Valentine's Day every year."

"I'm really touched. Thank you!" said Yi.

She put the roses in a vase, changing the water every day. Under her loving care, they bloomed for a long time. Ping called her several times after that, and each time she would tell him, "Our roses are still blooming."

"I see," said Ping.

"Do you smell the sweet roses?" she asked.

"Yes, I do," he said.

Yi smelled them herself, and found the fragrance in her home for the rest of the year.

Then Valentine's Day came again, and another bunch of roses was presented to her. Yi was still very excited. "Thank you for sending me roses again," she said to Ping when he called her afterward. She held them close to her face.

Three years had passed and Ping was supposed to return home, but he did not. Now she could only think of him. Then one day, while missing him, she suddenly felt that her love was far too remote.

When the next Valentine's Day arrived and when Ping had another bunch of roses delivered to her again, she was not excited anymore. She gazed at them as if in a trance.

When Ping called her afterward, she told him, "I don't want roses.

I want you back."

Ping did not come back, and he called less often now. Yi had not heard from him for a long time and simply forgot about him. Now she not only found her love too distant, she felt as if nothing had happened.

When she received roses that symbolized love from Ping on the following Valentine's Day, she was angry. "Why are you still sending me roses?" she shouted when he called her afterward.

"That's my promise," said Ping.

"I don't want any more."

After this, Ping called no more, and Yi seldom thought of him. There was no more love between them, and Yi felt Ping was not even like a real person in her memory now.

The only real thing was that bunch of roses on Valentine's Day. On the fifth lovers' day after he left her, Yi shouted angrily at the girl who knocked on her door, "Don't you ever come to bother me again!"

"You shouldn't say this to me, Miss," said the girl.

Yi thought the girl was right: "I should tell Ping instead." She decided to tell him exactly that when he called her later on, but he never did.

Yi lost her job that year and was struggling to make both ends meet, so she forgot about Ping altogether.

Then another unexpected Valentine's Day came, and again somebody knocked on her door and brought her a bunch of roses. Yi didn't even say a word this time. She simply threw them at the corner of the room after she received them, but immediately she picked them up. It was a very big bunch, which contained more than twenty roses, as she counted. "These roses must be pretty expensive," she said to herself.

Soon afterward she ran downstairs with the flowers. In the street she found many people of her sex carrying roses like she did. Whenever they saw a man, they would say, "Sir, do you want to buy a bunch of roses?" Yi followed suit, but every man she asked would shake his head and say no.

Finally Yi came to the man who was selling bread and said, "Sir, do you want some roses?"

"No," he said.

"I'll sell them to you cheap," she said.

"No," he said. "Not even if they are cheap."

"I could give them to you for two buns if you like. This is a big bunch. It's very expensive."

The man said nothing. Only then did she realize the real value of her roses. Gritting her teeth, she trampled on the roses.

May and Her Husband

By **Cao** Duoyong

May used to work in the same office as her husband, Xiang, but she was laid off two months ago. While Xiang still kept his job, they found it hard to make ends meet because he had hardly been paid lately. They had to eat three meals a day and they also had a child at school, and everything cost money.

It took the honest, decent May much determination to make this decision.

Only when she went to the job interview did she realize that many people were competing for the job. They were all girls around twenty years old, unlike her, who was approaching the threshold of thirty. Unexpectedly, she was hired as a Miss Entertainer in the Song and Dance Hall, or SD Hall.

May was not a beautiful woman, but she was tall, which gave her an extra advantage. Besides her height, she had no idea what other advantage her boss had found in her. He was a man of over fifty years old who did not speak much, but two invisible hands seemed to have stretched out of his pale yellow eyes measuring her body parts from head to foot. May felt his eyes were taking off her clothes one by one, so she could not help clutching her shoulders and trembling. Her boss narrowed his eyes into a smile which she felt like a stringy thorn.

"May," he said, "you may come to work tomorrow."

May breathed a breath of relief and turned round.

"Don't wear too much clothing when you come to work, May," he added before she left.

When May returned home that day, she burst into tears, crying out her grievances. However, when she dried her tears, she still decided to work as a Miss Entertainer.

The Miss Entertainers all worked at night, but the SD Hall required them to be there at 5:30 p.m. They were responsible for cleaning and decorating the dance hall as well. May started to prepare herself for her first day well ahead of time. She touched up her eyebrows, powdered her face, set her hair, and so on, until she could not recognize her own face and head. She knew that in the SD Hall it was a woman's youth that would sell. As best she could, being a Miss Entertainer, she had to demonstrate whatever youth she still had by showing it on her face, her head and the different essential body parts. She began to wonder whether to wear a long skirt or a short one. May knew that in such a place, a short skirt was more attractive than a long one, but she did not want to be too attractive. At least, she was not quite comfortable wearing a miniskirt for the first day of work, yet the SD Hall owner's eyes that could almost touch her like two hands seemed to be drifting before her all the time. May thought, "Men who go to the SD Hall must be the same as its owner. If they don't have hands in their eyes, why would they go there, anyway?" Somehow, she felt a chill in her heart.

May was still home when Xiang returned from work at six o'clock. He was shocked to see his richly attired and heavily made-up wife. May, dressed in the latest fashion, showing a delicate body with a beautiful face, threw herself into Xiang's arms, saying, "I don't feel at ease when I go to such a place."

"Don't go then," he said. "We live a poor life in a poor couple's way. You won't starve to death, anyway."

Now May was so excited that she began stripping herself and said, "That's why I've been waiting till you are home from work. Here I am, giving my real solid self to you again."

Xiang asked if she still wanted to go to the SD Hall, and she nodded.

That night, May returned home around 10:30. Xiang had been awake waiting for her. No drinker or smoker, he found the odors of smoking and alcohol disgusting. May came in with both odors.

"Did you drink?" he asked her anxiously.

May shook her head.

"Did you smoke?"

She shook her head again, but Xiang did not believe her.

"Come, let me smell your breath," he said. May really came over with an open mouth. The odors did not come from her breath, but from her clothes. Only after she took a bath did she join Xiang in bed.

"Do I look like a woman who smokes and drinks?" she asked him, sounding a little hurt.

In the bright morning, May wore her casual clothing without makeup. She went to the market for her groceries, then returned home and cooked lunch as usual. She also did the laundry and mopped the floor. Her morning passed quickly.

After lunch, she took a long nap. Anyone working in the SD Hall needed it. Otherwise they would collapse, for they all had to stay up late, night after night.

At almost five o'clock in the afternoon, May got up and began to dress and put on makeup, regaining her lost spirit bit by bit. Then she went to the SD Hall, well before Xiang returned, and again did not come home until late at night. Like before, Xiang lay in bed waiting for her.

That night, when May returned home, she went straight to the washroom and took her bath before she entered the bedroom with a steamy body.

"I have told you not to wait for me. Just sleep by yourself," May said in a blaming tone.

"How could I sleep without you in my arms!" he said in the same tone.

Though she had had her bath, she still smelt of smoke and alcohol.

"This time, you really smoked and drank," said Xiang.

"Manager Qian of Everbooming Company said he would give me one hundred yuan for each cigarette I smoked and two hundred yuan for every cup of wine I drank. I dug two thousand yuan from his pocket tonight."

May had surely drunk a lot that night, for she fell asleep before she could even finish her talking.

But Xiang could not sleep that night.

Now that May had lots of money, she found ways to spend it. During the day, she went to buy the latest fashions and cosmetics. She also went window shopping with a group of "little sisters." In short, she did not do her usual grocery shopping, cooking and laundry anymore. Since she did not prepare lunch for Xiang, she took him to a small restaurant and they ate out instead. Xiang went with her all right, but he just could not enjoy the restaurant food, one way or the other.

That night Xiang suffered from insomnia. It was one o'clock in the morning, but May had not come home yet. "It won't do if she goes on this way," he said to himself. "I need to talk it all over with her tomorrow."

A Relationship Long Broken

By **Yu** Rui

Finally, they buried the hatchet and reunited. This was directly attributed to the mediation of their helpful and sincere neighbors, friends, relatives, administrators and colleagues. It was with painstaking effort and out of obligation that the couple mended the "snapped lute string."

Suddenly, they became exceptionally polite to each other. For the first time, courteous terms, such as "please," "excuse me" and "thank you," which were just being promoted in society, found their way into the newly restored relationship. When the man came home with his rice and coal from the market, the woman would walk up to express her appreciation: "What a load you have there. Now do take a rest!" With this, she would make him a cup of tea.

"Thank you!" he would say as he received his tea politely.

If the woman splashed a few drops of water on the man when she was hanging up her clothes to dry, or if the man touched the woman's legs when he was moving the chairs, the former would say "Sorry," while the latter would immediately say "Never mind." When one finished work a bit late, upon returning home he or she would say to the other, "I'm really sorry. I was delayed at work."

Every morning, both would offer to buy the groceries. When they returned home from work, both would fight to do the cooking. After dinner, they would fight to do the washing up. They spoke very little at home, and they would think twice if they ever said something lest it be misinterpreted or rouse suspicion. The last thing they liked was touching their old wound.

Once the man misspoke: "Pork is getting increasingly expensive. We common people can hardly afford it now." He had no sooner said it than he started to regret it to himself— "Could she have mistaken it as a message of blaming her for buying too much pork?" Thus, he immediately explained in a sincere tone, "Anyway, whatever we need to eat we must eat. Health is most important."

Indeed, the next day, she only bought a few common types of vegetables, and no pork at all. The following day he offered to do the grocery shopping, bringing home over five pounds of lean pork.

"What for, anyway?" she laughed bitterly when she saw it.

After dinner he would ask her, "Should we go for a walk?"

"Great," she would answer. So they would walk out smilingly, but would soon return home. In fact, he preferred to walk by himself since he had a habit of pondering on things in his leisure walking, but out of courtesy and as a rule, he had to show her he really loved that she go when he invited her. As for her, she did not like walking at all. She was in the habit of staying home by herself. She chose peace and quiet before anything else, but also, out of courtesy and as a rule, she had to show him she really loved to go when she happily accepted his invitation.

Neighbors, friends, relatives, administrators and colleagues began to praise them for their fine qualities, noble sentiments and lofty ideals, never forgetting to mention the important roles they themselves had played in the couple's reunion. Soon after, as instructed by his boss, the secretary of the husband's department prepared a lengthy report of ten thousand words entitled, "How We Have Succeeded in Educating Our Staff Members and Their Families in Political and Ideological Aspects." Two hundred copies were printed and distributed to all the offices under its administration. Copies were also submitted to the upper municipal administrators, including the Department of Public Communications, the Women's Association, the Workers' Union, the Family Planning Committee, the Five-Four-Three Office and the Lecturing Group.

Not long after that, an administrator of the wife's department, in the shyest manner, told a general staff meeting about her valuable experience in changing the minds of the originally separated couple. Soon after, reporters from newspapers, radio stations and TV stations swarmed in, forcing the couple to tell them, again and again, how they had managed to turn a broken relationship into a happy reunion. They wanted to know what books and documents they had read, what useful reports they had heard, what uplifting influence they had received, and so on. Finally, the Women's Association, the Labor Union, the Lecturing Group and the Five-Four-Three Office jointly awarded them a "Five-Good Family" certificate.

The couple was noticeably losing weight, showing signs of poor health. They felt bored, depressed and suppressed—life was agonizing. They seemed like two strange but polite guests living in the same hotel, who would exchange pleasantries and give each other precedence, all for courtesy's sake. Each was living a weird life for the other: they could not do what they wanted to do or say what they wanted to say. They felt they were so hypocritical and wretched, playing a sickening tragic role in life.

Actually, they had cautiously been protecting their once-broken lute string. They were scared all day long that any accident would cause it to snap again. After all, because of its severe old wound, it was so weak and fragile. Covered with traces of old age, and never really durable or healthy, its muscles had been eroded badly by the days that had elapsed. It just could not stand another blow, not even the slightest one. The fact of the matter is, it was not the same string—it could not produce the same sounds anymore.

Eventually there came a day when he could not endure it any longer.

"Our life is really too tiresome, just too tiresome!" he said to her.

"Yes, it is." She nodded.

"Should we divorce then?"

"I've wanted to ask you the same question for a long time but was afraid you might feel hurt." She sighed deeply. "The string will snap again sooner or later, anyway."

On the third day, they were all smiles as they went to the neighborhood committee for their papers. The old lady in the office turned ghastly pale when she learned about the purpose of their visit, and said, "You both return home now. We have to study your request carefully. It also requires the approval of the upper level."

The following day, before they could get out of their door for their daily activities, neighbors, friends, relatives, administrators and colleagues, group after group, streamed into their home to persuade them to stay together. From six o'clock in the morning until twelve-thirty at night, with stiff smiles on their faces, the couple received thirty-two kind-hearted visitors.

On the fourth day, when they heard the first knock on the door early in the morning, they shouted to the visitor from behind the plank door, "Please go back. We won't divorce anymore!"

On the Lovers' Island

By **Liu** Wei

There is a clear river in the eastern suburbs of Xiaocheng, a small town. It is wide, and shallow, when the tide ebbs. On the other side of the river lies a small island covered with sand, weeping willows and unknown purple wildflowers. On summer days, lovers from town often trudge across the river, dating in the shade of the willows. For this, the island has been named Lovers' Island.

It was raining when Dayuan and Chunzi crossed the river—they had picked a rainy day for privacy.

Dayuan and Chunzi used to frequent the island, but they had not come for quite some time. For Dayuan had been feeling despair lately: he had contracted AIDS through a blood transfusion after a near-fatal traffic accident a year ago.

It kept pouring—perhaps they had watched the weather forecast on TV.

They came to the gourd shack on the southern part of the island. On the ground inside the shack was a shakedown made of straw. That was the "Garden of Eden" where they would make love, and where they would end their lives.

They had brought several bottles of whiskey, some canned food and a new type of rat poison. Separated by the heavy rain from the annoying outside world, the eager lovers stripped themselves. They twisted in each other's arms, clinging to each other's body like two naked snakes.

Time passed, and they had forgotten whether it was day or night. The rain did not stop until probably the third morning. That was when

290

they would stop their final madness as they had previously planned.

A ray of sunlight burst through the heavy dark clouds, looking fatigued and distressed. Chunzi got up, put on her clothes, then came to the little spring. Squatting down, she washed her face with care, tidied up her hair and flicked the straw fragments off herself. Then she took out her lipstick. She was so calm, looking as if she were doing her routine makeup before going shopping.

When she returned to the shack, she picked up the bottle within reach and sat facing Dayuan. She was gazing at him; he was also holding a bottle.

An unknown amount of time passed. Tears were oozing out of the corners of Chunzi's eyes.

"Let's drink it!" Dayuan howled mournfully.

Chunzi raised her head and drank up her bottle.

Somehow, Dayuan hesitated a little. It seemed as if he would not be at ease until he had seen her drink it up.

Chunzi's visible agony started to disappear as her body temperature gradually dropped. Over his shoulder, Dayuan glanced at the town bathed in the sun on the other side. His hands started trembling. He raised his bottle, then put it down. After putting it down, he raised it again. Suddenly, he threw away the bottle and screamed with terror, "Help!"

Dropping Chunzi's cold hands, he shot toward the riverbank. He failed to see the rapidly rising water and was soon lost in the roaring waves.

From their will, people learned that they had died for love. In fact, Chunzi had also been suffering in the past year. The year before, she had been sexually assaulted by her manager, and she had recently been tested HIV-positive. The two lovers not only had lost their jobs, but also their relatives and friends, who all abandoned them as if to avoid a plague. With no income or medical care, they had fallen into the abyss of desperation. To aggravate their pains, each believed he or she had infected the other with the deadly virus. Finally, they decided to die a happy death rather than live a painful life.

Lovers who visit the island often become quite emotional when they talk about their tragic story. Some girls even shed tears. Yet there is something they never understand: why didn't the lovers die in each other's arms?

The island is silent.

Yours Forever

By **Chung** Ling

The north wind was biting the old gentleman Mr. Shi's throat like needles, so he quickly buttoned up the collar of his blue cotton-padded coat. Mr. Shi went into the janitor's closet in the park, brought out his broom and bamboo dustbin, then walked over to the swing. He was about to sweep the leaves on the ground when he suddenly opened his eyes wide. He was surprised when he saw a mysterious object lying on the bench ahead of him.

"What's that weird thing on the bench?" he said. "A big black bag? But who's left it there? How come there's such a huge bag?" Only when he gazed at it did he recognize a human head on top of the large bag—it was a man's head with short black hair.

"Indeed, old age comes with bad eyes," he thought. "Definitely it's two lovers wrapped in the man's black overcoat. The park is a place for lovers, but I've never seen two dating at 8:30 in the morning, under the dark clouds, in the biting wind.

"That little world must be nice and warm inside." Somehow the old man thought of his old wife's plump body under his own quilt, but she had gone, for two years already. Broom and dustbin in hand, he turned about and started walking away from the lovers. "I'd better leave them alone."

Mr. Shi, instead, went to another corner of the park and started sweeping the ditch there. Covering the clear, shallow ditch were piles and piles of dark yellow leaves and orange leaves. He stopped at a spot where he saw paper fragments scattered all around, including an ID card crumpled into a ball and business cards torn into pieces.

"It must be someone who has cleaned out their wallet." He swept them away at a stroke, his broom bringing up a photograph. The photograph then flew back onto the clear ditchwater with a face smiling at him. It was a small black-and-white picture of a girl. He picked it up and found it had turned yellowish. It showed a girl with delicate features and with shoulder-length hair. Mr. Shi looked at the reverse and found the following words:

> *My dearest Guocai:*
> *It's yours forever!*
> > *Yours,*
> > *Liyun*
> *On this day of this month of this year.*

An invisible smile emerged from the curved corners of his mouth as the photograph fell drifting onto the huge pile of fallen leaves inside the ditch.

Red Scarf

By **Chen** Yonglin

After showing a day of despotic power, the exhausted sun dragging along its crippled legs gradually fell into the Poyang Lake. The lake immediately became a busy place.

The originally azure lake water was dyed with various colors: red, white, yellow and purple. In the lake there seemed to be red fish flying, white sheep running and yellow dogs jumping, with purple flowers bursting into bloom. Hovering over the lake was a flock of waterbirds looking for food, quacking like ducks. Occasionally one of them would dive into the water, soon emerge with a fish in its beak, then fly away.

The lake water, which felt pain, was groaning quietly, but before long it became peaceful and smooth as a mirror again.

A middle-aged man of dark complexion was walking toward the lakeshore with a hunting rifle. The sunset glow that had shrouded him dyed him dark purple and made him shine.

Treading on the wildflowers along the way, he left a string of large footprints of even depth on the shore. The footprints were filled with the fragrance of the wildflowers in various colors found in the thick green weeds around the lake.

His face looked like that of a sculpture that showed no emotion, so no one could tell whether he was sorry or sad, merry or mad.

Flying over the man's head was flight after flight of little birds, now tired after their search for food, that were returning home, chirping joyously. From the distance came dog barks; wisps of cooking smoke rose from a boat with a bamboo awning anchored in the middle of the lake. It was a hazy view that caused fatigue.

The man lay prostrate on the cogongrass, his sharp eyes like those of an eagle penetrating the waterweeds. A sudden sparkle flashed in his eyes: he had caught sight of two snow-white swans. Without a speck of another color, the swans were so white that they flickered and hurt his eyes, starting a current of warmth inside his heart. That's called touching.

Using their bills, the two white swans were preening each other's neck feathers. He held his breath, as he lay still there, the cogongrass blades rubbing his face like saw teeth. He felt pain, but he dared not move for fear he would scare the swans away.

The wind was blowing; the clouds were floating; the man was waiting. He wanted to kill the two birds with one bullet. It was now illegal to hunt white swans, which had caused the price of white swans to rocket. Each bird could be sold to the restaurant for two hundred yuan.

Before long one swan climbed onto the back of the other, both honking gaily, shaking the cogongrass violently around them.

The sky was beautiful; the water was clear; the wind was soft. The swans indulged themselves in the pleasant joy, unaware that a rifle was being aimed at them.

"Okay, I'll make your happy day!" the man cursed in hostility. He was reminded of his wife who had died many years ago. They used to be as wild as the swans, groaning with joy, but that belonged to the remote past. His finger on the trigger shook a little, then he closed his eyes and squeezed it. An enormous bang was heard.

Clusters of white feathers floated in the air.

The other birds on the lake all chirped in fear and flew away instantly. Only the reckless dogs in the distance kept barking at the bang of the shooting. The barking started with one dog, then the rest that did not know what had happened got scared and just joined in.

The man picked up the badly mangled bodies of the two swans and dumped them into his bag. Then he seemed to see somebody lying in the cogongrass. Walking closer, he found a dying woman whose face was tightly wrapped in a scarf red as fire. He found his legs too weak to support him, so he threw himself on the ground. It was the daughter he had raised, as a father and a mother, through aches and pains!

"Wake up, my child! You have my consent to marry him any time you like!" Holding her in his arms, he wailed in desperation; his howling penetrated the silence over the lake.

The sun had completely sunk into the lake, turning the sky and the earth into darkness. The heavy evening mist had now risen from the water, shrouding everything like a net.

Confessing or Attesting

By **Xing** Qingjie

The moment the light in the upstairs room in the opposite building went off, Qiao Zi said to himself, "It's time!"

He pushed the firing button, and off went the signal of the pager number which he had pre-saved.

Qiao shut the washroom window quickly, and hurried back to the living room, where several people were waiting for him to play mahjong. "Why did it take you so long to go to the washroom?" they all complained.

"Sorry," smiled Qiao. "I've been having some stomach trouble recently."

Boom! A deafening explosion shocked everybody in the house. Stupefied, they crowded toward the window, with Qiao among them, seeing the room in the building opposite them engulfed in flames.

Qiao was sure that the two people inside were killed. He knew that five kilograms of explosives was powerful enough to destroy everything there.

"God! Isn't that Hao Xin and Yue Xiaoshan's home? How come it has been blown up?"

"What caused the explosion?"

"Call the police at once!"

Immediately the living room fell into a state of chaos.

Hao and Yue were newlyweds, but Hao was Qiao's number-one enemy in life, for the bride used to be Qiao's girlfriend.

Qiao's hatred for Hao started from the first day they met. That day, when Qiao and his classmate and girlfriend Yue came to report for duty at the division office, they bumped into Hao, who had also come to report for duty. All three were assigned jobs in the same section. After they introduced themselves to each other, Qiao's girlfriend told him, "What a handsome and strapping man Hao Xin is!"

"Mm—" said Qiao, somewhat ill at ease, leaving her by herself.

As it turned out, Hao was a warm-hearted and open-minded person who soon became quite popular among his colleagues, who all thought well of him. Qiao, being an unsociable and eccentric man of few words, became a stark contrast to him. The hardest for Qiao to swallow was that even his girlfriend got mixed up with Hao. When she was with Qiao alone, she would always mention the hows and whats about Hao. Steadily, it led to an escalation of Qiao's jealousy and hatred of Hao.

Qiao then made up his mind to outdo his opponent—what a moment of pride and elation that would be! He thought his day would come soon, for their section director had just retired and the assistant director had filled his post, leaving vacant the position of assistant director.

Qiao was determined to seize the position by hook or by crook. On one hand, he asked his cousin who worked in the municipality to recommend him to the division director. On the other hand, he spent all his savings buying expensive gifts for the section director and the upper division director. Not long after that, somehow news mysteriously started to spread that the division was going to promote Qiao to assistant section director. Half jokingly, a few colleagues started calling him "Director Qiao." Though he said, "Don't tease me!" he was very pleased, saying to himself, "When I become the assistant director, I shall settle with this guy Hao Xin!"

The appointment soon came, but the job was for Hao, not Qiao.

That was just too much for Qiao. When he heard people in the office call his opponent "Director Hao" and ask him for a free dinner party, Qiao felt his heart aching as if pricked by bristles.

Blessings may not come in pairs, and mishaps do not come singly. Qiao's girlfriend decided to break up with him and was soon seen in tandem with Hao.

Qiao felt he could not stay in the same office anymore. Whenever he came to work, he always felt contemptuous and despising eyes staring at him. How he wished to sink through the floor!

On one of those torturing days in his life, Qiao quarreled over a trifle with another colleague, called Zhu. Seizing a target to vent his rage on, Qiao grabbed a paper knife from the desk and was about to attack Zhu but was finally subdued by his other colleagues.

"What a great man you are," cursed Zhu, "to have both your position of assistant director and your woman stolen by the same man! Nothing but a good-for-nothing!"

These words hit home. Qiao collapsed into the chair, instantly making up his mind to revenge himself on Hao. Now, he would not be a bloodless good-for-nothing any longer!

Soon Hao and his new girlfriend announced that they were getting married. That being the last straw, Qiao worked out a plan to retaliate.

Qiao, who used to study electronics and who had got the idea from the TV show *Immediate Chase,* spent a whole night turning his pager into an igniter. All he needed was a push on the button and the explosives would be ignited. The next morning he bought a pre-paid card from the post office which did not require any ID card, so whoever used it could never be found.

Mixed with his colleagues, the well-wishers at Hao and Yue's wedding party, Qiao secretly hid among the huge pile of wedding presents five kilograms of explosives carefully wrapped up as a gift parcel.

The deaths of the bride and bridegroom shocked the whole town. The police immediately started to investigate the case, but the explosion had destroyed everything in the home, leaving no useful clue for them. As their investigation progressed, the police officers learned about the feud between Qiao and Hao, so they summoned

Qiao for an interview. But Qiao had four "mahjong friends" who witnessed that he was home when the explosion took place. Also, the police found no proof that could point to Qiao's involvement in the blast, so they gave him up.

When Qiao returned to work, he found his colleagues talking about something excitedly, but they all stopped as soon as he stepped in. Yet he still overheard the last words: "I thought it was Qiao who did it, but it wasn't him after all." "I knew he didn't have the guts!" In the days to come, the mysterious explosion became the central conversation topic in the office. Everybody said the bomber was so smart to outwit the police. Qiao sat on one side away from his colleagues, as if he had nothing to do with the killings which he had contrived all by himself. This feeling soon dragged him out of the sweet pleasure of revenge, so gradually he grew gloomy. "I've avenged myself, and I've done such a beautiful job," he thought, "that none of my colleagues will ever know it. They even think I'm incapable of doing it. Doesn't my revenge mean no revenge then? In the eyes of my colleagues, I am still a double loser to Hao, both politically and in love affairs." This thinking had stubbornly clung to his mind, and could neither be dispelled nor shaken off. It soon turned into a horrific whirlpool that drew him in mercilessly. All of a sudden, Qiao shouted in a frenzy, "It was me who blew Hao to death!"

The whole office was first stunned, then burst into laughter. "What a capable man you are! Now, just look at yourself!" The dull-eyed man walked out of the office and did not come to work the next day.

On the third day, he finally surrendered to the police.

Qiao was sentenced to capital punishment. When the judge asked him if he had any request before his execution, Qiao said he wished to see his colleagues for the last time. Because he had surrendered himself and confessed, his request was approved.

On his day of execution, standing in front of his colleagues, his head shaven, Qiao just said, "It was me who killed Hao. Don't you believe me now?"

Love Bubbles

Lovers and Drugs

By **Ling** Dingnian

Three years ago, Cuihua met Alan Daron II when she was the owner of a restaurant. She admitted that it was his manliness and his boss-like airs that obsessed her. The problem was that Alan had plenty of girls around him, so he never really appreciated her sincere feelings for him. Cuihua racked her brains for ways to win his heart.

Then came the day when she heard about his going, for the second time, to the Drug Addiction Rehabilitation Center. Seizing the opportunity, she moved in with him.

It was the head nurse, a more alert worker, who was on duty that night. At midnight she heard strange croaking outside. After three croaks, she saw signals of a flashlight flashing from Alan's ward on the third floor. So she immediately informed the guards, who then seized a tiny flower basket Alan had pulled up from outside the window. In the little basket tied to a string, there were three grams of white powder wrapped in a piece of paper. Scribbled on the paper were the following words by Cuihua:

Loving you, missing you, kissing you.
Willing to do anything for you.
Cui

Perhaps she thought that was not sufficient to express her true feelings, so she had sealed it with a red kiss underneath.

Thus, Alan fell in love with Cuihua. Unfortunately, they had too little intimate time for each other. Whenever Alan craved a smoke, he lost interest in everything else. "No matter how beautiful a woman is, she won't interest me in bed even if she offers herself to me," he said. "I'd rather have a smoke instead."

In the beginning, Cuihua really meant to help him quit drugs by loving him, but then, when she could not bear to see his unendurable sufferings caused by his cravings, she would run out to buy some for him.

Like a bottomless hole, he soon smoked away all her 100,000 yuan of savings.

What she could not understand was how come such a strong man could not quit his addiction. She just would not believe it one way or the other. So she decided to set an example for him—to show him how she could quit it herself. Thus, she had her first smoke; it made her feel nauseated. She felt uncomfortable everywhere. When she had her second try, she felt like riding on the clouds, as if she was a happy celestial being. After her third smoke, she was hooked—there was no way she could quit now.

Within three years—just three years—her addiction had cost her everything she had. She had sold her restaurant, her car, her jewelry, worth 1.5 million yuan in all, and she had used up every penny. Her arms covered with needle holes, she looked a very unhealthy, fragile girl.

"Alan is dead now," she laughed bitterly. "It's like a nightmare. It's horrifying. Just horrifying!"

"Morning comes after a nightmare," I said, suddenly remembering that this was the name of a movie. I did not know whether I meant to comfort her or to encourage her to live.

"How miserably I regret all this! How stupid I have been!" she said tearfully.

"What do you regret? In what ways have you been stupid?" I pressed for a clear answer.

She burst out crying, wailing heartbrokenly, unwilling to utter another word.

Love's Retaliation

By **Bai Xiaoyi**

Nie Lu's wife called, so he left the meeting room at once. Cellphone in hand, he dashed to the corridor, where he started talking with her.

"Come home at once. Immediately. Right now!" she insisted in a commanding tone.

"What happened again?" he asked as he felt a chill on his back.

"Nothing. Just relax! You'll know when you come back. It's a great thing for you!"

With no time to guess, Nie rushed straight home. He even forgot to tell anybody at the meeting. Neither he nor his wife could stand another trauma since the ordeal of their daughter. Sitting in the taxi, he could not help imagining whatever might have happened again.

Luckily there was no traffic jam, so it took only ten minutes to get home.

His wife looked serious but somewhat mysterious when she opened the door for him. She dragged him in, closed the door and bolted it heedlessly.

"What's going on?" asked Nie, surprised.

Again, she said nothing. Hushing him in a mysterious manner, she led him to the bedroom by his hand.

Nie's first guess was she wanted to make love with him, but they had been married for so many years, after all. How could she have such a sexual desire that had to be satisfied in such a hurry? Before he could figure it out, he found himself already in the bedroom. He was astounded at the sight of a naked young woman lying across the bed. The woman was motionless. Only the rhythmical rising and

305

falling of her breasts showed that what he saw was not a corpse.

Nie was stupefied.

"Come on! What are you waiting for?" His wife gave him a push.

Nie had been well aroused, but not to the extent of having lost his wisdom.

"Where is this—this—from?" he stammered. "What on earth is going on?"

"She is that notorious gangster's daughter!"

"Ah!" Nie uttered in surprise.

"I tricked her into coming here. Then I drugged her. I want her father to know what it is like to have his daughter raped."

Nie Lu was speechless, his eyes wide open.

"Come on. Get on her now! What are you staring at? Are you a man or not? Don't you have blood in you?"

Finally, he seemed to have found a good reason for himself. He made up his mind and moved closer to her. He was slow, hoping his wife would leave him alone to finish the job, but his wife grew impatient at his slow move, so she unbuckled the belt for him before he did it himself.

"Let me do it myself—let me—" he said haltingly.

His wife stopped, stared at him angrily and said, "Do you want to have a good time with her? It is revenge! Don't forget what you are doing!"

Nie's face reddened. He did not want to argue with her, but he suddenly found his sex drive all gone.

His wife, who had just unbuckled his pants, also discovered the same problem, so she tried to arouse him herself.

After a long, silent attempt, she could not but scold, "I never knew you were such a good-for-nothing!"

How annoyed Nie was! He opened his mouth but could not utter a word.

"Where's that little drive you usually have? You miss it all when you need it most . . ." She began to complain as if she were doing the house chores.

Nie was so annoyed that he pushed away her hand, left the bed and went over to sit on the sofa.

Seeing her nearly successful revenge plot unexpectedly falling though, the extremely disappointed wife sat by herself crying at the bedside, her face buried in her hands.

For quite a while, her crying was the only noise that could be heard in the house.

In some unknown dreamy world or other, the girl peacefully sleeping on the bed showed all sorts of vivid facial expressions.

Sitting on the sofa, Nie found his head pretty numb. He could neither feel nor think. His embarrassment and suffering lingered on until the girl opened her eyes and suddenly sat up.

"What's going on here?" she asked, but heard no answer.

The wife went on crying while Nie remained silent.

The girl thought for a while and said, "I know. I've 'paid the bill' for my father, aren't I right? Can I go now?"

"No!" Nie's wife countered quickly. "He didn't do it! Not because he should not, but because my husband is not a beast. He's not like your father!"

This unexpected stimulus immediately excited the girl. "How could it be possible?" she said, her eyes flashing. "I don't even have that charm to attract him?"

The girl's response took them by surprise—it was crying and trouble they thought they would have to deal with. They thought she would call the police, and they were prepared to go to prison. Neither knew how to respond to her.

"I don't think this has anything to do with any 'beast.' It's your husband who has some psychological barrier." Now the girl was in control of everything. "I understand why you are doing this. Auntie, how about doing it this way? You leave me and your husband alone and let us finish the job. He will feel embarrassed when you see him doing it."

"And you don't feel embarrassed yourself?" Nie's wife thought something might go wrong. "You are just as shameless as your father!"

"I am just trying to help you," the girl smiled.

"Get out of here!" Nie's wife vented out her anger, feeling relieved that she had finally found a reason to kick her out. She was well aware the girl could be so unkind and unforgiving to the extent of throwing them in jail.

The girl walked away calmly, but before she got out of their house, she turned round and added, "My father may not be a beast, after all. I could tell that he and your daughter Xiao Xiang are in love with each other."

That Smile of Hers

By **Xiu** Shi

I was waiting at that bus stop again.

The bus shelter stood erect outside a fence that was at least seven or eight feet tall. The top of the fence was covered with barbed wire. Behind it was a two-storey house, the residence of a rich family. You could not live in such a place if you were a dollar short.

On the left was a large steel gate through which cars drove in and out. The gate, which was painted silver, glittered in the light. It was almost airtight, and only when I tiptoed could I peep at a thing or two through the narrow seams.

Because of my job, I could be at this bus stop in the morning, at noon, or in the evening. While waiting for the bus, I usually stood on the lawn, treading on the little yellow flowers that bloomed all year round on the roadside. Otherwise, I might raise my head and stare at the few trees with dot-like leaves swaying in the wind. Tall and thin, the trees seemed to be the resting stops for the flying birds.

One day, out of curiosity, I walked closer to the gate for a peep, seeing three cars whose brands were unknown to me parked on the road leading to the front door of the house. They must be name brands, of course. I was still looking when an unexpected shadow brushed past me.

I looked at her, stupefied. She was an extremely dignified and virtuous-looking woman with beautiful hair cut to her shoulders. Impeccably dressed, she gave people the impression that she was a noble lady of fine breeding.

She threw a glance at me, followed by a faint smile. Engulfed in her elegant fragrance, I gave a look of helplessness and walked away shamefacedly. Then her gate opened and she went in.

After this encounter, I paid special attention to this house on several occasions. Quite often, I would just walk toward the edge of the road, raise my head and look beyond the fence. Separated by the uneven tree shadows, as I saw, the windows on the top floor were always covered with white screens that blocked outsiders' view. When the rooms were lit at night, I could see a little better—namely, some dark shadows. I guessed that the cone-shaped outline had to be a gigantic crystal chandelier.

Sometimes I was so busy peeping that I would miss a bus. When I was late for work, I would be reproached by the supervisor of my company. Besides this, I would dream up romantic stories, yearning to visit the house one day, but this mostly happened only when I had nothing to do at home.

Another day, I walked up to the steel gate, stood on tiptoe and peeped inside. This time, I could see much more clearly. There were glass walls with a sliding glass door on the first floor, inside which were sumptuous furnishings. Outside was a garden with outdoor furniture that looked like what we sold in the agent company. New yearning began in my mind.

Forgetting where I was, I went on peeping, discovering an awning hanging above the doorway, both sides of which were decorated with colored lights. While I was enjoying my eyeful of discoveries, I heard a peal of dogs' barks, then felt a pat on my back from behind.

I turned about and saw a police officer. On his uniform was a police number glittering in the sun.

"Show me your ID!" he said.

I put down my briefcase and drew out my identification card.

He copied something, spoke into the walkie-talkie over his chest for a while, then returned the card to me. Then came a bus. I tried to leave, but he stopped me with his left hand and said rigidly, "Will you go to the police station with me, please."

"Why? I have broken no law, and I am not involved in any incident." I raised my voice gradually, indicating confusion and displeasure.

"You behave in a suspicious manner, which has to be clarified in the police station." He stared at me coldly. "I hope you will co-operate."

I said nothing, but did not move. "This family has complained about you!" he continued.

"I don't believe it." I stood still with no intention of going with him. Then I also showed him my employee identification card and said, "I work for this company. I have been waiting for the bus to go to work."

The big gate opened as I finished my explanation. The woman who had smiled at me appeared, leaning against the gatepost. "Yes. It was me who complained about him," she said to the officer as she pointed at me. "I have seen him wandering outside my gate several times. He is up to no good!"

I was taken aback. Thanks to that smile of hers, I had thought she would protect me by saying I had done it out of curiosity, not purposely. But I had woken up to disappointment!

"All right then. Let's go!" said the officer.

I followed him in silence to the police cruiser at the corner of the street.

My Secret Affair

By **Chen** Lifeng

When my turn came, the fixed stare of the three men meant to tear open my face, as if to unearth the secret they thirsted to know. I lit a cigarette, drew two sulky breaths, and slowly began my story:

That year, I went to a county town on business. The town was so small that I had nowhere to spend my spare time. But as luck had it, I found a turtle-shaped slope in the northern suburbs. So I would stroll there with a book under my arm. One day while I was walking on the slope, I caught sight of a girl sitting on the grass with her chin in her hands, lost in thought. From her figure, I could tell she was an extremely ordinary-looking girl, but due to my unendurable boredom, I was dying for any excitement.

With a nobleman's air, I strode past her without looking at her. Then I purposely dropped the book from my arm. As I expected, I heard her calling me from behind, "Sir, you've dropped your book."

Like a gentleman, I turned around and walked up to her. I thanked her politely. "Do you like reading?" I asked her as she handed the book to me.

She nodded.

Thus we started our conversation, meandering from books to life, from the catastrophic Mexican earthquake to the rise and fall of Brazilian soccer, from astronomy to geography. Mobilizing all my brain cells, I impressed her with whatever knowledge I had acquired. When she had come to adore me sincerely, I paused.

After a moment, in the saddest tone I could ever create I started telling her my tragic love story. I told her how a faithless woman had cheated on me, and how I had generously forgiven her lack of chastity and wished her happiness. In the end, I told the girl emotionally that I had buried my sad story in my heart, enduring the pain all by myself. I told her that somehow it was the sight of her innocent eyes that had triggered the release of all my secrets. She heaved a sigh of sympathy, and in a shaky voice she tried to cheer me up, comparing my future to a bunch of wildflowers as she pointed at them.

Night crept in quietly. I told her how lovers dated in big cities, taking her arm when the time was right. She shuddered but did not refuse me. Then arm in arm we started to talk love. While talking, I let my chest rise and fall sharply for a while, then grasped her in my arms all of a sudden and held her tightly . . .

Her head leaning against my chest, she started crying, crying in great pain.

I left the town for home the next day—a home composed of my wife and me—quickly forgetting my affair as if it had been a passing cloud.

But I returned to the county town on business again last year. Again, I felt bored and lonely, so I thought of her and went to the suburban slope again.

Like before, the slope was there, covered with lush green grass, but there was no sign of the girl. What I found was a grave mound by a freshly planted pine. Over the grave was orange soil glimmering in the light. Watching over the grave was a silent young man. My heart stirring, I walked over to him. He withdrew his gaze from the birds flying overhead, telling me in a hoarse voice, "Here lies a girl who has died of leukemia."

"Oh!" I said in shock.

"She was my classmate," he said. "I had loved her secretly, but when I finally told her about this, she said she already had a sweetheart. When I asked her who it was, she said 'It's a man I may never see again. I have his address, but I won't contact him, because I will leave this world soon. I love him so much that I don't want to him to

313

grieve over my death. He couldn't have suffered more from his last relationship . . ."

In the blue sky, a white cloud that bore her smile was walking leisurely toward me. When I remembered the false address I had given her, I found my heart in acute pain, as if rent by the sharp teeth of a demon. I wanted to have a good cry, but I did not, for fear I would disturb her underneath the ground. Instead, I added a handful of soil on top of her grave.

She was dead, really dead. Before her passing, she had insisted that her family bury her on this slope, where she had met her first and last lover. The young man said she died smiling, with two shallow dimples on her cheeks.

I don't remember how I left the slope afterward, or how madly I drank in the days that followed. I only remember swearing to myself after I woke up from a nightmare, "I must become a decent man." And that's when I started my literary career.

My listeners were all lost in silence, gazing at me in bewilderment.

"Making up" Dreams

By **Liu** Liying

People in Sunzhuang Village have a peculiar way of talking about "dreams": they say "make up a dream" instead of "have a dream." For example, if someone wishes to buy a lottery ticket in town and expects to win, the villagers will say, "Expecting meat pies to fall from the sky—you are making up a daydream." Another example: if a man with an itchy hand wishes to touch Xiaoshui's large black braid, the villagers will say, "You think everybody, man or devil, can touch her big braid, eh? You must be making up a dream."

Xiaoshui is Da'er's wife, and Da'er is a villager in Sunzhuang. The year when Xiaoshui was married to Da'er, the blind fortune-teller* Sun shocked the world by saying, "Her waist resembling a willow, she's as beautiful as a flower. Yet she's more lovely than a flower, for she is a talking beauty. She is fairer than jade, for she's pleasant and sweet."

Face reddening, Da'er cursed, "God damn you! So you aren't blind after all!" With this he kicked over the fortune-telling** stand. Sun was so scared that he wet his pants.

Xizi, a villager who loved Xiaoshui, told people in private, "I'd be glad to die right away if I could touch Xiaoshui's braid just once

---

* *Translator's note:* See "fortune-telling" below.
***Translator's note:* Fortune-telling is the practice of foretelling others' destinies, and picking "lucky dates" or best days for engagements and marriages, for building a house, and for other activities.

in my life." Having heard this from other people, the smiling Da'er walked up to Xizi and gripped his hands. Xizi was so hurt that he cried out. As noted by people later on, quite a few of his fingers swelled like carrots.

"I made up a dream last night. I dreamed of our black hen with feathery legs laying an egg with two yolks," Xiaoshui told Da'er.

"You are making up a dream. You are just making up a dream." Da'er's face looked like it was covered with a layer of ice. Xiaoshui would go to bed to make up dreams early at night. For days and weeks, she would not let him touch her in bed.

That day, their hen really laid an egg with two yolks.

Da'er found a weird expression in Xiaoshui's eyes.

"Last night, I made up a dream. I dreamed of seeing Xizi's pig eating the celery in our fields," she told him.

Again, Da'er found a strange expression in her eyes. Before he left home, he thought for a while, then decided to bring along the blunderbuss handed down from his ancestors. Doubtfully, he went to his vegetable fields.

"My God!" Da'er heard his hair crackle. There really was a bad pig in his celery fields. He was aiming his blunderbuss at the happy hog when Xizi appeared out of the blue. "Da'er, please don't kill my pig. I'm counting on it for the money I need for New Year."

"Damn you, Xizi, what about my vegetables?"

"You can kill me, but don't kill the pig."

"Kill you? That would foul my blunderbuss! I will have a sleep with your woman." That is the way men are in Sunzhuang. When two become bitter enemies, one will want to sleep with the other's wife. Once this cruel demand is made, what often follows is a rolling up of sleeves and a tearing of each other's cotton-padded coats.

But Xizi agreed readily. "If you want to."

Da'er had no way of retreating. If he did, he would not be called a man in Sunzhuang.

"Our pig has eaten Da'er's celery," Xizi told his wife. "Let him

316

sleep with you for once." With this he closed the door behind him, leaving Da'er rubbing his hands in his house until they were sweaty.

"Don't you want to sleep with me?" Xizi's wife said to Da'er. "Take off your shoes and get onto the *kang*." Da'er heard his hair crackle again.

"Foolish man," she said, "you've been kept in the dark. Xiaoshui and Xizi have secretly fallen in love with each other and have set up a trap for us."

Da'er was suddenly enlightened: so the double-yolk egg and the pig eating celery were simply tricks played on him by his wife and the other man! "Just like making up a dream. Making up a dream! They two have made it to bed, but I've been dreaming like a fool." Picking up his blunderbuss, Da'er said, "I'll finish off that dirty pair!"

"If you finish them off, you'll be shot yourself," said Xizi's wife. "They would do anything for their relationship. Talking about ideas, Xizi will beat ten of you, Da'er."

"To hell with Xizi! God damn Xizi!" cursed Da'er, his face changing from blue to red, then from red to blue.

"Isn't your wife a lamp-oil saver?* A dog can't get through a well-built fence. They are stuck with each other for life or death. Even if you kill them, you won't separate them. To tell you the truth, in the beginning, I even thought of committing suicide, but then I thought, maybe they were really meant for each other."

Da'er walked out of Xizi's house with uneven steps. The words "Foolish man. That's you and that's you!" kept echoing in his ears.

Later on, Da'er's wife lived with Xizi, and Xizi's wife lived with Da'er.

Still later on, when nosy men asked about the story, villagers in Sunzhuang looked aghast. "Men in Sunzhuang don't exchange wives

---

* *Translator's note:* "A lamp-oil saver" refers to an unusual woman who is difficult to deal with.

like that. You must be the ones who want to switch wives desperately. You are making up a daydream and talking dreamily." The nosy men still did not want to give up. They searched the whole village from corner to corner, but never found the woman with a large braid.

Every woman in Sunzhuang wore short hair, cut to the bottom of her ears, like that of an athlete.

Relationship by Fate

By **Tao** Ran

His bedsheets were white, his quilt cover was white, and so was his pillowcase. Lying on the bed, he glared blankly at the white ceiling, smelling the special hospital drug odor that was drifting toward him.

"Now, does it mean I will die soon?" he thought, terrified. He was not quite fifty years old yet. If he really had to go, one way or the other, he would find it pretty hard, especially when he had Jane to miss.

He had been with Jane for just about a year. He still remembered she called the day after his ad, "Girlfriend Wanted," appeared in the newspaper. Several women had phoned him previously, but strange to say, he showed no interest in them and had met none of them. Somehow, he fell in love with Jane's voice instead, which was not really much sweeter than the rest. Talking about the real reason, one could attribute it only to fate.

He met her in Chao Gang Cheng Restaurant for luncheon in Tong Luo Wan, so that he could see her clearly.

He found her a little coy, which reminded him of the saying, "That gentle temperament from her hung head is appealing."

When he asked her a question, she would answer it, but she never asked him a thing. "Thirty-five years old? She doesn't look that old! She seems more like an introverted girl than a divorced woman."

Probably because they had met for a clear purpose, neither held back their sexual desire in the course of dating. He was surprised at the return of his sexual impulse, and was more surprised at her embarrassment as a seemingly green-hand. He thought he ought to

319

play the role of an instructor, but didn't know what to say offhand, due to a feeling of strangeness.

Perhaps everything spoke for itself in the absence of their words. After their physical contact, Jane was not as restrained as before. "What a madman you are! Is your wife like you?" she whispered in his ears.

He was taken by surprise. "My wife? If she had not been in low drive for years, I wouldn't have been suffering! One way or the other, I am still a little boss. Why would I have secretly printed the 'Girlfriend Wanted' ad?" He forced a smile at her, shaking his head as if to get rid of his heavy memory.

Jane became increasingly important in his heart. She had never said no to him. Now the ill man longed for her all the more. Last night, he even made a special call to her. "Find a good man for yourself," he choked with sobs in the course of their conversation. "Originally I intended to take care of you for the rest of your life, but I can no longer do that . . ."

He knew that he was trying to goad the woman into feeling more pity for him.

He had just closed his eyes for a rest when the nurse suddenly pushed the door open and gave him a letter without a stamp. He recognized it as Jane's handwriting and opened it without delay. He gasped with astonishment at the few words in the letter: "You reminded me last night that even if you are cured, you cannot marry me one way or the other. We are done!"

Poet for Rent

By **Li** Jingwen

Poet Hu Pan has written numerous love poems, but fame is out of his reach. How many pennies is a love poem really worth these days? Especially when it comes from an unknown poet. Even a three-year-old can hum two lines of the well-known song "The Bright Full Moon"— "Doesn't that bright full moon cost the same as a spoon?" Isn't it what people often ask with a wry smile?

In the first place, Hu Pan is a human being who eats cooked food. He is distressed, knowing his poems are practically worthless. Yet Hu Pan is no ordinary man. He loves thinking and turning over ideas in his mind. A Miss Ceremony puts herself up for rent; pianists and singers are willing to leave the sacred, splendid music hall for the ballroom, which in a way is also a rental service. Why not put up a poet for rent as well?

So there was that day when Hu Pan made up an ad and had it printed in the newspaper:

Master love poet Hu Pan offers himself
For Rent

Really, on the same day a woman by the name of Shi responded, saying that she wanted to rent a poet and would pay him by the hour. The money she offered was one hundred times as much as the remuneration he got for the publication of his poems. With her hourly rate, it would not take long before he made a small fortune or even became a rich man. Hu Pan had never expected such generous pay, so he readily accepted her offer.

Shortly before noon the next day, Shi personally drove to Hu Pan's home to pick him up. She took him to the best restaurant in town, where she entertained him with a sumptuous luncheon, then she drove him back home. She had very few words when she was with him. Shi did the same the next two days, and Hu Pan, no matter how self-possessed and gentleman-like he was, could not remain silent anymore. "Miss Shi, please don't hesitate to let me know if there's anything I can do for you. I'd be delighted to serve you."

"Thank you!" Ms. Shi interrupted him very politely. "Mr. Poet, you have started working already." With this she sent him home, without saying another word.

For the next three days, Shi would take him to the beach swimming pool every day, take a bath in the sea water with him, then enjoy some fresh seafood before sending him back home. On his way home, the perplexed Hu Pan asked her, "Miss Shi, do you find me a poor and pedantic poet so you sympathize with me and feel sorry for me?"

"No way," she answered as she drove. "Your Respectful Excellency Mr. Poet, what I want is this unique feeling of being with you. For example, the common people all nickname us women whose husbands are studying abroad 'Wives on Hold,' but Mr. Poet, you call me Miss. You are different, just different."

For another three days, loving to be called Miss, Shi would drive him to the splendid ballroom of the International Club for a dance in the evening. In the dim candlelight of the luxurious box, feeling a strong poetic urge in him, Hu Pan blurted out, "My respectful miss, how I wish to recite a poem for you!"

"Never mind. If I wanted to have a poem recited, I could have hired an actor myself." She stretched out her hand toward Hu Pan. "Don't you have the feeling that we are writing a poem together?"

Moved to tears, Hu Pan grasped her hand as it reached him.

On the ninth day, when they finished their midnight snack after their dance, Miss Shi's luxurious car did not go to Hu Pan's home as usual. Instead, it took him straight to her own luxury villa in the suburbs.

"I want you to write a love poem just for me, but how can you do so without life experience?" said the drunk and drowsy Miss Shi, pointing to her expensive waterbed.

Hu Pan seemed to have woken up, feeling insulted. "So you—"

Miss Shi exposed her gauze skirt, which was as filmy as a cicada's wings, laughing with stunningly seductive charm, "My dear poet, may I remind you that you haven't got a single penny of your rent yet!"

The poet was outraged, denouncing her with the harshest words as he rejected her offer.

Later, under the name of Hu Pang, a long narrative poem entitled *A Poet Who Was Rented* was published in a poetry journal, which instantly revived the poets' circle that had been desolately quiet for years.

A Golden Girl

By **Yuan** Yaqin

Mr. Ding Bo, a bachelor in his fifties, drew out something he had long wanted to present to her, waving it before Miss Zuo, who was sitting on the other side of the tea table. "It's this. I have kept it for many years without showing it to anybody. Today, I want to send it to someone who I think deserves it. It's just a gift with no other intention attached. I only—"

Miss Zuo casually glanced at the little red packet he was holding, then buried herself in her reading again.

"Guess what's inside?" A line of naïveté emerged on his old face as he excitedly moved over and sat next to her, gazing at her foolishly. She shook her head without saying a word, so he began to entice her emotionally by playing some soft, elegant music on his VCD player. After a moment of indulgence, he said, "It's a thing that is priceless though it may have a price. It depends on whose hands it falls into. Do you know it's just like a tie of friendship—a treasure that's valueless." With this, he unwrapped his red packet, showing an object weighing at least one hundred grams. Out burst captivating yellow beams, but it failed to start a sparkle in her eyes. She looked indifferent, her smile as careless as usual.

"Has she seen too many of these to be excited, or . . .? No, that's impossible. She isn't very well off. I don't even see any decent jewelry on her." He was surprised at her indifference, so he decided to enlighten her. "Don't think it is low-grade taste. It is something many people dream of. Just imagine what you would look like if it was made into a large necklace and when you wore it around your neck!

You would look even more beautiful. Now take it. It's a token of my fondness for you."

"Sir," she said, standing up, "what do you mean by this?"

"You know it and so do I," he said in a low voice. "It's called tacit understanding between you and me."

"No. I can't take it," she said, taking a step backward.

He gave a deep sigh, then put down his gift, packed up his smile and discontinued his discussion with her on the research topic they had been engaged in.

Leaving his home, Miss Zuo felt her satchel a little weightier and her heart heavier. When she got home, she discovered the gift lying at the bottom of her satchel; she was unaware of when Mr. Ding Bo put it inside. She found no joy at seeing it, only a feeling of depression which was hard to describe. "Return it!" was the only thought she had, but she did not want to go to his home alone anymore.

The next day, she told him that she still had some issues to discuss with him and requested an appointment so as to talk with him outside his home. Mr. Ding Bo was overjoyed that a girl had finally requested a date with him, especially when it was the MBA student he had long been fond of, and that they would meet in a private cubicle of a pretty tasteful coffee shop!

"Looks like women love money more than themselves these days—Miss Zuo just didn't feel dignified accepting my gift in my presence, that's all." Thoughts thronging his mind, his excitement began to spill out of his heart, as he got closer and closer to the goddess of his heart. But when he arrived at the booth where they were supposed to meet, he found nobody there. Of course she had not come yet, so he sat down to wait for her. He had hardly sat down when he caught sight of something on the table: a beautiful jewelry box. Carelessly, he opened the lid a little for a peep. "Oh, my! It's glittering!" he said, his eyes brightening up, his heart pounding fast. "Oh, my baby, it's my day today. It belongs to nobody but me! What a wonderful girl she is! She is playing hide-and-seek with me!" How he wished he could take possession of the gift and put it into his pocket immediately.

At this moment, his phone rang and up came these lines: "The gift is to be returned to its original owner. Remember: it is sterling gold. Just like me, it must not be soiled." He quickly opened the box for a close look. "Why, it is the same bullion as mine!" he murmured, his face reddening. "What a rare golden girl she is!"

A Door Forever

By **Shao** Baojian

In an old town south of the Yangtze River, there was a poorly
maintained compound with an old well. Inside the compound lived
eight or nine working families. Their houses were old bungalows of
a type that had never been remodeled, but they were decorated with
an increasingly modern taste.

Of the eight or nine families, two were single people. These two
permanent dwellers were Zheng Ruokui, a bachelor, and Pan Xue'e,
a spinster. They lived next to each other.

"Good morning," he would say to her.

"Going out?" she would reply, as she brushed past him, never
slowing down.

How many times they had greeted each other! Yet those were the
only two sentences anybody would hear if they ever did. Such simple,
boring repetitions really disheartened their neighbors.

Pan, probably in her early forties, had an oval face. She had regular
features with fair complexion. She was so slim that she looked
somewhat skinny and fragile, but she was still a charming woman,
tastefully dressed in a simple style yet never out of touch with fashion.
Pan worked for the flower shop on Western Street. The neighbors
did not know why this pretty woman had chosen to remain single.
They only knew that she deserved love but had never married.

Following Pan's footsteps, Zheng had moved into this compound
five years ago. He was an artist working for a movie theatre. He was
said to be a responsible and overcautious painter without talent. At
the age of forty-five or forty-six, he already looked like an old man.

327

His hair was messy and unhealthily yellowish. One could tell he seldom combed it. He was somewhat stooped with a haggard face, skinny hands and narrow shoulders. Only his large eyes still glowed with youth and expectation.

Zheng often came home with a bunch of fresh-cut flowers, such as roses, Chinese flowering crab apples, winter sweet—anything available, all year round. He would put his flowers into a blue translucent vase with a high base.

He was not in the habit of visiting others. When he finished work, he would stay home most of the time. Sometimes Zheng did go to the well to do his laundry, wash up and clean the vase. After cleaning it thoroughly, he would refill it with clear water and carry it back home carefully, pouting his lips.

A thick wall separated Zheng's room from Pan's.

A very old bamboo bookshelf the height of a person stood against the wall of Zheng's room, next to the bed. The right end of the top shelf was where his vase was always placed. Besides this, there were some Chinese paintings and some foreign paintings—done by himself and others, hanging on or lying against the walls.

From the arrangement of his furniture and the thickness of dust, one could tell it was a home without a woman; it lacked that warmth only a woman could create.

But the home dweller's constant polishing kept that vase spotless, that vase whose water was always clear, whose flowers were always fresh and in full bloom.

The neighbors in his compound used to long for the day when they could see his flowers appearing next door, in Pan's room, but this never happened. Thus, his surely sympathetic neighbors felt really sorry for him.

It was raining early on a fall morning.

"Good morning," Zheng greeted her in the same old way as he opened his umbrella.

"Going out?" Pan gave the same old answer, an open umbrella in hand.

The rain stopped in the evening. She returned home, but he never came back.

Soon, news spread that while painting in his office, Zheng had suddenly suffered from irregular heartbeats, then had fallen down. He was declared dead when he arrived at the hospital.

The working people in that compound burst out crying. Only Pan was silent, but her eyes were indeed red.

Wreath after wreath was presented to him. The biggest one, woven with a large variety of flowers but without a traditional elegiac couplet, was from Pan.

The bachelor who had lived an ordinary life without love was badly missed by the neighbors.

Several days later, Pan moved away, suddenly and hastily.

When people were sorting out Zheng's belongings, they were greatly surprised. Though his home was covered with thick dust everywhere, his bright, shiny blue vase seemed to have been polished by someone not long ago and the white chrysanthemums showed no signs of fading.

Their eyes nearly popped out at what they saw on the wall when they moved away that old bamboo bookshelf.

A door! There was a door in the wall! Definitely, it was a purplish red door with a brass handle, elegantly made.

"So that was it!" Everybody's heart started to beat faster.

The neighbors became very noisy now. Disappearing like broken bubbles, their grief and the respect they had shown for the bachelor in the past few days suddenly changed into indescribable resentment.

"Wow!" somebody shouted while trying to open it. The brass handle was as flat and smooth as the wall, and so were the door and the door frame.

It was a door painted on the wall.

Wits at Risk

Underwear

By **Zhou** Daxin

A villager by the name of Dashuan was in the habit of sleeping without wearing underwear. "It's relaxing and comfortable, and you also fall asleep more easily," he would extol its advantage to others.

One day, Dashuan went on a business trip for his fellow villagers and had to stay in a hostel in town. He booked an economical quintuple room without a washroom. To his happy surprise, there were no other guests when he went in. "I paid for one bed, but got a whole room for myself," he said to himself. "Pretty good luck!" He stripped off all his clothes and was soon fast asleep.

The naked man woke up at midnight, for he had to urinate. Slipping off the bed, he opened the door and ran straight to the washroom outside. But when he returned, he found himself in a bit of trouble: the door had been shut in the wind and the built-in lock had locked him out. He was taken aback, groaning to himself—the key he had got on a deposit from the service desk was in his pants pocket! How could he get back in?

The wind in the corridor was rather cold. He stood there holding his arms, but was soon shivering. "No. I've got to get the attendant to open it for me." He started to walk toward the night-shift room where she stayed on call, only to realize he was completely naked. "No. It won't do. If I knock on her door like this, she will be scared when she sees me and will scream. She will think that I am a hoodlum or rapist." Halting his steps, he stood still again and continued to shiver. It was cold enough to freeze him to death if he waited until daybreak. "I've got to find a way out," he said to himself.

331

There, with the help of the corridor light, he saw some black ink and a Chinese writing brush on the service desk. He thought for a second, then relaxed his eyebrows: "I have a way out now!" Immediately he started walking toward the service desk, from which he picked up the writing brush, dipped it in the Chinese ink and drew a circle around his waist and one on each thigh, thus creating the shape of a pair of underpants. This done, he headed confidently for the attendant's room and knocked on her door.

The nearsighted girl was yawning and rubbing her eyes when she opened the door. Dashuan quickly turned around as he told her that the wind had shut him out and that he wanted her to open the door for him. The girl glanced at his clothing and, without a word, followed him to his room. After opening the door for him, she said, "Your underpants look very springy. Where did you buy them?"

"In the Eastern Department Store," he answered, suppressing his fear as he slipped into his room.

Mosquito Punishment

By **Sun** Fangyou

Chenzhou, nicknamed "Water Town," was surrounded by lakes covering tens of thousands of hectares. At the horizon, the water merged with the sky in one color. There was patch after patch of cattails and countless lotus leaves everywhere, infested with mosquitoes in summer. At dusk, mosquitoes would swarm from one spot to another, and wherever they gathered, they would blacken the sky, while their buzzing could be heard a hundred feet away.

With long stingers, large wings, clear bellies, and legs that resembled snakes, mosquitoes in Chenzhou were known as "snake-legged mosquitoes," or "flying snakes." Their bites were nearly painless, but would swell, then turn into hard lumps, the itching of which was simply unendurable.

Throughout the summer evenings, smoke curled up into the sky over Chenzhou from households burning mugwort to repel mosquitoes. Outsiders who came to Chenzhou had to learn to endure the mugwort; otherwise, they could not stay. You had to bring your burning mugwort when you took a bath. As soon as you made a circle overhead with your mugwort in one hand, you began to rub your body with the cleaning powder with the other. If you were too slow, you would find a black coat over your chest and back. When you hit them with your hand, you would get a handful of blood. When you had a bowel movement in the evening, you needed your mugwort all the more. After taking off your pants you held them with one hand, and with the other you swished the smoldering mugwort around the body. Otherwise your buttocks would be covered with a coat of black and instantly gain a layer of "fat." The worst that could happen was that the mosquitoes would bite your fragile parts. Once bitten, that parts would swell like a balloon and you would wet your shoes when you urinated. It is said that the famous Bao Gong had to endure this pain when he came to Chenzhou. Luckily, the common people didn't want to darken the name of the government official. That is why the story has been told by word of mouth only and never found in print.

Thanks to its unique effect, the local mugwort had great value.

In ancient times, Chenzhou was once a city, but in one unknown dynasty, it was reduced to the county administrative level.

The first magistrate of the county was called Jia. As for his given name, nobody ever knows, and there is nowhere to find it out. Jia was a vicious man who extorted money from his people by every means possible, so he was nicknamed "Snake-Legged Mosquito" by the locals. Every summer, he would engage in selling mugwort protected by his own policy that nobody, outsider or local, was allowed to engage in the same business. Being the sole business owner, he raked in shameless profits from easy sales.

Businessmen and the local villagers all coveted the fat returns from the cheap investment in the mugwort business. A wholesale bundle cost very little, but its profit was handsome, so some of them broke Jia's rules. Whenever a mugwort seller was caught, the magistrate would sentence him to mosquito punishment.

Mosquito punishment, as the name suggests, was being bitten by mosquitoes. Jia would have a prisoner stripped, then tied up, put in a boat and rowed to the middle of the lake. The guards would sit watching him from inside mosquito nets in separate boats surrounding the prisoner's. If the prisoner died of mosquito biting by five o'clock the next morning, he deserved it. If he was so fortunate as to survive, he would be released right on the spot. Nevertheless, most of those sentenced to mosquito bites could not stand it until dawn. Their bodies would soon swell up, and they would die.

The magistrate also punished bandits and hardened thieves in the same way. Though businessmen and the villagers who had secretly sold mugwort could not but receive Jia's punishment obediently, the bandits were no easy people to deal with. They swore to avenge their brothers on Jia if they caught him one day.

One night in July that year, a group of bandits launched a sudden attack on the town and succeeded in seizing the magistrate. After reaching a certain spot, the bandits pushed him out. The chieftain glanced at the magistrate and smiled bitterly, ordering, "Mosquito punishment for him."

On hearing the order, several bandits stripped Jia, exposing his white, fat body, which looked like that of a pig without bristles. One slapped him on the buttocks, the clear sound of which started a roar of merry laughter among the bandits, but when they stared at Jia, they found the same imposing appearance, with no fear of his imminent punishment. The furious chieftain then shouted, "Let his punishment begin!" Acting accordingly, the bandits tied up the magistrate, pushed him onto the deck of the boat and rowed him to the middle of the lake.

It happened to be a midsummer night, and there were numerous mosquitoes. The bandits all sat in a large boat protected by a mosquito net, eating meat and drinking wine as they laughed at the greedy official who would soon go to the other world. Jia's body was covered with three layers of mosquitoes that turned him into a beehive. Before long, Jia became much "fatter," as if a black snowfall had buried him completely. The deathly quiet Jia did not move until dawn, when the bandits untied him, thinking that he was dead. To their surprise, though he was so badly bitten that his face was almost beyond recognition, he was breathing. "How come you are still alive?" the bandits asked in astonishment, as he got up abruptly.

"Mosquitoes are lazy insects," he laughed. "They sleep after they've eaten and drunk their fill. I pretended to be asleep throughout the night in order not to scare them away. In this way, other mosquitoes couldn't land on me. Those over my body had already drunk their fill. It was they that saved my life. When I tell you how I managed to survive, you may not understand it. It's called 'Endure what you cannot cure.'"

"Nonsense!" roared the chieftain. "How come our brothers were bitten to death?"

"It was their own fault. The Mosquito Act clearly stipulates that 'those who survive until dawn shall be released.' Yet they couldn't stand it. When the first swarm had just drunk their fill, your brothers started to shake their heads and bodies, driving all of them away. Then came another swarm. Throughout the night, mosquitoes came and went, swarm after swarm. How could you save a drop of your blood this way?"

The bandits were all astounded.

The chieftain understood it now and immediately freed the magistrate.

A Mysterious Phone Friend

By **Chen** Dachao

Deng Qiuhong's job at Shengxun Radio Station was chatting with people in a sweet, coquettish voice. In the beginning, even she felt sick of hearing herself, but as time passed, she got used to it. Then not only could she prolong her chats with her callers by taking advantage of her coquettish voice so that she could collect more commissions, but she had also accustomed herself to male callers' teasing remarks and often lewd words. One day, as soon as he was connected to her, the girl, who was wasting her youth without knowing what her future would be, heard a man asking her for a good scolding. He took her by surprise.

"Scold? You want me to scold you? Are you teasing me?" What followed was a string of giggles sounding like silver bells. She was baffled when she learned that her stubborn caller really meant what he said. "Now, what a strange, strange, strange man you are! You are asking a new high school graduate to scold you on the phone. That's a very, very, very difficult thing for me to do. Now, how do I scold you? Call you a rotten man? Call you a blundering fool? What? I can call you whatever names I like? The dirtier the better?" So in search of curses, she started to recollect the scolding scenes in the Hong Kong and Taiwan movies she had seen.

"You son of a bitch!" She started to try a few names. "You good-for-nothing! You rascal! You will die in your boots!" Then she added, smilingly, "Sorry, sorry. Didn't I sound awful? I don't feel good about this." But the caller at the other end of the line said her scolding was terrific, asking her just to scold him that way, saying again that the

337

nastier her curses were, the better. He also asked her always to speak in a harsh voice.

After that, this talk friend would call her every three or four days for a sound scolding on the phone.

"Why do you pay to be scolded on the phone?" she would ask him after the scolding. "What do you do? Don't you have something else to share with me, besides getting scolded?" But each time she finished her scolding, he would only say "Thank you," then hang up. His mysterious ways interested her more and more. Once she even invited him to dinner, intending to talk to him in person, but he declined.

Her colleagues also found it pretty funny, speculating that he must be courting her with some kind of special strategy. Of course, there were other guesses as well, but whatever the guess, she could not bear to scold him again.

"You ask me to scold you. That's all right, but you need to tell me the reason," she told him when he called again. "Otherwise, I'll never do it again."

To her surprise, after a long sulky silence he told her the following: "You don't know this. I am in danger of sinking into degradation or even degeneration. So to avoid being despised and scolded in the future, I may as well get scolded from time to time now. This may be a wake-up call that can trigger a change in my life by encouraging me to accept challenges, while I am still young and have the time."

Hearing that, she became dumbfounded and did not speak to him again until quite a while later. "I should ask you to scold me, too. I could have gotten into university if I had repeated a year in high school, but vanity took over. My parents urged me to do so more than once, but I just would not. Later, after a bad quarrel with them, I left home and started working as a miss for Shengxun Radio Station. Honestly, this is a life with no respect and dignity."

After that day, Deng Qiuhong disappeared from the radio station. The following year, she passed the national college entrance examination and was admitted into a rather prestigious university. The only regret she had was that she could never find out who the phone friend was. It was he who woke her up and triggered off a change in her life instead.

Calligrapher

By **Si** Yusheng

At the Chinese calligraphy contest, people gathered around the visiting Bureau Leader Gao to ask him to write a few characters.

"What should I write?" asked Gao, smiling, as he picked up a brush and cocked his head.

"Anything. Whatever you are best at."

"All right then. Here I am, showing my incompetence." Gao muttered something to himself, shook his wrist slightly, then started writing. In an instant, two large and breathtakingly beautiful characters meaning "agree"* flowed onto the rice paper from the tip of his brush.

The amazed crowd murmured in admiration. "A few more, please!" someone shouted.

Gao looked up in the direction of the voice and said in embarrassment, "I'd better stop here. Those are the only two characters I write well."

---

* *Translator's note:* "Agree" is a word used as an acknowledgment of approval by a Chinese official on any official document, such as reports, applications and petitions.

Selling Books

By **Wang** Xiaoqian

My literary friend Wang Fushun bumped into my office with a stack of books, dropped them on my desk and said in distress, "This is the book I have just published. I have been trying to sell it, but haven't sold a single copy after trying several offices. I need your advice!"

"Nowadays, you need to cover the cost of the book you publish in most cases. Even if the publisher offers to publish it for you, they would prefer to pay your royalties in books, to follow their foreign counterparts, as they beautifully put it. Of course, your book won't be an easy sale . . ." I said as I glanced through a copy. When I saw its title, *Yinyang, the Professions, and the Chinese Characters,* out of curiosity I turned to the synopsis. The more I read, the more interested I became.

In the book, Wang said the work was the result of his five years of research on the unique features of the Chinese characters. The two basic philosophic concepts yin and yang, which originated from *Yijing,* or *The Book of Changes,* explained and represented whatever existed in nature and in society. Basically, yang represented the masculine and the positive, yin the feminine and the negative. For example, most of the 160 characters that were associated with "nü" (female) are derogatory, such as *yiao* for "demon," *lan* for "greed," and *jian* for "rape" or "wicked." By contrast, nearly all the fifty characters that were associated with "li" (force) that represented males are commendatory, including *yong* for "brave," *gong* for "merit," and *bo* for "vigorous." Doubtless, in the process of creating the Chinese characters, the ancestors fully demonstrated their view of yin and

341

yang by worshipping the sky, the male, and yang, while humbling the earth, the female, and yin.

"Man, you've done a good job! It's a great book that's worth reading!" I commented.

"But how should I promote it? I am already carrying a great debt because of this book. I know you are full of ideas. Your book *St. Idiot* was sold out within a short time. How did you do it?"

"It won't work for you, but I can tell you how I did it. I won't use the method again, anyway, but please do not tell anybody about it. In the beginning, I could not sell my books either, so I hit on the idea of selling them through a 'Girlfriend Wanted' ad. I wrote my ad this way: 'A twenty-eight-year-old man, multimillionaire, is seeking a woman as a future wife. Similar temperament as the character named So-and-So in the book *St. Idiot* required.' Before long, my book was sold out in all the bookstores in town. Just that simple."

"Wonderful! What a marvelous way! But I have no specific character in my book, and I can't use your method!" he sighed, looking helpless.

Hoping to help him in some way, I told him a story I had read in a book about how a publisher took advantage of the president when he created his advertisements.

There was an American publisher who had a book that did not sell well. One day, an idea struck him and he sent a copy to the president. He asked for his opinion again and again. Finally, the president, who was busy with the duties of his office, decided to free himself of the continual annoyance, so he wrote the publisher a simple sentence: "The book is not bad." Soon the book was sold out. Not long after that, the publisher had slow sales with another book, so he sent the president a copy again. This time the president, who had been taken in once, simply said, "The book is terrible." Learning about the president's reply, the publisher thought for a second and wrote up this advertisement, "The last book our president likes is now available for sale." Curious, many readers started to buy the book, so it sold out. The third time he received the publisher's new book, remembering the first two lessons, the president did not even write back. But the publisher still made full use of his silence: "A book that our president finds hard to comment on is available for sale. Buy it today before it is sold out." Again, the book sold out quickly.

Wang was all smiles, saying he knew what to do now. Dropping two copies on my desk for me, he hurried out of my office.

Two months later, an outraged Wang was sitting in front of me, a newspaper in hand. He even lit a cigarette, which I had never seen before. He did not speak until quite a while later.

"What should I do now?" he finally said. "I sent a copy of my book to a renowned linguist in our country, Professor So-and-So. He never wrote back, but today he has published his own article entitled, 'Chinese Characters Disclosing Ancient Chinese Philosophy.' He has made a few changes and published my research under a new title without even mentioning my name. Isn't it outrageous!"

Shocked at the news, I felt a nervous tic. "Boy," I shouted as I pounded on the desk, "it's your day now!"

"What do you mean?" Wang jumped to his feet with a start.

"Publish a statement in the newspaper immediately, saying the renowned linguist Professor So-and-So has lifted your research from *Yinyang, the Professions, and the Chinese Characters,* and so on. Also say 'The book became a best-seller the day it came out. Buy it today.'"

One month later, Wang came to my office again. This time he started talking before I greeted him. "Brother, your advice is really valuable. I have made a big profit from my book. Here's some money for you. A token of appreciation for your work," he said as he drew out an envelope.

"Forget it. I don't need this. You keep it for your lawsuits."

"Gee! You can really predict the future. That old man has written to me that he conducted his research from an angle different from mine. He wants me to withdraw my statement from the newspaper, or he will take me to court."

"Wouldn't it continue to help you sell your book? Perhaps you'll have some other happy surprises, you never know!"

We looked at each other and burst out laughing.

Fleeing a Banquet

By **Han** Ying

Mr. Qin did a pretty good job as the department director, so he was promoted to deputy secretary of the Party Committee.

When Qin was the director, he had his life routine. He would get up when he had to get up; he would eat when he had to eat; and he would sleep when he had to sleep. His daughter called him a robot in those days.

But shortly after his promotion, Qin's routine changed, especially his eating habits. He could not eat when it was time for eating, but he had to eat when it was not time for eating. He had to eat when he had finished eating; he had to drink when he had drunk his fill. He kept eating and drinking, again and again. It became torture for him.

April 7 was a Sunday. As an old habit, he got up at 6:30, and at 7:00 he went to the take-out counter of the Yingbin Hotel to buy three steamed vegetable buns. Then he went back to his office, made himself a cup of tea and started to eat his buns as he read his newspaper—it was just great. The simple breakfast was an enjoyment for him.

Then the assistant director of the Reception Office called. "Good morning! Is it Secretary Qin? I am calling to remind you that you have breakfast with the visitors from Zuyi Prefecture at eight o'clock, and breakfast with the guests from China Bank, Macao Branch, at nine o'clock."

"I haven't forgotten. I have written them down," Qin said, glancing at the calendar on his desk. Then he said to himself, "I have two breakfasts with visitors in the morning, three lunches with guests at noon, and I have to drink with an army of drinkers at dinner in the evening."

He laughed. As he walked out to the balcony, he lit a cigarette, drawing an enjoyable deep breath. "We owe today's good life to the open-door policy!" Outside the window was a banyan tree that had turned green in the early spring. "Now we have quickened our pace of work and life. We also have more visitors, and receptions are unavoidable, but this banquet . . ."

"Time to go." Qin hurried downstairs, rushing straight into the cafeteria.

The cafeterias were his battlefields. The east hall was a battlefield, and so was the west hall. From people who urged him to drink he had heard the following numerous times: "Rather hurt the body than friendship," "Our feelings are deep, but our mouths are cheap," "Our friendship is true; drink till you turn blue" and "Meeting an old friend in your hometown, you drink until you're down."

The only thing he had ever repeated was "Our feelings are deep, but our mouths are cheap." On some occasions he had gulped down with his visitors three glasses in one breath, which meant, "Welcome, welcome, and still welcome." For this, some people nicknamed him "Three Glasses Qin." Others said "You drown yourself for your friends."

"Friends have to be entertained, but you have to save yourself," he said. "Life is precious. We've got to cherish it."

After having three luncheons with three groups of guests, Qin felt exhausted. Walking into his bedroom, he fell flat on his bed without taking off his clothes or shoes. "It looks like your job, no matter how hard it is, won't kill you, but eating will," he muttered to himself. "And so will drinking."

After a good sleep, Qin came back to life. He washed his face, brushed his teeth, then shaved. After that he brought along his keys, cigarettes and a cigarette lighter, dashing toward the guest hotel like a shooting star.

"I'll have to face an army of drinkers this evening. What should I do? What should I do?" Arriving at the banquet hall, Qin shook hands and exchanged business cards with each and every guest. When the hosts and guests were all seated, Qin made an enthusiastic welcoming speech that marked the start of their banquet in a warm and cordial atmosphere.

"To show our sincere welcome to all our guests who have come to visit us from all the different places, here I drink up three glasses in one breath." He drank up a glass and said, "Miss, more whiskey, please." He kept his word, winning warm applause from the whole hall of guests as he gulped down the third glass.

"Please help yourself, everybody. I won't help today. Please help yourself to whatever you like."

"Great! It's great, this way," they responded.

Sitting in the chair, Qin shut his eyes gently in silence, his left hand pressing his stomach as sweat oozed over his forehead.

When his guests came over to toast to him, he rose to his feet with great effort. His hand trembled as he raised his glass. He stopped speaking even before he started. Suddenly, he fell onto the chair again.

"Quick! Send Secretary Qin to the hospital! Quick!" cried Huang, the deputy secretary-general, who immediately started to get ready for the emergency.

Two men carried Qin downstairs, as he looked back after each step taken and said haltingly, "I—I—am sorry. Your dinner—you—you eat—yourselves. Your whiskey, you—you drink—yourselves. Wait—wait till I come back. I'll—I'll eat with you—"

Everybody rose to watch him leave.

His car, an Audi, was taking him straight to the emergency in the city's central hospital, but he stopped his chauffeur when they reached the Tongji Bridge. "Drive me home!" he then ordered him, leaving no room for negotiation.

The chauffeur was stunned, and so was the secretary.

"There's nothing wrong with me," Qin said, smiling, as he opened

347

his eyes. "It was just a trick, the last one of the thirty-six stratagems—escaping. It is the best of the thirty-six stratagems, though it might not be the wisest. This means that if you are in an inferior position, you must not keep fighting.

"'Escaping' here means 'fleeing.' They are synonyms. So you can say it's best to 'escape,' or it's best to 'flee.' 'Escaping the banquet' means 'fleeing the banquet!'"

Mirror

By **Lin** Weisheng

Joy and laughter filled Room 308 in the staff residence on the school campus that lay in the tranquil suburbs of Canton.

Somebody, out of the blue, suggested that the room needed a big mirror that could attract neighbors and visitors. It would add fun and joy and . . .

Indeed, the campus needed more fun, and a mirror was a terrific idea. It would also serve me well personally: my mom had been complaining that I did not dress neatly and never quite looked like a teacher. My friends said my hair was seldom neater than a bird's nest or straw. My colleagues had told me that sometimes I walked like a baby and sometimes like an old man.

Yes, I should get a mirror to help me redesign myself, and I needed more fun, too!

The next day saw a big mirror, forty inches by twenty, professionally installed right in the middle of the south wall.

All my visitors would stare at it with admiration, telling me it was the best mirror on campus.

On a later day, after he had just recovered from a cold, Mr. Zhang, a teacher who shared all my conversation topics, asked to come to my place for some *gongfu* tea.* No sooner had he entered my room than he started to look in the mirror, just like any other visitor.

All of a sudden, he was lost in melancholy, looking solemn and disappointed. After a long moment of silence, he raised his hand slowly to comb his long grey hair. "I haven't really looked in the mirror for a long time. I almost couldn't recognize myself!" It sounded like joking, but he meant what he said. His original enthusiasm now lost, he left immediately after we exchanged a few pleasantries.

I secretly blamed the mirror for its cruelty in showing him his old looks.

Then a schoolmate two years my senior came to borrow a book from me—volume 4 of Xu Guozhang's English textbook. Though we both had been living in Canton, we hadn't seen each other for several years.

I was shocked when she stepped in—I simply could not believe that the past few years had turned her into an out-and-out "auntie." I was worried that she would look in the mirror, but she did anyway. With thin hair over a pointed skull, she stood there like a pair of chopsticks, lost in silence.

I woke her up. Then we started a hearty conversation—or rather, I listened while she talked. She kept talking non-stop while I listened.

Her husband had been cold to her; her daughter was left without proper care; her teaching load was too heavy. And she went on and on.

Rather than a treasured moment between two school friends, her visit turned out to be an opportunity for her to groan and grieve. Her tears dropped onto my smooth table and the rough floor. I passed my tissues to her one after another until the whole package was gone. Finally I had only a roll of Zebra toilet paper for her.

After she left, I borrowed a hammer and a pair of pliers and, in one breath, moved my mirror to the less noticeable north wall.

Not long after, my winter vacation started, and my dad came to visit me from my hometown. My father, who naturally cared about his son's decor, in no time discovered the large object on the north wall. He could not but enjoy looking in the mirror.

"How strange!" he murmured to himself. "My back looks like a bow, and my nose seems crooked." With this, he started to feel the mirror to see if it was flat.

Not knowing how to respond to the situation, I cleverly explained that I had bought it at a discount and perhaps it didn't reflect well. The Chinese teacher suddenly became speechless, leaving me alone to find new conversation topics.

I was lost in thought.

"Your mirror is a demon-reflector. It reveals the true colors of everybody, leaving nothing for anyone to hide," teased my next-door neighbor Xiao Liu. After hearing the joke, I simply covered the mirror up with a large 1992 calendar.

From then on, Room 308 on the quiet campus was filled with happy laughter again.

---

* *Translator's note: Gongfu* tea is mostly found in Chaozhou, Jieyang and Shantou of Guangdong Province, Fujian Province and Taiwan. Though the sizes vary, the tea set is usually very small but always artistically made. The tea pot, often made of high-grade clay, may be as small as a baby's fist, while the cups are around four centimeters in diameter and about three centimeters deep. Usually, the tea set consists of a pot, three (maybe two or four) cups placed in a round tray with a waste-water container underneath. Typically, it comes with a very small stove and a tiny kettle that boils water for immediate and repeated serving. The tea pot is first filled with *wulong* tea. Then boiling water is poured in until it spills. The tea pot is covered with its lid before serving. In most places, the tea is drunk hot in one breath. Anyone who sips it and puts it down for a break betrays him/herself as a non-tea drinker, or an outsider. Each pot of tea may be served up to a dozen times. Before the tea is poured into the cups each time, the cups are quickly washed with boiling water. It is required by the local custom that anyone who is sick refrain from joining the tea drinkers. Or he or she should bring his or her own cup, which is usually placed away from other cups. As described above, much expertise as well as time is required, thus, the name *gongfu* tea—*gongfu* in the local language primarily means "skills" and/or "free time."

More Like the Star Himself

By **He** Baoguo

Mapu Commercial Television, or MCTV, started a new game called
Who's More Like Me? during prime time on the weekend. Like oil
spread over fire, it set the whole city ablaze at a speed never seen
before. MCTV's ratings rocketed steadily; advertising customers
simply swarmed in.

The program was masterminded by Gu Ping, the most influential
person in this commercial city. He had won the first prize in a national
popular singers' contest at the age of twenty, and was immediately
recognized as a star. Later, he switched from singing to television,
continuing to shine until now as a hot TV personality. Whenever he
appeared on TV, he captured hundreds and thousands of fans. It was
said that the letters and postcards he received every day could almost
fill up a large gunnysack, which he could never finish reading one
way or the other.

Everybody could participate in *Who's More Like Me?* Whoever
believed they looked like a certain star could go to MCTV to sign up.
The program crew would then choose several of the applicants who
looked most like that star and introduce them to the audience in the
photo studio. The audience would rate them live. Whoever received
the highest scores—was believed to most resemble the star—would
be awarded prizes donated by sponsors. At least ten people had been
signing up for the program every day. Watching and talking about
the program had become a trendy activity in the city. What stunned
and elated the viewers was the large number of residents in the city
who resembled stars—some even looked more like the stars than the

stars themselves.

Its fifth program showed three people looking like Andy Lau, and its sixth, four like Jackie Chan. One of the participants, a local police officer, was rated one hundred per cent and declared to be "more like Jackie Chan than Jackie Chan himself." In its seventh program, six "Small Swallows," or Zhao Weis, walked out one after another, with the audience shouting "Bravo!" at every one of them.

Today was its eighth program, and the host was Gu Ping. Gu Ping walked toward the stage to the soft music and started the program by saying, "Hello friends! Welcome to another *Who's More Like Me?* program. Who's more like me—" As he spoke, he looked back and caught sight of a Gu Ping slowly walking toward him from the entrance, an out-and-out Gu Ping who wore the same clothing, had the same height and the same bearing. The latter's appearance made a stir in the audience.

"Wow!" The audience was stunned by the protagonist, a real, living Gu Ping appearing right before them.

"Take a look, folks. Does he look like Gu Ping?" Gu Ping asked the audience.

"Yes!"

"Let me ask him for some details then," smiled Gu Ping.

As a rule, what followed was identification-checking.

"What's your name?" asked Gu Ping.

"Gu Ping," said the man.

"You even have the same name as mine," said Gu Ping. "Where do you work?"

"I work as a host for MCTV," said the other Gu Ping.

The audience in the studio simply could not distinguish the two men, whose voices sounded the same when they talked. Boiling with excitement, the happy audience started to beat time to their dialogue. It turned out to be the most successful program MCTV had ever produced. The person who pretended to be Gu Ping got a record high rate of 120 per cent and claimed to be "more like Gu Ping himself."

The audience cheered and applauded over thirty times, which took up eighty per cent of the time. Viewers outside made 1999 calls to the TV station through the hotline. MCTV's rating set a record high.

When Gu Ping returned home that evening, his relatives in his hometown called, telling him his father had fallen ill and was hospitalized. Gu Ping took a bus early the next morning to visit his father. Though he was with his sick father in the ward, his mind was with *Who's More Like Me?* Though the preparation was done by his assistant, Gu Ping had to be present for the production that would start on Wednesday afternoon. But his father was still under intensive care. Thus, he had to call MCTV to ask them to reschedule it for Thursday morning. To his surprise, Xiao Fang, who received his call, hung up even before hearing his full request. When Gu Ping tried to call again, the line was always busy. His father's condition improved later that day, so Gu Ping returned to Mapu in the evening for the Wednesday production. He rushed into MCTV only to see the dress rehearsal of the weekend's *Who's More Like Me?* taking place at the film studio.

"Hello friends, I am Gu Ping," the smiling Gu Ping in the rehearsal spoke to the camera.

Gu Ping was astonished that the man was disguising himself as him. He was about to walk over to find out what was going on when the agile, sharp-eyed Xiao Fang stopped him sternly. "Hey! What do you want? We are doing the rehearsal!"

"I am Gu Ping—" Gu Ping became anxious now.

"You are like Gu Ping? Yes. I think you look like Gu Ping, but you should have come to register earlier! You have missed the deadline," said Xiao Fang. "Two people who look like Gu Ping are participating in our program. You can come for the next show."

"It's me who—it's me—" Gu Ping was too anxious to speak. At that moment, the man who looked more like Gu Ping swept his hand toward two men, and said, "Friends, do they look like Gu Ping?"

Up came two men who looked exactly like Gu Ping. Gu Ping

was stupefied. "God, how come there are so many men looking like me, or even more like me. Even I cannot tell!"

Getting Out of the Desert

By **Shen** Hong

Radiating hostility, the four pairs of eyes were again fixed on the water bottle hanging from my neck. I clutched the strap of the bottle all the time, in fear they would snatch it from me.

We confronted each other in this deathly desert. This had happened once at noon already.

Seeing their sallow faces with parched lips, I had thought of giving up and really wanted to hand over the water bottle to them, then . . . But I couldn't do it!

Two weeks ago, we had followed Professor Zhao on a folklore investigation trip along the Silk Road. Seven days ago, nobody knew what happened, but we got lost. Then we wandered into this inhuman desert. The dry and sweltering desert exhausted every single one of us. We had run out of food, but we feared thirst more. Everybody knows having no water in the desert simply means death.

Before we got lost, everybody had a bottle of water. After we got lost, to save water Professor Zhao collected all the bottles from us and redistributed them to us regularly, but he had passed away last night. Before he died, he removed the last bottle from his neck, gave it to me and said, "It is this bottle that will pull you out of the desert. You must try not to open it, not until death confronts you. You must carry on. You must get out of the desert."

At this moment, their eyes were still fixed on my bottle.

I had no idea when we could get out of here, and this bottle was our life support. So I would never give it away until we had reached a moment of life and death. But what if they tried to seize it by force?

I grew scared at their desperate looks. I tried to look calm and asked, "Do you—"

"No more nonsense!" the impatient, unshaven Meng Hai interrupted me. "Give us the bottle." With this he got closer and closer to me, the other three following behind.

We'd be done for! If they seized the water bottle, I could . . . I dared not imagine what might happen next. Suddenly, I threw myself on my knees and said, "I beg you not to be like this. Please do not forget what our professor told us before he died!"

They stopped, and I saw four hung heads instead.

"Right now, none of us really knows when we can get out of the desert," I went on. "And we have only this bottle of water left. We had better not touch it unless we really have to. There are still two hours before it gets dark. Let's walk on while we can still manage. Believe me, I'll definitely distribute the water to everybody two hours later."

With great effort, we started to trudge along again. Another day had almost passed, but evening would soon come. Then there would be the wee hours, then tomorrow. By that time . . . oh, let heaven decide our fate!

The endless desert was just as vast as the Buddha's palm in the novel *A Journey to the West*. We just could not get out of it no matter what. It was getting dark when we climbed a sand dune.

The rays of the setting sun at the edge of the horizon stretched out all over the desert. They were dark red, just like blood. How splendid the scenery was! At sunset, Meng Hai and the other three people confronted me again. They appeared ready to stage a life-or-death fight with me. I knew I had no other way out, so I would just give them the bottle. A thought of real desperation flashed across my mind. I was taking off my water bottle when I heard Yu Ping shouting, "Listen, guys. I seem to hear some noise."

Everybody plopped down on their stomachs at once. We listened carefully and concluded that it came from the sand dune on the left—

and that it sounded like running water.

I could not hold back my excitement. "There may be an oasis over there. Let's go. Quick!"

Indeed, on the left below the tall sand dune lay an oasis. Everybody ran toward the lake like mad.

The sun finally sank in the west. The green trees on the other side of the lake were full of life. The lakeshore was covered with wild fragrant flowers. Meng Hai and the others lay among the flowers, smiling contentedly. Perhaps they had forgotten about the water bottle on my neck, but I felt very sad. So I got them up and said, "I want to tell you something now. Do you know why I didn't let you drink the water from this bottle again and again? In fact, there is no water in it at all. It's just a bottle of sand." I took off the bottle and unscrewed the lid. Instantly, fine yellow sand ran out.

Everybody was dumbfounded.

I glanced at them and said in a sad voice, "We ran out of water yesterday morning, but Professor Zhao didn't tell us the truth. He was afraid we might become desperate. So he carried a water bottle so that we'd think there was still water. He had secretly filled it with sand so we wouldn't be suspicious. Later on, he knew he could not make it, for he had not had a drop of water for several days. He had saved his share for us. He told me about the bottle and asked me to keep the secret from everybody. He told me, 'The bottle would pull us out of the desert. If I die, you should take it over from me and carry on.'"

I could not continue anymore. Meng Hai and the others had already broken down. Only when we looked back to the deathly long road lying behind us did we understand what had got us out of the desert.

Chopping Chicken Heads

By **Ye** Chunsheng

A district court in Hong Kong heard a case of debt involving two moguls. Old Lee and Old Chen accused each other of repudiating a debt of half a million Hong Kong dollars, but neither presented any reliable proof. They had no receipt, no written transaction records and no witnesses. Nobody except themselves knew the truth.

"Go and chop chicken heads at the Wen-wu Temple," ordered the judge when he found no basis for a ruling. "Chopping Chicken Heads" was a popular service performed at an oath-taking ceremony in a temple about fourscore years ago, but it still had legal effect.

Placed in the temple were a kitchen knife, a chopping board, joss sticks, candles, ingots that looked like gold and silver, and a piece of yellow paper. Written on the paper were oaths for the plaintiff and the accused to swear.

Under the supervision of the private legal assistants and the lawyers, the ceremony started with Lee and Chen standing before the altar, lighting joss sticks and candles, kowtowing to the celestial beings.

Soon they would swear an oath, chop off the chicken heads, spread the chicken blood over the yellow paper, then burn it away, thus ending the presentations of the case.

Old Lee was staring at the oath, "With a clear conscience, I speak nothing but the truth!" Old Chen was looking at "If I ever lie, may heaven strike me down, and may my sons die with me!"

"Mr. Lee," the master of ceremony in the temple announced, "will you kneel down and swear now."

"No, he can go first," said Lee, pointing to Chen.

"Why me? You will go first," said Chen.

After much exchange of words and angry looks, followed by moment of silence, neither wanted to kneel down first. As a result, no chicken heads were chopped.

When they met again in court, the judge found Lee the plaintiff guilty, without explanation.

Because of That Mailbox

By **Lin** Rongzhi

Public order in the small town has not been too good lately. It is said that an unknown gang of robbers has been breaking into houses when the owners are at work. .

The day before yesterday, the owner of a private business, Wangma Software Centre, on Dongkai Avenue was ransacked.

Yesterday, a family business on Hongwei Street was robbed.

Today, the home of a government official on Aimin Lane was broken into.

Such news spreads fast, and everybody in town has become terrified. The police cannot crack any of the cases immediately. All they do is instruct the neighborhood committees to knock at every door and warn every household against break-ins.

Actually, even without the warning, everybody has been on alert. All my neighbors, for example, have installed new iron doors. From a distance, the bars look like those of strongly fortified prison cells.

"Should we also buy an iron door?" my wife asked me about a week ago.

I thought for a while and said, "I'm a teacher—I can't compare with our neighbors. Even if the burglars break into our home, they can only find books. An iron door costs more than two hundred yuan, or two months' income."

My wife did not insist. Meanwhile, the postman slipped our mail, including a newspaper, through the door. It was so thick a pile that it kind of got torn, and I thought of making a mailbox.

I had just started working on my mailbox when I heard three

knocks on the door. I was pretty scared when I opened it. A man was brandishing a glittering kitchen knife at me. "Buy it from me! It's a good knife!"

"No, no, no," I answered mechanically.

"You can pay me in grain coupons." He drew out another sharp dagger from his satchel, ready to enter by force.

With great effort, I managed to hold the door and keep him outside. He threw an angry look at me with threatening eyes.

"Sorry, but leave me alone." I became alert now.

I decided to have an iron door installed the next day, but the price shocked me when I went out to inquire about the cost: it had tripled. "I'd better wait until I get my salary next month," I said to myself, returning home, dejected.

When I returned home, I found the postman had again misdelivered mail to me. I simply brought out my writing brush and wrote as a reminder for the careless postman, "Mailbox of Lin Lin the teacher," on the mailbox I had hung by my door.

When I returned home from work late in the afternoon, I heard all my neighbors cursing and swearing. I walked up to them and soon learned they all had been robbed. The robbers were old hands who had even managed to break the iron doors. I went back to check my own door and found it undamaged. I had no trouble myself, so I uttered a deep sigh.

The police arrived. The captain walked from door to door, back and forth. Finally, he stopped at mine and said to himself, "How come every home has been robbed except this one?"

"That's right," another officer who had overheard cut in. "And they all had iron doors installed, except this family."

Hearing them, I suddenly grew rather nervous, not knowing what to do.

"That's the answer!" A sparkle flashed in the captain's eyes. "They have a protective talisman!"

"What talisman?" asked the officer beside him.

"It's this mailbox," said the captain. "Don't you see the word 'teacher' over there?"

Only after hearing this did I sigh with relief.

From then on, every one of my neighbors hung up a mailbox by the door with the word "teacher" on it.

Just a Joke

By **Sun** Chunping

Li Hairen, who used to be the director of the Office of the County Committee, was promoted to deputy director of a department of the upper-level City Committee. Two years later, he returned and caught everybody off guard by assuming the position of the county's deputy Party leader.

Late in the afternoon one day, when they had nearly finished work, Da Jiang of the Commission for Inspecting Discipline and Ma Heng of the Organizational Department invited him to the Dog Meat Restaurant for a Triple-Dog-Penis Soup.*

Hairen told them to bring along Lin Jingyuan, the present director of the Office of the County Committee.

After calling Jingyuan, who was hearing a visitor's grievances in his office, Ma Heng said, "Since we told him there is some emergency, we ought to give him something to worry about. He can't have Triple-Dog-Penis Soup for free. Hairen, show him the Party leader's power and airs. Use all your might to bluff him into confessing his illegal or wrongful doings."

What he said reminded Da Jiang, who quickly drew out an envelope that a township had sent to the county's Committee for Inspecting Discipline and placed it in front of Hairen. "Good idea. I have ready stage props here. I guarantee we will scare the shit out of him."

Hairen understood at once and said smilingly, "One is the

---

* *Translator's note:* Dog-Penis Soup is said to be capable of enhancing one's sex drive.

playwright and one is the director, so I am left with the role of an actor. When Jingyuan comes in, cooperate with me. Pull a long face and take your cue from me as I act. Nobody should laugh."

Meanwhile, they heard footsteps in the corridor. Hairen gave a gesture, so the other two immediately put on an ugly look, obediently sitting in the sofa opposite him. When Jingyuan pushed the door open and saw what was inside, his smile disappeared instantly. "Secretary Li, you wanted to see me?" he asked gently.

An indifferent Hairen threw a glance at him from the corner of his eye, still looking at the other two. "You two may go now," he said in a serious tone. "I saw you today in order to verify a few things. We talked about everything, but you have no duty to spread it around also. If anything is leaked, I will hold you both accountable."

Da Jiang and Ma Heng kept nodding like chickens pecking at rice. They acted very well.

Hairen waved at the two in an insufferable manner; they then rose and left. Neither said anything to Jingyuan. They even tried to avoid meeting his eyes directly.

"You may sit," Hairen finally said to Jingyuan, pointing to the chair opposite him.

Nervous and scared, Jingyuan sat down, noticing the letter on the Party leader's desk. He also saw Hairen carelessly pick it up, then put it down. The atmosphere was depressing, as both remained silent.

Hairen wore a taut expression on his face, trying to hold back his laughter. He knew that his improvisation was very successful. He did not have to act: all he had to do was make believe that the person before him was somebody who had broken the rules and violated discipline, and that he had nothing to do with him. "God! So that's how an actor does it!" he thought.

Jingyuan finally broke the silence, asking carefully, "Secretary Li, you wanted to see me. Is there anything you wish to raise with me?"

Hairen gave a deep sigh and said, "There are a few things the Committee for Inspecting Discipline has reported to me. I thought about it for a long time, and finally decided to talk with you in person—so that the situation may favor us. It will also help us in the next step, whatever should be taken."

Jingyuan who could not sit still found himself even more restless. "What—did they tell you?" he asked.

"If I tell you about it, how could it favor you then?"

"Is it something about eating and drinking?"

"If it is just about a meal or a drink, I wouldn't have bothered to ask you to come."

Jingyuan's face turned ghastly pale, his forehead covered with beads of sweat. Groping in his pocket, he drew out a cigarette but failed to light it with his trembling hands. Hairen's heart was filled with joy, so he showed an even colder face. His back leaned against the rotating leather chair; he indulged himself in the real fun of the game.

"Secretary Li, since you returned to our county recently, we—your old classmates—have all been overjoyed from the bottom of our hearts. If I really have made any small mistake, I hope you—"

"Am I not giving you an opportunity? If we weren't classmates, it would have been simple."

"I—just, just—" Jingyuan spoke haltingly, ready to confess something.

Suddenly, Hairen became mysteriously nervous. "No. I've gone too far. If Lin Jingyuan really confesses something, would I then be falsely acting out a true story or truthfully acting out a false story?" In his nervous anxiety, he covered his mouth with his hand and started to cough loudly. He tried to cough out a way to cope with the unexpected situation; he tried to call back the masterminds of the mischievous game.

"At that time, I—I didn't think—"

The door suddenly burst open. In came the two mischievous men, laughing and joking. They seized Jingyuan, patted him as they laughed non-stop.

"See how scared Jingyuan was!" said Hairen who also started laughing.

Jingyuan at once understood it was just a joke. His face turned pale, then red as he thought about scolding them. But after a quick glance at Hairen, he withdrew the curses from the tip of his tongue. Instead, he put on a smile, giving Da Jiang and Ma Heng each several heavy punches. Then he scolded them, laughing. "I knew it was you two little monsters who tried to scare your master. You think you are good at play-acting, and I can't carry another mile farther, eh?"

Rubbing his painful shoulder hit by Jingyuan, Ma Heng scolded, "Damn you! Call it play-acting. Why was your forehead covered with sweat then?"

"Don't you show off shamelessly!" Jingyuan said angrily. "If you were in the same scene just now, you might not have handled it as well as I did. We are neighbors of the same town—what is not known to others?"

Taking it easy for a second, Hairen hastily announced in a loud voice, "The show is over." Then, laughing heartily, he added, "All right then. It was a private little show for us old classmates only. Now let's go have Triple-Dog-Penis Soup!"

Humans and Animals

Selling a Horse

By **Yan** Xiaoge

The dark red horse owned by the production team was too old to work, so at a meeting the villagers decided to sell it.

"Go sell it. You know the market well," the team leader said to Cunshan, the old horse-keeper.

The old man nodded in agreement.

Giving Cunshan three hundred yuan, the team leader added, "This is all the money our production team has. Add it to what you get for the old horse and buy a foal that can help us when we go in to sow wheat next fall."

Again, Cunshan kept nodding as he received it with great care.

Cunshan had to travel thirty-five kilometers to the cattle firm in Luohe to sell the horse. Using a piece of red cloth, the old man wrapped up the money again and again. Then he asked his wife to tear open the lining of his ragged cotton-padded coat. He put the money inside, and asked her to sew it up for him. Only when he pressed it and was sure the money was inside did he relax and cheer up by opening his toothless mouth.

It was pitch dark when Cunshan started out with the old horse. He had filled his son's school bag with home-steamed buns that would last him the whole day. The head of the production team saw him off at the village entrance and kept telling him to be careful.

On the road, Cunshan took big strides one moment and small steps the next. Though the wind in early winter was cold, he felt drizzly warm sweat oozing all over his body. At cock's crow, Cunshan had crossed the railway into Luohe. He stopped walking and looked skyward to the east. It was still dark, not quite daybreak yet. Then he felt tired and hungry. Thinking there would not be people in the cattle firm until after daybreak, he squatted down against a hydro post for a break, grasping the reins. The horse leaned close to him intimately. Unintentionally, Cunshan fell asleep and began to snore.

It was the north-south Beijing-Guangzhou railway line. Trains came and went frequently. A train that was pulling into the station gave a long shrieking hoot. It really scared the old horse, which had been tilling in the fields all its life and never heard such strange noises. The horse struggled free from Cunshan's hands and started to run wildly. It was broad daylight when Cunshan woke up. He found his hands empty and his horse out of sight. He was stupefied. His sweaty body that had just dried up was soaked with sweat again. He got up and ran straight to the cattle firm. When he arrived, he found the firm was already very crowded. He elbowed through the crowds like an eel, hoping to see his horse, but failed. Instead, he went through the numerous streets in the city, asking anybody he met in a begging tone, "Have you seen a dark red horse?" But the answer was always no.

After lunch, when Cunshan's fellow villagers were sitting against the walls enjoying the warm sun, the old horse returned home. It was sweaty and was blowing out hot breaths through its nose.

"Why hasn't Cunshan sold the horse?" they wondered. They looked beyond the horse, hoping to find the old man, but he was not there. They called the team leader, and together they went to the road, looking into the distance. They stayed there until dark, but Cunshan never appeared. The villagers' hearts were heavier than lead. The worried team leader waited for him in anxiety throughout the night.

At the crack of dawn the next day, the team leader sent more than thirty men to Luohe to look for Cunshan. They went through all streets and lanes in the city, enquiring about his whereabouts. When they came to the south of the railway later in the day, they were told that Cunshan was seen leaving the city, but that was all the information they got.

The team leader and the other villagers waited for him for a few more days, but in vain. They then believed he must have died—he must have been robbed and murdered, for he had three hundred yuan on him. The team leader pounded his head with his fist as he burst into tears. "What a stupid fool I was! Why hadn't I thought of asking a young man to go with him!"

The team leader asked a new cattle-keeper to care for the horse in the best way he could.

He still recorded work points for Cunshan, ten (full) work points a day. This was the first time the production team had recorded work points for a dead man, but nobody complained. As time passed, they even got used to it. In the days to come, the villagers would drop by at the cattle hut to see the old horse. The shiny fur of the dark red horse would remind them of Cunshan. They would feel their eyes itch, followed by tears like earthworms crawling out of a can.

For the Chinese New Year, the farm in the neighboring village needed some meat to improve its workers' food quality. But that year meat was in short supply, and according to the by-law, it would be illegal to slaughter cattle for food unless they were a sick, disabled or old. So an official from the farm came to talk with the team leader, offering a plump and sturdy mule in exchange for the old horse.

"No," said the team leader. "Old Cunshan's life was tied to this horse. I don't want to give it away even for ten mules." The villagers also said they wanted to keep it until it died itself and bury it like a relative. So the visiting official left in disappointment.

Time flew. In the twinkling of an eye, the season for sowing wheat had come. The team leader lay sleepless in bed, wondering where to borrow a horse for the ploughing. In those days, there were few farm machines in the countryside and the horse was the farmers' life. Then, at midnight, the team leader heard strange neighs out of the blue. They were so clear and so close that he jumped out of bed, opened his door and ran out for a look.

As it was the fifteenth of the lunar month, the moon was full and bright. The team leader saw Cunshan standing in the middle of the village with a white horse, reins in hand. Cunshan looked much older: his messy hair and beard were grey, and his back stooped like a bow. The team leader ran over and circled him in his arms. "Brother, where have you been all this time?" he asked the old man anxiously. The other villagers also came out, gathering around Cunshan, who began to tell them why he had disappeared.

As the story goes, when Cunshan failed to find the horse, he felt he had let down his fellow villagers. So he went to Wuhan on foot, where he worked as a coolie at a harbor, finally earning enough money to buy this white horse. Tears started to trickle down the team leader's cheeks. "Good brother, the dark red horse came back at noon the next day. It's still in the cattle hut. We've been keeping it."

"Is that so?" asked Cunshan, his eyes wide open.

"Yes, yes, yes. You can go see for yourself."

Cunshan hastily staggered to the cattle hut, where he found the serene dark red horse feeding on night hay.

He held its neck in his arms, tears rolling down his cheeks non-stop.

The old man had been keeping horses all his life, but he had forgotten the old saying, "An old horse knows its way."

The Old Man and the Sheep

By **Zha** La Ga Hu

Slowly the moon unveiled its beautiful face, with bright beams stretching over the prairie. The sky was as clear as water, dotted with stars glittering in the cold. It was on this bright, charming night that I went to Dalanou to report for duty.

Suddenly, a faint light flashed in the distance, but it soon disappeared, followed by sheep's bleating. I had no clue what was happening, so I changed my direction and galloped my horse toward the noise. When I got to the sheep, I found no owner or shepherd there. What I saw was a sheep standing by the river with the rest of the flock bleating behind it. No less puzzled than just before, I dismounted from my horse for a close look. Only then did I find an old man lying in front of the sheep near the water. Next to him was a torch. So he must be the one who had flashed the light! I quickly tied my rope around the horse's legs and went over to help him up. His clothes were covered with ice.

Soon I found that his hat and beard were also covered with ice. I replaced his hat with mine, covering my own ears with my scarf instead. While I was removing his hat, I discovered a wound on his head, approximately the width of a finger, running from above his right eyebrow to the corner of his ear. His neck and cheek were covered with a large amount of blood—perhaps he had passed out from the fresh bleeding. I bandaged his wound with my handkerchief lest it worsen when further exposed to the cold. I was still wondering what to do when the old man unexpectedly threw down his hands after a brief struggle and opened his eyes.

373

"I'll send you home," I told him quickly.

"All right. Thank you." He stared with a bemused expression. "You are so kind."

"Where do you live?" I shouted.

"Just follow the sheep. They will take you to my yurt." The old man then shouted through clenched teeth, "Little Harri, lead the way home. Quick!" With this he closed his eyes again, breathing rapidly.

Hearing the order, the sheep next to him bleated and really started to lead the way. The rest of the flock followed it closely. I was amazed how smart the sheep leader was. How come it understood human words?

Giving the old man my saddle, I sat behind him, clutching him in my arms, and followed the sheep closely. We passed a hillock and were about to enter the reeds when a man on horseback, not far from us, appeared in the east. He was visible in the moonlit night, and I could see him coming toward us.

"My Little Harri, you are just as good as a young man!" he called out, reining the horse in front of the sheep. I didn't know what he was talking about. Neither did I know what to do with him.

"Who are you looking for?" I shouted to him. "And where are you from?"

He hesitated before answering me. "There! Aren't you Zha La Ga Hu from the Party Committee of the Hulun Boir Meng?" he cried as he came face to face with me.

"Why! It's you, Zhamusa," I shouted.

"What happened to Suguer?" he asked, staring at the old man.

After I told him the story, he said he had to take Suguer home immediately, asking me to follow the sheep myself. He also told me that their yurt was not too far away.

"Little Harri, lead the way home. Quick." Then he carried Suguer away.

Zhamusa rushed back to drive the sheep home after he had put Suguer in bed.

After the sheep got home, I also helped Zhamusa drive them into the pen. Then he invited me into the yurt, after which he went out to watch the sheep. I grew tired and sleepy, but I did not want to go to sleep. I wanted to wait until Suguer came to, yet he just would not wake up. Then I tucked in the bedclothes for him. After adding a few pieces of dried cow manure to the stove, I blew out the mutton-oil lamp and tiptoed out of the yurt to join Zhamusa.

"Where's Little Harri?" I asked him out of curiosity, my eyes sweeping across the pen.

"He sleeps in the middle of the flock. The same every day. Only when he lies down to sleep will the rest of them follow suit. He's Suguer's best friend." Zhamusa grew excited now. "Talking about Little Harri and Suguer, I've got a long story for you," he continued. "One day in the lambing season of the year when our stock-raising commune* was founded, Suguer was driving his sheep to the grazing land. On the way, one of the mother sheep, which was about to give birth to a lamb, foundered after treading over some mouse holes. She broke her front legs and could not get up. The sheep from behind pushed her down and ran over her. The mother sheep lay dying there with the lamb giving signs of coming out. Suguer stared at her, wondering how to save the unborn lamb. A moment later, he figured out a way: he squatted down to assist the mother sheep by giving her a touch here and a push there, and finally delivered a healthy little lamb."

The weather on the prairie was unpredictable. While we were talking, a biting northwest wind suddenly started sweeping all over the place.

"The mother sheep died after the lamb was born. Suguer then took the lamb back to his yurt. It had no milk, so Suguer would find time to milk the other goats for the lamb after he finished work, no

---

* *Translator's note:* A commune was an administrative division under the county level, which was gradually changed to "town" beginning in the 1980s.

matter how hungry and tired he was. When he returned with his milk, he would feed the lamb spoonful by spoonful. He took care of it like a mother caring for her baby. The lamb slept in the same bed with him every night. Under his meticulous nursing, it became as smart as a child, always getting off the bed when it wanted to urinate and defecate. His motherly care continued this way until the lamb could run. Suguer often spoke loudly to the lamb, turning the yurt into a noisy home. Gradually, the lamb learned to recognize his voice. Now, whenever Suguer goes out herding his sheep, all he needs is a shout. Then Little Harri will bleat to the flock and lead their way. The sheep leader Suguer has trained is just lovely. It has done so much for us."

Zhamusa and I returned to the yurt, only to find Suguer missing.

"He'll be back soon," Zhamusa said, looking at Suguer's bed. "He must have gone out to check the sheep." Then he continued with his story about Little Harri.

Before long, the door opened. In came a cold current, followed by Suguer with Little Harri in his arms. Only now did I realize that Little Harri was covered with icicles as if dressed in an ice coat. Suguer walked in halting steps—or, I should say, vigorous steps. Putting Little Harri beside his bed, he swept off the thick snow from head to foot. He was a small, short old man, dressed in a brown robe. One end of the strap that was attached to the robe was trailing on the ground. He looked like a man who was always busy but joyful. His eyes beamed with happiness under the black brows, his body imbued with vitality. He gave people the impression that he was an honest, kind-hearted and strong man. Sitting quietly on his bed, he expressed his thanks to me.

He then continued, "Already after midnight, and the wind started to blow again. I was worried Little Harri might catch cold, so I brought him in here. I was nearly frozen to death for him today. At sunset, I was driving the sheep to the Keerlun River for a drink. But all the sheep were afraid of the cold, so none of them wanted to get into the water when they got to the riverbank. Then I told Little Harri to take the lead. When Little Harri got into the shallow water, the rest of the sheep followed up, pushing him into the deeper water. Suddenly, a log that was drifting down the river struck him. It hit him so hard that he couldn't climb up. The next moment he was floating with the currents. Seeing he was drifting away in the waist-deep water, I couldn't care about myself anymore, so I jumped in to save him. It's early winter and the water is really cold. I was so cold, I couldn't think of anything except wanting to get Little Harri out of the water. After I reached him and secured him in my arms, another huge log came flowing down. This one struck me right on the head, tearing open my skin. Seeing a sudden flash of light, my head grew heavy and I fell down. I drank a lot of water, but I gritted my teeth and managed to get onto my feet, then out of the water. As soon as I got back to the riverbank and put down Little Harri, I lost consciousness. I couldn't remember anything else after that."

We asked the old man to lie down immediately so that he could rest comfortably. Then Zhamusa went out to watch the sheep while I lay down to sleep.

When I got up the next morning, Suguer was already out of bed. Again he wanted to graze the sheep. Zhamusa and I tried our best to stop him but failed. Suguer still left with the sheep.

When Suguer was driving the sheep to the grasslands, I watched him from behind, lost in joyful thought.

White Wolf

By **Peng** Sike

Stretching for hundreds of miles, Mount Tengly is a forbidden place inhabited by fierce beasts and venomous snakes. It is covered by primeval forests with luxuriant trees, steep cliffs and precipitous peaks piercing the skies. The forever turbulent Dalai River cuts across the mountains. Most noticeable are Tengly's countless caves, which can be seen high and low, for which it has been nicknamed "Mount Caves." Occasionally, decayed coffins are found in the caves. Nobody knows in which dynasty they were buried or why cave burial was observed. None of this, though, has ever scared the locals of the Mongolian and Han nationalities living in the vast prairie at the south foot. "Herd where there's grass; fish where there's water; hunt where the mountain is. It's a good place," they will say proudly.

The mid-1940s saw an outstanding hunter called Harbara, son of the well-known wrestler Buton Zana; Harbara was second to nobody in the 49th Qi.* In those days, thanks to its numerous caves, Mount Tengly was a kingdom for the wolves—the local white wolves, Siberian grey wolves, and black wolves that had crossed the frozen Bering Strait all the way from Alaska. In a matter of years, Harbara hunted down ninety-nine black and grey wolves. His fame spreading all over the prairie, he was duly nicknamed "Wolf King." At the peak of his fame, his close Han friend and herding mate, Liu Qingshan, lost his father to the mouth of a white

---

* *Translator's note: Qi is an administrative division of a county.*

wolf. The bloody, horrific scene was beyond description.

On hearing of the tragedy, the furious Harbara, thirsting for revenge, decided to kill the white wolf, but his nervous neighbors all tried to stop him. "You mustn't go. You mustn't. It was destined that his life should end that way. He couldn't escape the tragedy himself, but you must never, never provoke the white wolf. She is the Goddess of Wolves. Haven't you seen the Temple of the Goddess of Wolves? There's got to be a reason why it's been built. Never offend the goddess, or you will be in trouble. You've killed ninety-nine wolves, but they were all black and grey. Dare you provoke the White Wolf, you will regret it miserably when something happens to you!"

"I've heard of stories about killing white wolves in ancient times," said Harbara. "Why can't I try to kill one today?"

Learning of his decision, Liu Qingshan, who had been herding the same horses with Harbara, also came, but, fully aware that nobody—not even someone with the power of ten horses—could ever bend Harbara's will, Liu made preparation for him instead. He prepared for him some fried rice, butter, cheese, dry beef and mutton, and a large water bottle to be carried on his back. He also sent him an extra-large ancient Mongolian sword made of fine copper and inlaid with turkey stone and red coral. "No words can express my heartfelt thanks to you for your decision to revenge my dead father," he said. "But the white wolf is the Goddess of Wolves, and there will be no easy hunt. You are risking your life in a forbidden place. Please do take care of yourself. You can't afford to make the slightest mistake!"

Appreciating Liu's concern, Harbara nodded in agreement, but he knew what he was doing. It was the season when wolves littered, and as long as he caught the white wolf's young, he had caught her. The common saying goes, "Shoot the horse before you shoot the rider. Catch the ringleader before you round up the thieves. Hunt the whelps before you hunt the wolves."

An Anthology of Chinese Short Short Stories   Translated by Harry J. Huang

Indeed, the white wolf was no ordinary type—no wonder she was called Goddess of Wolves. Having had a premonition one way or the other, she had moved away all the whelps except one when Harbara arrived. No sooner had Harbara seized the last red-eyed white whelp—almost as tall as a calf—than its old mother returned to the cave only to encounter the unexpected intruder, whom she watched on full alert. Harbara was too close to the wolf mother and the cave was too narrow for him to use his weapon—a curly mace with a copper hammer. Holding the whelp in his left hand, he used his right hand to prick its skin with the pointed tip of his sharp sword, sending it into continuous howls. It was a serious warning to its mother: should she jump at him, he would kill the whelp first.

At this moment, something rather unexpected happened. Squatting on her hind legs, the fierce, red-eyed wolf raised her front paws to bow, her bloody red, triangle eyes flickering with tears. It looked like the pitiful old mother wolf was begging for mercy.

Harbara was stonehearted, knowing that he could not show pity to the wolf, let alone that she might be the one that had killed his friend's father, Mr. Liu Hui. A smart fighter, Harbara knitted his eyebrows, deciding not to kill the whelp but to hold it as a hostage and to wait to see what its mother would do.

There and then, the white wolf acted in the weirdest way, move after move. It might sound like exaggeration, but she almost gave him the highest salute of kneeling and kowtowing. Then she kept a proper distance from him, nervously walking down into the deep cave as if she were leading his way. She paused to check on him every few steps, looking pitifully sad as she raised her lower jaw to point to the front. The cave got darker and darker, so Harbara, a man who loved adventures, lit a torch made of white poplar bark. Following her calmly, he cursed to himself, "You won't get away with this, White Wolf! I wouldn't care even if this were a death cave. I dare you to leave your baby and run out of here."

The cave was extremely deep, with more than nine twists and

380

eighteen turns. There were smaller caves inside the bigger ones, branch caves within the main ones. Though they had walked a long distance no light was yet in sight, and still it got darker. It was only the torchlight that was showing Harbara's way. After they had covered nearly a mile, the white wolf suddenly leaned against a black object that looked like a huge rock, the size of a crouching ox. Standing on her hind legs like a human, she kept making bows to Harbara with her front paws. Harbara grasped his Mongolian sword firmly, ready for action.

The black object turned out to be a huge, ancient coffin, whose paint had all peeled off so he could not tell its color. Through the crack, he saw a human skull. "So that's where you've led me to," Harbara said to himself angrily, "a place where you'd bury me! Humph! No way! Too bad, neither will you or your baby leave here alive!" At this moment, he heard a loud noise—the white wolf had smashed a little jar she had fetched from the casket. Out came eight silver dollars that scattered around. She pushed one toward him with her mouth,.

Squatting in front of Harbara, the wolf mother kept making courteous bows which stirred up a sense of pity inside him, but he was a smart man and soon became himself again. He would be taken in should he let go of the whelp. If the white wolf ran off with her young, not only would he fail to revenge his good friend's dead father, but he would likely get lost in the cave as well. Then thirst, hunger and fatigue would ultimately lead him to demise in this death cave. His suspicion was well founded: the wolf mother could not but lead him out of the cave. In the light, Harbara indulged himself in joy and excitement, pressing his chest to make sure that the eight silver dollars were still there. How heavy they were! Suddenly he became softhearted, saying to himself, "This can't be Mr. Liu's killer wolf! She seems quite nice. She even gave me these precious silver dollars in exchange for mercy for her baby. I ought to appreciate it and be an honest and forgiving gentleman." With this, he released the whelp without hesitation.

Holding up her baby in her mouth, the white wolf stood up once more to make a bow of thanks instead of running away. Her triangular, blood-red eyes seemed to glow with friendliness and kindness. Out came some sort of mumbling from her large mouth that exposed sharp, long teeth that looked like fierce saw teeth. She seemed to show some sort of intimacy. Soon she was leading the way again, looking back from time to time to keep Harbara in close distance. By now Harbara had really changed into a different person, saying to himself with complacency, "Maybe she will send me some more funeral stuff. This white mother wolf isn't bad after all. She appreciates others' kindness and help." Thus, he followed her into the meadow. Suddenly a loud noise was heard. A giant iron trap that had been set up by a hunter for some time opened up and fell heavily onto Harbara's right leg, which would have been smashed had it not been wrapped in multiple layers of cloth straps and protected by the heavy cowhide boot.

Clearly, the cunning wolf was taking revenge by using somebody's trap. The pitifulness on her face instantly gave way to her real bloodthirsty look. Putting down the whelp she had been holding in her mouth, she opened her large mouth and jumped some eleven feet high into the air, aiming at Harbara. She created such a stinking wind that it could almost sweep a feeble person away.

From all her moves, Harbara finally figured out what she was up to. His right leg was now trapped, just like being shackled, and he could not stand up straight. Instead, he squatted down in a horse-riding position, his hands firmly grasping his sharp Mongolian sword that pointed into the sky. With the impact of her jump, the wolf slit her belly wide open on his sword. This tricky beast, the so-called Goddess of Wolves, fell dead after a howl and several somersaults.

"You have red eyes but with a vicious heart, you White Wolf. I'm sorry I have to be cruel and finish off your whelp as well!" The cursing man then threw his curling mace at the squirming whelp, killing it instantly. From that day on, the locals did not believe in the Goddess of Wolves anymore. Instead, the glorious story about "Wolf King" started to spread far and wide.

Being a Human Being

By **Wu** Wanfu

Dong Ye* was heirless. He was in his sixties without a disciple he could pass his knowledge on to. Obviously, all the invaluable herbal remedies and books of medical notes handed down to him from his ancestors would have to be shelved.

Yet people in and around the small town, far and near, all spoke highly of Dong Ye. He never refused any patient who sent for him, be it midnight or after, rain or shine. "Benefiting others means happiness" was the rule he followed when dealing with people. If he ever borrowed something from somebody, he would rather pay back more than what he had borrowed. Throughout his years of medical practice, nobody had ever uttered the word "bad" about him.

But one day Dong Ye experienced shame which he could never clear from his name.

It was drizzling that day when he walked with uneven steps out of the Maoshan Valley. As he ploughed his way through, he caught sight of a stout man lying on the ridge in the field. The man's nostrils were still moving, but he had lost consciousness. Dong Ye felt his pulse and discovered that he suffered from some acute disease, so he started to revive him by feeding him some medicine, accompanied by acupuncture. Instantly the man breathed out a slow, thin breath through his mouth and nose.

Unexpectedly, when the man woke up, he categorically accused Dong Ye of taking away the money from his pocket.

* *Translator's note:* "Dong Ye" literally means Grandpa Dong or Master Dong.

"I have saved your life. Why would I take away your money?" mumbled the ghastly pale Dong Ye.

"God knows what you were up to," said the man. "You must have forgotten about morals when you saw my money!"

"I have been a doctor all my life—" muttered Dong Ye.

"Being a doctor all your life! But can that prove you are a decent man?"

Dong Ye became tongue-tied. Then, out of desperation, he emptied his medicine chest and unbuttoned his coat and let the stout man search him.

"Humph!" said the man, throwing open his hands. "One man can hide something ten people won't find. You ought to know it was the food money for my family!"

Like a scholar running into a simple soldier, Dong Ye could not reason with him. The infuriated Dong Ye just turned round and got on his road again. The man followed at his heels straight into his clinic, then started crying and screaming.

Onlookers gathered outside the clinic, making all sorts of comments.

"Could Dong Ye have done that?"

"I don't really think so."

"Why would I have made up a story out of the blue?" the pitiful stout man said in tears. "Everybody has a head; you never know what's in it. Can you really read his mind? Can you guarantee he hasn't done it?"

The crowd was silent.

His body covered in mud, the stout man spun around on the floor, wailing in deep grief.

The onlookers found it somewhat believable, though it could be a scam.

Soon mumbling was heard: "No matter how well you stand, there's always a chance you may slip!"

"That's right," joined in another voice. "Dong Ye must have been beside himself with love for money this time."

Dong Ye's face turned purplish, his lips quivering. He staggered and nearly fell to the floor.

Trembling, Dong Ye brought out his 150-yuan savings, counting the 1,500 ten-*fen* notes before the stout man, and gave it to him. Money in hand, the man kept bowing at him with indescribable gratitude, then left Dong Ye's clinic.

Dong Ye's image was instantly ruined among all those who knew him. Then he fell ill. His wife stayed by his bed, looking after him and comforting him day and night. Dong Ye, however, just could not swallow this.

At noon on the fifth day, Dong Ye got up from bed. After cleaning his hands and lighting the joss sticks, the trembling old man carried out a sandalwood chest in both hands. Staring at the miraculous herbal remedies his ancestors had accumulated through painstaking efforts, generation after generation, he burst out crying until he lost his voice. Then he ripped up the remedies and burned them up in the incense burner one by one. He destroyed one page as he wailed a cry. While he wailed another, he tore up another. By the time his wife came out of the kitchen and snatched what he was tearing and burning, there were only a few blank sheets left. The dark ashes of the paper floating over the fire looked like butterflies hovering over flowers.

His old wife also burst out crying—she could never recover the invaluable remedies for later generations.

Dong Ye saw no more patients.

The common saying goes, "Gold has a price tag, but medicine is priceless." After practicing medicine for a whole life, Dong Ye had not saved even a penny.

Yet his life had to continue, and he still needed money.

One evening, when Dong Ye was strolling on the lawn in the suburbs of the town, he happened to see a dead dog, covered with grime, in a water hole. It had mistakenly eaten some distillers' grains. Obviously it had struggled before it plunged head first into the water.

The dog had been dead for some time, but it could still be saved. A dog's life is an earthen life. When it is with mud, it has a seventy per cent chance of revival.

Dong Ye bent down, held it up and placed it over his knees. He curled the dog up, then gave it a gentle push. Out burst a pool of foul waste from the dog's mouth that went in all directions, soiling Dong Ye's pant legs.

When the dog woke up, it gave a wild bark and snuggled up against Dong Ye. Then it fled, looking scared.

After a short distance, the dog halted, knelt on the ground and glanced at Dong Ye. After that it returned to him, lay down and raised its front paws to make a bow of thanks. It wagged its tail, making many sounds like saying "thank you" to Dong Ye for saving its life. When Dong Ye patted it, several muddy tears rolled down from the corners of its eyes. Only then did it reluctantly leave him.

Dong Ye was touched.

After he returned home, he decided to open a canine clinic, to treat canine diseases only. In this way, he could still make a living.

From that day on, irregularly, dog owners would take their pets to his clinic for treatment.

Somehow, keeping a dog became a trend in the small town. It was mostly the rich households that kept such pets. Some kept three or five, others just one or two. The dogs would follow their owners wherever they went. The sounds of the rattling iron chains around the dogs' necks filled the air as the dogs went through the street like commanding troops.

Dogs have their own characters, some like wolves, others like tigers. When they exposed their teeth, scared strangers would retreat hastily for safety. Thus, dog owners had indirectly improved their social status. Owners took advantage of their fierce dogs to bully others at will, by showing their might and displaying their power. People in town had been haunted to such an extent that they would be terrified at hearing about dogs. They would shudder at any dog barks.

But Dong Ye was not afraid of dogs. Those that he had treated would run over to wag their tails at him whenever and wherever they saw him. They would lick his hands and climb over him like intimate friends.

Everybody envied Dong Ye who could get along with dogs.

A Tale from the Snowfield

By **Ma** Duangang

It was a week ago that I invited Fatty Ren, a southerner, to dinner in the Wailou Hotel. I had long heard that he had become rich by raking in almost half a million yuan from reselling fur. Having eaten and drunk his fill, the sleepy Fatty Ren hiccupped with animated gestures, "You northerners are behind the times, with no talents for business. If you don't know the market, how can you get rich? Now the fur prices are rocketing in our place. Go and buy some from the Daxing'an mountain area in the northeast right away. I guarantee you will make fifty thousand yuan with each trip." Then, every cell in his body filled with joy and excitement, he added, "Girls there are not only sexy, but also cheap. That's called cheap and good. You buy their fur in the day, and enjoy dog meat with hot whiskey accompanied by beautiful girls at night. What kind of life is that?" He showed an air of satisfaction, water dripping from the corner of his mouth.

What damn luck I had! To arrive here to brave this heavy snowfall! Large snowflakes kept falling, and there was no sign of their stopping. I waded through the knee-deep snow. How could I have believed Fatty Ren's nonsense and come to this goddamned no man's place! The snow had covered the entire primeval forest. With a broken compass—I didn't know when it had been damaged— I could not tell my direction anymore. "Alas! When you are unlucky, even your teeth will block the water you drink." The fat snowflakes kept battering my face, and my chronic stomachache was now killing me. Clenching my teeth, I was like a desperate wolf running

389

aimlessly in an endless forest. Finally, I succumbed to the assault of the snowstorm. Seeing a patch of dark, I fell head first into the snow.

In the dark, I seemed to have seen Fatty Ren's slimy face with his cunning smile. "Fatty Ren, God damn your whole family!" I murmured. Then I heard faint dog barks from somewhere . . .

"He's awake. He's awake." Half asleep, I heard many people jabbering. In the oil-lamp light, I opened my eyes to meet a grey-haired old man, dressed in an Inner Mongolian costume, who was staring at me with a smile. The hospitable old man put a hot bowl of tea mixed with milk in my hand and chattered, "Drink it up. It's good for you." Only now did I realize I was lying on a warm *kang*. A black wolfhound was lying by the *kang*, licking my red face non-stop. Immediately, I drew out two hundred-yuan notes and thrust them into the old man's hand for saving my life. He pushed away my hand and said smilingly, "Young man, if I'm not mistaken, you must have come to buy our fur." From the old man, I learned that they still had no electricity or mail service. It was a typical poor area in the northeast, where every family made a living by hunting and by herding cattle and sheep. They all, though, had saved some pretty rare fur that could pull them through the hard times.

"Indeed, good fortune comes out of a mishap! God's will," I said to myself. "After tracking miles and miles in vain, the coveted fur comes purely by chance!" Seeing the bags and bags of fur I had purchased at very low prices, I jumped about merrily, beaming with joy as I forgot about all the worries and frustration in the past few days.

Before my departure, I invited the old man and his relatives to dinner, again to express my thanks to him for saving my life. I had long before learned that the men here were all straightforward and great drinkers. Today we would drink until everybody got good and drunk.

When I was half drunk, I suddenly remembered Fatty Ren's

enticing remarks. "I hear the dogs here have delicious meat,"* I said sleepily. "Why not kill one for me. I want to try it so that I can say I haven't wasted my time here." Seeing no response from the old man, I grew furious. "Don't be such a damn miser. I won't eat it without paying!" With the power of my whiskey, I threw out two hundred-yuan notes. The black wolfhound lying by the *kang* started to bark at me. Then the old man raised his cup and said, "Young fellow, maybe you don't know. A hunting dog is just like the hunter's life."

"What life? Money is everything and I have plenty of it." I drew out two more hundred-yuan notes. "Who wants to sell me a dog?" Money in hand, I swept across the crowd. The house, which was not very large, became silent. After a while, a man stood up, took my money and pulled over the black wolfhound. "Kill my dog," he said. I raised my sleepy eyes and found everybody staring at him in contempt.

Before long, a pot of steamy dog meat was brought up to me. It was as delicious as people said. Bite after bite I ate like a hungry wolf, oil dripping from my mouth and sweat from my body. Everybody stared at me in silence, so I immediately picked a piece and put it into the old man's bowl. Tears in his eyes, the old man said emotionally, "The dog was called Tiger Racer. Dear, people in poor places are just stingy."

I threw another hundred-yuan note at the old man. All my guests, except the old man, rose to their feet and left, hanging their heads.

Tapping the ashes from his smoke, the old man sighed, "If it were not for his two children's tuition fees, the owner would not sell his dog for the world. That dog was the life of his whole family. Young man, you don't know this: if Tiger Racer hadn't found you

---

* *Translator's note:* Though there are a few places in China where dogs are raised like pigs and cows to provide edible meat, most Chinese are horrified or disgusted by the idea of eating dog meat.

when you were buried in the snow that day—"

"What?!"

Alice Is Sick

By **Wu** Jinliang

The elevator had broken down, so Xiao Wang must have run all the way up. He looked deathly pale, his eyes rolling up. He gasped for breath, "Good—good new—news. Alice is sick!" Our general manager Mr. Zhao and I were baffled.

"Catch your breath first," I said, pouring him a cup of water. "That's no way to talk. It's not good, whoever is sick."

Sitting down, Xiao Wang sipped his water and smiled, "You are right, but you must know Alice is either Mr. Peak's wife or his daughter."

"Well?" Mr. Zhao finally cut in, apparently showing his disapproval of what Xiao Wang had said.

"It's true, it's true, Mr. Zhao." Xiao Wang was so nervous that his eyes rolled up again. "What I mean is, whether Alice is Mr. Peak's wife or his daughter I haven't found out yet, but I am sure she is very important. I overheard them again and again. Everybody there who toasted to Mr. Peak would also say 'I wish Alice good health, and hope she will recover soon.' You can imagine, if she were not important to him, those expert bootlickers wouldn't have uttered those sickening words."

After all, it did sound like good news. A smile emerged on Mr. Zhao's face. "Good. Xiao Wang, you've gathered great intelligence!"

"Really, Mr. Zhao. Thanks go to your good leadership."

"Even dog meat could become food if it's ever put on the table," I said to myself, feeling jealous that Wang had seized the opportunity to report on the case. In the past several days, all the companies,

393

except us, had been fighting to invite Mr. Peak to banquets held in his honor. We had been waiting for our opportunity, and had got it at last. Mr. Peak really respected women's rights. So it would work better to flatter the female members of his family than to lick his own boots. Indeed it was a pretty good opportunity!

"It is imperative that we act promptly," Mr. Zhao said, raising a finger. "Other companies aren't dummies. This time we will act before they do. As for what to send to him, it's up to you two to decide."

Grasping the real meaning of "act promptly," Xiao Wang and I rushed downtown like a whirlwind. Ginseng and pilose antler* were musts, while jewelry, especially jade, was the average woman's first choice. We were sure that Mr. Peak could cave in to pillow-whispering, too.

Finally, each carrying a bunch of fresh-cut flowers, we came to Mr. Peak's hotel with a large pile of gifts we had purchased for him— big boxes mixed with small ones.

"Mr. Peak, our boss hears that Alice—" Xiao Wang gulped, not knowing whether to call her Mrs. or Miss—something we had never thought about. I stood next to him in such anxiety that my palms began to sweat. "Alice, she, she—" Xiao Wang showed the whites of his eyes again.

Our smiling host was waiting patiently for him to finish his words, but perhaps because the signs of embarrassment were universal, Mr. Peak was finally touched by Xiao Wang's bashfulness and came to his rescue. "Mr. Wang, just take it easy. I don't avoid the word 'sick' myself. Yes, my little Alice is sick, but it's nothing serious. She has just caught a cold, but she is getting better."

Xiao Wang and I finally gave a sigh of relief. Since it was "little Alice," it must be his daughter, and definitely not his wife. We put down our gifts and held out our flowers solemnly in both hands as

---

* *Translator's note*: Used as a medicinal herb to keep one healthy and energetic.

we saw him turn and walk toward his inner room.

"Here, here, my Alice, wake up. See who has come to see you. They even have brought flowers . . ." Mr. Peak murmured as he walked out gently.

A dog? Called Alice?

We were stupefied when we saw a puppy in his arms!

Ancient Stories

Coming to Life

By **Tao** Qian (365-427)

The merciless outbreak of the plague in Xiangyang* took away Li Chu's life. Li's grief-stricken wife kept a bedside vigil from the time of his passing until midnight, when his corpse unexpectedly sat up and seized the gold bracelet she was wearing. Li's wife helped him, so he successfully removed the bracelet from her wrist.

Bracelet in hand, Li Chu passed away again, the dead body falling flat down. Puzzled, the wife kept watching him closely by his side, until early in the morning when his heart started to beat. His signs of life continued to improve till he was fully awake.

"When I was caught by the ghost official in the other world," he told his wife after he fully regained life, "I met many others who had also been captured. Then I saw people bribing him and having their names erased from the death roll. So I promised the ghost official that I'd give him a gold bracelet. He told me to go home and get it, and so I did. As soon as he got my bracelet, he set me free. So here I am—home again."

---

* *Translator's note:* Xiangyang is known as Xiangyang County in Hubei Province today.

Mr. Shen

By **Pu** Songling (1640-1715)

There lived a poor scholar by the name of Shen near the Jinghe River. He was so poor that he often ran out of rice. Husband and wife would sit looking at each other, not knowing what to do.

"We really have no way out," his wife said one day. "You may have to be a robber if you want to survive."

"As a learned man, I can't win honor for my ancestors, but would darken their names and ruin their reputation. I'd rather starve myself to death than be a robber."

"You want to stay alive, but you are afraid of losing face?" said the wife angrily. "In this world, if you don't own land or other wealth but you want to survive, you have only two options. Now that you can't rob people, do you want me to be a prostitute, then?"

Mr. Shen was furious and started to quarrel with her. His angry wife then climbed into bed to sleep instead.

Shen thought, "I am a man, but I cannot even earn two simple meals for my wife, who even thinks of making a living as a prostitute. I might as well kill myself!" So he snuck into the yard and tied a rope to the tree, deciding to hang himself.

No sooner had he put his head through the loop than he saw his dead father coming toward him. His father spoke to him in surprise: "Silly boy, why are you doing this?" He then broke his rope and continued, "You might as well be a one-time robber. If you hide yourself where the thick and tall crops are, one robbery will make you a rich man. You don't have to do it for the second time."

The sleeping wife, who heard something drop outside, woke up in fear. She called her husband but heard no answer. Then she lit a lamp and walked out to look for him, only to find a broken rope dangling from the tree. Her husband had passed out under the tree. The terrified woman immediately tried to rescue him by massaging him. It took her a while to bring him back to life. She helped him to bed, her anger vanishing instantly.

The next morning, using the excuse that her man was ill, she asked her neighbor for some porridge for him. After he finished the food, Shen left home. When he returned home at noon, he had a sack of rice on his shoulders. His wife asked where he had got it. "My father's friends are all wealthy people," he said. "I hated to lose face, so I never humbled myself to beg favors from them in the past. Our ancestors made the point: 'When you are unfortunate, tolerate a bit of shame and there is nothing you cannot do.' Since I wouldn't mind being a robber, what else would matter? Please cook for me now. After eating, I will go out robbing people as you told me to."

His wife thought he was still upset about what had happened the day before, so she remained silent as she washed the rice and cooked it. After he ate his fill, he hastily found a piece of hard wood and chopped it into a stick. When he was leaving with the stick in hand, his wife realized he was not joking, so she immediately tried to stop him.

"This is what you told me to do. Don't regret it if something happens and if you become involved!" Then he freed himself from her and ran away.

At dusk Shen was seen at the neighboring village. He chose a spot some half a mile away and hid himself, but a shower soaked him to the skin. Then he caught sight of a wood of luxuriant trees, where he decided to take shelter. He was starting to head for the wood when a thunderbolt lit up the sky, showing he was quite close to the village. Also in the light, he seemed to see a person in the distance walking toward him. Fearful of being discovered, he quickly snuck into the thick crops below the fence and squatted down to hide.

Soon he sighted a strong and stout man also coming toward the crops. Shen was so scared that he dared not move. Luckily, the man passed by the other side of the fork. Shen's eyes followed him secretly and saw him climb over the fence.

"On the other side of the fence is the Kangs' residence, the richest family of the village. It must be a thief. I'll wait until he comes out with a good loot and have my share," he thought. "The man is very strong. If I ask for a share politely, he definitely won't give it to me," he went on thinking. "Then we will have to fight, but I am no match for him. I'd better just knock him down with a sudden blow when he comes out."

Knowing what he was doing, he started waiting attentively. It was near cock's crow when the man emerged over the top of the fence. Hardly had he landed on his feet when Shen sprang up and struck him on the waist, knocking him flat on the ground. Shen looked at him and found him to be a huge tortoise with a wide-open mouth the size of a basin. The astonished Shen kept hitting the tortoise until it died.

As the story goes, the Kangs had a daughter, beautiful and intelligent, whom her parents loved dearly. One night a man entered her bedroom out of the blue and forced her to sleep with him. Before she could cry for help, the man had already thrust his tongue into her mouth. The girl passed out, so the man raped her in whatever way he pleased. The Kangs kept the incident from outsiders. All they could do after that was to gather the slave girls and servant women to guard her. They also bolted her door and closed her windows.

However, the door mysteriously opened when they were sleeping at night. In came the same man, and everybody in the room fainted simultaneously. So the man raped all of them one by one. The terrified girls and women told their master what had happened. Old Kang then asked all the men in his house to arm themselves with swords and guard his daughter's bedroom. He had the lamp lit in her room and asked her to sit through the night instead of sleeping.

Yet everybody, inside and outside the room, suddenly passed out again near midnight. A moment later, they all woke up as if from a dream. When they looked up, they found the girl had been stripped and was lying naked like an insane person. She did not fully wake up until quite a while later. The old man hated the rapist from the very depths of his heart, but could do nothing to stop him.

This continued for several months until the girl became a bag of bones. Seeing his dying daughter, the old man said, "I'll reward anybody who can drive away the monster with three hundred taels of silver."

Shen had heard about the monster, but only when he had killed the tortoise did he realize it must be the monster that had been harassing the Kangs. So he went to knock on the Kangs' door for his reward.

Old Kang was overjoyed when he heard the news. He invited Shen to dinner, offering him the most important seat at the table. He asked to have the tortoise carried into his yard and cut into slices. He also asked Shen to stay overnight. Indeed, the monster did not come that night. Thus, Old Kang rewarded Shen with three hundred taels of silver.

Shen carried his silver home. His wife, who had been worried about him throughout the two days and nights that he was away, at once started asking where he had been. Shen did not utter a word. Instead he threw the silver onto the table.

His wife was shocked at the unbelievable amount of money in sight, and said, "So you really went out robbing?"

"There! You forced me to, and now you are blaming me!" he said.

"I didn't mean it," she cried. "But now you really have committed a crime that deserves beheading. I won't be involved in this. I'd rather die before you are caught." This said, she went out to kill herself.

Shen ran right after her and dragged her back smiling, telling her the true story. Only then did she beam with joy. The couple worked hard and grew even richer year after year.

Han Ping and His Wife

By **Gan** Bao (317? -420?)

Han Ping, an imperial official working closely with King Song Kanwang, married a woman called He. She was so beautiful that Kanwang simply seized her for his own. Han Ping hated Kanwang for what he had done, so Kanwang took him into custody, sentencing him to guard the city gate in the day and to build the city wall at night.

One day, his wife sent him a secret letter, using their own secret language: "It is raining cats and dogs. The river is wide and deep. The red sun in the sky shines on my heart." When Kanwang seized Han Ping's letter, he showed it to those close to him, but nobody understood the secret language. Eventually, it was his subject Su He who figured it out.

"'Raining cats and dogs' means that she has been shedding tears," he told Kanwang. "That is to say, she is extremely miserable. 'The river is wide and deep' means that they have been separated and can no longer meet each other. 'The red sun in the sky shines on my heart' means that she swears to the sun for her devotion to her husband. It means she has made up her mind to kill herself."

Soon after that Han Ping took his own life.

When Han Ping's wife learned about the tragedy, she secretly frayed her clothes. Later on, when she had the opportunity to accompany Kanwang on his tour of the watch tower, she jumped off the tall structure. The servants tried to rescue her by grabbing her dress, but her damaged dress tore and she fell to her death. Afterward, a letter she had written to Kanwang was found inside her girdle:

"You think it's good for you when I am alive, but I think it's good for me when I am dead. I beg your permission to allow my remains to be buried with my husband's."

Kanwang was outraged when he read the letter, bluntly rejecting her request. He ordered the villagers to bury her remains opposite her husband's grave.

"You never stopped loving each other," said Kanwang. "All right then, if your graves could join into one, I wouldn't stop you!"

Overnight, a large catalpa tree emerged on top of each grave. Ten days later, the tree trunks, whose girth now equaled one's stretched arms, as well as their roots, began to intertwine with each other. Inhabiting the trees were an affectionate couple of mandarin ducks that never once flew to another place. Sitting against each other closely, they cried mournfully all day long.

People of what was then the Song State were sympathetic to them, so they called these trees *xiangsi** trees. The Chinese expression *xiangsi* thus came into use. Southerners believe that the two mandarin ducks were the reincarnations of Han Ping and his wife. In Suiyang,** there is still a Han Ping Town that was named after the devoted couple. Up till today, folk songs in praise of their true love remain popular among the people.

---

* *Translator's note: Xiangsi* means yearning between loved ones, especially lovers.
** *Translator's note:* It is Shangqiu County in today's Henan Province.

Naked Swimming Pools

By **Wang** Jia (317? -420?)

In the year 192, Liu Hong, last emperor of the Eastern Han Dynasty (AD 25-220), frequently indulged himself in pleasurable activities in the Western Palace. There he built nearly a thousand "naked" swimming pools whose steps were covered with liver mosses and which were surrounded by running water he had led from a nearby river. The water was as clear as a mirror, perfect for boating. Emperor Liu Hong would ask the royal maids to sit in the boat with him, picking the most beautiful ones to pole and paddle the boat. During the hottest summer days, he would ask them to pole him to the middle of the river, then capsize the boat so that he could view their fair, wet skin. Meanwhile, he would tell the maids to sing him the following song to make his summer days more pleasant:

> *The sun kisses the water as the breeze blows;*
> *Night sees lotus leaves open, but day, close;*
> *Time's too short for pleasure as this day shows.*
> *Light music and songs sweeter than cock crows,*
> *New joy arrives before our old joy goes.*

The lotuses featured leaves the size of a very large umbrella, ten feet wide. They were tributes paid to the imperial court by the south, known as "night-opening lotus," or "moon-watching lotus," as some people believed that they opened up at the moon. The leaves opened up at night and closed in the day, with some stems bearing four blossoms.

Emperor Liu Hong would spend the hottest summer days in the naked swimming pools, feasting and drinking all night. "It would be a heavenly life if one could live like this forever," he would say, his voice filled with emotion.

The emperor's maids were all between fourteen and eighteen years old, and every one of them was beautifully dressed. Often the emperor enjoyed seeing them around with no clothes on except panties. Sometimes they would bathe with the emperor in water perfumed with scent imported from or given by the Western countries. Afterwards, they would pour the bath water into the ditch, which they called Fragrance Ditch. The emperor also made the imperial boy servants bray like donkeys behind the north wall. A Cock Crowing Hall was built, where many cocks were kept. Whenever Emperor Liu Hong got drunk and did not wake up, his servants would all try to crow like cocks, in which case he could not tell whether it was cock crowing or human crowing. At the same time, they would also light up candle torches and throw them in front of the palace hall, which would easily wake him up.

Later, when Dong Zhuo rebelled against the emperor and successfully seized the capital, Luoyang, he drove away all the royal maids, burning down some of the structures. However, up until the year 264, every night, looking like flickering stars, sparks were seen in the place where candle torches had been tossed. The later generations believed they were celestial lights; they therefore built a small house at the spot, which they called Celestial Light Temple, where they would pray for good luck and happiness. The celestial light was seen until the later years of Emperor Mingdi in the Wei Dynasty.

The Sword Maker and His Son's Revenge

By **Gan** Bao

The king of Chu State had ordered two double-edged swords from Ganjiang Moye*, a well-known sword maker. Yet, the pair of swords—a male and a female—took Ganjiang three years to make, so the king was furious and decided to kill him.

Ganjiang had to deliver the swords to the king when his wife was about to give birth to a baby. Before his departure, he told her, "It has taken me three years to make the swords for King Chu, and he is angry with me now. I am sure he will kill me when I present them to him. If our child is a boy, tell him this when he grows up: 'Go out the door, and you will see the South Mountains opposite our house. You'll find a pine tree growing on top of a rock; hidden behind it is a double-edged sword.'" With this, he went on the road, bringing along the female sword for the king.

Indeed, the king was furious. Upon receiving the sword, he called someone to inspect it. This person told him that Ganjiang ought to have made a pair—a male and a female—but that he had delivered only the female sword. King Chu became more outraged and, as expected, had Ganjiang killed.

Ganjiang's unseen baby turned out to be a son, who was named Chi. When Chi grew up, he asked his mother, "Where is my father?"

---

* *Translator's note:* There is another school of thought which holds that Ganjiang Moye should be read as two names with the former being the husband, and latter, the wife, but no one, regardless of his or her opinion, is certain whether Ganjiang Moye refers to the man only or to the couple.

"Your father had to make two double-edged swords for King Chu, but it took him three years. That offended the king, and he had your father killed. Before your father left home, he wanted me to tell you this: 'Go out the door, and you will see the South Mountains opposite our house. You'll find a pine tree growing on top of a rock; hidden behind it is a double-edged sword.'"

As instructed, Chi went out the door and looked to the south, but he saw no mountains. What he saw was a pine post standing on the corner stone in front of the main room. He got his axe, hacked open the post from behind and found the male sword inside. From that moment on, he was thirsting to avenge his father.

One day King Chu dreamed of a child with an abnormally wide forehead, whose eyebrows were nearly a foot apart. The child was crying for revenge on the king. When the nightmare woke him up, he ordered that one thousand taels of gold be rewarded to anybody who caught the child. Hearing the news, Chi at once fled home, intending to hide himself in the depth of the mountains. On his way there he kept crying and singing. A stranger who saw him asked, "You are so young, why are you crying so sadly?"

"I am the son of Ganjiang Moye. King Chu killed my father, and I want to kill him for my father," he said.

"I hear King Chu has put up a reward of one thousand taels of gold for your head. If you give me your head and your sword, I will kill him for you."

"Wonderful!" In the blink of an eye, he chopped off his own head, and together with his sword he gave it to the stranger, his body standing straight, refusing to fall.

"I won't let you down," the stranger promised. Only then did Chi's body fall onto the ground.

The stranger took the child's head to King Chu, who was simply overjoyed. "It's a warrior's head," he told the king. "It should be boiled in a large pot." The king agreed, but it couldn't be boiled. After staying in the boiling water for three days and three nights, it jumped out of the boiling pot, its terrifying eyes popping out.

"The child's head can't be boiled," said the stranger. "I hope King Chu can come over and take a look. I am sure it will be subdued once the king sees it."

King Chu at once walked over to the pot and craned up his neck to peek at it. No sooner said than done: the stranger drew out his sword, aimed at King Chu's neck and, in one simple stroke, sent his head into the boiling water. At the same time, the stranger cut off his own head, which also fell into the pot.

The three heads were so badly boiled that none of them was recognizable. King Chu's subjects could not but divide the water and the flesh and bones into three shares and bury them next to each other. They named the joint tomb Three Kings Tomb, which can still be found in Yichun County in northern Runan Prefecture today.

Lost in Love Land

By **Liu** Yiqing (403-444)

One day in the fifth year of Emperor Mingdi's rule (AD 62) in the Han Dynasty, two villagers named Liu Chen and Ruan Zhao of Shan County, who had been gathering wild rice on the Tiantai Mountains, lost their way and could not return home. The little food they had brought kept them alive for thirteen days. The feeble men were pretty sure that they would soon succumb to starvation. As fate decided, across the mountains opposite them, they caught sight of a peach tree covered with fruit on a breathtaking precipice overlooking a turbulent gully. Finding no way to the tree, the brave villagers climbed upward by clinging to the twigs and rattan over the rocks until they reached the top. The two men helped themselves to a few peaches. In a moment their hunger was gone, their energy fully restored.

Then they came down from the cliff. When they were scooping up water with a cup, intending to wash their hands and rinse their mouths, they saw some mustard leaves floating out of the gully, followed by another cup. Inside the cup was some rice cooked with sesame seeds.

"We can't be too far from people now," they said to each other. With this they trudged about a mile ahead against the current, leaving behind the huge mountains as a large brook came within sight.

Standing by the brook were two extremely beautiful young women. Seeing the men coming out of the mountains each with a cup in hand, they smiled, "Mr. Liu and Mr. Ruan, could you give back our cups which drifted away from us just now?" Liu and Ruan were surprised that the two strange women called them by their names

410

and talked as if they knew them well. Soon they took pleasure in conversing with the charming young women.

"Why did you come so late, anyway?" the women asked, inviting them to their home immediately.

It turned out to be a house built with bamboo tiles and lived in by the two celestial hostesses. There was a large bed against the south wall, and one against the east wall. Both beds were covered with an imperial purple silk curtain. Dangling from its four corners were tiny gold bells and other gold or silver ornaments interlocked with one another. It was simply splendid. By each bed stood ten maids ready to serve their hostess.

"Our young men, Mr. Liu and Mr. Ruan, have trudged on forbidden mountain paths all the way here. Though they've eaten some celestial peaches, they are still tired and hungry. Please prepare dinner for them at once," the two women instructed their servants.

The hostesses entertained Liu and Ruan with rice cooked with sesame seeds, mutton, beef and other food, all exceptionally delicious. After food was served, they drank. Then a group of fairy maids, each with three or five celestial peaches in hand, came smiling at the two hostesses: "Congratulations upon the arrival of your husbands!" Soon everybody was nearly drunk; then music was being played. The two men were overjoyed, but were scared as well. Night fell, and each of them was asked to sleep in one of the two large beds, accompanied by one of the two hostesses. The hostesses' soft and soothing voices soon dispersed the two men's fear.

Ten days later, Liu and Ruan said they wanted to go home, but their hostesses disagreed. "It is good fate that has brought you to us, why do you want to go back?" So reluctantly the men stayed another half year, until spring, when the weather was warm, the grass and trees were green, and birds were singing. Again they were homesick, wanting to return home desperately.

"Earthly sins are still bothering you; you are both hopeless beings," said the two celestial hostesses, who then asked the two

411

score or so female servants to dance and play music as a farewell party for the earthly men, after which they told them how to find their way home.

When the two men finally returned to their village, they found that their relatives and friends had all died; even the houses in the county town were unrecognizable. Simply, there was nothing to match their memory. Only after painstaking efforts did they manage to find the descendants of the seventh generation of their two families.* "As the story goes," the descendants told the two, "once our ancestors went into the mountains, lost their way and never returned home."

One day in year 383, or the eighth year of the Taiyuan era ruled by Emperor Wudi of the Eastern Jin Dynasty, the two men suddenly disappeared again, and again nobody knew where they had gone.

---

* *Translator's note:* In Chinese fairy tales, as in this story, one heavenly day may equal one earthly year.

Yang's Dog

By **Tao** Qian

In the Taihe years of the Eastern Jin Dynasty (AD 366-371), there lived a young man by the name of Yang in Guangling, known as Yangzhou today. Yang kept a dog that he loved dearly and that followed him wherever he went.

One winter day, Yang, who had drunk too much liquor, was seen waddling across the marshes. Before long he fell down into a sound sleep. It so happened that the dry grass on the wasteland was on fire. The flames soon engulfed the marshes as a strong wind fanned the fire rapidly.

His scared dog could not but keep running around him, howling desperately, but the drunken man just would not wake up. The dog then ran into a pool of water nearby, returned with soaked fur and shook the water over the grass surrounding Yang. It ran back and forth until the grass around its master was all wet and until the fire died out, thus saving its master's life. Yang did not realize what had happened until he finally woke up.

Another day, Yang accidentally tumbled into a deserted well when he was walking in the dark. The dog kept howling by the well throughout the night until somebody passed by in the morning. The surprised stranger walked over, looked into the well and caught sight of Yang. "If you get me out of here, I'll reward you with the best I can afford," Yang begged him.

"If you give me this dog, I'll get you out," the stranger answered.

"I owe my life to the dog. I can't give away my dog. You can have anything else I have."

"If that's the case, you will have to stay there."

At this moment, the dog peeked down at Yang, seeming to tell him something. Getting the dog's message, Yang told the stranger, "All right then. You will have my dog." With this, the strange man got Yang out of the well immediately. Then he tied a rope around the dog's neck and walked away with it.

Five days later, the dog escaped from the new owner in the dark and returned home.

Fighting a Tiger

By **Yin** Yun (471-531)

One day, while Confucius was touring the Taishan Mountains, he asked his disciple, Zilu, to get him some water. On the errand, Zilu encountered a tiger near the brook and fought it fiercely. Finally he conquered it by seizing its tail, which he cut off and hid inside his robe against his chest. When he returned with the water, he asked Confucius, "How does a first-class fighter kill a tiger?"

"By seizing its head," answered Confucius.

"How does a second-class fighter kill it?"

"By grabbing its ears."

"How does a third-class fighter kill it then?"

"By seizing its tail."

Zilu was deeply offended. He drew out the tiger's tail and flung it on the ground. "You knew there were tigers near the water," he reproached Confucius, "but you told me to go get water there. You meant to kill me!"

He was about to kill Confucius with the stone he had hidden against his chest when he asked again, "How does a first-class killer kill people?"

"With a pen," replied Confucius.

"How does a second-class killer kill?"

"With his tongue."

"How does a third-class killer kill, then?"

"With a stone hidden against his chest."

Shocked at the last answer, Zilu drew out his stone, throwing it away instantly. He was much impressed by Confucius's wisdom.

Snake Killer

By **Gan** Bao

Somewhere in Minzhong, Dongyue State, there lay the gigantic Yongling Mountains, about two thousand feet high. Inside the cave in the northwest of the mountains was a huge snake at least eighty feet long and fourteen feet in girth. The locals were terrified of the snake: even the lives of the military commander, his soldiers and the county officials in Dongye Town were threatened. After many people had been eaten by the snake, the locals started to offer sheep and oxen to the snake, but that did not earn them peace.

The story goes that the snake made its request by appearing in people's dreams, or by simply telling witches and wizards who were praying for protection from celestial beings that it wanted to eat twelve- or thirteen-year-old girls. All officials, big or small, at the county and prefecture levels were outraged at the request, but they just could not conquer the snake to eliminate the fear of the people. With no other option, the officials started to adopt slaves' baby girls and infant girls born into criminal families. On August 1, the day when offerings were made, they would place a girl outside the snake cave. The snake would then crawl out and gulp her down. One a year, year after year, the snake ate up the nine girls available.

Another year came, and the officials had yet to find another girl for it. August 1 was approaching, but they hadn't found the right child. It so happened that Mr. Li Dan, a villager in Jiangle County, had six daughters with no son. His youngest daughter, Li Ji, said that she would offer herself as a recruit. Her parents, of course, disapproved of her decision, but she said, "Dad and Mom, you were born with no

416

happy lot. That's why you've got no son but six daughters. You have children, but it's like you have no children. I'm no Tiying,* and I can't free my parents from their sufferings. Nor do I have the ability to provide for you in your old age. I am a good-for-nothing for you, just a waste of clothes and food. The sooner I die, the better off you'll be. I will be happy if I am sold, so that we'll have some money for you both to buy food and clothes. Don't you agree?"

The parents, who loved her dearly, felt sorry for the poor child and just would not agree. Li Ji instead stole out of her house and sold herself before her family could stop her.

After she was recruited, Li Ji asked the officials for a double-edged sword and a dog good at hunting snakes. As scheduled, on August 1, she was taken to the Snake Temple as an offering. Armed with a sword, she sat inside the temple, holding the dog by the leash. As she had instructed, several loads of cooked glutinous rice were made into large balls, then filled with maltose and placed at the entrance to the cave. Soon the snake emerged from inside. Its head was as large as a grain bin; its eyes glowing like two foot-long mirrors. Following the smell of the sweet rice, the snake started to gulp down the rice balls.

Li Ji released her dog at once. It immediately jumped at the snake, took a deep bite and just would not let it go. Meanwhile, using her sword, Li Ji kept hacking at the snake's back with all her might until it was seriously wounded in many places. Unable to stand the pain, the snake shot out of its hole, landing dead in the yard outside the temple.

Li Ji went into the snake's cave for a look, discovering the skulls

---

* *Translator's note:* In the Eastern Han Dynasty, Chun Yuyi, who had committed a crime, was sentenced to corporal punishment. His youngest daughter, Tiying, then wrote to the emperor, offering to receive the punishment on her father's behalf. Touched by her letter, the emperor pardoned her father, freeing him from his due punishment.

of the nine girls who had been eaten. Taking them out, she said in a voice filled with emotion, "You were timid and weak. That's why you were eaten by the snake. What pitiful tragedies!" With this, the calm girl went back home as if nothing had happened.

When the King of Dongyue State heard the story, he proposed to Li Ji, who accepted and was subsequently crowned queen. He also appointed her father Magistrate of Jiangle County and rewarded her mother as well as her sisters. From then on, there were no more evil monsters in Dongye Region, where popular ballads have been sung in praise of Li Ji to this day.

Peach Woods

By **Tao** Qian

In Emperor Xiaowudi's years in the Eastern Jin Dynasty (AD 376-396), there was a man in Wuling who made a living by fishing. One day he was paddling his boat on a small river, following the ripples forward. Not knowing the exact distance he had covered, he found himself in front of a beautiful peach wood, hundreds of feet in width and depths, covering both banks of the small river. There were only peach trees, with no other type among them. The fragrant wild grass, exceptionally fresh and lovely, was dotted by the dazzling beauty of the fallen peach petals. The fisherman found himself lost in a breathtaking place he had never happened upon before.

He paddled on, intending to row past the peach wood. Leaving behind the peaches, he reached the end of the river. In sight was a mountain, where he saw from the distance a little cave with dim light. He left his fishing boat and headed straight for the cave. The first thirty feet of the cave was rather small, just enough for one person to walk through, but after that it became larger and brighter. Then came a vast plain with neat houses, lovely ponds, mulberries and basmboos dotting fertile land. Ridges connected the fields into a net. Dogs barking and cocks crowing could be easily distinguished. The farmers who came and went, dressed in clothes the fisherman had never seen, all looked like aliens. Everybody, old or young, was living a happy life.

The villagers were surprised to see the fisherman, asking where he had come from. He told them how he had found his way to their place. Soon they invited him to their homes, prepared dinner with freshly slaughtered chickens for him and served him with wine.

Learning about his arrival, the whole village rushed over to inquire about the outside world, telling him that in order to escape the persecution of the cruel dictator Emperor Qinshihuang (259-210 BC), their ancestors, together with some other people from the county, came to this place nobody had set foot in. "Nobody has ever left here, and we are totally cut off from the outside world." Then they asked him what dynasty it was. They didn't even know there was the Han Dynasty, let alone the Wei and Jin dynasties. The fisherman told them everything he knew. The villagers regretted their undeniably limited knowledge.

Other villagers also invited the fisherman to their homes, entertaining him with good food and fine wine. Thus he stayed for several days. On the day of his departure, the villagers said, "Please never tell anybody about our village."

Walking through the cave, the fisherman found his small boat and rowed back home by the same route. However, he deliberately marked the different spots as he left them behind. Upon his return, he asked to see the prefecture chief and told him about his rare encounters. The prefecture chief immediately dispatched a group of people, who tried to follow the route the fisherman had marked, but they got lost and failed to find the place. Liu Ziji, a reputedly learned man in Nanyang who was also interested in the fisherman's rare experience, took great pleasure trying to locate the place, but he never succeeded. Not long after, he died of some disease. Ever since then, nobody cared about this event anymore.

SUPPLEMENT

ESSAYS AND COMMENTS ON THE CHINESE SHORT SHORT STORY

Origins of the Chinese Short Short Story

By **Liu** Haitao

As a form of narrative literature, fiction existed back in ancient China. The old fairy tales show a thing or two about its narrative mechanism. The fairy tales about the gods and celestial beings, or historical legends that acquired such elements, in fact indirectly reflect the state of mind and expectations of the people at that time. No matter how mystical, changeable and deceitful, they all narrate a complete legendary tale in a "simple, direct prose style." The story "Kua Fu Chasing the Sun"* in *Shan hai jing,* or *The Book of Mountains and Oceans,* and another story, "Chang'e Fleeing to the Moon"** in *Huai nan zi* (a book consisting of twenty-one internal volumes and thirty-three external volumes), among others, contain the basic elements of narration. These works had a profound impact, of one type or the other, on the writers of later generations.

This narrative mechanism developed in the fables and prose of the early Qin Dynasty (221-206 BC) until the earliest short short

---

* *Translator's note:* The story goes that Kua Fu chased the sun till he reached its entrance. It was so hot and he was so thirsty that he drank up the water of two Chinese rivers, which was not enough. Consequently he died of thirst. The crane he left behind then turned into a forest.

** *Translator's note:* In the fairy tale, Hou Yi's wife, Chang'e, while she was a mortal being, stole some herb of immortality, took it and fled to the moon, where she became an immortal being but, as one version of the story goes, was cloistered forever.

story took shape. Stories such as "Waiting for Hares by the Stump"* in *Han fei zi* and "Nicking the Boat for the Lost Sword"** in *Lü shi chun qiu* were already popular tales. Such fables and prose are short, to begin with. They often contain thirty words or so, up to about one hundred words, but they tell a complete event or a complete act of a character. Next, the description of life had digressed from the mystical features of fairy tales. Closer to life, they might vividly depict some type of a character, so as to expose common social phenomena in a meaningful way, thus marking the essential elements of fictional characters and themes in the narrative mechanism.

The Wei and Jin Dynasties witnessed short short stories that conveyed real meaning. The literary narrative mechanism, supported by the rich experience accumulated through the long process of development, turned out a great variety of mature literary works. Liu Yiqing's *Shi shuo xin yu (A New Book of Stories)* in eight volumes about humans and Gan Bao's *Sou shen ji (Collection of Fairy Tales),* a collection of mystery tales and tales of the supernatural, are typical masterpieces of the time. *Sou shen ji* contains many unbelievable changes in characters. For example, the stories *"Ganjiang Moye"* ("The Sword Maker and His Son's Revenge") and *"Han Ping fu fu"* ("Han Ping and His Wife") have unusual and complex plots, with the same theme of exposing the cruelty of the rulers at that time. More important still, stories like *"Shi Chong yu Wang Kai zheng hao"* ("Rivals Shi Chong and Wang Kai Fighting to Be the Powerful Man") in *Shi shuo xin yu* not only have complete plots, but, through

---

* *Translator's note:* There was a stump in a farmer's field. One day while he was working there, a hare ran into the stump, broke its neck and died instantly. Picking up the unexpected gift, the farmer stayed by the stump every day from then on, waiting for more hares to bump into it.

** *Translator's note:* One day, while a man was taking a ferry, his sword slipped into the water. Then he marked where the sword had slipped through. When the boat got to its destination, he got into the water, trying to recover the sword.

meticulous, lively details, their characters are created with distinct personalities.

Influenced by *Shi shuo xin yu* and *Sou shen ji,* many literary sketches emerged after the Sui (581-618) and Tang (618-907) dynasties, stories which deserve historians' efforts at classification. A large number of rare short short stories are found in *Chao ye qian zai (The Court and the Commonalty Recorded Together)* and *Ye ren xian hua (The Wild People's Gossiping),* among others. While sorting them out, we found that the ancient Chinese short short story had by now broken away from fables and prose, starting to develop an artistic mechanism of its own. First, it had freed itself from the restriction of fables and prose by drawing materials from life—the populace and anecdotes. Second, its description of characters differed from that of fables and fairy tales, which focused on events rather than on characters. The short short story was capable not only of creating a character through a complete event, but also of highlighting the personality of a character through vivacious, exciting details. It not only steered clear away from the common practice of preaching through narration, but also, by means of lifelike description and exciting narration full of ups and downs, reflected the author's profound understanding of life and judgment on the issue of beauty. Third, in overall planning, unlike the fables and tales of the early Qin Dynasty that followed a model of simple recording, the short short story of this period shows some meticulous artistic concepts. The story shows not only maturing character and event development, but also artistic changes of fine fiction.

The Ming Dynasty (1368-1644) and the Qing Dynasty (1644-1911) mark the peak of ancient Chinese short short story writing. In this period, the well-developed writing style of fiction in general enabled the now mature short short story to thrive. Among the many collections of short short stories is the world-famous treasury *Liao zhai zhi yi,* or *A Collection of Weird Stories,* by Pu Songling. From Pu Songling's characters, such as Ying Ning and Wang Sheng, one can see that the Chinese short short story of this period was highly developed and diversified. As a short short story writer, Pu Songling succeeded in depicting not only vivid personality traits, but also typical characters. His stories contain not only beautiful dialogues and lifelike action, but also meticulous psychological description.

The highly developed short short story of this period was attributed to the release of the short short story from the restriction of straight recording and to its embracing of true fictitious artistry. Thanks to the merging of the authors' creativity with their artistry of narrative fiction, outstanding classics appeared, with characters readers love to talk about from generation to generation. Elegant, artistic structure became a feature, with realism and romanticism and other writing techniques radiating with dazzling brilliance. Pu Songling created monumental art works in ancient Chinese short short story writing.

Another Essay on "The Short Short Story Is a Populist Art"

By **Yang** Xiaomin

The Chinese short short story, which this author calls a "populist art," originated in ancient times, but it is still a relatively new form of literature in China.*

First of all, not only does the short short story differ in length from the novel, the novella and the short story, but its content also differs from that of a tale and a literary sketch. As a form of fiction, the short short story not only requires the basic elements such as characters and plot, but, more important still, it also carries spiritual guidance, as it should as a form of fiction. That is, it provides the reader with the ideological capacity to ponder on life and to learn about the world.

Though called a "populist art," its high level of artistry and literary value must not be neglected. "Populist art," in particular, may be further defined as follows: "That the short short story is a populist art means that it is a form of language art that most people can read (simple and unconventional), that most people are capable of writing (close to life) and that most people can benefit from (short but meaningful)." Few literary forms have all these three features. For example, the novel, the novella, the short story and non-fiction are not what most people are capable of creating. Poems do not make the best reading for the majority of readers. This being the case, the feeling of an invisible distance makes it unlikely that the great majority of

---

* *Translator's note*: Scholars may disagree with this opinion.

426

the population will benefit from these forms of literary art. Tales and sketches, on the other hand, though they contain all three features and are appealing to the populace, are in principle considered popular culture or sub-literature, and cannot be called "art" in most cases. In China, pure literature basically equals elegant art.

The contemporary Chinese short short story has been developing rapidly only since the 1980s. Nonetheless, nearly fifty writers, thanks to their successful short short story writing, have been admitted into the prestigious Chinese Writers' Association, while hundreds of others have joined writers' associations at the provincial and municipal levels. They all have been crowned with the honorable title "Author." Two score of short short stories have been included in national textbooks used in universities, colleges and secondary schools. Publications that represent various cultural levels rightly satisfy the needs of different readers. Be they prestigious publications or popular periodicals or magazines, each has an important role the others cannot play. Even publications of tales and sketches which are not too literary are capable of comforting the soul, dissolving conflicts and promoting education.

I am just the publisher of a short short story periodical, not a real short short story writer or researcher. Because of my job, I have been soaked in short short stories, realizing that the short short story, as a relatively new form of literature, has a limit in length (about 1,500 Chinese characters), a unique way of judging its beauty (degree of quality) and certain structural features (elements of fiction) as expected, and other regular boundaries.

Studying a literary form at the theoretical level will surely promote its healthy development, which will eventually lead to its maturity. When I define the short short story as a populist art, I focus on its double meaning: one is that it belongs to a rather high level of popular culture that can continuously improve readers' artistic taste, their interest in this form of art and their cognitive ability; the other is that, for its literary attainments, quality is an indispensable requirement. For this I have published a longer Chinese essay, entitled, "The Short Short Story Is a Populist Art," in which I discuss it in greater detail.

Finding Materials for the Short Short Story

By **Ling** Dingnian

Being a member in the family of fiction, the short short story, as characteristically known, can be made up. However, this does not mean you can fabricate or invent events at will. Generally speaking, the story is based on life, though it is re-créated by the writer with reasonable imagination, or by means of twisting or exaggeration, or by adding absurdity, magic, and so on. Yet its root should be inside the soil of real life.

With regard to the gathering of raw materials, my writing experience shows that they can be divided into direct materials and indirect materials.

A. Direct Materials
1. *Personal experience.* An event I have gone through. I become "the one" in the story, or the story may reflect my life.
2. *Personal observation.* People and events happening in my family or around me, or whomever and whatever I have seen or have contacted and have perceptual knowledge about.

B. Indirect Materials
1. *Overhearing.* What I hear while chatting with family members, colleagues, classmates and friends, or overhear from people in public, etc.
2. *Inquiries.* Asking acquaintances and strangers about and for the particulars of an event. This is a method Pu Songling, of the Qing Dynasty, used. He would ask people at the village entrance

or passersby near the fields about what happened in their homes, anecdotes and fun events. The renowned scholar of the same dynasty, Ji Xiaolan, once even spent money buying stories from the residents, which is called "collecting folk tales," or *caifeng,* in contemporary Chinese literary terms.

3. *Reading books and newspapers.* This is another way to obtain materials and find inspiration. The world is big and full of strange things and funny people. As long as you set your mind on it, the daily news often can be used as raw material. It all depends on whether or not you have the exceptional ability to discover it. Many non-literary books also contain a lot of excellent materials that are awaiting the interested writer to discover and use, to process and transform.

4. *Imagining.* The ability to imagine is always an important quality a writer should possess. With regard to this issue, in the case of the short short story, "image" should come before "thought," for the practice of "theme first" was once under attack. Nevertheless, it cannot be denied that authors may hit on an idea first and try to find materials later, or simply make up the content accordingly.

In my opinion, we don't have to stress either personal experience and observation or collecting folk tales everywhere, but setting your mind on it seems a must. That is called committing yourself to whatever you do. As long as you keep your eyes open, suitable materials will come to you. If they do, you should write them down. Otherwise, you may forget them before long.

Gathering materials should be a routine practice. Never wait until you are about to start writing, or you will waste time or write bad stories.

The Art of Ending the Short Short Story

By **Sun** Fangyou

All fiction writers—not only short short story writers, but also novelists, novella and short story writers—care much about the ending. A good ending has the readers reflect on the enlightenment or inspiration received from the story, even long after the reading. Liu Qingbang says that the short story is a naturally grown product, while Bi Feiyu believes it is a "baked" product. I, for one, tend to accept Bi's word "baked."

A good story has to be baked over and over again until it shocks. My story "Mosquito Punishment," from the conception of the idea to the product, took over ten years. Traced back to the day I first heard the folk tale, it would be almost twenty years. I did not write the story earlier merely because the hidden meaning and the ending had not been properly baked. In the past, when film directors listened to somebody's scenario, they would ask you to begin with the ending, or the "real story," as they called it. You can see how important the ending is for films and television.

An unsuccessful beginning may be easily forgotten by the reader, but a successful ending stirs the reader's soul. The dagger is deadly only when it stabs you at a vital point. In the story, the vital point is the ending. If a short short story is to win by its size and length, it has to rely on its hidden meaning, condensing the most thought possible inside the smallest space available. Also, the author has to wittily merge his or her unique opinions into the story in a way that can win a shout of "Bravo!" from the reader.

Believe in the power of the word, which is no ordinary

431

transportation tool. It can create sentence after sentence that carries profound meaning. Examples are texts written by Confucius, Mencius, Lao Zhuang and Zhou Yi. They range from a few thousand to twenty or thirty thousand Chinese characters, but they are all classics containing rich content. From this, one can see that the length of the short short story is sufficient for it to be classic. If you want the reader to shout "Bravo!" with his or her thumb up, one important art lies in the ending. In the end, you shake out from your "bag" your unique hidden thought and the final distillation of the story—just in a few words. Yet the few concluding words will feel as heavy as a mountain and as powerful as thunderbolts.

Needless to say, because the form is so short, the narrative language of the short short story cannot contain unneeded fabrication of any kind. It has to read like Faulkner's, like nails. The ending is like a heavy hammer striking the last few nails deep into the reader's heart. In 1,500 or so Chinese characters, the story has to have ups and downs, the material and viewpoint have to be refreshing, and a character has to be created. Then there is the aspect of technicality. The martial art masters reach the acme of perfection only when their "techniques" are found inside their souls. The art of ending the short short story is no exception. If you seek perfection before it comes, you will, instead, expose your "technical" weaknesses and face more difficulties. Only after years of practice will you find it at the tip of your pen.

The Short Short Story Has Its Own Advantage

By **Zhou** Daxin

I have not written many short short stories, but I enjoy reading them.

Sometimes, the pleasure you experience in reading a short short story is no less than that in a novel. Some short short stories are extremely succinct and meaningful, and leave a long-lasting aftertaste. Some have exceptionally novel scenes that shock you with delight. Some have unique characters that are capable of terrifying you. Things that you cannot find in a novel may be found in the short short story.

The short short story writer, actually, faces more or less the same pressure as that of the novelist in the creation of the work. A novel usually has a large number of characters, so if one is not well created, the blemishes may be covered up by the rest. By contrast, a short short story, which usually depicts only one or two characters, will be ruined if one of them is not well done. A novel tells a long story with a complex plot, so if some scenes are not that lively, they may not be very noticeable. A short short story, on the other hand, narrates a very short one, so anything imperfect may be easily exposed. A lengthier novel contains much more dialogue, which can conveniently cover up language deficiency, but any poorly constructed sentence or awkward use of words and expressions in a short short story will not likely escape the eyes of the reader.

The relationship between the novel and the short short story is not a parent-child relationship, and never one between a grandfather and a grandchild. They are equal members in the family, and neither is superior to the other. One is just larger in size than the other, that is all. You play your role in the family, and I, mine. I may respect you, but you cannot belittle me.

The status of the short short story has been respected in Chinese literature since ancient times. Literary sketches in Chinese literature are in essence short short stories. Though the short short story is small in size, the ancestors never abandoned it. In modern times, when democracy and tolerance are being advocated, we have more reason to provide the space for the creation, growth and flourishing of the short short story, so as to meet the reader's needs.

What I Think of the Short Short Story

By **Tao** Ran

About fifteen years ago, after I had been publishing novels, novellas and short stories for many years, an editor friend working for the supplement of a newspaper unexpectedly asked me to write some short short stories for him, and so I did. After that, I could not tear myself away from the short short story: I had simply fallen in love with it.

If we can say that the short story is a transverse section of life, then the short short story is often the product of an idea flashing across the author's mind. Wherever you are, whatever divine light flashes in your mind becomes good material for a short short story. The short story, with an obvious, distinct feature of being short, wants no fabrication and pretentiousness, any of which may easily be exposed, be it in its structure or plot. In contrast, the short short story has to be even more succinct. A slight loss of control over its length may easily turn it into a short story.

The short short story contains all the basic elements of fiction, though it is the shortest form, or the smallest brother in the family of fiction. Completing it with the presence of all the basic elements within the extremely limited length is a challenge for the writer. It will not do without details, yet it cannot have too many. Thus, the writer has to make choice after choice. Its plot may be simple, yet it has to be well developed with rich content. Perhaps that is what makes the short short story peculiar. In order to successfully reduce a novel into a short short story, the writer has to bear in mind that he or she is writing a short short story and avoid turning it into a short story.

Some writers think the short short story is a waste of plot, saying that themes and plots are hard to find. They believe that one would benefit more by turning a short short story into a short story or a novella or even a novel, instead. That makes sense in a way, but personally I think that each form of fiction—the novel, the novella, the short story and the short short story—requires different materials and plots that suit itself. They do not conflict with one another. As long as you observe what is happening around you in real life, you will find plenty of themes for your short short stories.

Of course, though the so-called idea flashing across the author's mind is not a castle in the air, it is also no guarantee of a successful short short story. That idea only triggers your inspiration. To turn it into a good short short story, you have to bring into full play your life experience and your ability to imagine. Otherwise, the idea is unlikely to sustain a fine story with literary value.

The Short Short Story Beats the Novella

By **Xu** Xijun

I never agree with calling the short short story the little brother of novellas and short stories.

The difficulty of short short story writing is fully understood only by those who have long been writing it. My experience in writing short short stories throughout the past years can be summarized into one word: "hard." With the same material, if you soak it in water gently, it may become a sizeable loaf of bread, but as a short short story writer you have to rack your brains so as to make it into ship's biscuit. The reader can easily tell which is easier than which.

Nevertheless, from my long years of writing I have also gained something that can be summarized in another word: "ease." That is, I feel at ease, knowing that when a story which I want to write is completed, at least I won't waste that much of the reader's time, whether it is well received or not. The reader may utter a word of flattery or simply curse it. Careless readers may laugh through it quickly, while serious ones may ponder over it for a long time.

Probably because I have written "too many" short short stories, readers mistake me as a short short story writer only. I don't know whether it is meant to be fun or respectful; critics have called me a "short short story professional." The public also seems to have forgotten that I have written quite a lot of novellas and short stories. In a way, as I take it, that just proves the superiority of the short short story.

Needless to say, the novella has a bigger capacity, usually with a more complex plot that can reflect an important aspect of life. Probably this is where the novella's superiority lies, yet in the final analysis, it is still the protagonist's life, in part or in full, that reflects the social phenomena of a certain period in history and that reveals just the characteristics of some social aspects. Yet that is not beyond the short short story's reach. On the contrary, the latter performs extremely well in this particular aspect.

A limited capacity determines a simpler plot, but, similarly, the short short story reflects the most typical examples in life. An event, a character, very common materials or a rather common citizen's life may contain rich social content that starts the reader thinking about matters of principle. Of course, in today's society, where writing is paid according to the number of words, short short story writers are the sure losers. If I had altered them a little bit, many of my short short stories could have become stories of thirty thousand words, or even longer. For example, my story *"Pai fu,"* about one thousand Chinese characters long, which is claimed by critics as one "that goes against tradition, yet is contained in tradition," might not have been as effective had it been written as a novella. As a matter of fact, it was originally written as a novella, but I felt it would only torture the reader with its length and waste his or her time. Therefore, I abandoned it and rewrote it into a short short story.

I write short short stories and express sincere feelings in honest words. I need not list a specific vocabulary or decorative words for extended length, which is probably a superiority over its counterpart— the novella. That a short short story or a group of short short stories may achieve or outdo what a novella does does not require any theoretical inference or research. It is a fact that has been proven by practice.

Biographical Sketches

(The author's country of residence and nationality is China unless indicated otherwise.)

Ah Zhu (1957-), pseudonym of Liu Xuezhu, reporter and writer, who has published news articles and reportage. He has also co-authored *An Introduction to the Culture of Tourism.*

Bai Xiaoyi (1960-) works for a literary magazine in Shenyang, Liaoning. A recognized short short story writer, he has written many short short stories.

Cao Duoyong (1962-) was born in Dahe Village, Anhui. A Literary award winner, he has published a novel, *The Dahe Bay,* and several novellas as well as short stories.

Chen Dachao (1958-) was born in Nanzhang County, Hubei. Winner of six awards for short short fiction, he has authored a thousand literary items, which include short stories and poems besides short short stories. He has published in China's mainland, Hong Kong, Macao, Taiwan, and other countries.

Chen Lifeng (1958-), born and brought up in Henan, has published stories as well as essays on social issues, totaling more than one hundred pieces. He is the associate editor-in-chief of a college journal in Henan.

Chen Yonglin (1972-) is an editor working for the prestigious

Chinese magazine *Selected Mini-Stories*. Winner of a national short short story contest, he is an active writer who has written many short short stories.

Chung Ling (1945-) was born in Chongqing but grew up in Taiwan. She received her PhD in comparative literature from the University of Wisconsin. A National Literary Award winner, she has written more than three collections of stories, including *Short Short Stories by Chung Ling,* or *Miniature Short Stories of Chung Ling* as originally introduced *(Chung Ling ji duan pian), The Predestined Lovers (Sheng si yuan jia),* and *The Great Wheel of Life (Da lun hui).* She has taught at New York State University, Hong Kong University, and National Sun Yat-sen University, and has been director of the Teaching Affairs Department of National Kaohsiung University in Taiwan.

Feng Jicai (1942-), born in Tianjin, is one of the best-known authors in China, having written many books, including novels, collections of short stories, and literary non-fiction. He is presently in charge of the compiling and editing of eight thousand volumes of Chinese folklore and folk literature, four volumes on each county in China. Besides holding two important literary positions, Mr. Feng also serves as member of the Standing Committee of the Chinese People's Political Consultative Conference and as vice-chairman of the China Association for Promoting Democracy.

Gan Bao (317?-420?), a talented literary man and a knowledgeable historian, author of *Collection of Fairy Tales (Sou shen ji),* during the Eastern Jin Dynasty (AD 317-420). His original work has long been lost. The version available today was put together by later editor-scholars. More than four hundred of his stories have been collected, published in twenty volumes.

Gao Weixi (1933-) is a lifelong professional literary editor, associate editor-in-chief of the prestigious Chinese bimonthly *The Novelist* and director of its editorial department. He has published many works, including a collection of short stories *Sailing in Love,* and two collections of literary non-fiction, *Irrational Passion* and *A Stormy Life*. He now lives in Toronto, Canada.

Gui Qianfu (1964-) was born in Luochuan, Shaanxi. He has published various literary works, totaling about six hundred pages.

Han Ying (1939-) was born in Liaoyang, Liaoning. A lifelong government official in Guangdong, he has published more than one thousand literary pieces—poems, literary non-fiction, short short stories—writing more than twenty books. He has won two prestigious national awards for his short short stories.

He Baiyuan (1943-), also known as **Yuan** Bai, was born in Nanhai, Guangdong. Multiple literary award winner, he has written four books and many other literary publications. He works as associate editor-in-chief for the *Foshan Literary Paper*.

He Baoguo (1966-) works and resides in Nanjing, Fujian. He writes short short stories, among other things.

He Peng (1960-) was born in Qingshuihe County, Inner Mongolia. He has written a collection of short short stories entitled *Strange Disease* and three collections of literary reportage, including *Candle Light* and *Green Romance*.

Holmes, Lynn (1935-), professor of English, has coauthored with Elizabeth Holmes a college communications textbook, among other books and essays he has proofread and copyedited for colleagues and friends. After retiring from teaching literature and writing at Seneca College in Toronto, his home city, he taught English for a year in Nanning, at the Sino-Canadian International College at Guangxi University.

Huang Fei (1946-), officially known as **Li** Huangfei, was born in Mianchi, Henan. He has written several collections of novellas and short stories. Some of his stories have been turned into TV plays. He works as a reporter for the *Luoyang Daily*.

Huang, Harry J. (1956-), or **Huang** Junxiong, also known as Freeman J. Wong, bilingual (English and Chinese) writer and translator, has published more than ten books, including three collections of short short stories entitled *Nothing Comes of Nothing, Morality, Eh?*, and *A Bride in Washington*. He has also published university and college textbooks, as well as early childhood education materials (under another pseudonym, Will Strength). Winner of a social science award, he is the translator of the 1986 version of the National Anthem of the People's Republic of China. He became a Canadian citizen in 1993, and has been teaching English in Seneca College in Toronto.

Jiang Han has written various literary works, including novels and short stories, with the short short story being his most recent focus of literary creation.

Jiang Zilong (1941-), one of the most prominent writers in contemporary China, has published more than seventy literary works, of which *Factory Director Qiao Starting His Job* was turned into a popular movie loved by viewers throughout China.

Li Jingwen (1961-) works and lives in Jiangdu, Jiangsu. He has published short stories, short short stories and other works.

Li Yongkang (1964-) resides in Wenjiang, Sichuan. He writes short short stories and other forms of fiction.

Lin Rongzhi (1958-) was born in Zhanjiang, Guangdong. Winner of several national awards for fine fiction and non-fiction, he has written seven collections of short stories and literary non-fiction.

Lin Ruqiu (1947-), senior editor, was born in Minqing, Fujian. He has published short stories, non-fiction, tales and short literary critiques, totaling about two thousand pages. He has written and edited eight books, including two collections of short short stories.

Lin Weisheng (1967-), also known as Linser, writer, translator and associate professor of a college, published his first book in his early twenties. He has taught himself in practically the same way as his ancient Chinese counterparts did. Through self-study, he first earned a college diploma, then a BA degree, leading to an MA degree, and he is presently reading for his PhD.

Ling Dingnian (1951-), one of the best-known, most prolific Chinese short short story writers, top winner of World's Chinese Short Short Stories Contest, has written thousands of short short stories, including fourteen collections. He has also edited or co-edited dozens of collections of short short stories.

Ling Junyang (1985-), is an outstanding representative of the numerous active young writers who began to publish in their teens. "Dr. Song" is one of the most recent of his stories, which show great creativity.

Liu Fengzhen (1963-), winner of China's National Short Literary Works Contest, has published dozens of short stories and short short stories. She has also co-edited *A Collection of Poems by North Shaanxi Women Poets*.

Liu Gong (1960-), officially known as **Liu** Enrui, is a literary editor-in-chief, writer, calligrapher and poet. He has written three books, including *New-Styled Short Short Stories*. Since 1993, he has published approximately four thousand pages of literary works. He has collected fifteen awards and prizes at the provincial and national levels.

Liu Guofang (1957-) was born in Linchuan, Jiangxi. He is a two-time first-prize winner of the National Short Short Story Contest (1990, 1996), with a long list of publications.

Liu Haitao (1955-) was born in Zhanjiang, Guangdong. Professor and vice-president of Zhanjiang Teachers' College and winner of the National Excellent Teacher Award, he has published more than two hundred research essays in various journals inside and outside of China. He has written ten books on special subjects, including *The Chinese Short Short Story: Theory and Writing Skills*. He has devoted himself to theoretical research on the short short story, the science of writing and the study of overseas Chinese literature.

Liu Liqin (1966-) started his literary writing in the 1990s. He has published more than one hundred stories in different literary periodicals. He works for the Cultural Centre of Zhenan County, Shaanxi.

Liu Liying (1960-) is a full-time writer. National short short story award winner, she has published 120 short short stories and forty other literary pieces, including novellas and short stories.

Liu Wanli was born in Hanyin, Shaanxi. Winner of two national short short story contests, he has published more than three hundred stories, including short short stories, short stories, and novellas. He works for a newspaper in Shaanxi.

Liu Wei (1960-) has published poems and stories, besides four collections of prose. He lives and works in Benxi, Liaoning.

Liu Yiqing (403-444) was the author of many works, including *A Collection of Tales of the Other World (You ming lu)*. This work, said to contain thirty (or twenty) volumes in its original form, was lost in the late fifth century, or in the Sui Dynasty (581-618). Over two hundred stories are still available, many of which are sketches, though some are fairly complete story-lines. Though the majority are ghost stories, some originated in folk tales. His writing style significantly influenced many writers in the later generations.

Lu Fuhong (1960-) is an established short fiction writer. He has published many short short stories, including "A Little Bird" and "My Third Uncle," winners of two annual national short short story contests.

Ma Baoshan (1948-) was born in Fuxin, Liaoning. Also known as **Bu** He Au Si Er, fiction writer and associate editor-in-chief of a literary magazine in Inner Mongolia, he has published three collections of short short stories, including *The Crying Sun* and *Ma Baoshan's Short Short Stories*. He started writing fiction around the age of thirty, devoting himself to short short story writing from the early 1990s.

Ma Duangang (1970-) was born in Baotou, Inner Mongolia. He writes mostly fiction and has published a collection of novellas entitled *Sunshine in the Afternoon*. He works as an editor for a literary magazine in Inner Mongolia.

Ma Fengchao (1935-) was born in Sanmenxia, Henan. He once worked as the associate editor-in-chief of the *Sanmenxia Daily*. A literary award winner, he has published short stories and reportage, totaling almost one hundred items.

Ma Shaoxian (1938-), lifelong literary editor and writer, has published many literary essays as well as stories, including a book of literary non-fiction entitled *Heartfelt Love.*

Meng Meng (1948-) was born in Xianyang, Shaanxi. Winner of more than ten municipal and provincial awards, he has written four books and other works, including two novels, a collection of novellas and short stories and two collections of literary non-fiction as well as three scenarios.

Mo Bai (1958-), born in Huaiyang, Henan, started his literary career in the late 1980s. He has written more than forty novellas and novels, including *A Sleep Walker* and *A Midsummer Ditty,* as well as many short stories. He has also published a collection of short short stories entitled *The Lonely Man.*

Peng Sike [si-ke] (1930-), writer, editor and one-time journalist, has written many publications, including a novel entitled *Battles in Yihetala* and a collection of short stories and novellas, *The Golden Mt. Xingan.* He has won many literary awards.

Pu Songling (1640-1715) was born in Zichuan, or today's Zibo, Shandong. For the greater part of his life, he was an impoverished teacher, but he published many works, including fiction, poems and books for the undereducated public. His masterpiece is *A Collection of Weird Stories (Liao zhai zhi yi),* which has been claimed to be a monumental book of short short stories full of literary imagination. Some critics believe it is not only an important book of Chinese short stories, but also one that belongs to world literature. "Mr. Shen" is an average story taken from this book.

Ru Rongxing (1958-) was born in Jiaxing, Zhejiang. Winner of forty literary awards, he has, since 1982, published more than six hundred short short stories and critiques, including two collections of short short stories.

Shao Baojian (1946-), born in Huzhou, Zhejiang, is an award-winning writer. He has written two collections of short short stories. He works for the *Huzhou Daily* in Zhejiang.

Shen Hong (1959-), a national prize winner, has authored a collection of short short stories. He works for the *Huzhou Daily* in Zhejiang.

Shen Zulian (1951-), one of the best-known Chinese short short story writers, two-time Chinese national book award winner, has written six collections of short short stories, including *Third Day of the Honeymoon, Men's Scenery,* and *108 Mini-stories by Shen Zulian.*

Si Yusheng (1956-) is the associate editor-in-chief of *Jingjiu Evening News*. He has published novellas, short stories and short short stories, totaling more than one thousand pieces, including two collections of short short fiction.

Sun Chunping (1950-) is a well-recognized author. His collection of novellas and short stories won China's Fourth National Literary Award for Minority Writers.

Sun Fangyou (1950-) is claimed by critics and readers to be one of the best short short story writers in China. He has written many short short stories since 1978, including one collection entitled *Women Bandits* and another, *Assassin*. A top short short fiction award winner, he has won sixty literary awards. He became a full-time writer in 2002.

Tao Qian (365-427) is believed to be the author of *Another Collection of Fairy Tales (Sou shen hou ji),* despite all doubts raised. This work, which consists of ten volumes, by its name appears to be the continuation of Gan Bao's *Collection of Fairy Tales (Sou shen ji)*. An outstanding poet in Chinese literature, **Tao** Qian did not care for fame or money and had a free sexual life. After being an official for eighty days, he quit his job because of his resentment of government corruption and hypocrisy, and resumed a simple life in his home village.

Tao Ran (1943-) born in Bandung, Indonesia, is the editor-in-chief of Hong Kong Literary Press. He has written twenty-two books, including three novels, eight collections of literary non-fiction, two of short short stories, and many novellas and short stories, as well as two collections of non-fiction and poems. In 2000, Professor **Cao** Huimin of Beijing University published a book entitled *Reading Tao Ran: Essays on Tao Ran's Literary Works*.

Teng Gang (1962-), first-prize winner of a Chinese short short story contest, has written *Teng Gang's Short Short Stories,* among others. He is one of the few Chinese short fiction writers who also explores sex-related topics.

Wan Qian (1959-), a three-time national short short story contest winner, lives and works in Kunshan, Jiangsu. He has written four collections of short short stories and non-fiction.

Wang Jia (317?-420?) is believed to have lived somewhere between AD 317 and 420. His story included here is taken from his *Collection of Anecdotes (Shi yi ji),* which consists of ten volumes, most of which record stories about the emperors from ancient times up until the fourth century.

Wang Kuishan (1946-) was born in Queshan, Henan. A three-time winner of national short short story contests, he started to publish literary works in 1981 and has written a collection of short short stories entitled *Wang Kuishan's Short Short Stories*, among others.

Wang Xiaoqian (1964-　) was born in Fushun, Sichuan. He has published about two thousand pages of literary works, including a collection of short short stories, one of literary non-fiction and one of reportage. He has also co-written a TV series script, which has been produced and broadcast. He has won many awards and prizes, including a third prize at the national level.

Wong, Freeman J., pseudonym of Harry J. **Huang**.

Wu Jinliang (1955-　), winner of several literary awards, has written five books and many stories, including a collection of short stories, a literary biography, two novels and a collection of short short stories entitled *Wu Jinliang's Short Short Stories*. Some of his works have been turned into films and TV plays.

Wu Wanfu (1969-　), born in Guanshan County, Henan, started writing in 1989. Besides two collections of short short stories, he has published novellas and short stories, as well as poems and literary non-fiction, totaling more than three hundred items. Some of his works have been turned into short TV plays.

Xia Xueqin (1963-　) started to write in 1987. Third-prize winner of the first National Short Short Story Contest (2001) in China, she has published in many literary periodicals and newspapers. She works for a district cultural centre of Hangzhou.

Xie Zhiqiang (1954-　) is a first-prize short fiction winner with a long list of publications. He has published a collection of short short stories entitled *War Between Shadows*.

Xing Ke (1937-), originally known as **Xing** Guoxi, was born in Qixia, Shandong. Also published under the pseudonyms **Ke** Ren and **Zhu** Xinkang, he used to work as an editor, then as associate editor-in-chief and later editor-in-chief for a literary magazine in Zhengzhou until retirement. Since 1958, he has published more than five hundred literary items, including novellas, short stories, short short stories, poems and critiques. He has written four books including *A Selection of Xing Ke's Short Short Stories*. He has collected more than twenty literary awards at the local and national levels.

Xing Qingjie (1970-), born in Yucheng, Shandong, has published novellas, short stories and short short stories in more than two hundred periodicals and newspapers across China. He has written two collections of novellas and short stories, one of short short stories and one of reportage. He has won a provincial TV broadcast award, and is the first-prize winner of two national short short story contests.

Xiu Shi (1954-) is a Hong Kong poet, literary non-fiction writer, fiction writer and critic. He has written five books of poems, four of non-fiction, three of criticism and one of short short stories, entitled *A Certain Woman in Houston*. Xiu pursues a style that is "common but realistic, pedestrian but true." He detests any type of "cosmetic and pretentious" writing.

Xiu Xiangming (1958-) was born in Jimo, Shandong. Winner of two important national short short story contests—one at the national level and one at the international level—he has published many short short stories, winning several literary awards.

Xu Huifen (1952-) is an award-winning short short story writer. She has published stories in various newspapers and magazines in China and overseas.

Xu Xijun (1960-), born in Guanyun, Jiangsu, used to be a TV producer and director. Winner of two literary awards, he has published two thousand pages of literary works, including three books. He now works as an editor for a polytechnic journal.

Xu Xing (1923-) was born in Yixian County, Liaoning. He has written more than ten books, including a collection of poems entitled *Hard Journey,* and two collections of stories, *The Fourth Maple Leaf* and *Wild Roses.*

Yan Chungou (1948-), Hong Kong resident and editor working for Cosmos Books, has also published under three pseudonyms: **Mu** Yi, **Si** Ren, and **Leng** Ying. He has won two literary awards in Hong Kong and one in Taiwan. He writes mostly literary non-fiction and short stories, and has published three collections of short stories, including *Red and Green Lights,* one of non-fiction, and a literary scenario entitled *Bloody Rain.*

Yan Xiaoge (1968-) was born in Xihua, Henan. Teaching as a profession, he started to publish short short stories in 1995 and has won several prizes.

Yang Xiaomin, editor-in-chief of the prestigious monthly *Selected Short Short Stories*, has edited many collections of short short stories, including *A Collection of the Prize Winners of the Past 15 Years: From the Monthly Selected Short Short Stories*. He also writes short short stories.

Ye Chunsheng (1939-) is the author of many works, including *Tales About Canton* and *A Collection of Guangdong and Hainan Customs*. He is a Chinese professor and folklorist supervising PhD candidates in Sun Yat-sen University, and is well known for his profound knowledge of southern Chinese culture and customs.

451

Ye Dachun (1956-) was born in Wuhan, Hubei. He has written a novel, a collection of short stories, a collection of literary non-fiction and one of short short stories, among others, totaling five thousand pages. He is a three-time winner of the Chinese Short Short Story Contest.

Ye Qingcheng, also known as **Hu** Qingzhi, lives and works in Wuhan, Hubei. A short short story prize winner, she has authored six collections of literary non-fiction and three collections of stories.

Yi De Er Fu (1944-), originally known as **Ye** Fu, started his literary career in 1972, writing many books, including a collection of short short stories entitled *Classified Reference Open to the Public,* two of short stories, *Springing Out* and *Stories by Yi De Er Fu,* and one of novellas, *Whose Fault*. He has published many other works, such as short plays, TV scripts and literary non-fiction, as well as a book of his own calligraphy. He has collected nearly forty municipal, provincial and national literary awards. He has worked as an editor for several literary series.

Yin Quansheng (1955-), well-known short short story writer, was born in Neixiang, Henan. He has written a collection of short stories and four collections of short short stories.

Yin Yun (471-531) was the author of the thirty-volume *Stories,* which have been lost. His stories were popular tales of his time, with a distinct feature of folklore. "Fighting a Tiger" is one of those that remain. As recorded, Yin was "a man who doesn't care about particulars, but well read and diligent at learning."

Yu Rui, officially known as **Fang** Yurui, was born in Liu'an, Anhui. A multiple short short story prize winner, he has published more than one hundred short short stories, including a collection. He works for a museum as director and associate researcher.

Yuan Yaqin works as the editor-in-chief for the *Hunan University Journal*. She has written a collection of stories entitled *Red Beetles,* and a novel, *Give Women a Chance*.

Zha La Ga Hu (1930-), well-known novelist, has written twenty books, including *The Fall of the Golden Family* and *Legend of Gadamei Village*. He has won ten literary awards at the regional and national levels. Some of his works have been translated into different languages or included in national textbooks. His name appears in *International Authors and Writers Who's Who* as Hu Zha La Ga.

Zhang Jishu (1951-) was born in Feixiang, Hebei. He has published many short short stories, including four collections entitled *A Strange Dream, A Drunk Dream, A Story That Can't Be Told,* and *A Love Dream*. Some of his works have also been published outside of China.

Zhang Kaicheng (1958-) was born in Jiyuan, Henan. He has published stories, literary non-fiction and reportage in various publications, totaling about two thousand pages.

Zhang Ke (1979-) was born and grew up in Hebei. Winner of a national short short story contest, she has published more than one hundred literary items, including a collection of short short stories entitled *Young Dumplings*.

Zhong Zimei (1942-), born in Bandung, Indonesia, graduated from Sun Yat-sen University in Guangzhou, China. He is best known as a short short science-fiction writer. He works and lives in Hong Kong.

Zhou Daxin (1952-), widely respected author, has published more than thirty books and won many prestigious literary awards. More than ten of his works have been turned into plays, including TV plays, radio plays and films, one of which won the Gold Bear medal at the 43th International Film Festival in Berlin.

Zong Lihua (1971-) is winner of the Annual Best Chinese Short Short Story Award. He has published nearly two hundred stories in different literary periodicals and other publications.

Glossary

The following terms occur more than once in the anthology. They are explained in endnotes/footnotes when they first appear. This glossary is given as a convenience to readers who may encounter them without footnotes.

Bonus: Apart from the regular month's salary, nearly all salaried employees receive additional income known as "bonus" from their employers. Bonuses differ greatly from place to place, depending on how well off the employers are. Generally speaking, the better off the employer is, the higher the bonuses the employees are likely to receive.

Confucius (551-476 BC): A sage in ancient China, born in the feudal State of Lu, or today's Shandong Province. He advocated a system of morality and statecraft that would preserve peace and afford the people stable and fair government. The influence of his doctrines has spread from generation to generation and far beyond China itself.

Cultural Revolution: Short for the Great Proletarian Cultural Revolution, which was started in 1966 by Mao Zedong, then chairman of the Communist Party of China; it ended in 1976.

Family planning: Family planning—or rather, "population control"—has been a fundamental policy of China for decades. Late marriage and late childbirth are encouraged. Generally speaking, couples in the cities and towns are allowed to have one child only, while those in the countryside may have a second one if the first one is a girl.

455

Fen: See **yuan**.

Kang: An earthen bed that is heated in wintry nights, mostly found in the cold regions.

Party secretary: The Party secretary is the director of a Party branch or committee, the most powerful person of a province, county, factory, school or department store, for example. He makes the decisions and approves or disapproves anything of whatever unit is under his control. Chinese Party secretaries may be ranked as follows:

- General secretary of the Central Committee of the Communist Party of China
- Secretary of a provincial committee of the Communist Party of China
- Secretary of a county committee of the Communist Party of China
- Secretary of a town committee of the Communist Party of China
- Secretary of a district general branch of the Communist Party of China
- Secretary of a village branch of the Communist Party of China
- Head of a group consisting of fewer than three members of the Communist Party of China

Different organs and institutions other than those mentioned above are generally classified as provincial-level units, county-level units, and so on, and Party secretaries of such units are granted power and receive benefits accordingly.

Yuan: One yuan of the Chinese currency, Renminbi, which contains 100 *fen*, or 10 *jiao*, is equal to about 12 cents (US) at present.

How to Pronounce the Most Difficult *Pinyin* in the Wade System

Pinyin	Wade System	Example
c	ts	cao — ts'ao
g	k	gai — kai
i	yi [i:]	li — lee
j	ch	jiang — chiang
q	ch	qing — ch'ing
x	hs [s]	xiao — hsiao
z	ts [ts]	zang — tsang
zh	ch	zhong — chung

Authors' Names and Titles in Chinese

下列作品多数由原作者（或授权译者）修订过，几篇有大改动。汉英对照时以译者的汉语原稿为准。

目　录

Table of Contents by Title

462

图书在版编目（CIP）数据

中国小小说选集 / 周大新等著；黄俊雄译. 一北京：外文出版社，2005
（熊猫丛书）

ISBN 7-119-03881-8

Ⅰ.中 ... Ⅱ.①周 ... ②黄 ... Ⅲ. 小小说－作品集－中国－当代－英文
Ⅳ. I247.8

中国版本图书馆 CIP 数据核字(2004)第 126724 号

外文出版社网址：
http://www.flp.com.cn
外文出版社电子信箱：
info@flp.com.cn
sales@flp.com.cn

熊猫丛书

中国小小说选集

作　　者	周大新等	
译　　者	黄俊雄	
责任编辑	陈海燕　李　芳	
封面设计	蔡　荣	
印刷监制	张国祥	
出版发行	外文出版社	
社　　址	北京市百万庄大街24号	邮政编码　100037
电　　话	(010) 68320579 (总编室)	
	(010) 68329514 / 68327211 (推广发行部)	
印　　刷	北京蓝空印刷厂	
经　　销	新华书店 / 外文书店	
开　　本	大32开（1450×2100毫米）	
印　　数	0001－5000册	印　张　15.125
版　　次	2005年第1版第1次印刷	
装　　别	平	
书　　号	ISBN 7-119-03881-8	
	10－E－3645P	
定　　价	22.00元	